^the Speech

the Speech

Andrew Smith

URBANE
Publications

urbanepublications.com

First published in Great Britain in 2016 by Urbane Publications Ltd
Suite 3, Brown Europe House, 33/34 Gleaming Wood Drive, Chatham, Kent ME5 8RZ
Copyright ©Andrew Smith, 2016

A CIP catalogue record for this book is available from the British Library.

ISBN 978-1-911129-51-6
EPUB 978-1-911129-52-3
MOBI 978-1-911129-53-0

Design and Typeset by Julie Martin
Cover by The Invisible Man

Printed and bound by
CPI Group (UK) Ltd, Croydon, CR0 4YY

urbanepublications.com

The publisher supports the Forest Stewardship Council® (FSC®), the leading international forest-certification organisation. This book is made from acid-free paper from an FSC®-certified provider. FSC is the only forest-certification scheme supported by the leading environmental organisations, including Greenpeace.

For Isabella, Poppy, and Harriet

For Jennifer, Rowan, and Winter

A MIGRATION

To know Hedayat requires us to know his father, to understand the father means we travel labyrinth streets to the grandfather, to understand whom requires us to move back still to great-grandfather unto mist and the origin of things: to once upon a time.

Fire in the Unnameable Country, by Ghalib Islam

March, 1916

John Enoch Powell's grandfather, Old Enoch, was woken by the sputtering of a blue flame, the rowdy release of gas among glowing coals in the grate. He'd been dreaming of his Welsh-born father, Sawyl ApHywel – young John Enoch's great-grandfather. Old Enoch remembers a wistful quality in his father's voice when he reminisced about his childhood home in the somnolent Welsh border country of Radnorshire. It was obvious Sawyl's migration to England had been no execration of his birthplace, but was made out of perceived necessity – an escape from poverty. Old Enoch's father first searched for rewards that the Industrial Revolution was said to offer in the coal mines of South Wales, but remuneration was less than bountiful. Eventually, after hours, days, and months of darkness, dust and drudgery, every ounce of coal that could be reached was stripped. Sawyl and his fellow miners were dismissed by English mine owners with less consideration than pit ponies sent to the knacker's yard.

Many of them looked east, across the border, for the good fortune they'd anticipated. The first passenger railways had begun operation in the northern counties – the Liverpool and Manchester, Stockton and Darlington lines. But there was no rail transport to take Sawyl and his newlywed wife to the English Midlands, where industry was reputed to be booming. They walked the twenty-odd miles from Merthyr Tydfil to Newport. From there they caught a horse-drawn mail coach to Birmingham. On steep hills they were obliged to dismount and walk, to save the horses. A broken axle delayed them for a day-and-a-half outside Tewkesbury. Eventually, bone-shaken, bitterly cold, dazed, and disoriented, young John Enoch's great-grandparents were deposited outside the Hen and Chickens Inn in Birmingham, strangers in a strange land. Native Welsh speakers, they had no more than a dozen phrases of English between them. 'Coalmine' and 'miner' were two words Sawyl had picked up in the English-owned pit in Merthyr Tydfil. Not surprisingly, he was offered a job mining coal in Wednesbury. Not what he'd dreamt of, but at least it was a start.

On his first day at the Wednesbury mine he was asked his name. 'Sawyl ApHywel.' The man in the pit office made him say it twice more. Eventually the man wrote 'Samuel Powell' and waved him away. Sawyl grudgingly began to use the name the man had given him. It made little difference, he was still called a 'cursed forrainer' by local miners and neighbours. It was no comfort to hear others – Irishmen – called worse for no other reason than their origins. Despite there being paid work for all, Sawyl and other Welsh miners who'd gravitated eastward were ferociously enjoined to 'hasten back whence yow came.'

Sawyl pleaded for a Welsh name for his son, even if it was only Dafydd, difficult for locals to mangle. But his wife insisted on an English appellation so that their boy would 'fit in.' Enoch was chosen because it was much favoured among the locals. After a few months at school the whining dialect of the Black Country that so grated on Samuel's ear issued from his own child's mouth. The fruits of the industrial revolution never fully ripened for Samuel – he worked in the mine all his life – but at least he saw his progeny reap the benefits of his migration to England. His grown son grew unimaginably wealthy dealing in scrap metal. He became the owner of a grand house in Smethwick.

Old Enoch – unappreciative recipient of his father's largesse, never having grasped the complexities of his migration – shuffles bony buttocks to armchair's edge to poke the coal that woke him. He thought he'd miss his spacious house after the blast furnaces began to close and his lucrative scrap metal business fell on hard times, but he's content in his 'miner's cottage,' as his son likes to call it. How would Albert know? He isn't the one who grew up in one. When Old Enoch was forced to move from double-fronted mansion to two-up-two-down terraced house, he transported rolls of fanciful wallpaper, left over from plush decoration of his former dining room. Now that the block-printed paper lines his otherwise modest parlour, he enjoys the illusion of trellis walls, where lissom roses meander. Whimsical birds, yellow finches perhaps, perch among peach-coloured blossoms.

Real birds roost around the room – a dozen examples of ornithological taxidermy. Some are imprisoned beneath domes of gleaming crystal. Others are confined in glass-fronted boxes, appropriate habitat painted on interior surfaces. An approximation of a Brazilian forest surrounds a crimson, yellow, and cobalt Macaw. A pair of British Kingfishers scrutinize a confusion of daubed wavelets rushing under their sturdy twig perches.

Albert has imparted his vast knowledge of British birds to his son, but young John Enoch's only information on alien genera is gleaned from scant descriptions in the Harmsworth Encyclopaedia. The lad pores over the volumes as assiduously as a sea-captain examining ocean charts – as if afraid he'll flounder and sink should he fail to memorize every word. Old Enoch finds the endless display of erudition that goes on in Albert's household unsavoury. But with both parents' vocation as teachers, their only child couldn't help but learn even if he were resistant. Old Enoch always found his daughter-in-law to be resolute, but the doggedness with which she stuffs her son's head borders on the obsessive. Her admonishments are forceful and frequent as a puppy trainer. "What you start you must finish!" She urges John Enoch to be "thorough at all costs." Fortunately the boy is like a sponge, and the more scholarship he absorbs the more eager he is to show off his newfound knowledge, feverish for his parents' approval. When they call him 'the professor,' as they've begun to do, John Enoch grins maniacally.

Despite the disparity of John Enoch's knowledge of domestic birds versus foreign species, visitors are stunned when the pre-schooler delivers lectures on the avian collection. He describes in detail the behaviour, habitat, and breeding habits of Barn Owls, Bearded Tits, and other British breeds. Whereas the Toucan, the Antillean Euphonia, and other exotics are dealt with in a couple of short sentences. Seemingly untroubled – to the point that he appears unaware – by the gap in his knowledge, the lad speaks authoritatively, standing erect atop a high stool. A shrewd tactic for one so small – making himself the same height or taller than his audience. Born during a violent thunderstorm, John Enoch Powell sometimes looks like he's been struck by lightning. Blue eyes glitter like one of the new electric light bulbs. If Old Enoch dare contradict his grandson – a four-year-old is sometimes mistaken no matter how clever – the lad's eyes ice over. That degree of confidence laced with arrogance in one so young is disquieting, even for Old Enoch, who's known his share of hubris.

TEN DAYS IN APRIL

DAY ONE

Easter Sunday, April 14, 1968

As Brigadier John Enoch Powell, Conservative Member of Parliament for Wolverhampton South West, approached a fork in the street, he allowed himself a rueful gaze to the right, down solidly middle-class Compton Road. He'd have thought his older daughter, Susan, might be too fatigued from an afternoon of horseback riding to notice his momentary inattention to the road ahead, but in the rear view mirror he glimpsed her questioning eyes. After Enoch managed to ease the car to the left, toward their house on the less desirable Merridale Road, he glanced in the mirror again. Susan was gazing out of the side window. He was aware that his dubious driving skills were noted within the family, though rarely mentioned. He prayed his daughter's mind was cantering across a Shropshire field rather than dwelling on his shortcomings. That his daughters – or anybody else, come to that – might consider him lacking was anathema to Enoch. His flesh crawled at the very idea.

Compton Road, the object of Enoch's hankering glance, marked the boundary of an area where many of Wolverhampton's professionals lived. Doctors, bank managers, and lawyers. Apart from a couple of enterprising Asian families, residents were exclusively white-skinned. To the left, on Merridale Road and adjoining streets, more modest houses had been built. Opposite the semi-detached Powell residence sat a row of narrow terraced houses. The neighbourhood, Enoch had noticed, was becoming home to an increasing number of West Indians, Indians, and Pakistanis.

Enoch stopped the car outside the house he and his wife, Pam, bought in 1954, the year Susan was born. The cost was £1,500, exactly his annual salary at the time. Perhaps they could have stretched to a more expensive location, but Enoch was aware of the precariousness of political life and insisted they save for the inevitable rainy day. And it wasn't as if they'd be there permanently, they lived in London when parliament was in session. The Wolverhampton house was perfectly serviceable, especially after Enoch's skill in carpentry provided improvements. A modest bay window provided some light to the front room, although the rest of the interior was gloomy. On first inspection of the house, Enoch – ever the Classics scholar – was charmed by carved stone leaves on the capitals of two square columns supporting the roof of a narrow porch. The property boasted a back garden, where Enoch planted lettuces in regimented rows, the distance between seedlings carefully calibrated to ensure each was perfectly equidistant from the next. But as he held the front car door open for eleven-year-old Jennifer, Enoch wondered if his investment would have been more secure in the middle-class enclave bordered by Compton Road, rather than in the humbler Merridale Road neighbourhood, more susceptible to an influx of immigrants and the resulting reduction in property value.

Monetary loss was never Enoch's overarching concern,

however. In the same year he bought the house, he was part of a group who succeeded in pressuring Churchill to defer the provision of an annual £500 to MP's for expenses. How could you expect voters to approve when you took more of their tax money than they'd reckoned on when they elected you? No, it was the possibility that he'd made a mistake that irked Enoch. The actual nature of the mistake was secondary. Added to this was the feeling that, once again, he was an outsider, a state so familiar to him he was rarely conscious of it. But in this case – being of his own making – it was galling to think he'd put himself and his family on the wrong side of the tracks, so to speak.

"Jeffa," Enoch called after his younger daughter, Jennifer. "You've left your riding hat on the front seat. A purposeful and deliberate act is one thing, but if done through carelessness, you'll waste time looking for it next time you need it."

Jennifer retrieved her hat and marched into the house after her sister. Enoch was pleased to see she appeared to bear him no ill will. A lesser child may have been resentful. Enoch was not oblivious to the fact that he talked to his children differently than most parents. But his goal was to always get his point across as precisely as possible, no matter who he addressed. Otherwise, what was the point? Enoch made sure all the car doors were locked before following his daughter. As he turned he caught sight of a woman, who appeared to be Indian, emerging from one of the terraced houses across the street. The collar of her nurse's uniform was clearly visible under her navy blue Macintosh. When their eyes met, the nurse waved. Enoch waved back.

Obviously encouraged, the woman glanced left and right before hurrying across the road.

"Mr Powell, sir. I want to thank you for bringing me to this country."

Enoch understood immediately. The woman had obviously arrived under his watch when the Party had been in power a few years earlier.

"I'm not sure I'm deserving of your gratitude," he said. "Certainly, I was Minister of Health. But recruitment was in the hands of the hospital authorities. Given there was no bar upon employment to those, like you, from the Commonwealth, they were able to employ whosoever they wished, as long as the likely candidate was qualified."

"But as Health Minister, you must have ..."

Enoch cut her off by addressing her in Urdu. He asked her how much longer her training was to last, and to where in India she planned to return. The nurse took a few seconds before replying.

"I don't know what you're saying or where you think I spring from."

Enoch frowned. Eyebrows, normally sloping up to his temples, became glowering horizontal lines. Creases scored the high dome of his forehead beneath a gleaming quiff, oddly luxuriant in the centre of his receding hairline. His mouth, wider than most, was a rictus gape beneath his moustache, which he kept clipped to expose an ambiguously sensual top lip. Most would describe his mouth as cruel, some may say it appeared generous, and a very few might think it attractive, even sensual.

"I was born in Jamaica, my mother and father too," said the woman. "Their fathers were brought from India to work in the plantations. But I never been there in my life."

Damn! Another mistake. Enoch swallowed, took a breath.

"Nevertheless, your thanks remain misplaced, for the reasons I outlined," he said.

Enoch turned as if to disappear into his house, but at the last minute he spun on his heel.

"How much longer do you have to train before returning home?" he asked.

"Train? I've been a Staff Nurse at the Royal the last three year. My husband and I just bought that house over there." She nodded her head across the road. Then she hesitated for a second or two, appearing to be searching for the words. But then she blurted, "We're here to stay."

"Really? Well, good day to you," said Enoch, and he strode the few steps to his front porch.

Out of the corner of his eye he could see it was the nurse's turn to frown as she stood, staring at his retreating figure.

After he closed the front door after him Enoch repeated a phrase he'd uttered more than once as Health Minister during the nurses' strike, when opposition MPs tried to make recruitment from overseas an issue: "the best available figures show that less than seven percent of nurses have come from the Commonwealth." What he didn't add at the time, but said out loud at that moment, standing in his shadowy hall, was: "and they were a bloody sight cheaper than British nurses. I saved the government thousands."

"Tea, Enoch?"

He looked up to see his wife, Pam, standing at the end of the hallway. His irritation drained away. God, but he was lucky to have found her. He couldn't have come across a better candidate if he'd posted a personal ad – something like:

Brigadier and future Viceroy of India wishes to meet private school educated young woman with a lively interest in politics, preferably the daughter of an officer of the Indian army, with first-hand knowledge of the sub-continent. She should be a natural Tory, have professional experience in the higher echelons of Westminster, be able to type, and enjoy travel. Social graces are a must. An open face, good teeth, and a short but full figure are preferred.

Pam ticked all the boxes, plus more Enoch hadn't been aware of until he encountered the sum total of her endearing qualities. She was eternally good-natured, and seemed to flourish when she came to work as his secretary. He hadn't minded when he discovered her effusive morning greetings were a ruse in a wager with the other secretaries to see who could be the first to make him say good morning. He hadn't known he was aloof until then. Later he overheard Pam telling someone she thought Enoch "very attractive, his eyes are very blue and mesmeric, and he's great fun." He deduced he'd become more affable. But it was some time before romance developed. Not until Pam was helping with his second election campaign in Wolverhampton. When she returned home to London for a weekend, Enoch found himself missing her. So much so that he went to meet her on Sunday evening only to find her train had been delayed. That October night, as he waited for Pam on a cold, foggy platform, he realized he wanted to marry her. Fate had provided a better strategy to win her affection than any Enoch could have devised. Pam's expression, when she stepped down from her severely overdue train to find he'd had been waiting hours for her, couldn't have been more gratifying. But first things first – he delayed proposing to her until he'd won the election. After the unfortunate misunderstanding of his last and only other marriage proposal, Enoch made sure Pam understood exactly what he was asking of her and the likely consequences if she accepted: grinding poverty and a husband who was a permanent backbencher. His modesty hadn't been completely false – he recognized he was an anomaly within the Tory ranks and might be side lined at any point. Labour's defeat coupled with Pam's acceptance – on the stipulation that she'd never be asked to cook tripe – made 1951 a very good year for Enoch.

"If you want to go up I can bring your tea," said Pam. "I've left the transcript on your desk."

Although she always typed his speeches from his handwritten draft, Pam had been reluctant to give up her role as driver in order to type his latest effort. Enoch never conceded his driving was as inept as Pam claimed. He'd hoped his account of learning, during World War II in a thirty-hundredweight army truck while travelling 3,000 miles across North Africa, might have excused his erratic driving style, but Pam was unimpressed. He'd learnt to ride a horse too, but was a much more accomplished rider than a driver. He threw himself into fox-hunting the minute he got back to England, often taking the Underground dressed in jodhpurs and hacking jacket to ride to hounds at a Hunt on the outskirts of London. After a number of minor motor collisions he tacitly agreed Pam should take the driver's seat whenever possible.

The idea for the speech took shape during a shadow cabinet meeting Enoch had attended before leaving London. The discussion about the proposed Race Relations Bill was a complete fiasco. Ted Heath in particular had galled Enoch. He waffled about how, if they opposed an Act that banned the refusal of housing or employment on the grounds of race or colour, they'd be labelled fascists. But as each of his colleagues agreed the best plan was to take the coward's route and merely table an amendment rather than outright oppose the Bill, Enoch began to realize the situation was ripe with opportunity. The speech he was to give the following Saturday would allow him to ignite the fuse the Act provided and blow the issue wide open. He held his tongue, knowing it would lead the others to believe he was in agreement with them. Immediately after the meeting they motored – Pam driving – to Wolverhampton where Enoch started in on the speech that would surely change his fortune. After several handwritten drafts he'd been desperate to see it typewritten. Pam reluctantly agreed to type it that morning while he drove the girls to riding class.

The warmth of Pam's voice told Enoch she approved – or at least she didn't disapprove. Despite the unshakeable conviction that he had no option than to go ahead with the speech, Enoch had to admit to a feeling of relief. But despite his wife's tacit approbation, Enoch knew the speech needed something in addition to heartfelt expressions of selflessness and the drama of classical allusion. He'd included a barrage of attention-grabbing statements, designed to appeal to hoi-polloi, as he sometimes referred to the majority in a nod to his knowledge of Ancient Greek – πολλοί, meaning 'the many.' But to make certain these devices didn't sail over the heads of a large proportion of the population – those with little or no higher education – whose understanding was vital, he needed an anecdote or two, morsels from what he believed everyday life had become. Stories that even the most benighted would understand. Time was ticking. He had less than a week before the Conservative Political Centre meeting in Birmingham. He may have no option but to resort to the source he'd consulted for his Walsall speech. He was reluctant to return to that particular font, but if needs must, he would.

DAY TWO

Monday, April 15, 1968

The latch made a harsh crack, the metal door flew open. Bumboclaat! Nelson Clarke stood up so fast the blood rushed from his head – he swore he'd pass out. Sounded like a whole heap of bones hit the concrete floor behind him. How a falling chair make so much noise? A white man strode through the door. Seemed like he filled the room. Nelson stepped back, almost fell over the chair. Behind the giant hovered a lank duppy of a man. His ashen skin and bumpy cheeks, scarred by sickness, reminded Nelson of the pitted belly of a Caribbean fish he used to catch.

"You seem a little edgy," said the older man.

Nelson thought the stretched vowels of Black Country voices sounded like griping. This brute whinged like the rest of them, but he looked like he could easily fix things that troubled him.

"Cause of how you going on," Nelson said.

He held one hand tight with the other. If they saw his fingers shaking it'd just make matters worse. He watched as the heavyset one sat at the table and placed some papers in front of him.

"Pick up the chair and sit down," he said.

Them take him for a half idiot to turn his back? Nelson moved to the far side of the chair before picking it up.

"I'm Detective Inspector Gorman," said the giant. He didn't introduce his ghost of a friend.

"What were your movements between eight o'clock and noon yesterday morning, April fourteenth?"

Wha' happen yesterday? Wha' the bloodfire happen?

"I won't ask again," said Gorman.

"I was at me Auntie Irene house."

"What's the address?"

"22 Newcombe Road, Handsworth."

"Can anyone substantiate that?"

Nelson knew the word, but what if he had the meaning wrong?

"For fuck's sake, boy, you speak English or not? Can you prove you were at that address all morning? Was anyone else there?"

"Yes sir, me Auntie Irene. We flex there with a few fren'."

Gorman turned his head in the direction of the ghost.

"He and his aunt relaxed with a couple of friends," said the man.

How come this one understand more than that one?

"Why weren't you at work?" Gorman asked.

"I take a little break."

"You on the dole?"

This giant think him a worthless bait? Nelson felt a prick of triumph to prove the detective wrong.

"No, sir. The boss between contract, so him lay me off for a week or so. I going back to work tomorrow."

"Really?"

One word, but said so sarcastic it was clear to Nelson it

was the rass policeman who'd decide if he ever worked again, never mind tomorrow.

"You were with this ... Auntie Irene and your friends all morning?"

"All mornin', all afternoon too."

If whatever they dragged him out of bed for happened yesterday morning surely he was in the clear – home free – no?

"How did you get that scar? In a fight?"

So he was right, it was his pussy claat scar got them thinking. Hard to miss, a shade or two lighter than his skin. At that moment Nelson could have sworn it tingled. The length of it, from one eye to the corner of his plump lips.

"No sir, it wasn't no fight. Some bad bwoys hold me up back in Jamaica, and tief everything, then cut me up. I was just bad luckied. Just salt."

Again Nelson watched the inspector turn his meaty head toward the skinny man.

"Ruffians accosted me and stole everything, then cut my face. I was unlucky that's all," translated the man.

"You got a bad temper, son?" asked Gorman.

"No, sir. I was minding me own business when them come humbug me."

It felt like an hour passing. Nelson heard a car drive by on the street outside, gears grinding. How long this brute going to do nothing but look down at the rass papers? Nelson was aware of the other man's eyes staring out from his rotten face. Suddenly Gorman lunged forward, more bull than man.

"You mean to tell me you were nowhere near the Sunrise

Boarding House in Wolverhampton yesterday morning? Come on boy, admit it! You were there weren't you?"

Nelson jerked his head back, but still he felt Gorman's spittle hit his face. The palms of his hands grew clammy. Partly because of the detective's screw face, but also Nelson realized he knew the place. Fifteen shillings a week just to lay his head while he was working too far from Auntie Irene's to go home at night.

"Something happen over there so?" Nelson asked.

"Just answer the question."

"As there is a God, sir, me no go near that place since last year."

"But you're familiar with it?"

"I board there for a coupla month last summer."

"You're acquainted with the owner, Mr … Raman …jit … Singh," said the inspector, reading from his papers.

Nelson could picture Mr Singh's plump cheeks bulging above a hair net that held his beard tight to his chin. Nelson often wondered how the net was held. Must be hooked around the landlord's ears, hidden by his turban.

"He is known to me. Why? Is what happen?"

Nelson held Gorman's gaze for a full five seconds. He was damned if he'd let this rass detective break him down.

"Mr Singh was beaten senseless at the Sunrise Boarding House yesterday. He's in hospital now, fighting for his life."

The inspector continued to stare at Nelson, eyes as cold and hard as the steel rods Nelson hauled up and down ladders all day long. Nelson's guts heaved. So much for his resolution. He felt he might throw up, or shit himself.

"You can't think me have anything to do with that. Me tell you true, I was in Handsworth dawn to dusk. Ask Auntie Irene and the rest ... them can tell you."

* * *

When the telephone rang in The Vine, the public house of choice for Wolverhampton's art students, Frank McCann's eyes remained glued on the half dozen black-and-white photographs he'd arranged on the bar's gleaming wooden surface, pristine as freshly frozen ice. As usual, the young student had been the first customer of the day. He enjoyed his solitary occupancy of the pub, savouring the faint disinfectant smell of recently mopped tiles. He'd been miffed when two second-year students, Pete Scallion and Mick Collins, from his own department, graphic design, had wandered in. At least they sat well away, at the other end of the bar. After a while Frank barely noticed them. His head, a tangle of dirty-blonde hair, several shades lighter than his chestnut sideboards and Frank Zappa moustache, was bent over the photo prints he'd laid out. Frank was so intent on his photographs he was hardly aware of Barry, the brawny publican, standing right in front of him behind the bar, muttering an occasional "ah" and "all roight" into the telephone. But when the landlord exclaimed "never" with disgusted incredulity, Frank glanced up. Barry was staring at Frank's prints. He cut his caller off with an abrupt "Call you back layter" and returned the receiver to its cradle with a loud clunk.

"Give us a shufty at them photos," he demanded of Frank, who obligingly turned the half-dozen prints around so Barry could examine them more closely.

Frank felt the unfamiliar sensation of pride. Unused to prodigious production – he was the first to admit he was no model student – Frank believed he'd done an impressive job of photographing the previous day's student demonstration, his first live-action photographic project since he learned the workings of the college's Rolleiflex camera. He'd captured the mood perfectly in the way he'd framed marchers' belligerent expressions and angry gestures. Not that he shared his fellow students' concerns. The issue of the day could be racial injustice, the war in Vietnam, or the price of beans on toast in the college cafeteria – Frank couldn't give a toss. His only interest was in displaying his photographic talents. He was planning on showing the prints to the editor of *VoxPop,* the student newspaper in the hope he'd agree to run a shot or two in the upcoming issue.

Barry asked Frank where and when the photos had been taken.

"Here in Wolver'ampton? Yesterday morning, you're sure?" asked Barry.

"Of course I'm sure. Just down the road, on Darlington Street. You can see Beatties' windows in the background … see? What do you think?"

The normally obsequious landlord was uncharacteristically critical of Frank's efforts.

"They'm boring as fook. Look like a bunch of Persil-white whiners."

Frank's fellow students at the other end of the bar guffawed. Pete, caught in mid swallow, choked on his beer. Frank was too stunned by Barry's comment to react. He was the pub's most loyal customer, for fuck's sake. Barry seemed harmless enough when he adopted his normal fawning attitude toward his student customers in an obvious attempt to relieve them of their government grant money. But this unusual display of belligerence from the six-foot, fifteen-stone landlord made him more of a bully boy than a sponger.

"It's all very well them marchin' about saying they're for racial equality, but you can't tell it from these bloody photos, can you?"

Frank was slightly less offended when he realized it wasn't the quality of the work that disappointed Barry, but the content.

"There's a sodding big sign trumpeting 'Racists Out!' What more do you want?"

"All I'm saying is, it'd look better if one of them marchers was coloured, that's all," said Barry.

"But there are no coloured students. Jock Sinclair looks like he might have a touch of the tar brush, but he's from Scotland. He's got a Glaswegian accent you could cut with a knife."

Late morning sunlight sliced through The Vine's Victorian stained glass windows. Geometric shapes of colour fell across bottles of spirits, some of which outshone with their own vivid hues – incandescent amber of Pimms, the electric cyan of Peppermint Schnapps. Frank stared at Barry wondering what in God's name was going through the publican's greasy head. Barry kept his eyes fixed on one of the prints, his straw-like eyelashes bristled with every blink.

"What 'appened to that mate of yours? West Indian chap you used to bring in 'ere last summer … the one you took all those photos of?" asked Barry.

"Nelson Clarke? I haven't seen him since the beginning of the school year."

Frank met the young Jamaican immigrant when he became an employee of the construction company that hired Frank and a couple of other students during the summer months to help speed completion of a block of flats being built on the eastern fringes of Wolverhampton. If Frank were honest he'd have to say that part of the attraction of befriending a coloured person was that he thought it would contribute to the raffish image he liked to project. He'd even considered taking his new friend to meet his parents – to see the expressions on their face. But that wouldn't have been fair to Nelson. Despite his initial motivation, Frank had become genuinely attached to his Jamaican pal. He'd even spent a few weekends with Nelson at his Auntie Irene's house. Part of Frank's enjoyment was the expression of awe on his fellow students' faces when he dropped into conversation that he'd been partying in the West Indian stronghold of Handsworth.

When summer ended, Nelson and the full-time building crew moved on to a new project somewhere in Birmingham, leaving Frank and the other student workers to return to college.

"Anyway, Nelson isn't a student," Frank told Barry.

"Student or not, it's a shame your coloured pal wasn't marchin' along with that lot," said Barry, indicating a line of marchers in the print he was holding.

"That'd make a crackerjack photo that would. Give it some teeth."

"Well he wasn't with them, was he," said Frank.

Barry scowled at the photograph. From the jukebox Jack Bruce of Cream chanted, 'I'm so glad, I'm so glad, I'm glad, I'm glad, I'm glad.' The sound of Ginger Baker's cymbals and Clapton's guitar riffs reverberated around the room. Out of the corner of his eye Frank caught the two graphic design students draining their glasses at the end of the bar.

"But just the other day you was in here boastin' about how you'd been taught to do tricks with photos. Doublin' up negatives. Printin' stuff on top of other stuff. You showed me that photo you'd made of a pig with a man's head."

Frank knew he'd been a bit of a dick when he superimposed the head of a tutor he particularly disliked onto a pig's body, but he was annoyed all the same when nobody in his class found it funny.

"Shouldn't be difficult should it, to pop the coloured feller in one of these photos? Make it look like he was at the march?"

"That's way beyond Frankie's talents," said Pete Scallion as he and Mick Collins passed Frank on their way out.

"Fuck off," said Frank.

"You have to admit, you're not exactly known for your work ethic. No way you could pull off what Barry's suggesting," said Mick, examining Frank's photos on the bar.

Frank bristled. Who the hell did these cocky second-year students think they were? Casting aspersions on his abilities. It was probably his own fault for his devil-may-care attitude to college work, but Frank was sick of the reputation he'd fostered. He'd show the bastards.

"How much do you want to bet?"

"Five quid?" said Pete.

"Each," said Mick.

"And you've got twenty-four hours," said Pete.

"You're on," said Frank.

He might have appeared to be acting rashly but Frank had been thinking on his feet. He remembered the shots of Nelson that Barry had mentioned. He recalled the weather had been cloudy, similar to the day of the march, so the light was consistent with that of the demonstration. Not a sharp shadow in sight. Frank was fairly certain the angle at which he'd snapped Nelson was identical to that of some of the photos he'd shot at the march. He didn't see why it wouldn't be possible for him to position Nelson's figure in place of one of the aspirin-white demonstrators. Nelson wouldn't have any objection. In fact, Frank reasoned, his immigrant friend would probably welcome an opportunity to help the cause against racism. He swallowed a mouthful of Guinness.

"You've landed yourself right in it now, haven't you, my son?" said Barry, reverting to his usual sycophantic self. He grinned at Frank as he polished a glass.

* * *

Through the open door of his lair in the back room of the shop-front constituency office, Enoch Powell heard the postman's voice.

"I must be barking mad to be walking defenceless into

enemy territory."

There was a resounding slap of the afternoon delivery of letters as they landed on the desk of Mrs Georgina Verington-Delaunay – Georgy, to those who passed muster – who held the official title of administrator and the unofficial post as advisor to Enoch.

"Better watch out, Bert. We're planning to sell off the Royal Mail. And then where will you be?" said Georgy.

"You lot may flog the steel works, but the day'll never dawn when the Post Office is up for grabs," said the postman.

Enoch could guess the gist of Bert's parting shot. His and Georgy's double act was the same every time the post was delivered.

"You know why, duck? 'Cos you'll never get back into power. It's Labour all the way from here on in."

The sound of the front door closing signalled the postman's triumphant exit.

Enoch felt a pang of disappointment. He thought back to the days immediately following his Walsall speech when the post came in bags rather than bundles. The sheer volume of letters – ninety-nine percent in support – had given him a kind of spiritual gratification. Enoch would have to be tortured first, but even he would have to admit to the occasional sliver of doubt. The torrent of letters had given him a feeling of sublime confidence that he was on absolutely the right path.

Bert was wrong about it being 'all the way' for Labour. Not if Enoch had anything to do with it. Only two years, in fact – until the next election. It was unlikely Harold Wilson would call one sooner, even with a healthy majority of ninety-six seats. But then, if Enoch remained steadfast, there'd be a changing of the guard. With that thought in mind he applied himself to Pam's typescript of his speech. He changed a phrase here, a word there. How many speeches must he have written since he was first elected? Eighteen years worth. Hundreds of them. A twenty-minute speech took him an average of a day to prepare. Preparation time alone must total years. And a good proportion of speeches destined for the House were never delivered. Debates often ran out of time before he had a chance to gain the floor.

"Please do excuse me, I hope I'm not intruding but I wonder if I could leave this invitation for Mr Powell?"

Enoch leant to one side to see past the door jamb. A moth of a woman hovered in front of Georgy's desk. She hesitantly proffered a pink envelope.

"Certainly, may I ask what it's an invitation to?" asked Georgy.

"Our Society, the Wolverhampton and District Choral, is giving a recital on May eleventh. We were very much hoping Mr Powell would be the guest of honour."

Enoch grimaced. He could see Georgy flipping pages of his appointment book. She was a handsome woman. Good cheekbones. A magnificent bust, cosseted in a lamb's wool twin set. Enoch liked that Georgy didn't run to pearls like most of the other Tory women. He felt a wave of affection for her. She'd been a fixture in the Wolverhampton office since before he was first elected in 1950. Georgy had worked alongside him every minute of that initial gruelling campaign. As well as her other chores, she insisted on going through the drudgery of finding out the names and addresses of those who voted by post, something Labour didn't seem concerned about. She sent out appeals to postal voters outlining policy and asking for their support. Enoch squeaked in with a mere six hundred and ninety-one majority. The twelve hundred postal votes may well have won him the election. He'd been grateful to Georgy ever since. Constancy of friends and acquaintances often eluded Enoch. Georgy was the exception.

"Brigadier Powell will be in town that weekend, and as far as I can see he's free, said Georgy. She disagreed with Tory strategists in Westminster who thought it best Enoch drop his military title. She continued to use it whenever possible. "Tell you what? Why don't you ask him yourself? I'll just get him."

Damn! Enoch quickly straightened and studied typewritten sheets in front of him. He rarely refused if somebody wandered into the office wanting to see him, although he could see little point or benefit of the encounters.

"All MPs detest their constituents to a greater or lesser degree," he'd once told Georgy.

They were at a public meeting at the time. Georgy had hissed at him to keep his voice down. Enoch was surprised by her reaction. He thought she'd have known him well enough to realize he was perfectly aware of the ramifications should he be overheard. He may lose a couple of votes, but he was confident of his overall majority. Enoch never said anything without calculating its effect, therefore he rarely regretted a single word he uttered. If he ever did, he certainly never admitted it.

"I hope I'm not being a pain," said the woman, visibly

fluttering, her hand at her throat, the other adjusting its hold on her handbag.

"It's very kind of you to ask, but I'm afraid I couldn't possibly accept," said Enoch. Although by no means thin, Enoch had once been described as gaunt. He'd disliked the description, believing it indicated a sloppy stance. Nevertheless he was aware of a physical awkwardness. His limbs sometimes behaved more stiffly than he'd have liked, his fingers occasionally plucked at his thigh of their own accord. As he fixed the woman with a stare, he straightened, realizing his shoulders were hunched. "I avoid things of that nature, concerts and recitals, because they tend to interfere with one's heartstrings. I avoid works of fiction for the same reason. It simply doesn't do to awaken longings that can't be fulfilled."

The woman looked at Enoch, eyes narrowed. He recognized the expression, it often flickered across people's faces after he'd spoken. Disbelief, incomprehension, irritation.

"I think you overestimate the abilities of our choir," said the woman, her hands now still.

"I wish your event every success," said Enoch. He gave what he thought was a warm smile, teeth bared, eyes narrowed.

"Another happy customer," said Georgy once the door closed after the woman.

If there'd been anyone else working in the constituency office Enoch would have been inclined to make some kind of riposte. But they were alone, so he forgave Georgy her sarcasm.

"One can't help but wonder what it is exactly that might interfere with your heartstrings. What longings do you have that can't be fulfilled?"

Georgy looked expectantly at Enoch. He knew immediately her implication. It was probably something she'd wanted to ask him for some time, but had only now been supplied with the opportunity. He couldn't remember when he was first aware there was a rumour, but he recalled feeling not displeased that one existed – he'd obviously achieved some recognition if people were speculating on his sexuality. Perhaps the talk began after he'd voted for the decriminalization of homosexuality, even though his vote was motivated simply because he didn't believe sex between consenting adults to be a proper area for the criminal law to operate. Only three other Tories had voted in favour. As far as he knew they weren't being tarred with the same brush. Perhaps it was Enoch's poetry. His poems were so obviously influenced by A. E. Houseman. Although aware of Houseman's predilections, Enoch couldn't remember a hint of sexual overture from the poet when he was his tutor at Cambridge. Photos from those days portray an intensity of sensitivity in Enoch's pale features, which must surely have been attractive to the great man. Perhaps Houseman's deep-seated suppression of passion, the severity of which was obvious in his poems, had come to bear. On his part Enoch had always been wary of the lack of control that would surely accompany unbridled lust. When not at lectures, Enoch spent eighteen hours a day in his room studying. During the colder months he wrapped himself in an overcoat and scarf rather than light the gas fire. Would he respond frankly to Georgy's question? Confrontation was something Enoch never shied away from. In fact he relished it as an opportunity to hammer home his points of view. And he considered Georgy a trustworthy friend, although he doubted the sentiment was reciprocated in those exact terms. Enoch judged Georgy unlikely to understand completely, although he was certain she'd empathize.

"My longings now are many and various, but none are of the variety you insinuate, as others have done – all off the mark, of course. Nevertheless, even at the risk of being misunderstood it would be wrong to deny the fact that I have been, and remain, romantic, to use the wider sense of the word. It's a mistake to discount the emotional factor in politics and politicians. One can't fully understand events in history without taking it into account."

Then, at the risk of fuelling the fire of Georgy's insinuation, Enoch quoted the last lines of a poem he wrote during the war, some six months after Tommy Thomas was killed. It perfectly illustrated his romanticism surrounding the ultimate sacrifice of dying for one's country. When he and Tommy parted in Singapore he'd known it was the last time they'd see each other. It was the most painful parting of his life, and had haunted him ever since.

"That I for ever and alone remain
On this side of the separating flame."

As if on cue, Enoch's eyes filled with tears. He thought back to the time he visited Thomas's parents, a year-and-a-half before his death. He was keen to meet the combination that produced the miracle. But Enoch left Tommy's home in Sittingbourne feeling desolate. The ordinariness of the Thomas family had acted as a catalyst for the revelation that he'd spent the previous five years in a love affair that was not only one-sided but likely to be the only one he'd ever experience. And with a member of the wrong sex to boot. Enoch knew he'd been naïve about matters of the heart. He still was to a certain extent – there was that unfortunate misunderstanding of the engagement he thought he'd had with Barbara Kennedy during his early years in Wolverhampton. The only woman except for Pam he'd had romantic feelings for. Nevertheless he still thought of his relationship with Tommy as a love affair, albeit unconsummated. After his visit to the Thomas household Enoch was left in a strange stew of negative emotions. He realized he'd experienced in his twenties what most men, if they encounter it at all, only feel in their teens. He added arrested development to the other disadvantages of being an only child. After his visit to Sittingbourne, Enoch hadn't allowed his bitterness to change his treatment of Tommy, who was an unwitting participant after all. He remained a beloved hero. After he was killed, Tommy Thomas became symbolic of the bravery of war. The regret that he hadn't been killed himself had never completely left Enoch – rooted in the loneliness of separation expressed in the two lines he'd quoted from his poem.

"One's love at the time was for a whole generation that was doomed. Although does one not also love young men from being young?" Enoch asked Georgy. "It was only after the war, when life stretched ahead of me, that I saw women for the first time. Before then, Greek deities were more familiar to me than the opposite sex."

"No surprise there. Women are alien creatures to most men," said Georgy. "But I'll just add one thought. Which is that, should one want to fulfill certain longings, you only have to look at Ted Heath to know it's perfectly possible in politics as long as you keep your head down. Although it must be easy for him, being such a cold fish. The man doesn't appear to have a passionate bone in his body."

Enoch laughed uproariously. Georgy's ability to take the sting out of a situation was remarkable. It was obvious she knew only too well that if she played to Enoch's intense dislike of Heath she'd lighten the moment. But Georgy wasn't smiling, she eyed Enoch.

"The danger is, I suppose, that if one were insistent on denying part of oneself, how much easier it might be to deny other aspects of one's character, or those of the rest of the world come to that," said Georgy.

Enoch's amusement faded. However, he admired Georgy's ability for packing a punch having created a smokescreen of levity, making the ensuing strike so much more devastating.

"Yes, I concede that might be a danger ... for some people," he said.

Georgy eyed Enoch for several seconds, her hazel eyes buzzing with intelligence.

At that moment the sound of the front door opening provided a merciful interruption. An overweight man with sparse straw-coloured hair filled the doorway, visibly perspiring.

"Mr Dangerfield, just the man I need," said Enoch. "Come into my office, such as it is."

The back room was more cupboard than office. Barely room for a small desk and two chairs in among shelves of posters, newsletters and postal supplies.

"Wouldn't you be more at home out here? There are lots of spare chairs to spread out on," said Georgy, studying their bulky guest.

"It's perfectly alright. We'll be quite comfortable in here," said Enoch, ushering the man into the room. By moving a box of envelopes he managed to close the door behind him. Enoch squeezed himself into a chair up against the desk to give his visitor room to sit across from him.

"Now, what have you got for me?" he asked.

*　*　*

Nelson felt like a bone being gnawed on by D. I. Gorman. If the policeman asked Nelson once he asked him a hundred times if there'd been any disagreements, quarrels, fallings out, squabbles, scraps, run-ins with Singh. How many ways to say the same rass thing? It was almost as if Gorman knew about the one and only time Nelson and Singh locked horns. But Nelson would be damned if he was going to admit to a little trace-off that soon blew over.

When he was in lodgings Nelson tried his best to go home to Auntie Irene's for Saturday and Sunday nights, as he did the weekend of his spat with Mr Singh. On the Monday morning Nelson dragged himself out of bed before dawn to catch a train from Birmingham to be on the building site in Wolverhampton by seven-thirty. When he reached the Sunrise Boarding House at the end of the day he was looking forward to a good sleep. But his bed wasn't made up. There were fresh sheets on the bed belonging to Charlie, the man Nelson shared a room with, but none on his.

Nelson would never forget the first time he boarded with his fellow workers. Not one of them wanted to share with the only coloured boy they'd had on the crew. After a lot of argument the men pulled straws to decide who'd be stuck with Nelson.

"Like me was something to scorn," he told Auntie Irene.

The loser, Charlie, wasn't happy. But he soon changed his tune once he discovered Nelson didn't snore. The other men made enough noise to rattle the windows.

The only time Mr Singh ever showed up was on a Friday, when he hung around to pick up rent. 'Strictly emergencies only' was scrawled in big letters above the landlord's phone number, which was posted above a coin-operated phone in the hallway of the boarding house. Nelson considered the situation enough of an emergency. What him pay all that rass money for if not for sheets on his bed? But Mr Singh had a different opinion. The cupboard where he stored clean linen was locked, he had the only key and he was damned if he was going to run all the way over to the Sunrise to make up one bed. Nelson could sleep under the blankets for one night and the bed would be made up the next day. The argument ended only because Nelson ran out of pennies for the pay phone. As he went back to his and Charlie's room, Nelson cursed the landlord up and down – everyone in the place must have heard.

When Nelson complained to Charlie he said, "Fuck that nonsense," and stalked off.

Charlie vex? Nelson never knew in the Mother Land when what he said might give offence. Charlie came back ten minutes later with clean sheets.

"Which part you get these from?"

Charlie tapped the side of his nose and grinned.

"You broke into the cupboard? You mad or what? Them going think is me do it."

Despite sleeping between clean sheets Nelson tossed and turned. He knew he'd be blamed for breaking open the linen cupboard. Sure enough, despite Charlie insisting it hadn't been Nelson who'd forced the lock, Mr Singh threatened to call the police. Nelson managed to put a lid on his frustration and offered to pay for the repairs. Afterwards Charlie slipped Nelson a couple of pounds towards the cost. His friend – which Charlie was by then – had come a long way since the day he'd pulled the short straw and been forced to share a room with a coloured boy. But that was small comfort to Nelson.

He didn't know how he found the strength to resist the onslaught of Gorman's questions. But the more the detective persisted the more Nelson denied he had anything to do with the assault.

"Tell why me go all them miles to Wolverhampton just to mess with that rass Sikh when me relaxin' at home in Handsworth."

Gorman picked up his papers and stalked out of the interview room.

"Don't think we done, bwoy," said the skinny ghost. He slammed the door shut behind him.

Nelson heard the whoosh of tires, another car passing on the road outside the room. He glanced at sunlight seeping through the frosted glass of a window not much bigger than a toilet's. If he can't see out, then nobody passing by can see the goings-on inside either. Marks on the concrete floor didn't look like bloodstains, but hard to tell. Seats of chairs were worn through to bare wood. Nelson guessed hundreds, maybe thousands, of people's backsides sat there. What happen to them in this room, all those people?

Nelson was losing his battle with fear. The stench of an ashtray on the window ledge crammed with cigarette butts sickened him. He moved to the other side of the table and sat down in Gorman's chair. Nelson hoped to hell they weren't looking into how he got his scar. He couldn't protest his innocence so easily about that. But them can't find out what happen in Jamaica from Birmingham, surely? The only person in England who knew was Auntie Irene and she would never breathe a word.

The only time Auntie Irene brought it up was when she met Nelson at New Street station, when he arrived from Jamaica, New Year's Day before last. So cold he believed he'd lose his nose, ears, toes, and fingers too. It was July before the chill in his bones eased. The time before he arrived in England wasn't easy – the robbery, rough voyage, seasick 'til he feel like dying. Not to mention the strangeness of the Mother Land. In all his twenty-one years Nelson had never seen so many houses. Rows and rows of them, stretching cheek by jowl for miles along the railway. Then, when he saw how Irene favoured his mother, he almost broke down right there on the station platform.

"My Lord, people must think twice 'bout boxing with you," Irene said.

Perhaps then she mistook his eyes watering for him hurting, because then she spoke kindly and said it was not a bad thing for people to treat him with care, and if anything the scar made the rest of him look more handsome. But no matter how many times Nelson looked in a mirror his forehead puckered when he saw the angry gash bisecting his cheek. Nelson wished more than anything in his life he hadn't fought against the three robbers after they took the billfold his dead father gave him. Bad enough he was robbed and cut, without making matters worse. It was after he saw red – his own blood, rage, or both – that he lashed out.

Nelson glanced around the interview room and told himself to ease up. He closed his eyes and tried to conjure up the heat of Caribbean sun on his shoulders. He imagined the chair seat was a wooden step outside his mother's door in the hills above Port Antonio. He managed to summon up the sweet and sour scent of rotting mangoes. Nelson strained to hear palm fronds rustling above his head. He saw a cloud of dust motes drifting in sunlight, propelled into torrid Jamaican air by a passing friend. He called out to him, "Wha'ppn my yute?"

Nelson took a breath, shoulders slumped. But his few seconds of relief were soon shattered by a snap of the latch. A thickset uniformed policeman with a ruddy face loomed in the doorway. Is wha' this 'pon me now? But Nelson knew the answer only too well – this one was obviously sent to beat a confession out of him.

"You're free to go. But don't leave the country. No cruises to the Caribbean, you hear?"

Nelson didn't need telling twice. He was past the officer and down the hall before anybody changed their mind. But, not believing he could just walk free, he hesitated in front of a wooden counter that ran the length of the foyer. The pockmarked skeleton of a man who'd hovered behind Gorman, silent as the grave unless giving a translation, stood behind the counter with a telephone to his ear. He stared back at Nelson and winked. But it was a wink so full of malice it made Nelson's guts churn all over again.

"What are you waiting for, Sambo? The banana boat doesn't stop here, you know," said the uniformed policeman, who'd followed Nelson down the hall.

* * *

When Nelson came out of the police station he worried he'd break out crying. Partly from the relief of sun on his face – even weak English sunlight – but mainly because Auntie Irene stood on the pavement waiting for him, rooted and solid as Tom Cringle's cotton tree.

"Wha' you doin' here, Auntie?"

"I got a call to come tell 'bout your whereabouts yesterday mornin'. And I make sure put myself together nice. Next thing them think we don't come from nowhere."

Auntie Irene and Nelson's mother looked like twins

though a full year separated them. But his mother never wore a dress with a riot of red roses all over it like Irene's. She could never afford it. Nor the white-leather handbag dangling from Irene's elbow. A pink straw hat crowned with a silk hibiscus flower perched on top of Irene's tight waves. Her right hand gripped her left wrist while fleshy forearms rested on the curve of her belly. She could have been any one of her five sisters back home – Nelson's mother and his four other aunts. If Nelson came within reach of any one of them, they pulled him to them, strong as any man. The smell of cocoa butter almost choked him. Then they kissed him, despite him pretending he didn't like it. Nelson thought one of those rib-crusher kisses would be welcome right then. But, dressed as if for church, Auntie Irene acted accordingly and just pecked Nelson's cheek, though he felt a glow because it was the scar side she kissed.

Ever since Nelson could remember, he heard stories about his mother's older sister. Every Christmas while he was growing up a gift arrived for him from England wrapped in brightly coloured paper. One time the paper showed dark green leaves with red berries covered with gobs of white guck. Snow, according to his mother. His favourite present from Irene was a plastic contraption with a lever he pulled to make silver ball bearings shoot round and round and, if he was lucky, fall into one of the holes with a number next to it. Otherwise they fell to the bottom to be shot around again. Nelson's mother told everyone her sister had been one of the first to leave Jamaica for the Mother Land. Sometimes she hauled out Auntie Irene's old letters and postcards. Nelson remembered a picture of the King of England, crown and all. On the back, in her even script, Irene described sailing into Tilbury on a sunny June day after twenty-two days aboard the Empire Windrush. She often described to Nelson how she saw whole streets of houses smashed to pieces, debris from the air raids of World War II.

"I tell you, when I came here there was hardly any buildings standin' and as far as you see everything bomb up and burn down through and through. Still and all, it was easy those times though, compare to how it stay these days. They did want us bad back then. The National Health Service just start and they was cryin' for nurses, any colour, black or white."

As Auntie Irene explained to Nelson how she came to be standing outside the police station she kept her eyes fixed on a point behind him. When he turned to look, he saw the pallid, pockmarked man standing at the window staring back at them.

"Come, make haste, make we go home," said Auntie Irene. She took his arm and steered him up the street. "That one always make me skin scratch me," she said, looking straight ahead towards the bus stop that stood a hundred yards or so down the road.

"You know him?"

"I've seen him around the hospital. When you see him you know trouble set like rain."

"Him talk like we, you know."

"Like you, you mean."

Auntie Irene was always scolding Nelson for using slang.

"Is Jamaica him come from. Spanish Town," she said.

Nelson was aware that white-skinned Jamaicans existed, he'd seen white nyegas before. But they at least had a little colour. The man in the police station looked like the sun never kissed his skin, let alone lingered on it to stain it like it did with white people back home.

They sat downstairs on the bus because Auntie Irene, even after twenty years of riding British double-deckers, was convinced the thing might tip over.

"Does no harm to be safe and sit inside" she always said.

Nelson thought there must be some sense to this – Irene was a qualified nurse after all – but he couldn't see how sitting downstairs would be any less of a calamity if the bus did indeed topple over. But he knew not to argue with Auntie Irene.

"His name is Fowler. According to what I hear, they bring him up from Jamaica so them can know what Jamaican saying in patois," explained Auntie Irene.

"Him a police now?" Nelson asked. He thought the man seemed more like a paid thug.

"Yes, but law don't mean much when it comes to that one. You wouldn't believe the stories I hear from some of the blood-up patients who come to Emergency."

Nelson's idea of British detectives came from polite plainclothed policemen in Sherlock Holmes novels he'd read at school. Fowler didn't fit at all. Neither did D.I. Gorman come to that. But it came as no surprise – Nelson already discovered a whole heap of things he'd been told about the Mother Land were all pure lies.

"Anyway, we don't need to worry about Fowler no more.

I told Inspector Gorman you was home with me all day long from the moment you get up out of bed, and enough people can back me up."

Nelson wasn't so sure so many people could swear he was home as Irene thought. He could only remember three who'd dropped in. An older man named Cecil had come inside for a few minutes to leave the church magazine. Irene's friend Delilah came by so Irene could style her hair in the kitchen. Nelson kept out of their way in the living room and read the *Gleaner* to catch up on news from back home. And a handyman called Charles spent an hour or so at the house mending a tap in the bathroom upstairs.

"They ask 'bout your scar?" Irene asked.

"Yeh, but I only tell how me tief and cut."

"Good. Make sure it stay that way."

Nelson prickled with irritation. She think him run back to the police and tell everything? But he knew she meant well, so he sat still and said nothing. As the bus neared Auntie Irene's place, Nelson peered out of the window at people crowding the streets of Handsworth. Seeing West Indian faces usually made him feel better. But all he could think about was hundreds of thousands of roads and avenues running all over Britain full of white people. Thousands, maybe millions of them. It made those few Birmingham streets – the ones where his fellow Caribbean islanders lived – seem smaller than his village back in Jamaica.

Despite the warmth of Auntie Irene's arm pressing against his, Nelson felt chilled. He ached for home, like the worst hunger pains possible. But his mother's warm wooden step drenched in dusty Jamaican sunshine may as well have been on the moon.

***

Enoch walked his guest to the front door of the constituency office. Not something he'd normally do, but he didn't want Barry Dangerfield to feel unappreciated. He'd had to reject the stories Dangerfield had come up with thus far. They were too obviously smoke and mirrors – Enoch didn't want a repeat of the fiasco that unfolded after his Walsall speech back in February. Since then he'd received letters rife with lurid stories, but nothing he could use. They were too imbued with intolerance and/or undisguised hate to be taken seriously. He needed an anecdote that rang true, with no obvious agenda, but would get to the heart of the fear he was convinced many people felt. An account that would guarantee an avalanche of righteous indignation.

"Tomorrow then?" asked Enoch.

"Tomorrow," said his guest.

Enoch watched as Barry Dangerfield made his way towards Chapel Ash, surprisingly nimble for such a large man. Before he turned back to the office Enoch stood to inspect the buildings on the other side of Tettenhall Road. He gazed admiringly at a handsome row of three-storey terraced houses, not unlike his own late-Georgian house in London. Directly opposite was a double-fronted detached mansion with lawn on either side of an imposing front door portico. Admittedly some buildings had been converted to offices or flats, but to Enoch they still screamed gentility. His interest in architecture didn't stop with the physical features of a building. Enoch rather saw style and structure as an expression of their owners and the lives they lived.

"What's your opinion on property values on my side of the divide?" Enoch asked Georgy.

"The divide?"

"Compton Road," said Enoch.

"I never think of it as a divide."

"Perhaps that's because you own a house on the smarter side," said Enoch.

Georgy looked at Enoch, her head to one side.

"I suppose property in your immediate neighbourhood is worth less than in mine, but it always was. Your house suits you, doesn't it?"

Enoch doubted Georgy capable of harbouring any of the usual Tory discrimination toward his lower middle-class background, but he wondered about her use of the word 'suits.' Did Georgy's question imply he belonged on Merridale Road? Or was it an innocent question about his fondness for the house? A glimmer of doubt must have shown on his face.

"It's only your constituency house after all. Your proper house is in Belgravia, for Heavens sake. And smart side or not, you never know about people's lives. Look at us, we're as poor as church mice since Humphrey had to take early retirement from the bank."

Georgy's husband, Humphrey, was hampered by crippling arthritis. Not the agile young man Enoch had once known in India, where they'd first met during the war. Enoch hadn't recognized him when Georgy re-introduced them. It was only when Humphrey sheepishly reminded Enoch of their first meeting in 1943 that the penny dropped. Enoch had just returned to Delhi from a reconnaissance along the border with Burma. Young Verington-Delaunay, wet behind the ears but keen as mustard, had turned up at British HQ in Enoch's absence. Enoch arrived back from his mission and demanded that Humphrey, who'd been assigned to keep track of such things, show him plans for the invasion of Burma. Humphrey downright refused until he'd phoned military intelligence to see if Powell was genuine. Eventually somebody came along and put matters straight. It turned out Humphrey suspected Enoch, who had a touch of jaundice at the time, of being a Japanese spy. As well as his yellow skin, Humphrey pointed to Enoch's dark spiky hair and the fact the he wore the entire pukka khaki drill – tunic and tie, long trousers, the lot – while all the other British officers wore open-neck shirts and shorts, a dispensation for the hot as Hades weather. Enoch persisted in wearing full uniform no matter what the temperature – and he always worked through the worst heat of the day, while everybody else wilted on barracks cots. It was his way of proving that he could adhere to army protocol better than any Eton-educated, Sandhurst-trained officer. Enoch had never understood why Humphrey mistaking him for Japanese caused so much hilarity among his fellow officers.

"If you deduce that I'm asking about property values because my concern is for my house as a form of investment, you are mistaken," said Enoch. "I'm simply wondering what the effect of an influx of immigrants might be on prices."

"I suppose it may have a negative effect but you're not

going to lose, are you? Not at the low price you paid for the house almost fifteen years ago."

"Again, my concern is not with my own property."

"Of course not," said Georgy. Then, before Enoch could belabour the point, she said, "Who was that fellow? Wasn't he knocking around a couple of months ago, at the time you gave the Walsall speech?"

Georgy had made no bones about her low opinion of his Walsall speech. She'd been disgusted when the story he'd quoted, about a solitary white girl in a class at one of the local schools being swamped by coloured children, proved to be a flagrant misrepresentation. It had emerged that the girl wasn't the only white child in the class at all. It was just that other locally born pupils were off sick on the day in question. Those with an axe to grind still took the story at face value. It came as no surprise to Enoch that people continued to believe an untruth if it suited their purposes. Fabricated story or not, he'd made his point. But not as cogently as he'd have liked. Despite popular local support and the spate of letters there was hardly any press coverage. He was desperate to make sure his Birmingham speech would garner more widespread attention.

"Is your plump friend perhaps one of the hopeless and helpless?" asked Georgy.

She was referring – somewhat mockingly, Enoch noticed – to a line in the Walsall speech in which Enoch had claimed there was "a sense of hopelessness and helplessness" thereabouts because the authorities paid no attention to the fact that people were being inundated by immigrants.

"You may be joking, but he is in fact feeling somewhat hopeless and helpless. He feels he has little power over an illegal nightclub in Whitmore Reans, which he claims is damaging his business."

"His business?"

"He owns a pub in the town centre. Students mostly. Who seem to be finding the exoticism of this nightclub hard to resist."

"What does he expect you to do about it? Surely it's a town council concern."

"Exactly what I've told him," said Enoch.

"It's a wonder students have either time or money to frequent nightclubs. Shouldn't they be studying, for heavens sake?" said Georgy.

Georgy had once told Enoch she'd emerged from Benenden in 1933 with top marks in her school matriculation, good enough for a place at any university in the land. Whether her father would have allowed her to attend became a moot point when he lost his fortune. He blamed Labour Prime Minister Ramsay MacDonald for the economic downturn that led to his insolvency. Whatever the reason, Georgy's academic aspirations disappeared along with her father's wealth. There were no government hand-outs for further education in those days.

At that moment one of the volunteers arrived to spend the afternoon printing out a newsletter that carried Enoch's memoranda and other tidbits of news relevant to his riding. Enoch disliked the smell of the Gestetner duplicating device. The ink smelt pungent and slightly putrid. It reminded him of smells he'd experienced in the alleys and side streets of Delhi. He'd enjoyed many of the heady aromas India offered, but this wasn't one of them. Enoch decided to head for home, where Pam could make a clean transcript of his altered pages. As he gathered his things from the back room he could hear the volunteer and Georgy in a heated discussion about a report in the newspaper on the rise of sexually transmitted diseases.

"I blame the permissive society," said the volunteer.

"I do wish people wouldn't use that term pejoratively," said Georgy. "On one hand we treat innovations like the birth control pill and miniskirts as portents of social erosion, and on the other hand we belittle them as insignificant. Why can't we just see these things as emblematic of the massive transformation that's happening before our eyes? We Tories should be learning from the phenomena, instead of decrying a complete generation's behaviour."

"But young people aren't interested in politics," said the volunteer.

"Then we should bloody well make them interested. Just look at the number of people born since the war. And it won't be long till the voting age is reduced to eighteen. If we don't start appealing to them PDQ it'll be too late."

As he left the office Enoch couldn't resist joining the fray.

"But Georgy, I often talk to the pupils of the Wolverhampton schools of which I'm a governor."

"Addressing the pupils of the Girls High and the Boys Grammar on Prize Day once a year isn't exactly engaging with young people, is it Enoch? We're sending the message we don't care about them. For example, you once dismissed the Beatles by saying you had 'nothing against' them. I'm amazed that – as a poet, let alone a politician – you're not more interested in what they have to say, especially given their popularity. If they ran for parliament they'd win by a landslide."

"We should be grateful then that neither they nor the Rolling Stones are likely to seek an elected position any time soon. See you tomorrow."

As Enoch left the office he could sense more than see Georgy's expression of frustration. He smiled as he let the door close behind him. He decided to take a long route home. The walk would do him good. There hadn't been any opportunity for one of his restorative countryside rambles during the Easter weekend. He assumed his normal brisk clip, shoulders slightly stooped, brief case in one hand, the other swinging somewhat stiffly at his side. But when Enoch reached the once-genteel square aptly named Park Dale, he slowed to admire blossom thick as cream dripping from ornamental apple trees. Most of the mansions on either side of the grassy rectangle of land had been divided into warrens of flats and bedsits, inhabited mainly by students. Gardens were unkempt, driveways weedy. Here and there paint peeled from window frames. Nevertheless the leafy park, bordered on both sides by imposing 19th-century houses, appealed to Enoch's lingering infatuation with Britain's imperial past. Gazing at blue-slated mansard roofs rising above treetops, he could easily imagine chauffeured motorcars coming and going. Servants polishing door knockers, gardeners mowing manicured lawns. It was hard for him to accept those halcyon days were finished forever. Impossible for him to come to terms with that fact that there wasn't a British ship on every ocean of the world with three funnels and 16-inch guns, ready and able to blow out of the water any other navy it was likely to face. If it was true, and *Pax Brittanica* – British dominance in the absence of any challengers – was indeed a thing of the past, he feared for the world. On a less emotional level he knew only too well, of course, the Empire was finished. But that left him wondering, who on Earth was going to keep things in order? God forbid it would be the Americans.

"Mr Powell, good afternoon."

Enoch was yanked from his reverie by a short woman with gleaming black hair pulled back into a bun so tightly crafted it appeared hard as ebony. He'd known Signora Macchia since he was first elected. Born in Wolverhampton of Neapolitan immigrants, who'd come to Britain after World War I, she acted as Italian Consul for the Midlands. She'd worked on his election campaigns, browbeating the local Italian population into supporting him. As well as her own house she owned four others in Park Dale, all rented to students, who she controlled with an iron fist.

"*Buonasera, Signora. Molto felice di vederla,*" said Enoch. His morose thoughts about the end of the Empire were instantly vanquished by the schoolboy thrill of being able to show off his Italian. As a child he'd taken to languages like a duck to water, maybe because his mother had tutored him rigorously in Greek, having taught it to herself when she was young. She didn't let up until young Enoch had a comprehensive grounding to take to his prestigious new school. He never forgot the exquisite pleasure of seeing his mother's shining eyes when she received a letter announcing that he'd won a scholarship to King Edward's School for boys. Her prodigy had begun to fulfill her fierce ambition for him as a scholarship-winning, knowledge-devouring student. Her aspirations were overwhelmingly accomplished when he later won fistfuls of prizes and scholarships at Cambridge, and was finally awarded First Class Honours with Distinction. On arriving at Kind Edward School Enoch announced to his new classmates that he intended to better them all in Greek. His pronouncement proved true, but despite the satisfaction of achievement and the thrill of his mother's approval, whenever Enoch looked back at his time at school he experienced twinges of sadness. Reaching the apex of scholarship left no time for socializing with his new classmates, and he rarely saw the few acquaintances he'd left behind at the local secondary school. When he considered the years he travelled by train alone back and forth from his home in Kings Norton to his exclusive school in the centre of Birmingham a feeling of desolation threatened to overwhelm him. Enoch often wondered about the long-term consequences of deprivation of early experience in social relationships. He found it difficult to make friends once he arrived at Cambridge. He spent university holidays roaming around the British countryside alone.

"Good to see you too," said Signora Macchia.

Enoch was irritated when she didn't respond to his Italian by speaking it back to him. He'd once commented on it. She'd replied that it had been difficult growing up with parents who barely spoke English.

"It was stupid of me, but as a child I was actually ashamed of my mother and father. To this day I feel slightly embarrassed to be speaking Italian to an English person."

"But it would be a great shame to lose the advantages of culture and language which your patrimony supplies," Enoch had replied.

Signora Macchia agreed, explaining that she later realized what a rich and interesting heritage she had at her fingertips.

"Which is why I work within the Italian community to preserve our traditions and customs."

"I'm well aware of the intensity with which you work," said Enoch, who'd attended some of the events she'd organized. "You are to be applauded for it."

"I'm looking forward to Saturday," said Signora Macchia.

"You're attending the CPC meeting?" asked Powell.

"The CPC?"

"I'm addressing the Conservative Political Centre's annual meeting in Birmingham on Saturday afternoon."

"I hope you haven't forgotten you're coming to address our group that evening," said Signora Macchia.

"On the contrary," Enoch lied. "I've been revelling in the joys of Italian in preparation for my talk."

"*Bravo! A presto,*" said Signora Macchia.

"*A Sabato,*" said Enoch,

As he walked away, beaming in the flush of his exchange with Signora Macchia, Enoch considered translating the speech he was to make earlier on Saturday for her group later the same day. But he quickly discounted the idea of regurgitating a speech about the perils of a large immigrant population – half the room would be immigrants and the other half children of immigrants, albeit Caucasian. He'd have to come up with something else.

There was something vaguely feline about Enoch's features, and at that moment a passer-by may have thought he resembled the cat that drank the cream as he considered his linguistic skills. Accomplished in Greek and Latin obviously, but also Urdu and Hindi, both of which he'd learnt while in India. He tried to avoid memories of polishing his Urdu at the School of Oriental and African Studies once he returned to England. They evoked fresh disappointment at having his hopes for high office in India bitterly dashed when the country was prematurely – in his opinion – handed independence. He'd been convinced he'd be Viceroy of India, never dreaming the position could vanish in an explosion of secular violence when India was handed its independence. Out of curiosity in his forebears Enoch taught himself mediaeval Welsh. Russian too. He had a good amount of French, France being a place he and Pam escaped to regularly. "Because God takes his holidays there," Enoch always said. But it had been German that gave him the most pleasure. When he discovered German he found the language he'd dreamt of but never knew existed. Hard-edged, jagged, with words of such complexity and structure they were the embodiment of precision, yet imbued with romance. Sentences in everyday German seemed to Enoch so full of melody they struck him as more poetry than prose. He was liberated – transformed – when he spoke German. He could express emotions that were impossible to articulate in any other language. He immersed himself in the culture, progressing from Goethe to Wagner and finally to Nietzsche. Enoch embraced the philosopher's 'God is dead' maxim with zeal, having already eschewed Christianity, recognizing it as just one of many faith systems dreamt up by a person or group of people in order to control society. Enoch so idolized Nietzsche he grew a moustache like his.

His disillusionment with German and Germany hit him as precipitously and as drastically as a lightning bolt when he heard the news about Hitler's purging of the Brown Shirts in 1934. Many were murdered, including their leader Ernst Röhm.

"Turning my back on Germany and German was one of the hardest things I've ever had to do," he told a producer at the BBC Radio overseas service for whom he'd prepared broadcasts in German. "But I no longer believed that Germany could be my spiritual homeland when there is no justice, where justice does not reign. Overnight my spiritual homeland disappeared."

"But aren't you rather throwing the baby out with the bath water," said the producer. "Admittedly recent events tend to colour one's view of the German character, but the culture endures. Goethe, for example, isn't guilty of any wrongdoing, his life and work remain the same."

"I don't see it that way," said Enoch. "To me it's all been illusion, fantasy, a self-created myth. Music, philosophy, poetry, science and the language itself – everything has been demolished, broken to bits on the cliffs of a monstrous reality."

"But the political machinations of a country are often a

totally different kettle of fish than its cultural life. You have to view them separately. I think you're overreacting."

But Enoch couldn't be persuaded.

"I'm not condoning Hitler's methods by any means," said the BBC producer. "but it sounds as if Röhm and his nancy-boy army were out of control."

"The fact that Ernst Röhm may have been assassinated for his sexuality only makes matters worse. By that standard a good portion of the politicians in Britain would be put to death," said Enoch.

Walking up Compton Road toward his house, Enoch came within sight of the crenelated tower of the Grammar School. It reminded him that he owed a letter to the deputy headmaster, a Classics scholar. He and Enoch had been writing back and forth about the inefficiency of the bin men who came to pick up the school's rubbish. Normally Enoch wouldn't concern himself with something so insignificant. He'd suggest an approach to the town council, but the man had written his introductory letter in Ancient Greek. Enoch replied in the same manner. He was tickled pink by the idea of correspondence about such a mundane contemporary problem being conducted in Ancient Greek. He couldn't wait to get home to compose his next missive.

* * *

After wolfing down a steak and kidney pie for his lunch, Frank left The Vine eager to try out Barry's idea of doctoring one of the photos he'd taken at the demonstration. He worked through the afternoon in the rubicund murk of a stuffy darkroom, tucked under the roof of the Victorian building that housed Wolverhampton College of Art. Frank had to admit he wasn't known for spending time doing anything *during* classes, let alone after. Nevertheless he was quite hurt when his photography teacher, Dave Bishop, feigned heart-stopping astonishment at his request to use the darkroom for a few hours after class. Frank was anxious to have a print ready for the editor of *VoxPop,* who he'd arranged to meet later that evening.

A rust-coloured safelight dangled inches above Frank's unkempt hair. He watched intently as an image gradually emerged on a stark white rectangle of photo paper lying in a bath of developing fluid. Puppet On A String played on a tinny transistor radio. Songbird Sandy Shaw was too perky for his taste. He flicked off the radio, then gently raised and lowered one end of a black plastic tray, sending slow undulations of clear developer along the surface of the photograph. With each surge the image strengthened. It seemed to Frank as if a column of demonstrators, in lines five abreast, were trudging in slow motion toward him out of a dense white fog. As each ripple of developer crested along the length of the print the mist became less opaque.

Transistor silenced, the only sound was a steady drip from a tap with a faulty washer. A daubed slogan on the print turned gradually from pale blur to darker clarity on a placard: Racists Out! Frank could see a rivulet of black that dribbled from the point of the exclamation mark and disappeared off the bottom edge of the sign, giving the illusion that wet paint was dripping onto a mop of frizzy hair belonging to the demonstrator who brandished the banner above her head.

It wasn't difficult now for Frank to detect the dark-skinned face on the photo print that he'd keenly anticipated. In his excitement he raised the developing tray higher than intended. Fluid slopped over the end furthest from him, liberated developer made its escape down the sink's drain with a loud trickle. Frank lowered the tray and stared intently while the shadowy spot assumed distinct areas of light and shade. Dark flares of wide nostrils were slowly delineated. Frank could make out sensuous curves of high cheekbones, each bordered by a scimitar of impenetrable, black whisker. Once the developer had worked its magic Nelson's scar was clearly visible, noticeably lighter in tone than the dusky skin surrounding it. The weather at the demo had been frigid for the beginning of April. In comparison to Nelson, the neighbouring marchers' faces appeared wraithlike. The strongest attributes of the chilled physiognomies of the four white students in the front line were shadowy saucers of open mouths. The marchers' strident chant could almost be heard: Down With Racism! Racists Out!

The photo looked completely natural. Nobody would ever suspect that any meddling had taken place. Frank felt a warm glow of gratitude towards the publican of The Vine. He had to admit that Barry's idea to manipulate – Frank couldn't bring himself to use the word 'fake' – the photo had been a stroke of brilliance. As more subtleties in shades on the black-and-white photo print became obvious, stripes in varying tones of grey separated themselves from each other on college scarves worn by a couple of the marchers who strode toward

Frank. The stripes could have held the insignia associated with any campus in England – perhaps the London School of Economics, for whom the local students were marching, to show their solidarity in protest over a new director with links to Rhodesia's racist regime. But Frank, who owned an identical scarf as the ones in the photo, knew that they bore the purple, yellow, white, and black stripes that identified them as belonging to students from Wolverhampton College of Art.

Realizing the print had achieved its optimum strength Frank plucked the rectangle of paper out of the developer and plunged it into the stop bath. Vinegary fumes of acetic acid tickled his nostrils. Battered fish and soggy chips wrapped in newspaper came instantly to Frank's mind as he scooped the print out of the stop bath and slid it beneath the surface of the fixer fluid. It had been a long time since his steak-and-kidney-pie lunch. Since then he'd devoted several hours of hard graft to this single print. Now he could relax and admire his handiwork framed by the background of the black plastic fixer tray. He flicked on the radio. The smooth tones of Otis Reading singing Dock o' the Bay seeped into the windowless room. Frank was ecstatic that he'd managed to execute the deception so effectively. It was usually only professional retouchers who undertook such expert work, and few of them achieved the successful result that Frank had engineered. His eyes watered – and not only because they were tired from demanding darkroom work. He wasn't used to the emotions that achievement can generate. For perhaps the first time in Frank's life endorphins frolicked freely in his brain cells. That'd teach him for taking the piss out of hippy-dippy students when they claimed to have experienced a 'natural high.'

The labour had been painstaking. Frank first made a photo print of Nelson so that his body was the same scale as those of the protestors in the photo Barry had seen. With precision worthy of a surgeon, Frank made an incision around Nelson's figure. Then he carefully peeled away the micro-thin layer of paper that held Nelson's image. He glued Nelson on top of a white lad who was slightly smaller. Then Frank shot a negative of the composite picture. He made a new print from the freshly shot negative and used an airbrush to obliterate any peripheral traces of the original student and make Nelson blend in perfectly. Frank could have left it at that and presented the retouched print for reproduction in the newspaper, but he was nothing if not canny. Someone might detect the roughness of airbrush paint on the smooth surface of the print and become suspicious. So Frank made another negative of the retouched print and then used it to make a final, consistently smooth print – the one that now floated gently in the fixer tray in front of him.

Frank wondered briefly if he could use the photo print for part of his final mark at year's end. God knows he'd got little else to show for a winter's worth of study. But he immediately discounted the idea. It might not be a good idea to advertise the fact that he'd doctored the photograph. Although he was sure it happened all the time – half the documentary photos in magazines like *Nova* and *Life* were probably faked or staged. Frank glanced at his watch. Shit!

He was a few minutes late for his meeting with the editor of the student newspaper. He hastily stuffed all his working material – the few strips of original film, the print with Nelson's figure cut out, copy negative, and retouched print – into an envelope.

* * *

When Frank met Steve MacDonald in the Vine an hour before closing time, he was reminded of how much the *VoxPop* editor resembled Bamber Gascoigne, the gangly host of the TV show, University Challenge. Especially when Steve's eyes shone behind tortoiseshell frames of his spectacles, as they did when he saw Frank's photo.

"Excellent. Front page material for sure," he said.

As well as his editorial chores at the student newspaper, Steve undertook the duties of president of the Student Union and organizer of the local arm of the Campaign for Nuclear Disarmament, added to which he sat on more committees than there were days in the week. Frank put Steve's agitprop attitude down to him having been raised a Quaker. In his heart of hearts Frank knew that coming clean was the honourable thing to do, but he was certain the upright editor would reject the photo if he caught even a whiff of tampering. Frank's ambition overcame his qualms – he decided to keep mum about inserting Nelson into the photograph. Steve hadn't attended the demo. He'd been at a CND rally in Birmingham and would have no idea there hadn't been a West Indian among the marchers in Wolverhampton. There was a danger that one of the students in the shot might cry foul, but it was more likely they'd judge the manipulated photograph as 'cool,' and think no more about it.

"This'll show them at LSE," said Steve, sliding his glasses back onto the bridge of his nose with a slim index finger.

It seemed to Frank an odd thing for the *VoxPop* editor to say. He was under the impression the Student Union was showing solidarity with the London School of Economics, not vying with it. But it came as no surprise to Frank that even Quakers could be competitive. Steve grabbed his Donkey jacket, black serge with a band of shiny PVC across the shoulders. The current fashion for art students although designed for navvies and other manual labourers.

"I'll drop this off at the Tech. With a bit of luck we'll find room in this week's issue. Better rush, the inky-fingered boys in the printing department will be starting work about now."

Frank felt a surge of excitement to think his photo was going to be reproduced – actual ink on actual paper.

"It should hit the streets by elevenses tomorrow morning," Steve called as he headed for the door of the pub.

"I'll get a credit next to the photo, right?" Frank yelled after him.

The lanky editor's assurance could just be heard over the slamming of the door. Frank was left to savour his success in solitary jubilation.

Steve had been laying it on a bit thick when he claimed the student rag would 'hit the streets.' Instead of any public thoroughfare, piles of the flimsy four-page tabloid were left lying in strategic positions around college buildings. One location was the smoky, sweaty-walled student common room where an ancient tortoise of a woman named Sadie and her equally wrinkled husband, Bill, prepared massive urns of brackish tea and cups of watery Nescafé. There, as in other places, the weekly newspaper was largely ignored.

An occasional zealous student sometimes made a show of assiduously examining *VoxPop* and then strode off with the newspaper tucked ostentatiously under his or her arm. But most of the copies were scooped up by Sadie or Bill to cover the wet red-tiled floor of the common room once it had been mopped at the end of the day. Frank couldn't remember ever reading any of the editorial content of *VoxPop*. He occasionally glanced at advertisements for student dances to check which lame group the Student Union had cajoled into playing. But, although aware of Steve's exaggeration of the student newspaper's profile, Frank was glowing with a sense of pride – a unique experience for him. He'd be able to say he'd had his work published, even if only a handful of readers came across his photo.

Frank was relieved that Steve hadn't asked for information about any of the people featured. Frank assumed the newspaper would run a general caption under the photo without identifying any of the participants by name. Despite his excitement, Frank couldn't shake a last glimmer of guilt about using Nelson's image – especially when he recalled the good times they'd had the summer before, many of them in the room where he was sitting.

Once Frank discovered he and Nelson were both born on the same day, August 18th, 1946, he cajoled Nelson into joining him for a drink at the Vine after work on the building site. Nelson was reticent at first, but soon seemed to be enjoying his blue-eyed acquaintance's company. Especially Frank's introduction of him to the regulars.

"I'd like you to meet my twin, Nelson. Born just minutes apart."

It never failed. Frank was always rewarded by a puzzled or sceptical expression. At which the two lads pissed themselves laughing. They developed the habit of dropping into the Vine at the end of their working week – payday. As it happened, their twenty-first birthdays fell on a Friday that year. To mark the occasion Frank insisted they follow their usual pints of Guinness with celebratory shots of dark rum. After a couple of beer and rum combinations Nelson switched to lemonade, claiming he'd be sick if he carried on throwing back such a potent mixture.

"It wi' wreck up me insides," he said.

Nelson also maintained that he had to save some of his earnings to pay rent to his Auntie Irene.

"And me sending money to me mother 'pon top of it."

Frank, who wouldn't dream of offering his mother any of his earnings and regularly ignored her farcical advice that he should 'never do anything he wouldn't do in front of her,' continued to drink beer and rum until the bell rang for last orders, by which time he could barely stand.

The Vine was a livelier place back then. Frank glanced around the half-empty bar and told himself that the chances of Nelson ever seeing the student newspaper were zero. Conscience salved, he quaffed his Guinness and reflected on his recent achievement. He finally knew what turned him on, rang his bells, got his motor running. He'd always been envious of kids at school who had an unshakeable conviction about what they wanted to be when they grew up. Frank had no enthusiasm for any particular subject so saw little point in working hard enough to qualify for university. He didn't have a lot of interest in art, but he was sure he had enough talent to be accepted into art school (good composition and excellent colour sense, according to his comprehensive school teacher). He would qualify for a government grant, which made possible his escape from the parental home without him having to work for a living. Becoming an art student would piss his father off. And last, but by no means least, at Art College he could wear whatever he wanted every single day. No more shirt and tie for Frank.

He knew not one of his rationales was legitimate enough for the life-defining choice of a subject for further education. But from now on there'd be no more trivial motivation – not after today's events. No decision in his life thus far had even come close to being as conclusive as the one he'd made in the darkroom that day. He'd had a road-to-Damascus revelation of absolute certainty that he wanted to spend his life taking photos. Not any old photos, but snapping events and people that had some kind of meaning or message, and were bound to attract attention. Okay, so he cheated a bit with the Nelson device, but in future he'd seek out the real thing, ferret out situations that had genuine significance and interest and shoot the shit out of them. When he thought of the possibilities and opportunities ahead of him, Frank felt his heart accelerate.

And what better place to celebrate than a pub? Frank had

loved public houses ever since he bought his first illicit pint as a tall sixteen-year-old. There was no music more pleasing to him than the refrain generated by a well-populated bar – the rumble of contented conversation and sporadic peals of laughter punctuated by the occasional thump of a dart as it hit the board. All underlaid with the hiss of froth-topped beer being pumped into a pint glass and the ka-ching of the till when libations were paid for. And finally, at closing time, with a congenial female companion at his side and 'last orders' having been called, Frank delighted in the general atmosphere of feverish intemperance with its suggestion of uninhibited after-hours intercourse.

Frank's mother and father thought differently, they considered the consumption of alcohol to be an occupation of the devil. The same went for smoking, gambling, and, as far as Frank could tell, partaking in any sexual activity whatsoever. God knows how he was conceived. Doubtless a slip of the puritanical pall that shrouded every aspect of his parents' lives. Whatever had occurred, they never let it happen again. Frank was an only child and, as his father was fond of telling him, the biggest disappointment in his parents' life. Which led Frank to deduce: a) that it only took the mildest of human failings to qualify as an object of disenchantment, and b) his mother and father must have had some kind of expectation of progeny. Perhaps he'd been wrong about his parents and their lack of a sex life, but the thought of the two of them *in flagrante delicto* made Frank feel queasy, so he tried not to think about it.

Frank heard the clatter of change being deposited in the

jukebox. A hurdy-gurdy keyboard introduction was followed by Jim Morrison's trademark sullen style as he began the lyrics of Light My Fire. The door swung open and a blast of cool air propelled a gaggle of painting students into the pub. They tottered to the bar, bellowing with exuberance. It was obvious The Vine wasn't their first drinks stop of the evening. Although not usually chummy with painters, who tended to be contemptuous of graphic design students, Frank was pleased to see them. They livened the place up.

As soon as one of the students, Christine Baker, spied Frank, she wove her way over and plopped herself down on the vinyl-covered seat beside him. With one deft tug she pulled off the black cape she habitually wore. When her copious honey-coloured hair fell languidly back into place over the shoulders of a body-hugging sweater, Frank's gut fluttered. His eyes glided over knees caught in fishnet tights. His stare slid between shapely thighs to a tantalizing shadow cast from the hem of a black leather mini-skirt. Christine was more intense than Frank's usual female companions, but he'd fancied her the minute he'd seen her, in heated debate with a couple of other painting students in the college common room. She was defending her style of art, throwing around phrases like 'legitimate acquisition of popular imagery' and 'good draughtspersonship alone does not an artist make.' Frank had never before heard anyone substitute the word 'person' for 'man.' Christine was fiercely beautiful, cheeks flushed, eyes flashing. She exuded more fizz than firework night. Frank was smitten from the get-go. When he asked someone who she was it seemed like an omen – positive or not, but rife with consequence either way – that she shared the same surname as Frank's idol of a drummer, the mercurial Ginger Baker.

Just days after he first noticed Christine, Frank spied her again at a college dance. Modest but confident of his dancing talents, he tripped the light fantastic right beside her. Frank knew his boogie panache would pay off and wasn't surprised when Christine eventually engaged with him on the dance floor. But he couldn't believe his luck when, despite his graphic designer status, she invited him to go home with her at the end of the evening. Frank, who'd been fairly sober, remembered the events of the night vividly and with considerable gratification.

Christine fixed Frank with a meaningful stare, eyes glistening between lids heavy with black eyeliner.

"Mine's a half of cider," she said.

'Try to set the night on fire,' urged Jim Morrison, as Frank rose, grinning, to fetch Christine's drink.

DAY THREE

Tuesday, April 16, 1968

"For you and Pam, with my regards," said Georgy.

She placed a jam jar on Enoch's desk. A cellophane cover, taught as a drum skin, was held in place by a red rubber band. Enoch picked up the jam jar, held it up to the light, and peered into it. A pale emerald sea appeared to teem with shoals of slender green fish.

"Lime marmalade. Made by my own fair hand. It's amazing what you can find in the market these days."

"The new market?" asked Enoch.

"Yes, such as it is," said Georgy. "How is it possible the same generation of architects that built the new Coventry Cathedral can build such a boring monstrosity like the new market hall? Pure function with absolutely no regard to form."

"One presumes the architects who designed the cathedral were provided with particularly powerful inspiration," said Enoch.

"From God, you mean? I don't know, Enoch, I have trouble swallowing the idea of deity as motivation. But then, I've never really been a believer. Christmas Carol Service and Harvest Festival is as far as I'm willing to go. Bit hypocritical of me I suppose, but it's damn hard to buck those traditions. And I have to admit I enjoy the occasional dose of High

Church of England for the spectacle, its bells and smells. A belief in God seems superfluous."

Enoch was not unsympathetic to Georgy's agnosticism. Hadn't he completely forsaken God during his German phase and his infatuation with Nietzsche? He'd been more than willing to denounce Christianity as no longer a viable source of absolute moral principle. But those convictions had been swept away together with his disenchantment with German culture. Which left the door wide open for his Saul of Tarsus conversion. He seemed to go through transformations every now and then, but usually involving policy rather than religion. He was aware that his occasional *volte face* might be considered convenient inconsistency by some, but he countered the criticism with either downright denials that he'd ever held any view but the current revised version, or by inciting the Conservative creed concerning value of experience. He quoted the maxim that past events were a better guide to policy than theory, even though he didn't necessarily believe it, being at times a consummate theorist himself. If, despite his best efforts to persuade people otherwise, his metamorphoses were still labelled as blatant flip-flopping, so be it.

Rather than the road to Damascus, Enoch's spiritual revelation came to him on Lichfield Road slap bang in the centre of Wolverhampton. And instead of Jesus's voice he heard the bells of St Peter's Anglican Church. The revelation occurred as he was walking home from the railway station. His conversion – more of a reversion – to Father, Son and Holy Ghost was as comforting as a homecoming. A warm embrace of everything he considered truly dear after a fascinating but distracting dalliance.

St. Peter's ancient sandstone tower loomed over the old market site. Enoch had always imagined the haphazard maze of colourful stalls selling traditional English fare and household goods would be there forever. The idea that such a longstanding bastion of British way of life could be cleared in just a matter of days made him distinctly uneasy. The vibrant old market had been replaced by a desolate car park, with long-term plans to build new municipal offices on the site. Enoch reached for some papers on his desk, hoping Georgy might take the hint that he'd prefer not to discuss the old market's replacement, but she was in full flight.

"I suppose the Church is rich enough to pay for ornamental gewgaws by the likes of John Piper and Grahame Sutherland while municipalities can barely afford to mend holes in roads. But surely it's not just about money? Creativity doesn't always have to come at a cost. Especially these days, when design conventions are smashed daily. I'd have thought all kinds of affordable innovations would have been possible to brighten up the dreary new building."

"I hope the same vendors are there," said Enoch.

He hadn't had the heart to visit the new premises, but liked to think they housed the same doughty stallholders selling the same dependable goods.

"Ironically, the mausoleum-like atmosphere is somewhat relieved by a few colourful newcomers. There's a stall that looks like Aladdin's cave, packed with amazingly exotic fabrics. The woman who owns it sits like a maharani in a sari shot through with silver threads while her two assistants run around serving customers. I bought the limes from a West Indian, a mountain of a man. He let me pick the limes out myself. You wouldn't get that with an English greengrocer, you'd have what you were given. He had mangoes too, can you imagine? If I'm feeling brave I might give mango chutney a try."

"If indeed you do, you must be sure to save a jar for me. It was one of my favourites in India," said Enoch. He wondered why Georgy was being uncharacteristically chatty.

A look passed her eyes. Enoch was sure she'd suddenly remembered to whom she was talking.

"I have to admit to feeling a bit ambivalent about the newcomers, but I must get on," she said and turned as if to return to her desk.

"What were you referring to? Why would you be of two minds?"

Georgy turned back to him. A little too quickly? She didn't hesitate in her answer.

"I doubt you've ever experienced this, being such an accomplished linguist, but don't you think it odd that one is perfectly willing to stumble along with foreign Caucasians even though they can barely speak English, when one is reluctant to interact with a coloured person who in all likelihood speaks the language fluently. The argument that a Caribbean or Indian accent might be hard to understand simply doesn't hold water, does it?"

"Of course it does. Communication is key and if dialect is an obvious barrier to intercourse it would be quite natural to be reluctant to instigate a conversation, whether it's with a Geordie or a Jamaican."

"Let me phrase it another way. Why was I wary to approach the West Indian greengrocer who in all likelihood spoke perfectly good English, while I had no qualms whatsoever in addressing the Polish sausage maker who I'm well aware can only speak half-a-dozen words at best?"

Enoch recognized immediately what Georgy was up to. Ever since the Walsall speech she'd been testing him. But he refused to take the bait. The last thing he wanted to do was to enter a discussion with her about prejudice surrounding colour of skin. There was nothing to be gained and much to be lost. Her loyalty, her friendship – but most of all, her approval.

"I'm not qualified to answer that question since it concerns the inner workings of your psyche, with which I'm unfamiliar. Neither am I particularly interested in hearing any answer you may supply. Now, if you don't mind, I have work to do, and I presume you do too."

Georgy smiled. At least she didn't smirk, thought Enoch.

He was relieved to hear the sound of the front door opening. Georgy went to see who it was. Conversation mercifully ended, Enoch picked up the phone. He'd promised Pam he'd invite Clem Jones, his wife, and whichever of their sons were in town to the house on Merridale Road. Susan and Jennifer had heard it was the Jones's dog, Topsy's, birthday and they wanted to host a garden party. Enoch knew his colleagues in Parliament would be astonished to discover he'd helped arrange a dog's birthday party. But over the years Topsy had become the Powell girls' surrogate pet. His family's peripatetic life, moving regularly between London and Wolverhampton, meant Susan and Jennifer were only allowed hamsters, which were easily transported by car or train. When Enoch and Pam were in town they saw a good deal of Topsy, along with Clem Jones and his wife Marjorie. Clem was editor of the largest-selling regional newspaper in Britain, the *Express & Star*, and Marjorie was a local magistrate. The couple were a breath of fresh air among the generally stultifying circle Enoch encountered in Wolverhampton. Most people were reserved in his company. He presumed they were too intimidated to engage with him on more than a superficial level. The Joneses seemed to have no inhibitions at all about displaying lively minds and keen intellects. Enoch looked forward to their weekend jaunts together into Shropshire or the Welsh borderlands so he and Clem could indulge in a shared love of the countryside. They spent considerable time nosing out locations featured in Housman's cycle of poems, A Shropshire Lad.

Admittedly Enoch was suggesting Topsy's celebration for his daughters, but he was fond of Clem and Marjorie and had every reason to believe he'd enjoy the occasion. Enoch didn't like people to think of him as austere. He was hurt when Andrew Faulds called him "this knight of the sad countenance" in one of his attacks in the House. Enoch usually took comments from the opposition with a pinch of salt, especially criticism from Faulds. How could anyone take an ex-actor seriously? But the jibe struck a chord. Did Enoch think of himself as an unhappy person? Before he met Pam, perhaps. He overheard

Colonel Ledingham, the Tory area agent in Wolverhampton, telling someone that since his marriage Enoch had displayed "gleams of humanity that have brightened his rather sombre personality." He even took the odd glass of wine, having been staunchly teetotal until he started seeing Pam. As a matter of principle Enoch did his best to relish his life. After all, wasn't enjoyment of privilege what Toryism was all about? He was dialling Clem's number when he heard Georgy talking to whoever had opened the door.

"Is he in?" asked the visitor.

"Brigadier Powell is on the phone just now. I'll put a note in front of him if you'd like. Who shall I say it is?"

"Just put Dangerfield."

Enoch hung up the phone.

"First name?" Georgy asked.

"It's B. Just B. Dangerfield."

"Bert, Bill. Maybe Beauregard?"

The sweetness in Georgy's voice was laced with strychnine.

"Beauregard? What kind of a bloody name's that? It's Barry. Barry Dangerfield."

Enoch made a beeline for Georgy's desk.

"It's perfectly alright, Georgy. Mr Dangerfield has an appointment."

"There's nothing in the book."

"I omitted to tell you," said Enoch.

Enoch knew it irritated Georgy when he didn't tell her about his appointments, but he wasn't prepared to apologize. He considered the word 'sorry' to be grossly overused. People said it when they weren't remotely regretful. He wasn't contrite for not informing Georgy about Barry Dangerfield's appointment – he'd purposefully not mentioned it, so how could he be? He supposed he could say he was sorry for having discomfited her, but that struck him as obvious.

Once Barry Dangerfield had wedged himself into a chair Enoch closed the door and squeezed behind the diminutive table that served as his desk. When he started to read a copy of a letter Dangerfield handed him, his scalp tingled. The more he read, the more heightened his senses became. He was aware of the smell of cardboard and paper emanating from boxes of stationery on shelves just inches behind his head.

Eight years ago my friend was living at number 4 . Maybe you know it, it's a little cresent with half a dozen fairly big houses. After she was widowed my friend let out rooms. Number 6 was the first house to be sold to a Negro. Now they're all coloured. My friend is the only white person in the cresent.

"I blacked out the names and that. They wouldn't want to be identified so better you don't know, yeah?" said Barry Dangerfield.

"Yes, yes," said Enoch, head bent over the letter.

was anxious at the best of times but when the rest of the houses was bought by coloureds she got scared. It got noisy, and in the end all her white tenants moved out.

Enoch lifted the letter so that crepuscular light from a single low wattage bulb dangling from the ceiling would better illuminate inexpert handwriting. The notepaper trembled in his fingers.

She's got a bit saved but after paying the rates, she doesn't have more than £2 per week. She went down the council office but when they heard she had a seven-room house the girl told her she should rent part of it out. When she told them the only people she could get were Negroes, the girl told her it was no good being prejudiced these days.

Enoch's eyes raced along sentences, eager to take it all in but afraid he may find something that would dull his excitement.

Now my friend's afraid to go out. Her windows was broken. And before they left another white family had turds pushed through their door. If she goes shopping the coloured kids call her names. They don't speak proper English but she says they call her all sorts.

His body slumped with relief. He couldn't have crafted a more fitting story if he'd written it himself. He read the text again, more slowly. It might need a bit of editing but apart from that it was exactly what he'd hoped for.

"That's more what you were after, isn't it? Fits the bill, that, doesn't it?"

"It certainly does," said Enoch.

"So you'll be able to look into this jungle-bunny club that's taking all my business," said Barry Dangerfield.

"I'll do my best," said Enoch.

Enoch again walked Barry Dangerfield to the door. He clapped the publican's shoulder blade appreciatively as he said goodbye. When he turned back to the office Georgy was standing in front of her desk holding the open appointment book.

"Your friend looked pleased with himself. I see he was in to see you last February, just prior to your Walsall speech. *That* appointment seems to have made it into the book."

"It's entirely possible. The problem he brought to my attention about illegal drinking dens is an on-going irritation for him."

"But I thought we agreed. The town council is the place for matters of that nature."

"He's dissatisfied with their lack of attention and has asked me to intervene."

"I see," said Georgy, although it was clear from her tone of voice and the way she clutched the appointment book to her bosom she didn't 'see' at all.

"Your friend wouldn't have anything to do with that appalling story about the lone white schoolgirl in a class of coloured children, would he?"

Enoch felt a flash of irritation, he hoped his eyes didn't betray him. He decided to call Georgy's bluff.

"What do you imagine his connection might be?"

Enoch was relieved to see an uneasy expression on her face. She lowered her eyes.

"I've no idea," she said. She moved around her desk and sat down.

* * *

Frank and Christine started their walk into town from her place in Park Dale without talking, which rattled Frank. He was fairly certain the night had gone well, given Christine's reactions. He couldn't remember any other girls he'd gone to bed with who so obviously enjoyed his attentions. Some never uttered a sound, but Christine was at the other end of the spectrum. Her appreciative outbursts made the experience all the more satisfying. With other girls Frank invariably experienced what he called 'post-coital *tristesse*' and couldn't wait to get the hell away. But with Christine he was anything but sad. He found himself wishing he could spend all day with her. But his euphoria was threatened by anxiety that she might not like to do the same. He knew their first night together, a week or so before, had been fuelled by little more than a few pints at a college dance. Maybe he meant nothing more to her than an inconsequential screw. Frank was in an unfamiliar state of mind. He cast desperately around for something to say.

"I'm really glad we ended up dancing together the other week."

"You didn't so much dance as pulse," said Christine.

"Yeah, I've been told it's rather a distinctive style."

"You barely move your body. The only sign of life is the odd twist of the hips and the bizarre head-nodding."

"Well, you didn't seem to mind it," said Frank.

"It was less the dancing and more your total lack of self-consciousness. And the hair. You have great hair. Very leonine."

Frank threw his head back and shook his dark-at-the-roots dirty-blonde mane in an exaggerated expression of hirsute pride. They were walking past the Banks brewery in Chapel

Ash. Frank revelled in a deep inhalation of air rich with the aroma of malt and hops.

"It was kind of an experiment too," said Christine.

Frank exhaled noisily.

"What the hell kind of an experiment?"

"To see if there really was such a thing as an interesting graphic design student."

"So I'm just a guinea pig to you. Is that it?"

"You were at first. And you failed spectacularly. Never shut up all the way home about how little work you'd managed to get away with without being chucked out of college and losing your grant money. I almost dumped you."

"Why didn't you?"

Christine grimaced, the expression of someone pretending to have trouble remembering.

"I wasn't going to let you in, but when you massaged the back of my neck outside the front door I thought if I could just shut you up it might be worth it."

"And was it?"

"Let's just say most boys don't know a thing about women's bodies. What's worse is they won't take any direction. You turned out to be not like most boys."

Frank couldn't help feeling smug. He must have looked it.

"Don't get ahead of yourself. What I meant was you're a good learner," said Christine.

"Is that why you came to sit next to me last night?"

"I have to admit I was pleased to see you. And then it was a bonus to find I was mistaken about the oxymoron of an interesting graphic-design student. It was amazing how passionate you were, banging on about wanting to be a photojournalist. What was it you said? You wanted to shoot the kind of photography 'the world needs to see, whether they like it or not.' When your eyes got all bright and sparkly ... let's just say it was a real turn-on to discover you might have one or two convictions after all."

She laughed, eyes flashing with amused affection. Frank was surprised he'd come across so strongly about his photojournalist ambitions. He was bloody glad he had though.

They walked past the Milano coffee bar, a magnet for Wolverhampton's youth, from sixth-formers flirting after school to a late-night Bohemian crowd, huddled self-importantly over their frothy coffee. Frank had once been enamoured of their Paris Left Bank style. The women emulated Juliette Greco, the French chansonnière, with heavy eyeliner and hair died impenetrably black. They all smoked Gitanes as furiously as any Pigalle poet while talking loudly over each other about *nouvelle vague* films or the pros and cons of Sartre over Camus. But Frank realized if he embraced the Gallic highbrow lifestyle he'd be forced to forego his sojourns in the pub – he decided to stick with his own idiosyncratic style, at least until the Milano started serving absinthe. The coffee bar's door was locked, its gleaming Gaggia espresso machine and black-and-white photomural of the Duomo in Milan barely discernible through shadowy plate-glass.

"What are you working on today?" asked Frank.

It was the first time he'd dared bring up Christine's college work. In asking around he'd heard the story of her narrow escape the previous year. The trio of male teachers who formed the senior faculty of the fine art department had tried to throw her off the course.

"I'm doing a series of silkscreens. I had an idea when I woke up this morning for a new print. The Three Little Pigs probably won't like it, but fuck them."

Frank knew she was referring to her three senior lecturers, but feigned ignorance. He worried she might think he was creepy for snooping around, digging up the dirt about her.

"Three Little Pigs?" he asked.

Christine related the whole story of how the Three Little Pigs, as she'd christened them, claimed she wasn't 'benefitting from their instruction.'

"Which basically meant I wouldn't do the style of work they thought I should. As far as I'm concerned my art should say what I want it to say in the way I find most effective. I use collage – magazine pages, newspaper cuttings – as well as painting. The Three Little Pigs seem to find it threatening."

She told Frank she thought she'd been the victim of regional prejudice. Christine hailed from London, while the three instructors were all Black Country born and bred.

"Or maybe it's an age thing. Not one of them is under fifty," she said.

"I'm not sure that's a legitimate gripe. Look at Picasso, still pumping it out at eighty-seven. I know he's been criticized for not being as interesting as he used to be, but I think the new stuff looks as fresh and ground-breaking as ever. Not all old men are old farts, you know."

"You're right of course. It's just that the whole affair has made me a bit paranoid."

Frank breathed a sigh of relief. He was getting the hang of things where Christine was concerned. And it was invigorating to talk like a grown-up for a change.

Christine told Frank the only supporter within the college had been her art history teacher. He'd judged the end-of-course thesis she'd almost completed on British pop artist, Pauline Boty, as being 'so far, so brilliant.' The Three Little Pigs huffed and puffed, but Christine refused to let them blow her house down. She approached the Student Union to support her in requesting an appeal. The Union president – Steve MacDonald, editor of *VoxPop* – had pushed hard for an outside assessor to be appointed. A printmaking tutor at the Royal College of Art was brought in and deemed Christine 'a thoughtful and dextrous young artist, full of promise.' The Three Little Pigs had no option but to let her stay and finish the course.

"Not a hope in hell of a passing mark at the end of the year. But I forge on regardless."

Frank marvelled at Christine's enthusiasm when she went on to tell him, cheeks flushed, how she'd had an idea when she woke up that morning for a print using a collage of advertisements featuring a salesman, a smiling housewife, and an array of beds in a shop.

"I'm going to call it 'Satisfaction Guaranteed.' I can see it in my mind. I'm really going to play up the covert sexuality used in advertising slogans."

"Odd that you dreamed up the idea after last night don't

you think? Where the hell could it have come from?"

Frank, frowning but his mouth smiling, studied Christine's face.

"Very odd. I can't think of a single event in the last twelve hours that might have inspired such an interesting concept," said Christine.

She dug her elbow into Frank's ribs, threw her head back and laughed. God, but she looked fantastic – chock full of life. He experienced a brief moment of panic. What if she became bored with him? He ached to drape his arm around her shoulders or hold her hand as they continued up the incline of Darlington Street. He wouldn't have thought twice with past girlfriends, but with Christine he worried such a gesture might be fraught with possessive overtones. In bed that morning she'd told Frank that her mother's biggest disappointment was being born too late to be a suffragette. She read Simone de Beauvoir – who Frank had never heard of – out loud to Christine and despaired of the '50s ideal of the nuclear family with Mum as housewife and Dad as sole breadwinner. It was her mother's suggestion that Christine start taking the Pill when she went to Art School. Christine's father had been a conscientious objector during World War II. He continued to work as an administrator at the Red Cross after the war. With parents like that Frank knew he needed to watch his step with Christine. So rather than any premature presumption of a public display of physical affection he just smiled as winningly and lovingly as possible. He was overjoyed when he was rewarded with a resounding smacker on the cheek.

Frank and Christine strolled through Queen Square, past the equestrian statue of Prince Albert, the testicles of which students regularly painted red. The horse's, not Prince Albert's. Frank had been told the construction of the grimy limestone building that housed the art gallery and Art College had been funded by an affluent local contractor not long after the Great Exhibition. It was impossible to move a few yards in the Midlands without being reminded – consciously or not – of the prosperity of the Victorian era.

"Maybe see you in the coffee break," said Christine as she and Frank stepped through double front doors.

"Just try avoiding me," said Frank, heading for the wide stone stairs that wound up to the graphic design department, which was housed on the upper floors of the draughty building. He grinned as he looked back at her, aware that he probably looked insufferably self-satisfied. Christine smiled back at him nonetheless. Frank bounded up the steps, the rubber soles of his desert boots squeaking on every step.

* * *

Later that morning, when Frank sought Christine out in the crowded common room, he was aware he was grinning idiotically.

"You look weirdly smug ... like a teenager after his first shag," said Christine, eyes narrowed.

Frank held up *VoxPop* and pointed to his name running up the side of a large photo on the front page.

"Why didn't you tell me?" Christine asked.

She snatched the newspaper so that she could examine the picture more carefully.

"I wanted to surprise, amaze, and impress you," said Frank.

"Consider me amazed and impressed. Not necessarily surprised though. I knew you had it in you after last night."

"Really?" said Frank, a syrupy edge to his voice.

He put his forehead against hers. Christine pulled away.

"I mean I knew you had the ability to take such a great photo having rattled on about it for hours. The rest I'm not so sure about."

"Cheeky mare," said Frank.

"It's a fabulous shot. Look at the emotion in their faces. The coloured guy doesn't look quite as het up as the others, but it doesn't matter. Just him being there is what makes it such a powerful photo."

"Thank you," said Frank.

"Who is he anyway?" asked Christine.

Frank bent to peer at the shot, as though he needed to check Nelson's identity.

"Not sure. I think he might be from the Tech," he said. "Hey listen, let's go and have a proper drink, to celebrate. Come on."

Frank half rose in his seat as if to leave.

"Now? It's only eleven o'clock in the morning."

"Exactly ... opening time."

"No, I want to spend the whole day working on my print. Otherwise I'll never be finished in time for the end of term exhibition."

Frank plopped back down in his seat, stuck out his lower lip and frowned.

"Later. This evening. I'll meet you in The Vine," said Christine.

Frank brightened.

" Great. But not The Vine, it's been dead as a doornail lately. It's Folk Club night at the Giffard Arms, that's always good for a laugh."

After Christine left there seemed little reason for Frank to linger in the common room. He'd stuck his photo under the noses of everyone he knew, but he didn't think anybody except Christine had expressed enough wonder and awe. He was pissed off when a first year student had given the shot a cursory glance and pronounced it "fab."

"Fab? You sound more girly than Cathy McGowan. It's not some snap of a fucking rock group, it's an exceptional example of serious photojournalism."

"Get over yourself," somebody muttered.

Exasperated by the lack of enthusiasm, Frank made his way along the narrow corridor that led to the main staircase, where he and Christine had parted earlier that morning. An untidy pile of *VoxPop* newspapers sat to the side of one of the wide steps. Frank cursed Steve MacDonald's distribution methods, wondering why he didn't dragoon some Tech. students to get the weekly into people's hands more effectively. He bent to tidy the pile and scoop up a few more copies. He may as well take a bunch upstairs and scatter them around a bit. And he wanted to make sure his photography tutor, Dave Bishop, saw his published handiwork. Frank hoped it wasn't too late to change his final course project to a photography-based exercise instead of the typographic work he'd barely begun.

At the top of the stairs Frank bumped into Dave Bishop with, as luck would have it, his course tutor.

"Could I have a word?" asked Frank.

The course tutor looked suspicious.

"I was wondering if I could change the subject of my final project from fairground typography to documentary photography."

"You really are a waste of space, Frank. It's far too late in the game to be chopping and changing now."

"It's just that I'm really keen on the photography route. See, here's an example of the kind of thing I'd like to do."

Frank held up an issue of *VoxPop*.

"Is this what you were doing in the darkroom after hours?" asked Dave Bishop.

"After hours?" repeated the course tutor.

Dave Bishop explained that Frank had requested permission to use the darkroom after classes so he could finish an urgent project.

"Wonders will never cease," muttered the course tutor.

"It's a pretty impressive shot. What speed film did you use?" Dave Bishop asked.

"It was a bit of a dull day so I used four hundred ASA. But I pushed it in the developer. I wanted a bit more contrast."

"Why didn't you just use a higher-grade paper?"

"I did that too. I used a number five. Combining it with pushing the film I got that really stark newsy look I was hoping for."

The course tutor glanced at Dave Bishop, who nodded his head slightly.

"Put it in writing," said the course tutor.

Frank considered hugging him.

"And not just 'I want to change my end of course project 'cos it's Tuesday.' I expect a full and articulate rationale for switching."

Dave Bishop beamed at Frank and gave him a wink.

When Frank walked into the third-year studio he was surprised to find classmate Jock McAffrey bent over a drafting board. Jock was a smoker. Smoking wasn't permitted in the studio so Frank found it odd that Jock wasn't spending his coffee break in the common room puffing away with all the other smokers. Frank could see his fellow student was engrossed in work on yet another illustration of a battle re-enactment. Jock lived and breathed the English Civil War. He belonged to a re-enactment organization called the Sealed Knot. It was no surprise to anyone when Jock chose to design a recruitment campaign for the group as his final course project. Dressing up as a defunct soldier and pretending to fight long-dead battles seemed to Frank a bloody stupid way for anyone to spend their spare time. Also Jock was short and slight. It was hard to imagine him waving around one of those bloody great weapons that Roundheads and Cavaliers wielded.

"Seen this week's *VoxPop?*" asked Frank and nonchalantly tossed a copy onto Jock's board.

"Great photograph," said Jock immediately.

What the fuck was wrong with people? Jock had hardly

glanced at the bloody photo. Nevertheless Frank warmed to the compliment.

"Took it at the demo, day before yesterday."

"Congratulations," said Jock, but he didn't give the newspaper a second look. He kept his head bent over his illustration.

Frank gave up. He went to his desk and began to make notes for his application to switch his final project. Trouble was, he couldn't count on any more demos to photograph before the end of the academic year. More out of desperation than design, and prompted by the drama that Nelson's figure had provided, Frank decided his theme should be the recent influx of immigrants to the area. There'd certainly be no trouble finding subjects. Frank spouted rhetoric about the burgeoning immigrant presence in the region. He wrote a lot of stuff that he hadn't realized he ever thought about, let alone knew. He concluded with a paragraph underlining the importance of recording this 'momentous period in British history,' blah, blah, blah. He drafted what he thought was a pretty convincing argument. He'd been so engrossed he hadn't realized what time it was. Most people had left for lunch, Jock included. Before Frank went over to The Vine for his lunchtime pint of Guinness, he thought he'd retrieve his working material for the *VoxPop* photo, original negs and test prints, from his drawer in the grey metal plan chest that the third-year students shared.

When at first he couldn't find the large manila envelope containing his material, he pulled everything out of his drawer – proofs of lithos and etchings he'd made, old sheets of Letraset, a couple of sketch pads, coloured pencils, sheets of mounting board, tissue paper, a box of watercolour paints. But no sign of the envelope. He removed the drawer completely, thinking that perhaps it had slipped down to the drawer below. He pulled all the drawers out to see if the envelope had become trapped at the back of the chest. He came to the uneasy conclusion that he must have taken the *VoxPop* photo material home.

* * *

Frank plonked the student newspaper on the bar of The Vine in front of Barry Dangerfield and demanded his usual tipple.

"That's good that is," said Barry, nodding at the front-page photo as he pulled Frank's Guinness.

"That's an understatement, but thanks for the idea," said Frank.

Barry placed the pint glass carefully on a bar towel in front of Frank. Thousands of tiny bubbles teemed upward as the treacle-dark beer slowly cleared.

"We'll say no more about it. It's you what done the work, after all."

Frank fumbled for some change.

"On the 'ouse," said Barry.

Frank was amazed, Barry wasn't known for handing out free drinks.

"Wow, thanks a lot, Barry," he said, turning to scan the pub for a free seat at a table.

"Not so fast, cock. Take a seat on that stool. I want to know what's been said about it."

Barry was strangely insistent. The least Frank could do was stay and talk to him. But as he turned to sit in front of the bar, he could have sworn he'd seen Jock McAffrey, classmate and civil war re-enactor, making for the door. Frank had the impression another lad was following immediately behind. By the time Frank turned for a second look he could only see the other bloke's back as he disappeared through the doorway behind Jock. He was massive. And he carried a khaki knapsack, the type sold at army and navy supply stores. That wasn't unusual, lots of students bought equipment there – bags, clothes, boots – the stuff was cheap. Frank himself had a similar knapsack in RAF grey. Jock's companion was probably another Sealed Knot nutter, thought Frank. But there was something about the back of the man's head that rang a bell with Frank.

Despite his insistence that he'd wanted to hear about reaction to the photo, Barry was more intent on complaining about how his pub seemed to be losing favour with the art student crowd. As he whined on about it, Frank realized who it was that the man walking through the door behind Jock McAffrey had reminded him of – Dennis Perkins.

Dennis was a hulking twenty-two-year-old from Birmingham who'd been working on the building site where Frank met Nelson. He had ginger hair cropped so short that the contours of his skull were clearly visible. The only students Frank could think of with hair almost as short were a couple of interior designers. And the retreating figure was wearing the hiked-up Levis, braces, and black boots the interior designers sometimes wore. But neither of the interior

design students was as big. And it was doubtful they'd be
chummy with Jock McAffrey. Whoever it was had the same
ginger fuzz as Dennis Perkins. And a prominent ridge of bone
just below the crown on the back of his head.

Frank had groaned inwardly on his second day at the
building site when he was teamed up with Dennis to shovel
wet concrete – a sodden concoction of cement, sand and gravel
– into a portable skip each time a load was dumped at their
feet from a deafeningly noisy mixer. Frank's back and arms
were aching from the unaccustomed physical labour of his
first day on the job. Once the skip was filled, Dennis signalled
to the crane driver to hoist it up to the top of the incomplete
building where the concrete was used to form floors or walls.
Frank was embarrassingly aware that the skip had been filled
with more than twice the amount of Dennis's shovelfuls than
his own. He wasn't exactly pulling his weight.

"You're puttin' too much effort into it," said Dennis,
when they were resting on their shovels, having dispatched
the first skip load. Frank wasn't sure he'd heard correctly
over the ear-splitting rumble from the cement mixer. That and
Dennis's elongated Birmingham consonants made it difficult
to understand.

"What?" Frank yelled, moving closer.

"You lean over too much. You ought to keep your back
straight. Let your legs do some work," shouted Dennis, his
breath moist in Frank's ear.

When the empty skip returned, hungry for more concrete,
Dennis showed Frank what he meant. Rather than bend over
and push his shovel from above into the heavy sludge, Dennis

bent his knees, keeping his back straight. Then he used his right knee against his right hand, with which he gripped the shovel handle, to help propel the implement horizontally into the concrete mixture. Dennis hardly bent his back throughout, using his legs, arms, and lower body to lift an impressive amount of semisolid concrete. With his clipped, red-haired skull, powerful limbs, supple muscles expanding and contracting beneath freckled skin, Dennis appeared awesomely powerful. Frank thought about throwing in his shovel there and then, but after a couple more skips-worth he began to get the hang of Dennis's technique. His backache eased and, apart from a new blister on his right hand, Frank felt more comfortable altogether.

"We'll make a navvy of you yet," quipped Dennis, but he remained unsmiling, unblinking. He regarded Frank with cool blue eyes.

"Thanks for the tip, mate. You really know what you're doing," said Frank.

He cursed himself for sucking up to Dennis so clumsily. The ginger giant gave a hint of a nod and leaned on his shovel and examined his new workmate with narrowed eyes. Frank was relieved when another empty skip arrived and Dennis's attention was diverted to shovelling more concrete.

"Am you bloody listening?" asked Barry.

Frank was tugged back from memories of the building site by Barry's aggrieved tone of voice.

"Sorry, miles away. What were you saying?"

"Ah'm saying they'm all goin' to that bleedin' jungle-bunny club in Whitmore Reans."

"Who? Where?"

"You got cloth for ears? I've been going on about the bloody Montego Club for the last five minutes."

"What Montego Club?"

"Place in Whitmore Reans. They'm stealing all my best customers. All them fine art mob are going there."

"I never heard of it," said Frank.

"You must be the only bugger what 'asn't," said Barry.

* * *

Charlie heaved himself off the top rung of a ladder and let drop a bunch of steel reinforcing rods he'd been carrying on his shoulder. He was panting slightly, having climbed five storeys of unfinished building, ladder by ladder.

"You been a naughty boy then, Nelson?"

"Wha' you talkin' about?" asked Nelson.

Charlie find out about him and the police? Nelson hadn't mentioned it, he didn't want people knowing he'd been pulled in. In fact he'd hardly spoken from the moment he and Auntie Irene reached home from the police station. One thing about Irene, she was never slow to say when she thought he was acting stupid.

"Is no good you dwellin' on what happen, you know. You got to take the rough with the smooth and jus' carry on."

Nelson knew Irene was right, but it seemed to him things weren't as smooth in England as promised. Nelson tried to count the good things about being in the Mother Land. There was Irene's cooking. And a regular wage. All very well, but he missed hearing Jamaican music live. Dribs and drabs of the latest recordings made it to Britain, although Nelson was scornful of performers like Johnny Nash, who may have had the down beat, but was American. Nelson even had doubts about Toots and the Maytals. Although from Jamaica, they were suspiciously popular with English lads with closely-cropped hair and heavy boots.

"Wha' make them bwoys like Jamaican ska yet still them no like Jamaican people?" Nelson asked Wesley, who owned Sounds Good, the record shop round the corner from Irene's.

Wesley had no answer for him.

It was in Wesley's shop that he first heard The Pioneers singing Long Shot. It smooth so! Nelson was torn between excitement at the sheer novelty of the slower tempo and crushing disappointment at not being able to hear the Pioneers sing it for real. There was little consolation in the rumour that they might be coming to Britain. Nelson couldn't imagine how that would work. How could he let the music take him when he was in the gloom of a British dance hall?

"You must be outdoor fi hear music good so," Nelson told Wesley.

Charlie started weaving steel reinforcing rods across the next section of floor they were to construct, ready for a load of concrete.

"As I walked past the site office the foreman stuck his 'ead out the door and told me to tell you you're wanted. There was a copper in there with him, and another feller, nasty piece of work, plain clothes by the look of it."

"This other one, him whiter than white and skinny?" asked Nelson.

"All policemen in England are white, in case you 'adn't noticed. But yes, skinny as a rake. Poxy-looking face too."

Nelson's stomach flipped over like the cassava bammies his mother tossed in a frying pan.

"Don't look so fuckin' scared. If you've done nothing wrong, you've got nothing to worry about, have you," said Charlie.

Nelson wasn't so sure, He looked around for an escape route, but the only way down was by the ladders Charlie had just climbed.

"You haven't, have you? Done something wrong?"

"You think that make a difference?"

"This isn't darkest Africa, Nelson. We don't throw people in jail for no reason."

Scowling, Nelson went to peer over a finished section of roughcast concrete floor, but all he could see, five floors down, was the flat roof of the site office. Them have time from yesterday to talk to Jamaica police? Perhaps he should throw himself off and be done with it.

"The longer you hang around up 'ere the worse it'll be. Best go and find out what they want," said Charlie.

Nelson climbed down each of the five ladders. Charlie had turned out to be a good workmate, but his wife and kids got in the way of him being a real friend. Nelson wished he was still in touch with Frank McCann. Nelson was suspicious when the white student first started talking to him. Wha' him want wid Jamaican youth? But after a while it was obvious Frank was just being friendly.

"Him mi only key fren' in the Mother Land," Nelson told

Irene when she looked askance at him for inviting Frank for the weekend.

Frank said things that made Nelson think like he'd never done before. When Nelson inadvertently started singing one of his compositions Frank egged him on. He made Nelson sing it a couple of times over.

"Fantastic! You've got to get those words down on paper."

It had never occurred to Nelson to write his lyrics down.

"Today Handsworth, tomorrow Detroit! Motown won't know what's hit them," said Frank.

Nelson laughed it off, but for the first time in his life the thought occurred to him that maybe he could be like some of them boys back home who made records. Why not?

Nelson wondered if Frank was still living in the same bedsit. He'd slept on the floor there a few times, after he made sure Frank reached home safely after a night in the pub. Nelson had called Frank's number a couple of times during the winter. But he knew it was a coin operated phone shared with the rest of the house. The first time he called, he spoke to a man who didn't seem to understand when Nelson asked him to take a message. The same man always answered, so Nelson stopped trying.

As he walked across the building site, Nelson tried to heed Irene's advice not to let the situation with the police get to him – he'd done nothing wrong after all – but he was filled with trepidation. A sudden memory of the murmuring of his mother and aunts as they sat outside mending clothes on a balmy evening, the air heavy with the fragrance of flowers, threatened to overwhelm him. Maybe there was no work and no money back home, and mostly only food they could grow or catch, but there were things to be said for it. Nelson couldn't think of anything better than walking down to the sea in a pink sunrise to go fishing, the water flat and silvery as polished metal. Nelson longed for the calm of those God-given mornings. When he set off he sometimes worried he may not catch anything – it was hard to take the disappointment in his mother's eyes the few times he came home empty handed. Even so, once he started flinging his net and hauling it in, peace took over every muscle, bone and tendon. In England worry stiffened his shoulders, made his head a little muzzy. Especially now, with policemen bothering him every time he turned around.

Nelson knocked hesitantly on the site office door. A voice called out for him to come in.

"Handcuffs," barked Fowler as soon as Nelson walked through the door.

A uniformed policeman seized one of Nelson's arms and twisted it behind his back before reaching around for the other. No time to struggle or speak before the handcuffs locked into place with a sickening click. The cold metal cut into Nelson's wrists.

"Rhaatid! That hurt, man!"

"We're taking you into custody for further questioning concerning the aggravated assault of one, Mr Ramanjit Singh, on April fourteenth, nineteen sixty-eight," said Fowler.

"I tell you before, I was at Auntie's in Handsworth when that 'appen."

"This tells a different story," said Fowler, holding up a

newspaper in front of Nelson, his pockmarked face so close his sour breath seeped into Nelson's nostrils. Fowler rapped his knuckle on the front of the paper.

"Seems someone took a snap of you ... in Wolverhampton on April fourteenth. Not a mile from the Sunrise Boarding House. And it had to have been around eleven o'clock in the morning, just a half hour or so before you beat the hell out of Mr Singh, nuh?"

Nelson could see the photograph was of some kind of procession. There was a single coloured man in the front row.

"It might look like me, but is not me. I was in Handsworth. Me tired fi tell you."

"Take a closer look, bwoy. Even your foreman recognized you."

Nelson peered, disbelieving, at the newspaper. It was him in the photo, no mistake.

"See how nice and clear your cut look," said Fowler thrusting his rotting face even closer to Nelson's. He ran a fingernail slowly down the length of Nelson's scar from eyelid to lips.

Nelson had only once or twice smoked ganja – it made him dizzy. He was barely aware of the existence of LSD, mescaline, or any other hallucinogen. He'd never been blind drunk, two or three alcoholic drinks were as much as he could take without feeling nauseous. But at that moment he couldn't have felt more disoriented if he'd downed a whole heap of drugs and drunk a bottle of rum. Where he was when his body walk with white people waving banners? Everything in the shed's stuffy interior – fluttering architect's plans taped to the wall, his foreman's worried face, silver buttons against the funeral-black fabric of the policeman's uniform – bulged and wavered before Nelson's eyes. His legs threatened to give up on him.

"Steady, son," said the policeman.

Nelson breathed heavy, struggled to clear his mixed-up brain.

* * *

There came a point in the afternoon at that time of year when the sun slanted through the shop-front window of the Conservative office and shone directly into the back room, the door almost always standing open. Enoch was bathed in golden sunlight as he transcribed the letter Barry Dangerfield had supplied onto a clean sheet of paper. Almost believing himself blessed by the Greek god Helios, who drove the chariot of the sun across the sky each day, Enoch penned each paragraph with the ecstatic fervour a religious zealot would have recognized. Despite the late-Spring warmth, he was dressed in his habitual three-piece suit and tie. As he'd said many times, he intended to wear a waistcoat to the end of his days, and he eschewed any suggestion of removing his jacket in public.

Enoch couldn't imagine reciting the letter about the old lady verbatim, as originally written. As he rewrote each sentence he tinkered to make the language more literate, but still retain the sentiment. How could anybody fault the addition of a touch of eloquence? Finally Enoch's revised sheets were ready for a volunteer to type. A clean copy of the entire speech would be Xeroxed and sent out to various media – newspapers, TV, and radio. Clem Jones, Topsy the dog's owner and a newspaper man, had advised Enoch on a method to ensure the parts of a speech he wanted publicized would gain the attention of editors. "Journalists can be a lazy lot of so-and-sos," said Clem, who ought to know, having worked in the business for years. "So pick out the key paragraphs and put them on a cover page. I can almost guarantee they'll be what you see reproduced in print or quoted on TV." Thrilled as he was with the letter, Enoch left it to speak for itself, extracts wouldn't do it justice and in its entirety it was too long for a cover sheet. He circled three passages of his own composition.

Those whom the gods wish to destroy, they first make mad. We must be mad, literally mad, as a nation to be permitting the annual inflow of some 50,000 dependants, who are for the most part the material of the future growth of the immigrant-descended population. It is like watching a nation busily engaged in heaping up its own funeral pyre.

He was certain the second paragraph he circled would appeal to the thousands of British people he believed feared for their jobs, their Health Service, their homes – their entire way of life.

The discrimination and the deprivation, the sense of alarm and of resentment, lies not with the immigrant population but with those among whom they have come and are still coming. This is why to enact legislation of the kind before parliament at this moment is to risk throwing a match on to gunpowder. The kindest thing that can be said about those who propose and support it is that they know not what they do.

Finally an allusion to the socio-political groups – Sikhs, Muslims, Hindus. The factions people were afraid would overwhelm the country. He added a dig at the Labour party for having the gall to propose the Bill.

For these dangerous and divisive elements the legislation proposed in the Race Relations Bill is the very pabulum they need to flourish. Here is the means of showing that the immigrant communities can organise to consolidate their members, to agitate and campaign against their fellow citizens, and to overawe and dominate the rest with the legal weapons which the ignorant and the ill-informed have provided. As I look ahead, I am filled with foreboding; like the Roman, I seem to see "the River Tiber foaming with much blood."

Enoch debated back and forth with himself about whether to use the translation or leave the line from Virgil's *Aeneid* in Latin: *Thybrim multo spumantem sanguine.* He believed the prophesy of the strife ahead for Rome would dramatize his vision of the same for the future of Britain, so perhaps it should stay in Latin. And in Latin it would be more obvious the words were spoken by the Roman he referred to – Sibyl, the all-knowing prophetess. But in the end he decided he'd say it in English, since he was appealing to the masses, few of whom were likely to know the language of Rome.

Enoch looked up from his desk to see a startling vision of himself staring from the front window. An oversize poster, attached to the glass and unavoidable to passers by, was backlit by the sun, still streaming above roofs on the other side of Tettenhall Road. The white paper acted as a cinema screen, the sun a projector's bulb. A full- size, black-and-white Enoch Powell sprang to life before his eyes. He saw himself as he would in a mirror. His blue eyes met his grey eyes. His stance in the poster was stately, standing with one hand in his jacket pocket, the other resting on the desk beside him – but not in a supportive gesture, heaven forbid he should look as if he needed to prop himself up. He'd never appeared stronger, or more resolute. It was exactly how he thought of himself. Enoch stood and adopted the same pose. He stared back at himself. He could almost feel a flare of light in his eyes, bright as the reflection of a photographer's flash. Any sliver of reservation Enoch may have had about his speech dissolved. He was convinced he was on the right track.

Enoch took his annotated pages and left them on the desk of the volunteer who would retype and copy them the following morning. By the time he returned to the back room the sun had slid a little further down the sky. As he picked up the phone to call Clem Jones and extend the invitation he'd meant to deliver earlier, he was enveloped in the shadow of a chimney on the roof directly opposite. Clem was delighted by the suggestion of a birthday bunfight for his dog, Topsy, in the Powell's back garden. Enoch felt slightly relieved. He realized he'd been expecting resistance from Clem at the idea of coming to Merridale Road. Enoch should have known better than to think that even if Clem shared his reservations about the neighbourhood he wouldn't let them get in the way of his relationship with the Powells. Both the Joneses could always be relied upon to be enthusiastic about getting together. As he returned the receiver to its cradle Georgy appeared at his door.

"Enoch," said Georgy in a questioning tone. She held the copy of his speech in her hands. "What's this?"

"It's something I need retyped, copied, and distributed to the media early tomorrow. It's already a little late."

Georgy leafed through the pages.

"Please tell me this isn't the speech you plan to make on Saturday."

"I would be misleading you were I to tell you that. It is indeed the address I intend to deliver at the CPC meeting in Birmingham this weekend."

Georgy slowly nodded. She returned to an earlier page.

"I see," she said. "This section you've circled, the bit about making the Gods mad?"

"That is one of three excerpts I'd like set out on a cover sheet, with an introduction outlining where and when the speech is to be."

"It's you who are mad, Enoch. This is exactly what Ted Heath asked you not to do ... after the Walsall speech."

Enoch wasn't surprised that Georgy knew about the warning Heath had given him. He could well imagine the office was abuzz when news filtered down, as it always did, that the Leader had raked him over the coals, and warned him of the consequences should he repeat the performance. Enoch considered for a few seconds how to respond to Georgy's statement. He was well aware from an early age of the power of his stare. He'd honed and improved it over the years until it spoke volumes. He skewered Georgy with the most cryogenic look he could summon. But Georgy was made of sterner stuff.

"It's no good you looking at me like that, Enoch. Even if we forget about Ted's warning, and even if you truly believe what you're implying to be true, you simply can't go around whipping up the kind of overwrought emotions this is bound to generate. Your language is far too incendiary. What with mention of 'funeral pyres' and 'matches on gunpowder.' Its not a bloody poem for God's sake."

Enoch supposed many people would be irritated by Georgy's criticism, but he felt a glow of satisfaction. What Georgy was displaying was exactly the extreme reaction he hoped to generate – and she'd only glanced at the sections he'd circled. Just think what the full thing might achieve. He fairly sizzled with excitement. Nevertheless, he felt the overwhelming urge to correct Georgy's assumption about poems versus oration. His compulsion to insist that he never put a foot wrong was as natural a reflex as taking a breath.

"You are mistaken about a distinction between my poetry and my politics. Poetry is something which I say to other people in the conviction that they will feel the same, if they hear those words, thus arranged and thus ordered. And that's what I do in politics too. I say to people, 'This is how I feel, surely you must feel the same.'"

"Do you honestly believe immigrants will 'overawe and dominate,' as you put it, as a result of the Race Relations Bill?"

"Certainly. We see glimmers already. Look at Sikh bus conductors, agitating and campaigning for the right to wear turbans instead of regulation caps. Under the Act any dismissal as a result of their demand could be said to be discriminatory and thus illegal."

"But, Enoch, thousands of poor chaps wearing turbans died fighting on our side during World War II. A full one third of our forces were taken from the colonies," said Georgy. "It beggars belief that people are kicking up a fuss about a few bus conductors not wearing caps when nobody gave a damn what their relatives wore on their heads when they were dying for Britain during the war."

"I see no reason that that regrettable situation in history should colour what happens in England during peacetime. The wearing of a turban is, as I mentioned at Walsall, a custom inappropriate to Britain and the British way of life."

"I'm as British as the next person, and I couldn't care less if they wear potties on their heads and paint themselves blue as long as they get me where I want to go," said Georgy.

"I think you'll find that you are very much in the minority," said Enoch.

"I knew you must be up to something. I couldn't believe my ears when I heard you'd kept mum at the shadow cabinet meeting."

Enoch knew perfectly well that goings-on behind the closed doors of Westminster often became common knowledge within minutes of those same doors opening after the event. He was aware of colleagues who benefited from a few supposedly confidential morsels whispered into a well-chosen ear. Enoch believed himself above such tactics. He could be artful – he'd once heard someone refer to him as 'foxy' – but nobody could accuse him of being Machiavellian. His political career may have gone better if he were.

"It's completely out of character for you to keep quiet about policies you disagree with" said Georgy. "I understand Quintin Hogg was so amazed you didn't fight to downright oppose the Bill he confronted you after the meeting to make sure he hadn't missed something."

"Your sources are meticulous in their accuracy. I told Hogg when he asked me what I thought of his plea for an amendment that he couldn't have put it more fairly, which is perfectly true."

Georgy stared at Enoch. He could almost see the light dawn behind her eyes.

"'He couldn't have put it more fairly.' An opaque and ambiguous statement if ever I heard one. It's all about what you didn't say, isn't it? You didn't actually say you agreed with what you would call their 'lily-livered' amendment strategy, did you? You just kept quiet."

Enoch held up his hands. He grinned. Lips pulled back, teeth bared. His eyes verged on amused twinkle rather than their normal malevolent glitter.

"But why?"

"I would have thought that was obvious. We go back to the similarity of my poetry to my oration. I believe in expressing exactly what it is people should be thinking about. "

"With the language you're using you might just as well leave off the last word. Rather than thinking 'about' something, you want people to think exactly what you think, believe what you believe. And you're fear mongering in order to achieve it. Despite your insistence that – and I quote – 'a savage reliance on the working of your own intellect renders you impervious to intellectual isolation,' you do realize that Ted Heath will have your guts for garters?'"

At the suggestion of censure from his Leader Enoch felt pressure in each temple. There was little he could do to prevent his eyes becoming cool as an iceberg, as Pam had often told him they did when he was irritated.

"I deliberately include at least one startling assertion in every speech in order to attract enough attention to give me a power base within the Party. Provided I keep this going, Ted Heath can never sack me from the Shadow Cabinet."

"So it's about a 'power base?' Not what people should be thinking … about?"

"As you well know, Georgy, politics is never straightforward, simple, or uncomplicated," he said. "All to say I'm respectfully concluding our conversation, fascinating though it may be, and leaving now for the bosom of my family. Susan has some homework with which I promised to assist. After the girls' bedtime I intend to watch a Marx brothers film on TV, my favourite form of comedy, as you know. So I'll bid you 'good afternoon,' and leave you to lock up."

Enoch recognized the Marx brothers' brand of humour was somewhat puerile, but he never laughed so much as at one of their films. He felt some misgivings about preferring Americans to English comedians, but the Goon show just seemed silly, and the pathos of Tony Hancock or Steptoe and Son didn't strike him as particularly amusing.

* * *

The capacious upstairs room of the Giffard Arms was already packed with folkies huddled around tables when Frank and Christine arrived. Billows of blue-grey cigarette smoke hung in the air from the roll-your-owns folkies preferred over commercial brands. It seemed to Frank they made a perverse performance of the cigarette-rolling chore, making a point of only using Rizla liquorice papers. Despite the smoke, patchouli was the dominant aroma in the room. The dark wood-panelled walls and heavy oak furniture were a good match for the traditional English ballads that were trotted out at the Giffard. It struck Frank that folk clubs were often brightly lit, as was this room, with numerous multi-pronged sconces jutting from the walls at regular intervals. Frank preferred the murk of a shadowy jazz club, like the one held at a pub opposite the old market site. Not that he was particularly fussy about which drinking establishment he frequented. He often said, 'Pub is a pub is a pub is a pub,' believing Gertrude Stein would have approved of his version of her reflection on a rose to take the piss out of pseudo-intellectual posers who reverentially uttered the poet's line for all the wrong reasons.

Frank wasn't particularly a folk music fan, but he was always entertained by the earnestness of the folk club crowd. Along with a solemn expression, folkie women tended to wear their hair long, often painstakingly straightened, usually parted in the middle. Almost all the men sported bushy beards. The garment of choice for both men and women was an Aran fisherman's sweater, hand-knitted, often ineptly, in gnarled cable stitch. The doleful story that each island fisherman had his own unique design created by his wife so that, should he drown, she could identify her husband by his sweater seemed appropriate for the folk crowd, who tended to be gloomy, except on the odd occasion when they swerved toward ribaldry. Frank couldn't understand why the identifying patterns would be necessary. Did drowned fisherman always have their faces eaten off by predatory sea creatures? And when wet, wouldn't the sweaters render the possibility of retrieving a body unlikely? Surely their sodden bulk would drag a man down to Davy Jones locker and keep him there, languishing on the sea floor for eternity. Frank was tickled by the idea that the story behind personalized Aran sweaters was a hoax, dreamed up in the Woolmark advertising department by a trendy London executive wearing a Carnaby Street suit. A marketing ruse to encourage frantic knitting among folkies and their nearest and dearest.

"Is this seat free?" asked Frank of a group sitting silently at a table. It was the only vacant chair in the room.

"Mmm," muttered one of the men mournfully, leaving the distinct impression in Frank's mind that the chair's occupant might well be recently deceased.

Once Frank had secured he and Christine a drink each, she perched on his knee with one arm encircling his neck. Frank held her securely around the waist. He examined the crowd to see if there were any fellow art students to witness their uninhibited display of attachment. He'd be chuffed if word got around college that he and Christine Baker were now an item. Frank was disappointed when he didn't recognize a single face.

As soon as Frank and Christine were settled, two charcoal-bearded men and a woman with the biggest gold hoop earrings Frank had ever seen stepped onto the small stage. It was little wonder the place was packed. Jon and Michael Raven, with Jean Ward joining them, were among the better-known folksingers in the Midlands. The subdued clapping that greeted them seemed to Frank a tad limp, given their reputation. The crowd had no trouble settling into a reverential hush. Guitars twanged and Jon Raven launched into the first song. He had a velvet voice, deep and dark. It would have been ideal in a commercial for the glass of Guinness Frank held in his hand. Frank was unfamiliar with the ballad, but Raven's enunciation was perfect.

When gentle love first fired my breath
I rode from fair to fair.
No shepherd swain was 'ere so blessed
or so unknown to care.

All eyes were directed toward the three performers. Why was it, wondered Frank, that a roomful of people with the average age of twenty-five, were riveted by a song about a shepherd wandering the English countryside a hundred years or more before they were born. As far as he could tell most of the songs that folkies revelled in were about a bygone age. And it wasn't as if they were full of sweetness and light either, most ended in horrible tragedy. Sure enough, the shepherd swain and his true love were destined never to marry. Jon Raven finished the song in a suitably mournful tone.

Her parents thought our love amiss,
We vowed to meet no more.

Three quarters of an hour later Frank was still musing about the fascination with an England that no longer existed when Jean Ward sang the last number of the set, Cold Blows the Wind, about an unfortunate young girl weeping over her dead lover's grave. When Christine went off to the Ladies, Frank headed to the bar for another round, leaving Christine's cape draped over the chair to signal its occupancy. Despite guarded glances from other people at their table Frank grinned cordially when he returned with replenished glasses.

"Great evening. Those Raven boys really rock, don't they?" he said.

"If you say so," said one of the women, trying her best to smile. The others stared mournfully into their drinks. Frank was relieved when Christine appeared at his side, but when he looked up he was peeved to see a thickly bearded giant with his arm around Christine's shoulders.

"This is Al. Al, Frank."

Frank's imaginary hackles quivered with resentment.

"Cheers," said the giant, extending a huge mitt. Every one of Al's fingers proved to be a vice attempting to release the marrow from Frank's knuckles.

"Ow!" said Frank, shaking his hand in a show of semi-mock pain. Christine frowned at him. Al grinned, eyes fiendish, canines glistening. Christine explained to Frank that

Al was a fiddle player in a folk group based in nearby Dudley, but – Frank noticed – she didn't mention how she knew him. She did, however, regain her seat on Frank's knee, which placated him somewhat. But he smouldered with rage when Al crouched down to talk to Christine, steadying himself with a hand on her thigh.

"Why is it you lot are so fond of songs about Ye Olde England?" asked Frank.

He made a point of visibly tightening his grip on Christine's waist.

"They're not all mediaeval, if that's what you're getting at. In fact most were written as recently as the Industrial Revolution."

"Not exactly Bob Dylan or Joan Baez though are they?"

Frank was gratified to see Al's muscled fingers nervily explore whorls of whisker in his beard. He was sure he had the pedantic prat on the defensive.

"First of all, you're talking about American performers. And second, they sing mostly protest songs, not folk songs."

"Bit more relevant though, don't you think?" said Frank, going for the coup de grace.

"Not to me," said Al.

Frank was triumphant when Al took his hand from Christine's thigh and stood to his towering six-foot-something height.

"See you soon," he said to Christine.

"Yes, see you around," she replied.

Even though Al was vanquished, his implication that he and Christine would soon see each other again pissed Frank off as much as the giant's hand on her thigh.

"So how long have you known Big Al?"

Christine frowned and stared at Frank for a second or two before replying.

"Al," she said.

"That's what I said … Al."

"Not Big," said Christine. She emphasized each word, as though talking to a toddler.

"That's a relief," muttered Frank.

Christine rolled her eyes and removed her arm from around Frank's shoulders. He had to hold her tighter to prevent her falling off his knee.

"Look, if you're going to play the jealous little boy, constantly worrying that his penis doesn't measure up, we may as well break it off here and now."

"I'm delighted to hear we have an 'it' to break off … or did you mean my penis?"

Christine, obviously puzzled, pulled her head back to take Frank's measure. Frank tried his best to suppress a grin. Then, when Christine broke into gales of laughter, he beamed like an idiot.

"I'm really sorry. Won't happen again, I promise."

"Forgiven," said Christine. She returned her arm to his neck.

Frank gratefully stroked the back of her other hand with his fingertips.

"And I have to admit, it wasn't all your fault … Al can be a devious wanker," said Christine.

She pressed her forehead against Frank's. He felt an

ecstatic, but vaguely disquieting, sensation of being completely overwhelmed.

Then Frank noticed that the rest of the table were staring at them with undisguised curiosity. He winked at the woman who'd tried to smile earlier. She looked away, to where the Ravens were picking up their instruments for the second set. Despite the folksingers' laments, Frank couldn't have felt more euphoric. Christine had as good as admitted that there was something, presumably more than the obvious physical attraction, between them. And he'd handily turned around their potentially damaging first tiff. That, and the buzz from his second Guinness of the evening, put him in a mellow mood. He gave Christine a contented squeeze. She reciprocated by nuzzling his ear.

Some forty-five minutes later Jean Ward announced her final song, the story of a poor lass who slaved away in a coal mine. Frank had no idea women worked as coal miners. He suspected it was a story dreamed up by an inventive folkie to make a sad song even more depressing.

And though we go ragged and black are our faces

As kind and as free as the best we'll be found.
And our hearts are more white than your lords' in
high places
Although we're poor colliers that work underground.

What the hell was meant by 'more white' hearts? wondered Frank.

Jean was on the last verse when a kerfuffle broke out at the back of the room. Her final lines were barely audible over raised voices and insistent wrangling to which people responded with vehement shushes. As soon as she'd strummed the last chord, Steve MacDonald pushed his way through spectators who'd been standing at the rear, obviously preventing the *VoxPop* editor from barging in before the end of the song. He lunged toward Frank and Christine brandishing a copy of *VoxPop*. His face was flushed and his eyes, behind his tortoiseshell rimmed specs, appeared massive. At first Frank couldn't make out what Steve was yelling, the applause and cheers were loud and heartfelt now that the evening's performance had drawn to an agreeable close. But as the clapping and whistles diminished, Steve's voice could be clearly heard.

"I've been to every one of your bloody watering holes, looking for you. What the fuck is this photo all about?"

He held up the front page of *VoxPop* in a white-knuckled fist. Although the paper was crumpled and creased with the force of Steve's grip, it had been folded so that Frank's photo was front and centre. Folkies who'd normally be making for the door lingered to gawp at the unfolding drama.

"The coloured lad is in deep shit because of it. I've had his aunt on the phone threatening to sue us. Failing that, she swore there were people who'd be only too glad to chop my fucking head off with a machete."

Frank stiffened with panic. Steve's fury obviously had something to do with him inserting Nelson into the demo photo.

* * *

A muscle-bound barman ejected Steve for using bad language.

"Fucking students," said the barman, as he strong-armed the *VoxPop* editor down the stairs. The irony of his obscenity wasn't lost on Frank, despite being sick with dread. He, Christine and Steve stood outside the pub in a steady drizzle. Undeterred by the ignominy of being thrown out of the pub Steve continued his rant.

"The police are accusing the Jamaican woman's nephew of beating the shit out of someone here in Wolverhampton on the day of the demonstration."

Rage-induced spittle bubbled and dribbled on Steve's lips.

"According to her the police are saying the photo proves he was in town at roughly the same time as the assault, when the demo parade was moving up Darlington Street past Beatties. But she swears black and blue he was in Birmingham all day. That the photo must be wrong. So what the fuck is it all about?"

Frank felt as if someone had dropped a block of ice right inside his guts. He had difficulty making his mouth work.

"He probably was in Birmingham," he mumbled.

"What the hell does that mean?"

Veins stood out on Steve's temple.

Frank glanced at Christine. She was staring at Frank, her mouth a single taut line.

"It means I faked the frigging thing, alright?" Frank tried to sound defiant.

Christine continued to stare. She crossed her arms. Steve cocked his head, eyes narrowed, obviously straining to understand.

"I put Nelson in the demo shot from an old photo I'd

taken, to make it look more ... more ... interesting."

Frank's voice trailed off. By then Christine was looking everywhere *but* at Frank. Her face appeared drained of blood.

"You faked a photo that ran on the front page of my newspaper," Steve said slowly, as if repeating the words might make them easier to swallow.

Frank thought about pointing out that *VoxPop* wasn't exclusively Steve's baby, but decided against it. A car sped past, tires hissing on waterlogged tarmac. Why, for fuck's sake, had he let his ambition get the better of him? It was just a stupid college newspaper.

"I'm really sorry, but I didn't think you'd run it if I told you it was doctored," said Frank.

Christine wrapped her cape more tightly around her. Frank willed her to at least look at him.

"Don't forget you're a pacifist." Frank yelled when Steve MacDonald grabbed him by the front of his shirt and threatened him with a clenched fist. Folkies leaving the pub gave them a wide berth. Steve, clearly worried he may not be able to control himself, strode angrily away.

"How was I supposed to know he was under suspicion of grievous bodily harm?" Frank shouted after him.

Christine finally looked at Frank, eyes narrowed – Frank couldn't remember a stare cutting him so keenly, he felt as if he'd been stabbed through the heart.

"I had no idea, I swear."

Frank trailed after Christine the hundred yards or so to her bus stop. He felt like a dog disowned by its owner but refusing to believe it.

"Just leave me alone," Christine said, whenever he attempted to speak.

Frank cursed when a bus hove into view as she approached the stop. The one time he didn't want the bloody bus to come. As Christine hopped on she glanced back at Frank. Pale-faced and eyes laced with contempt, she couldn't have appeared more shocked if Frank had smacked her face several times over.

* * *

Frank was staring tearfully at the lights of Christine's bus as it disappeared down Darlington Street when he heard a familiar voice.

"Are thou alreet, Frank? Thou look bummed owt."

One of his classmates, Pete Gormley, a Yorkshire lad, stood examining him, forehead furrowed. Toward the end of first year Pete had declared himself a free but tortured spirit and taken on the quintessential trappings of the American beat culture – he wore faded loose-fitting Levi's, denim shirt, and frayed Converse baseball boots and carried around a dog-eared copy of Jack Kerouac's On The Road, like a talisman.

"What?" Frank asked.

"Are thou alreet? Thou look bummed owt," repeated the Yorkshire lad.

Unlike his father, who bitterly resented the Yanks for muscling in on World War II and claiming to have won it single-handedly, Frank held no prejudice against Americans. He could easily imagine the expression 'bummed out' would sound perfectly normal coming from the pen of a depressed Jack Kerouac holed up in some fleabag hotel in Middle America. But when repeated by the likes of Pete Gormley, the jargon of the American beat generation sounded ridiculous. Frank regularly derided anyone who pronounced phrases like 'crash at my pad,' or 'out of sight' in a Scottish brogue, a cockney twang, or with vowels clipped by a Geordie accent. But at that moment Frank hadn't the heart to take the piss out of Pete for repeating Yankee vernacular in a Yorkshire accent you could cut with a knife.

How was it possible that only an hour earlier he'd been deliriously happy? He'd had Christine on his knee, a beer in his hand, and an amazing career in the offing – not a care in the world. Perhaps one needed to have been so high to feel so low. Even though Frank was chilled to the core he couldn't face going home to his dreary bed-sitter. He thrust his hands deeper into his pockets. He could murder a Guinness, preferably followed by a rum chaser, but pubs were closed. He thought about the West Indian club Barry had complained about, the one he claimed fine art students now favoured instead of drinking in The Vine. The word 'club' suggested after-hours booze in abundance.

"You know a Jamaican club, Pete? The fine art mob are all going there apparently."

"Not really my bag, Frank lad," said Pete.

Frank rolled his eyes.

"It might not be 'your bag,' but do you know where the fucking place is?"

"I think it's on Fawdry Street in Whitmore Reans. Off

New Hampton Road a few streets down from the football ground," said Pete.

Frank wandered away feeling dazed – not his usual pleasant alcoholic stupor but an unfamiliar muddle of distressed confusion.

"Look after thaself," shouted Pete.

Frank picked his way through relentless drizzle, past lighted shop windows, parts of which were reflected in ragged-edged puddles. Now that patrons had been disgorged from pubs and staggered homeward, the town centre was deserted. Traffic lights flashed red, amber and green but with no traffic to comply they appeared no more commanding than fairy lights. Frank stopped to gaze at a display of flared velvet trousers in a boutique, but after a few seconds wondered why the hell he was looking at them. At the corner of Darlington Street and Waterloo Road he sheltered in the doorway of the vast Midland Electricity Board shop. Among gleaming new stoves and shiny fridges stood a large blow up of an advertisement. In the coloured photograph a hip young housewife lifted the lid of a red-enamelled casserole while a bevy of her friends, all dressed in the latest fashions, stood around a canary yellow Formica countertop. The women wore mini dresses, the men sported satin shirts with gargantuan collars, some with ruffles. A mop-haired husband filled an ice bucket – an ice bucket! – alongside pre-dinner cocktails adorned with slices of lemon. Lurid signs pasted to the window of the MEB shop featured starbursts and fluorescent typography promising: 'MAKE YOUR DREAM A REALITY TODAY. LOW, LOW, LOW HIRE PURCHASE PAYMENTS!' It occurred to Frank that the whole shebang – florid posters, shimmering appliances, the pretentious poshos depicted in the ad – could be one of Christine's trenchant artworks brought to life. At the thought of Christine he swallowed to try and rid his throat of a massive lump.

Frank edged his way past the sheer walls of Molineux, Wolverhampton Wanderers football ground. Unlit floodlights loomed above him, black silhouettes against indistinct clouds. Rivulets of rain trickled down his neck. He shivered, whether from cold or shock he wasn't sure. He still couldn't believe Steve MacDonald's fury. The editor's normally placid features had been distorted with rage. Frank was convinced he was about to have the shit beaten out of him. Terrorized by a sodding Quaker!

Frank almost missed the Fawdry Street sign sitting high up on a shadowy brick wall. A hundred yards or so up the street he passed an alley at the far end of which a doorway was illuminated by an overhead light. When he stopped to consider if it might be the place, he heard the telltale sound of a thumping bass rhythm. The door opened more easily than he'd thought. Frank almost fell into a small hallway. He was confronted by a voluptuous West Indian woman wearing a tight silver dress and perched on a barstool behind a folding table, miniature by comparison. The music – a thunderous low-pitched beat followed by a higher emphasis, ka-chink, ka-chink – was so loud Frank could barely hear the woman when she demanded half-a-crown for his membership fee. He was given a small card with the words Montego Club printed in letters made from bamboo sticks. The word 'MEMBER" sat at the start of a dotted line, where the woman indicated Frank should write his name. He also received a raffle ticket, which, the woman explained with gesticulations more than words, could be exchanged for a drink. It had better be a bloody big drink for that price, thought Frank.

The club's interior was almost as dark as the alley. The place comprised a series of three large shadowy huts joined to each other and linked by doorways. The chain of modest spaces led to a larger space, which was more brightly lit. As he moved toward the light, Frank could make out clusters of people on either side of him. All West Indians as far as he could tell. He experienced a degree of masochistic gratification from the hostility he imagined coming at him in waves from the dark-skinned figures he passed. He deserved to be despised. What a complete fuck-up he was, to have gone, in twelve hours or less, from the euphoria of seeing his photo in print and basking in the glow of Christine's adoration to the crushing disappointment of completely losing her respect. Not to mention that his fraudulent behaviour was bound to be frowned on by his tutors and the world in general. His embryonic career in photojournalism was clearly aborted a mere twenty-four hours after its conception.

The final, spacious room was lit by a half-dozen bare bulbs dangling from the ceiling. At one end sat a long table, piled with beer crates, which Frank took to be the bar. It was so dark in the smaller rooms it had been hard to tell what the walls were made of, but in the larger space Frank could see a rough surface of red brick. A few tattered posters depicting sandy beaches, azure seas, and graceful palm trees were taped to the bricks. Monolithic speakers reared up, one in each of the four corners. Wires snaked along the walls from each speaker to a DJ's console, behind which sat a man, inscrutable in a large pair of white-framed sunglasses. The speakers vibrated with a loud languorous beat. In the space between relaxed bass notes there was a distinct more vigorous note sharply detached from the main refrain. For a few seconds Frank felt hypnotized by the music. He wasn't sure he'd heard anything quite like it before. It was impossible for him not to move, his hips loose during the slower section but then marking each intermittent dissonance with a restrained jog of his leg. Couples – all Caribbean – were dancing with less inhibited, fluid moves and rhythmic thrusts. Rather than being stared at malevolently, Frank was studiously ignored. He wasn't sure which was worse. When he presented his ticket at the makeshift bar, the tall skinny barman eyed him suspiciously.

"You got any rum?" yelled Frank.

The skinny man reached into a beer crate for a bottle, flipped the cap off, handed it to Frank and fixed him with a penetrating stare that could easily have been an out-and-out challenge. Was he inviting Frank to object? Frank held the beer up to examine the label. Red Stripe, a brand with which Frank was unfamiliar. Since there appeared to be no alternative he decided to make the best of it. Frank nodded a thank you to the barman, who closed his eyes, languid as a lizard, in cool acknowledgement. Frank moved away and stood some distance from the bar surveying the dancers.

The beer was like gnat's piss. It had been a mistake to come to the Montego Club. The only good thing about it was the music. Frank was cold and damp. And to cap it all he felt excruciatingly alien.

It wasn't as if it was the first time he'd been the only white person in a crowd. Frank hadn't thought twice about not seeing another white face from Saturday afternoon until Monday morning when he'd spent weekends with Nelson in Handsworth. He didn't experience a moment's awkwardness the whole time he was at Auntie Irene's. It helped having Nelson along playing the proud brother – the 'twin' they'd joked about in the Vine.

It dawned on Frank that he'd been so wrapped up in his own misery he'd hardly given Nelson a second thought. The realization that it was his fault Nelson was in hot water prompted another surge of self-loathing in Frank. He resolved to go straight to the police the next morning to set the record straight about his photograph. Decision made, Frank couldn't wait to get out of the club. He put his half-full beer bottle on the bar and walked purposefully toward the door. But as he passed through one of the darkened rooms on his way to the exit someone grabbed his arm.

"Who let you in, Graphics boy?" the person shouted in his ear.

Frank turned to see a white face, moon-like in the gloom. He'd assumed four or five figures huddled to one side were West Indians, but they were sculpture students, for fuck's sake. Frank detested sculptors. They always looked pissed off. And they were invariably filthy, clothes and boots caked in clay or covered in stone dust. But worse, they wore the grungy evidence of their endeavours with too much of a swagger for Frank's liking. He ignored them and kept walking.

How utterly screwed in the head he must be, thought Frank as he made his way home through desolate, rain-drenched streets, to have imagined waves of hostility coming from coloured customers at the Montego Club when, if they existed at all, they were more likely to have come from white-skinned sculpture students.

DAY FOUR

Wednesday, April 17, 1968

"How much time me fi tell you? Me never at a demonstration the whola me life."

Nelson persevered now he had a solicitor at his side. Although he'd been disappointed when a woman was assigned to him. How this winji gyal wi' dirty hair a go help? But he was less upset after she shook his hand – hers warm and dry. When she told him her name was Ruth Barton he looked into her eyes, green as a deep Caribbean bay. As far as Nelson knew he'd never been the victim of any Obeah magic, but he believed he could be spellbound if he looked at Ruth's eyes long enough. He was jolted out of his state of wonder when, despite Ruth's best efforts, Gorman continued to hammer away at him about being in Wolverhampton on the day Mr Singh was assaulted.

"People saw me at me auntie place! Cecil. Delilah. Even Charles. Them can vouch fi me," said Nelson.

"We've interviewed those witnesses. Not one of them can say for sure they saw you in Handsworth on April fourteenth."

Nelson wasn't surprised. The ghoulish Fowler was the one sent to interview them. Nelson could imagine the kind of treatment Irene's three friends would have had to deal with.

"Well ask me auntie then. She know say me was with her all day."

"I'm not sure anyone will be persuaded by your aunt's story – not when there's clear proof you were in Wolverhampton that day," said Gorman.

When Nelson opened his mouth to object again about the photograph, Ruth Barton held up her hand. Nelson might have been upset, but being silenced by her reassured him she had things under control. She glanced at some papers in her file folder.

"I understand at the time in question Mr Singh's son left the Sunrise to go to a laundrette, leaving his father alone. When he returned half-an-hour later Mr Singh was lying, beaten unconscious, in the hallway. Is that correct?"

Gorman nodded, eyes narrowed.

"Nobody saw who was responsible, and Mr Singh hasn't yet recovered consciousness. Right?"

Gorman didn't even bother to nod.

"Since there are no witnesses to the assault you obviously have insufficient grounds to charge Mr Clarke, so I suggest you allow us to leave."

Was it any wonder Nelson was experiencing a sensation like warm honey flowing through his veins, delicious and comforting? Then, when Ruth Barton laid in to Gorman, berating him for harassing her client – him a client! – Nelson knew without a shadow of doubt he was smitten for life. Ruth might have been skinny with lank hair, but Nelson would be happy to gaze into her Miss World eyes forever. How it happen in a rass police station, a feeling big so?

After Ruth's reprimand Gorman said nothing for a second or two. He smiled, but his eyes remained steely as ever.

"You're free to go."

Nelson could have kissed Ruth, but was too awed by her
– not to mention too shy to kiss a white woman. White or
coloured, Auntie Irene didn't seem to care. She was waiting
in the foyer of the police station, and when she saw Nelson
smiling and without handcuffs she grabbed the slender
solicitor by the shoulders and pulled her into her ample
bosom.

"Just doing my job," muttered Ruth, blushing.

Nelson grinned at her. Jesum piece, she a look good wid
pink cheek!

"I have a feeling this isn't the end of it. Any more problems,
be sure to ask for me specifically. Make sure I'm present
before you say anything to anybody, OK?"

Nelson didn't like the sound of that. He glanced around. A
door opened a few yards down a hallway. Nelson was shaken
when Fowler stepped into the corridor. But then he was
astonished to see Frank McCann, his student workmate from
the previous summer, close on Fowler's heels. Man, it good fi
see a friend face! Ruth Barton, and now Frank. Things were
looking up. When Fowler saw the huddle of Ruth Barton,
Nelson, and Irene he stood squarely in front of Frank, but
Frank walked past Fowler and made a beeline for the group.

Nelson didn't believe he'd ever replace friends he'd left
behind in Jamaica. Especially not by the method Auntie Irene
was always pushing, urging him to come to church with her.

"You no need to pray, is just to mix up wid people," she'd
said.

But now he had Ruth Barton fighting for him, and Frank

here to support him. Nuff bredrin fi beat any rass policeman!

"What the blouse and skirt you doin' here, man?" he asked Frank.

"You! Wha' you bother come for? You a go make matters worse ..."

Auntie Irene spluttered, momentarily lost for words, but she soon recovered.

"You damn ginnal. Is your samfie picture cause this."

Nelson couldn't believe it. Auntie Irene obviously stone vex, to speak in patois!

Fowler watched from a distance and smirked as Ruth Barton ushered them out onto the street. Once outside, Auntie Irene laid in to Frank all over again. At the same time Frank told Nelson over and over again how sorry he was.

"Sorry fi what?" asked Nelson.

He looked from his downcast friend to his irate aunt.

"Is him take camera trick and put you where you never was or even belong," said Auntie Irene.

"You're the one who took the photograph of the demonstration?" asked Ruth Barton.

"That's why I'm here. To tell them it was a fake," said Frank.

"A fake?" repeated Ruth.

"I tell you so," Irene shouted.

Frank launched into his sad story. He started by saying it was the owner of the Vine who put the idea in Frank's head.

"But 'im always friendly so. Why 'im say do it?" asked Nelson.

Frank didn't answer, but started to explain how he made

this print and that negative. Nelson didn't understand a word. Like he was watching a film he couldn't follow. Eventually Frank eased off a bit and said simply how he altered a photograph to put Nelson in a demonstration that happened in Wolverhampton when he wasn't there at all. Frank was there to tell the police how he'd done it, but he didn't sound too hopeful that Fowler had swallowed his story. He mentioned something about working material, whatever that was.

"But it should be easy to produce the evidence – this working material – to prove the photo is a fake, shouldn't it?" asked Ruth Barton.

The police station was a red brick building on the corner of two residential streets. Nelson watched Frank's face as he hesitated. Frank glanced left and right towards rows of terraced houses, but his eyes didn't settle anywhere.

"Yeah, sure. Of course," he said.

Nelson knew Frank well enough – the student wasn't so certain as he claimed.

"Good," said Ruth.

At that, Auntie Irene seemed less excited, muttering under her breath.

"It shouldn't make a difference 'bout no photo. Nelson was home with me ... all damn day."

"If that's the case, why is it so important to prove the photo's a fake?" asked Frank.

"Gorman is calling Irene's story into question. If it ever went to trial the crown would imply she was lying, particularly if they had evidence to disprove her story ... like the photograph," said Ruth.

Nelson slumped a little, hung his head. He felt more sad than angry.

"Me never know you woulda treat me so, you know, Frankie. Wha' make you do it?" he asked.

"I'd never have done it if I'd known it would land you in trouble, Nelson, I swear. It was just that when Barry suggested adding you to the photo it seemed like a good idea. I honestly didn't think you'd mind."

Frank looked sick – pale and tearful. Nelson felt for him, never mind what he'd done.

At that moment, the front door of the police station opened and Fowler stuck his head out.

"Thought you might like to know. We just heard from the hospital. Singh died half an hour ago. We're looking at a murder case."

Fowler grinned and ducked back into the police station.

"Wherever bad things 'appen you find that man, happy like he won the pools. I swear 'im is the angel of death," said Auntie Irene.

"You know him from somewhere else?" asked Ruth Barton.

Irene explained how she knew Fowler from visits he'd made to the hospital, and from stories she'd heard about him.

"Them hang people for murder in England?" Nelson asked.

"Not any more," said Ruth.

They stood silent for a moment or two.

"But now it's murder, Gorman will be under the gun to

make an arrest. Make sure you phone me if they give you any more trouble."

"Lord keep him far from us," muttered Auntie Irene.

Amen, thought Nelson.

As they parted outside the police station, Nelson gripped the back of Frank's neck and shook him in mock chastisement to show there were no hard feelings. Then they shook hands, a loose-fisted finger shake, the way they'd always done.

* * *

It had been an unusually chilly night for late April. A fragile web of hoarfrost had settled on frigid pavements. Slabs warmed by the sun were enlivened by beads of melt water quivering in a crisp breeze. But as Enoch Powell walked past gardens on Larches Lane he was aware of the scents of Spring – fragrance of hyacinths, odour of freshly composted soil, the distinctive smell of a hawthorn bush coming into flower. A vaguely sooty aroma exuded from damp bricks, which, before the Clean Air Act of a decade earlier, had been wreathed in Black Country smoke for centuries. Enoch had been a huge supporter of the Act. He even floated the idea of shaming homeowners with offensive chimneys by publishing their names and addresses in the local paper. "Isn't that a bit like the mediaeval practice of putting people in the stocks?" Georgy had asked.

Enoch felt invigorated by the sharp air. His normally pallid cheeks took on a rosy tinge. It wasn't merely Spring that these sensations – sights, smells, and stimulus to his skin – evoked, but a quintessentially *English* Spring. It's what he'd missed as a young academic teaching in Australia, his first extended absence from his country of birth. And every day he spent in the aridity of North Africa during the war he yearned for the green haze of an English meadow, resplendent with fresh grass. He longed for an English Spring even when surrounded by the fecundity of India, the British Empire's jewel in the crown with which he was so infatuated.

Enoch always enjoyed holidays in France for the distinctive national characteristics he encountered, but French sights, smells, and sensations weren't his. He didn't own them. Whereas situations that were the essence of Englishness belonged to him, and he belonged to them – strolling on a village green, perhaps in the company of a local whose family name appeared on ancient gravestones. Sipping tea from a Thermos in the lee of a centuries-old castle wall, or the cut and thrust of debate in the chamber of the House of Commons, where time-honoured conventions and regulations dictated how one behaved. These were his birthright. What he considered to be the Englishness of townscapes and countryside supplied him with a pleasure verging on ecstasy. Sometimes, as he observed native English going about their business, or as he gazed at mediaeval castle walls in forays throughout the English provinces, he thought of the continuous life of a united people stretching back to the Magna Carta and came close to tears. But his passion was for England, not Great Britain. For all the leeks, thistles and shamrocks imposed on the national psyche by Wales, Scotland, and Ireland, it was the English rose that Enoch firmly grasped, like a talisman with immutable power to ward off exotic evils. He may have held a British passport, but England was his home.

When Enoch pushed open the door to the office he saw a man wearing a tan Mackintosh coat sitting in front of Georgy's desk. His brogue shoes were exceptionally shiny, the perforated pattern contrasted with their polished surface.

"Enoch I'd like you to meet Mr Ayres, he's liaison officer at the Commonwealth Welfare Council," said Georgy.

The man stood and thrust his hand out to Enoch. Mr Ayres had a firm handshake, with a particularly warm hand. Laugh lines radiated from the corner of iridescent green eyes. He appeared to be younger than Enoch by perhaps ten years. Mid-forties perhaps.

"Reginald, is it not?" said Enoch.

"No," said the man. "Geoffrey, actually."

"You're thinking of Reginald Eyre, MP for Hall Green," said Georgy.

Geoffrey Ayres smiled at Enoch, obviously not the least bit offended by Enoch's mix-up.

When confronted by affable self-confident people like Geoffrey Ayres, Enoch experienced a mix of attraction, envy, and, despite his dominant position, a need to prove himself. An expression of interest seemed the best plan to make up for his mistake.

"The Commonwealth Welfare Council is what exactly?"

Georgy gasped. Geoffrey Ayres studied his brogues.

"I simply can't believe you've never heard of it," said Georgy.

"I'm delighted to be able to add to your sense of childish wonderment," said Enoch.

Georgy sighed. Enoch was somewhat mollified to see Geoffrey Ayres smile quizzically. He clearly wasn't disturbed by the gap in Enoch's knowledge. Enoch, on the other hand, was struggling not to show embarrassment at his own faux pas.

"Geoff has been holding clinics in various towns in the Midlands to help immigrants who need advice. He's been at it for more than ten years, for Heavens sake," said Georgy.

"For my sins," said Geoffrey Ayres, smiling. He had what people were calling 'star quality.' He put Enoch in mind of the young actor, Albert Finney.

"As you understand," said Enoch. "My primary concern has been the change in the citizenship laws. It's been useless for me to devote a lot of time to the broader issue of community relations before dealing with the more urgent requirement of changing the legislation."

"I understand, sir," said Geoff Ayres. "I know you were very much a part of passing the Commonwealth Immigration Act a few years ago."

Was Enoch imagining, or was there a slight tone of disapproval? Labour, who were in opposition at the time, branded the Act a cruel and brutal anti-colour legislation. Had Georgy brought a Labour supporter into his office? And if so, why?

"But now you seem to be concerning yourself more with immigrants themselves, so I thought Geoff might fill you in on his experiences dealing with them every day of the week."

Georgy's voice trailed off slightly. She was clearly sheepish, obviously aware she might be overstepping the mark. During all the years Enoch had known Georgy she'd proved herself astute and useful time and again. First by rounding up the postal votes that doubtless won him his seat, but many times since. If Georgy believed talking to this man might be useful – whether Labourite, communist, or Trotskyite anarchist – Enoch would be foolish to refuse her.

"I'm amenable to hearing whatever pearls of wisdom you have to offer," said Enoch to Geoff. "Please take a seat in my cave back there. I'll be in directly."

Enoch turned to Georgy, who raised her eyebrows questioningly.

"I don't hear typing," he said, looking around at the volunteer who seemed to be stuffing envelopes. "Is my speech finished?"

"We thought we should get the newsletter out first," said Georgy.

Enoch examined Georgy's face. It was completely out of character for her to give priority to a task that could be done at any point in the next month over one he'd mentioned was urgent.

"What? Why are you looking at me like that?" Georgy asked.

"It's beyond my comprehension that you would think the newsletter more important when I expressly told you yesterday copies of the speech were already late in being sent to the media."

"I'll get on it right away," said Georgy.

When Enoch joined Geoffrey Ayres in his back room office he left the door open. It was only with Barry Dangerfield that he felt the need for privacy. Enoch supposed a more appropriate word might be 'secrecy.' Nothing whatsoever wrong with that. Politics often necessitated the holding of one's cards tight to one's chest.

"Now tell me about some of the problems you've experienced with the immigrant population," Enoch said.

Geoffrey Ayres frowned. He uncrossed his legs and shifted in his chair.

"I'm not sure I can do that. The town has been blissfully devoid of serious problems. Immigrants in Wolverhampton have been settling in nicely. I told Norman Manley when he visited here after the Notting Hill race riots of '58 there was absolutely no reason to suspect there'd be riots in Wolverhampton, and there still isn't. There's been the odd housing problem, but nothing major. And all the immigrants seem to have found work. They make good workers. Employers and fellow employees have only praise for them on the whole."

"But they must experience insurmountable hurdles in adjusting to our way of life."

"You're right in thinking adjustment is a challenge," said Geoff. "Not so much for Indians and Pakistanis. The ones coming here tend to be from urban areas. They're used to towns. And many are middle class and quite entrepreneurial, not unlike British owners of small businesses. But most West Indians in Wolverhampton are from rural Jamaica. Can you imagine if somebody from here picked up sticks and moved to a job tending a sugar cane plantation in a little village in the hills of Jamaica how difficult it would be for them? Well, the reverse is several hundred times more true, especially if the men come alone. When groups of male immigrants, discombobulated and absolutely clueless about living in England, come here without their families, problems often seem to surface."

Enoch sat forward in his chair. Geoffrey Ayres met his piercing gaze without blinking or averting his eyes..

"But the majority of West Indians in Wolverhampton moved here with family, or family followed soon after," he said. "And the kids, who tend to be more able to adapt, often help ease the difficult transition period for their parents."

This wasn't what Enoch wanted to hear. He didn't want to know that there were no insurmountable stumbling blocks or setbacks, so he did what he habitually did – ignored the statement.

"That brings us to another set of problems …"

"I don't know what you mean by 'another set of problems' when I just told you there weren't any to speak of."

Geoff Ayres was becoming less attractive by the minute. His self-assurance, which Enoch had found appealing, now bordered on belligerence.

"I bow to your experience and I'd like nothing better to believe the path to assimilation is as smooth as you say, but it beggars belief that these people can integrate so readily."

"Well, they need some help, which I hope I supply, but most of them adopt to our way of life with very few bumps in the road. Don't forget the rationale for immigration is often to leave a society that holds no future. Why would anyone cling to vestiges of something that served them badly? But I concede immigrant adults will probably always hold on to some aspects of their former lives. It's the kids who'll become bona fide Britons, probably not very different from your own daughters."

"The differences would be larger than you suppose," said Enoch.

He silently cursed Georgy. What the hell did she hope to achieve by exposing him to this socialist maniac? Was the man completely colour blind?

"And another thing, I was amazed when you spoke in your Walsall speech of a threat in schools from immigrant kids."

Geoffrey Ayres stared at Enoch with a questioning frown. Enoch looked down at his desk.

"I'm sure you'd be the first to admit there are large – and ever growing – numbers of immigrant children in schools" he said. "It must be difficult for teachers, having to coach children who may be behind the rest of the class and would surely hamper progress for other students."

"That would be true of newcomers who don't speak English," said Geoffrey Ayres. But almost all immigrant children come from the Commonwealth and speak passable to excellent English. Some of the Indian kids are more articulate than the locals."

Enoch had had enough. He now detested Geoffrey Ayres.

"Well, you've been most illuminating. Thank you for your time."

He stood and walked out to see how the typist, who was a volunteer, was progressing with his speech. Geoffrey Ayres wandered out of the back room. Georgy stood up when he approached. They moved toward the front door and spoke in low voices.

"Goodbye, then," called Geoff.

"Good day to you," said Enoch.

Georgy resumed the seat at her desk. Satisfied that the volunteer had almost completed the final draft and could soon start making copies, Enoch headed toward the back room.

"I hope hearing about Geoff's experiences gave you food for thought," said Georgy. "It's not too late for alterations, you know. I'm sure Betty won't mind a bit of retyping."

Georgy smiled, but grimly. The light dawned for Enoch. Georgy must have snaffled his speech after he'd left the office the day before and read it in its entirety. Geoffrey Ayres had been enlisted in an attempt to persuade him to moderate it. The animosity she'd displayed about the cover sheet passages obviously extended to the whole thing. Enoch skewered Georgy with his stare. Georgy held his gaze, jaw clenched.

"I can't imagine why you thought Mr Ayres' work would be of interest. It's no good me paying attention to the details of immigration when the root of the issue isn't touched," said Enoch.

"These aren't *details,* they're real people with real challenges. And how can you possibly know the extent of any so-called problem, or claim there are overwhelming racial issues, here – as you've done in your speech – when you aren't informed or don't concern yourself about such *details,* as you call them."

The volunteer dropped her hands from the typewriter keys. She stared at Georgy and Enoch.

"I have good reason to believe the beginnings of the current immigration problem have been very much in evidence in Wolverhampton during the whole of my candidature. Contrary to what you may think, they've been matters about which I've been very much on the defensive."

"It's odd that Geoff is unaware of any serious disturbances or racial disputes," said Georgy. "On the contrary, with his organization's help, integration has been largely achieved without any flare-up of racial prejudices. I really don't see how you can claim to be on the defensive about a situation that doesn't exist. Exactly what 'current immigration problem' are you referring to?"

Enoch stared at her for a full five seconds. The typist sat immobile, silent. A horn blared from a car on the road outside.

"I suggest you leave questions of that nature to Members of the Opposition and get on with the task at hand," Enoch eventually said.

He spun on his heel and strode into his office, slamming the door behind him. But he wasn't as angry as he might have appeared. Impassioned opposition like Georgy's wasn't completely water off a duck's back, but the effect on Enoch was less irritation and more steely resolve. As he'd insisted on more than one occasion, he had a strong conviction in his own capability of being right when everyone else was wrong. His exaggerated rage was an attempt to put an end to Georgy's harangue. He found her disapproval disquieting. His normal instinct would be to do anything possible to get back in her good books. He supposed it was odd that he was reluctant to lay out his entire rationale and strategy for the speech, but he'd known from the beginning it was an unconventional route, to say the least. The scepticism she was bound to have mattered little if he held his own counsel and carried on regardless. Georgy would come around eventually – when his goals were achieved. Enoch reached for his newspaper and sat back to try and enjoy an hour or so of reading.

* * *

"Enoch, you've missed out Tory Central Office on this list."

Enoch didn't look up from his newspaper.

"The meaning to which you attribute the word 'missed' is mistaken. It was purposely done."

"But I thought all speeches were to be sent through Central Office in London."

"Then you are again mistaken."

Georgy hesitated. Enoch could almost feel her eyes boring into the top of his head.

"So definitely no copy of the speech to Tory Central Office in London?" she said.

Enoch looked up from his paper. He didn't utter a word, just stared.

"All right, Enoch, if you say so."

Enoch went back to his newspaper. Georgy, although clearly not convinced, returned to addressing envelopes.

Georgy and the volunteer beavered away for the rest of the morning stuffing envelopes ready to be sent out to newspapers as well as radio and TV stations to arrive before Saturday's meeting in Birmingham.

At lunchtime Enoch heartily thanked the volunteer as she headed out to the post office, clutching a shopping basket full of envelopes, for her hard work in dispatching his speech. He was well aware he hadn't always been so appreciative of those who worked for the Party for altruistic reasons rather than any monetary gain. There'd been a huge brouhaha just after he was first elected when James Beattie of Beattie's department store, Wolverhampton's largest retailer, had taken offence to Enoch's brusque treatment. Colonel Leadingham told Enoch at the time that he may be "an able and most hard working Member but you are quite inhuman and arrogant in personality with little or no knowledge of human psychology." Enoch was stunned. Nobody had ever talked to him so directly. His first reaction was to deny the accusation outright. But after Beattie, who was influential within the local Tory party, kicked up a fuss, Enoch realized he was in danger of being ousted as a candidate in the next election. He changed his tune and became a tad more agreeable. It had been a life lesson he'd never forgotten. Sometimes he liked to embellish his gratitude with an inspirational sentence or two. On the spur of the moment, and with his speech very much in mind, he decided to cap his display of gratitude to the volunteer with a statement about how politicians, and by extension the volunteers, ought simply to echo the public mood.

"It's as well to remember that we aren't always the cause, nor the masters, of changes of opinion, but the exponents, representing to the public, in a kind of dialectical drama, what is passing in its own mind."

The volunteer looked slightly puzzled. Perhaps he hadn't quite got his point across. He decided to quote one of his favourite allegories. This one to illustrate a trap politicians often fall into – an overblown sense of self-importance.

"'What dust do I raise!' said the fly as he sat on the hub of the wheel. 'What a dust!'" Enoch recited.

The volunteer thanked him, and disappeared, clutching her basket of envelopes. When Enoch turned away he was confronted by Georgy sitting at her desk, wordlessly staring at him.

* * *

On the journey from the police station Frank took scant pleasure in sitting on his favourite perch in the bus, front seat upstairs. As the bus trundled towards Wolverhampton through the urban sprawl of West Bromwich and Tipton it occurred to Frank there were few sights more depressing than street after street of brick semi-detached houses. It wasn't only their appearance – it was the mind-numbingly boring lives they represented. Traffic was at a crawl. Frank squirmed in his seat with exasperation at the slow progress. He was intent on turning the Art College upside down until he unearthed his missing negs and prints. He didn't like to think what would happen if he couldn't find them.

To divert himself he debated the pros and cons of telling his tutors about his deception. The more Frank thought about the situation the more indignant he became – as far as he was concerned the ramifications of what he'd done shouldn't matter. Why should morality come into it? He should only be judged on the dexterity of his work, which was flawless. If it fooled the police it must be bloody good. But when Frank thought about the rationale he'd written for changing his year-end project, his indignation turned to despair. Nobody would trust him to accurately portray immigrant life in a realistic and unbiased manner, having inserted Nelson into a situation in which he'd never appear in a million years. He supposed he could rethink his project, but change it to what? An exploration of forgery techniques?

Frank's despair turned to anger. Why was he so bent out of shape about his college work anyway. He still had a longing to become a documentary photographer, but you didn't need a diploma for that. He had a good mind to piss off down south, take his chances with some of the newspapers in London. But he knew he didn't stand a chance without a decent portfolio of work to show he was up to the task. For that he needed college equipment – cameras, darkroom. And what about Christine? He didn't want to give up on her – and it was unlikely he'd get back in her good books if he took the easy route and dropped out. No. Crashing and burning wasn't the answer. He was going to have to make a clean breast of it. He prayed he'd be able to argue that the tainted print had no bearing on his ability to complete his year-end exhibition. In fact he could say he'd learnt a valuable lesson: to always portray situations as honestly as possible. If not, it was sure to come back and bite you on the bum. He suspected Dave Bishop would be on his side, but he wasn't so sure about his course tutor.

When did life become so fucking complicated,? Frank glared out of the window as his bus trundled past the grim redbrick walls of New Cross Hospital, originally built as a workhouse for the destitute. He tried to ignore the obvious answer that popped up, courtesy of his conscience. But, having been reminded of what he'd done to Nelson, he saw his Jamaican pal's face everywhere he looked – his expression of hurt and disappointment when he realized that his white friend's actions had been the trigger for his problems with the police. God knows what he'd undergone in the hands of the pock-marked detective. He'd certainly given Frank short shrift.

"You can't really expect us to believe this rigmarole about a doctored photo, coming from a bosom pal like you," Fowler said.

The corners of his mouth twitched in what Frank supposed was a knowing smile.

"You and Nelson Clarke may not be two peas in a pod but I've been told you're close as twins, nah?"

Fowler looked like the meanest cat imaginable who'd just mauled a flock of canaries and was now playing with their broken bodies prior to killing them.

"Close as twins," he'd repeated, leering.

Then, when Frank had again insisted he'd faked the photo, Fowler demanded to see evidence.

"Where are the original negatives? Bring those along and then perhaps we'll talk."

The rain that soaked Wolverhampton the previous evening and all through the morning had let up, but a dense pall of cloud cast a gloom over the landscape. Frank gazed disconsolately out of the bus window at abandoned factories with smashed windowpanes and collapsed roofs that foundered between railway embankments clogged with litter. It had never occurred to Frank to ask Nelson why he'd come to Britain. As he peered out of the grimy bus window at scenes of dereliction under lowering skies, he wondered if Nelson, Auntie Irene, and all those who'd left sunnier climes had realized what they were letting themselves in for. Why, for God's sake, would they give up white sand beaches, turquoise seas, and waving palm trees for frigid pavements, polluted canals, and concrete lampposts?

* * *

"Well, it's not as if you failed an ethics course, although, given your screw-up, maybe we should introduce one as part of the curriculum," said Dave Bishop after Frank had spilled the beans about faking the demo photo.

"I can't believe what a convincing job you made of it," he said, examining the front page of *VoxPop*.

Frank's course tutor wasn't as easily won over.

"I can see the headlines now. 'Wolverhampton College Of Fraud, Students Instructed On How To Make a Perfect Fake.'"

At least he called it perfect, thought Frank. The rest of his rant was a bit over the top though. Frank couldn't imagine any newspaper worth its salt giving a shit about the ins and outs of a poxy art college like Wolverhampton. Dave Bishop eventually prevailed upon the course tutor to give Frank a chance.

"If he applies the same talents to a legitimate project he may well have the best end-of-course photography exhibit we've seen in years. Which wouldn't go amiss with the examining board, not to mention the review the department is due for at year's end."

"So your West Indian pal has been set free? That's the end of the affair?"

"Yes, said Frank, trying to sound confident."

"Okay, but on your head be it," said the course tutor, stabbing his forefinger in Dave Bishop's direction.

Once outside the course tutor's office, Frank was feeling buoyant. He glanced at Dave Bishop as they walked back to the graphics department.

"I suppose it's definitely not on to include the *VoxPop* print in my year-end exhibition?"

The normally sunny photography instructor pushed Frank up against a gloss-painted wall and held him there, one hand lodged against Frank's sternum.

"Very fucking funny, Frank. If you screw this up, it's just your pathetic little life going down the toilet and nobody will give a shit. But I've gone out on a limb for you, and if you let me down I'll be forced to fucking crucify you, you hear?"

Frank could only nod repeatedly. Dave Bishop relaxed his grip. He tugged Frank's shirtfront back onto place, like a parent with an untidy child. Then he patted Frank once on the chest and beamed one of his beatific smiles.

"You've got talent Frank, make sure you use it for the right reasons."

Frank reeled upstairs to the third-floor studio, not sure if he should feel threatened, or flattered, or both.

There was almost a riot when Frank tore apart the studio in his search for the envelope that contained all his material from the demonstration.

"What the hell are you doing, McCann?" bellowed a beefy male student, who played prop forward for the Technical College rugby team, as Frank pulled the boy's drawer from the plan chest and dumped the contents on the floor.

"Don't get your knickers in a knot. I'll put everything back," said Frank.

Frank had always thought it inappropriate for an art student to play rugby – it showed a lack of sensitivity. But it also meant the lad wasn't averse to a bit of rough stuff . Frank made sure he kept his promise and returned everything to the drawer in good order, despite his heavy heart at not having found the elusive envelope.

Frank spent the rest of the afternoon conducting a thorough search of his bed-sit, although he almost never took work home. And it wasn't as if there were many places to look. He all but crawled under the single bed, but emerged empty-handed with dust-laden cobwebs in his hair. He laid bare his wooden coffee table of old magazines and newspapers, and pulled out all the plates and pans from shelves under his sink and hotplate. Frank scoured inside and on top of the wardrobe that came with the furnished room, he even pulled it away from the wall to make sure the envelope hadn't slipped behind. Frank felt physically ill when it occurred to him that he'd put all the original negatives of Nelson on the building site in the envelope as well as his material from the march. He was left with absolutely sod-all to prove he'd faked the final photo.

His last hope was the College darkroom where he'd done the work to make the print. He chivvied a couple of first-year students out of the place before turning on the overhead light, but the missing envelope was nowhere to be found. He considered turning off the main light and examining boxes of undeveloped photo paper under the amber rays of the safelight. But that was pure desperation, there was no chance he'd have stashed anything in boxes of unused photo paper. When he realized he'd exhausted all the possibilities, he felt nauseous with apprehension. He needed a drink.

* * *

"As little as you go to church, you in a haste fi forgive that damn ginnal," said Irene once she and Nelson reached home.

What was Nelson supposed to do? He was certain Frank had no idea that messing with the photo would land him in trouble. And he didn't want to lose the only good friend he'd made in the Mother Land.

"Me hungry, Auntie. Mek we eat something?"

Nothing like food to take Irene's mind off trouble. A hurricane might be raging, but Irene wouldn't care so long as she could cook. Sure enough, she seemed to forget about Frank's woes once she started preparing food. Nelson moaned and writhed with exaggerated ecstasy over one of her beef patties.

"Stop! You make me choke," said Irene, her stomach rolls jiggling with laughter.

After they'd eaten, Auntie Irene switched on TV.

"I read how that Ray Langton turning up on the Street again. See what Ina Sharples have to say 'bout that."

Nelson couldn't understand half the people on Auntie Irene's favourite soap opera. It was bad enough sorting out what Midland people said without bothering with Northerners. He sat quietly and worked on his latest song. Since Frank's suggestion of writing down his lyrics Nelson had got them all on paper. And now he started right in with new ones, writing them down from the get go. It made composing so much easier. Nelson always started by repeating the same line twice. Not exactly original, but all the songs by the big boys, like the Pioneers, did the same thing.

You gotta love, no pick and choose
You gotta love, no pick and choose.
You gotta love, sisters, brothers too.
The path not always smooth,
And you not always in the groove,
So don't go accusing others...

Nelson came to a full stop. What the pussyclaat rhyme wid others? He stared at the flickering television screen, where a trio of old ladies was sitting in a pub. Mothers!

The path not always smooth,
And you not always in the groove,
So doan go accusing others,
Like you, they got mothers.

Not so good. Nelson scratched out the last line. He strained to think. Maybe lovers was a better rhyme.

The path not always smooth,
And you not always in the groove,
So doan go accusing others,
Gotta make them all your lovers.

That was better. Nelson was on a roll.

Some do their best to change you,
Even rearrange you,
But it all up to you,
You gotta stay true.
You gotta stay true.

"Yeah, man!" Nelson whooped.

"Shh!" said Auntie Irene.

Nelson worked away for the next twenty minutes or so. He wrote and scratched out until he had three or four verses he liked. Just as the closing theme for Auntie Irene's programme began to play, a knock came at the door. So loud it threatened to take the door down. Irene looked up from the TV. Nelson knew she was thinking the same as him.

Given his earlier panic Nelson felt strangely unemotional when Fowler charged him with murder. He supposed he'd been expecting it. But Irene became hysterical when they clapped Nelson in handcuffs. Nelson had never heard her cuss so much. She followed them out the front door demanding an explanation from Fowler.

"New evidence has come to light," was all Fowler would say.

The police car probably caught people's attention, but Irene's shouts brought them out from behind their net curtains and onto the street. Nelson was more worried for his auntie than for himself. If it hadn't been for their next-door neighbour holding on to her she might have torn Fowler limb from limb.

"Just call Ruth Barton. Tell Ruth what happen," Nelson told her.

Nelson's terror, the stomach-churning dread he'd felt the other times they'd taken him in, was oddly dulled. Instead of razor sharp emotion, he felt numb. It reminded him of the robbery back home. As soon as them rude bwoys cut him he experienced a similar brain-dead sensation, as though he'd been suddenly plunged into an underwater dream. When he made it home with his white shirt a mess of crimson, he'd been unable to talk, neither had he cried.

"Him is in shock," one of his aunts said.

Being cool didn't mean Nelson wasn't devastated about Fowler arresting him. Bumbo claat! Arrested for murder – his nightmare from the day him did tief back in Jamaica. It was just that he wasn't overwrought like the other times. If anything, he felt humiliation. Most of Irene's neighbours were probably sympathetic, but Nelson would have done anything for them not to see him taken away in handcuffs. Least he can do is act proper.

* * *

When Frank arrived at The Vine, he was surprised to find himself disappointed that Barry was nowhere to be seen. The realization that the oily publican was the only person who might have any sympathy for his situation made Frank more depressed. But then he grew irritated. He wouldn't have had any working material to lose if it weren't for Barry's bloody stupid brainwave.

"Where's the boss?" Frank asked Tina, the barmaid, as she pulled his Guinness.

"Upstairs," she replied, jerking her head toward the archway next to the till that led to the private area of the pub, where Barry lived. Neither Frank nor anyone he knew had been granted entrance to Barry's inner sanctum. A glittering curtain of silver strips covered the opening, protecting the private space beyond from prying eyes. Whenever Barry pushed his way through the silver strips they made a faint metallic clatter and for a few seconds, before the strips fell back into place, anybody who cared to look could see a short hallway leading to a set of stairs.

Frank had always thought the metallic curtain appeared out of place in a Victorian pub. Barry had added other touches of jarring modernity in an attempt to convince youthful customers there was nothing square about the place. The jukebox of course, with its neon and chrome. And Barry had replaced the handsome old clock above the bar with a digital device. It featured numbers that clicked over every second. If it was quiet in the pub on the hour, when all the numbers flapped noisily over at once, all eyes turned to the clock.

Frank couldn't summon up the energy to find himself a table, although there were plenty vacant. He slumped onto a barstool. The pub wasn't exactly hopping. Two old ladies in hats sat at a table sipping Mackeson, and one of Barry's regulars was hunched at the end of the bar staring mournfully into his pint. The man pulled a cigar from a packet of Hamlets and lit up. Frank rested his elbows on the bar's polished wood. He kept his head in his hands except for the occasional lift of beer glass to his lips.

Behind the bar, but immediately in front of Frank, the silver curtain shimmered slightly. After a couple of minutes Frank could hear voices coming from behind the metallic strips. Barry's Wolverhampton drawl was easy to recognize. There was something familiar about the other voice too – the whine of a Birmingham accent, but Frank couldn't put a face to it.

"Why didn't you tell me he'd kicked the bucket, if you knew? Why did I have to read about it in this afternoon's fucking newspaper," said the Brummie.

"It don't make no difference, does it? Dead or alive? All you have to do is keep your 'ead down 'til it all blows over."

"It's not going to blow over so fucking easy now, is it Uncle Barry?"

Uncle Barry? Frank wasn't aware that the publican had a nephew, but then he knew nothing about Barry's life outside the public bar. For all Frank knew he could be keeping a harem and several eunuchs behind the silver curtain.

"It was your stupid idea for me to go and blab to the cops about the wogs' bloody quarrel. I was well off the radar until then. I could have been kept right out of it, and you fucking know it."

After this outburst all Frank could hear were shushes and mutterings. Frank thought he heard Barry say they 'needed to make sure' about something or other. Then the publican's voice rose. He was obviously losing patience with his nephew.

"You shouldn't have got so carried away with that bloody Paki in the first place, should you? So stop your blarting."

Frank continued to stare at the shimmering strips, straining to hear more snippets of conversation. When Barry suddenly pushed his way through the silver curtain he looked distinctly taken aback to find Frank sitting at the bar directly in front of him.

In the second or two before the strips settled back into place, Frank had a clear view beyond them. He saw Dennis Perkins, his shovelling partner on the building site, standing at the end of a short hallway. Unlike the day before, when he thought he saw the back of Dennis's head as he left the pub with Jock McAffrey, Frank had a full frontal view. Dennis was clearly lit from an illuminated lampshade dangling from the ceiling a few feet in front of him. There was no mistaking the burly Brummie's freckled face, closely-cropped head, and powerful frame. The only way Frank could have been more certain was if Dennis had been holding a shovel full of wet concrete.

Although obviously unsettled by Frank's presence at the bar, Barry nodded. He managed a tight smile.

"Alroight, cock? Want another?" he asked, an aggressive tenor to his voice.

"I'm OK, thanks," replied Frank, surprised to be offered a refill – his glass was still half full. Frank was convinced that, if he'd had a clear view of Dennis, the navvy must have caught sight of him too. Dennis had been staring straight down the hallway towards the strip curtain.

Barry was holding the local newspaper, the *Express & Star*, folded up in his hand. The paper would have hit the streets, as Steve MacDonald might have said, that afternoon. Barry seemed not to know what to do once Frank refused his offer. He slapped his meaty thigh a few times with the folded paper, and then threw it in a rubbish bin behind the bar.

"You look a bit peaked, my son. You need a rum chaser, put the colour back in them cheeks."

Despite his attempt at geniality, something about Barry's manner – the set of his lardy lips perhaps – gave the impression he was peeved to have discovered Frank at the bar.

"No thanks, Barry. I have to be somewhere. Already late."

Frank downed the rest of his Guinness in a couple of strenuous gulps and walked out of The Vine. He felt Barry's eyes drilling into his back before the door closed behind him. He felt as though he'd had a narrow escape, although he wasn't sure from what. One thing was certain – Barry was the last person he'd tell his troubles to now. The tone of the overheard conversation and Barry's reaction to seeing Frank at the bar had transformed the publican from harmless prat to enigmatic menace. As he made his way along Lichfield Street Frank realized he was heading for Park Dale. He needed to talk and hoped to hell Christine would agree to hear him out. A car horn blared. Frank started in alarm when he realized he'd crossed a side street without looking. He'd narrowly missed being mown down by a van. The driver yelled something unintelligible. Frank threw him an adrenalin-fuelled V sign.

It began to rain as he continued down Darlington Street. By the time he reached Chapel Ash it had become a steady drizzle. Deep in thought about the conversation he'd overheard, Frank barely registered the damp on his shoulders when his jacket became sodden. He remembered that, when he and Nelson had worked together, Dennis had been a boarder at the Sunrise Boarding House along with the rest of the full-time crew. Nelson had mentioned Dennis being there, and Frank recalled Dennis arriving at work with the other boarders, having walked with them the half-mile or so from their digs. An uneasy feeling overcame Frank that the overheard conversation in the Vine must somehow be related to Nelson's troubles.

As he made his way down Tettenhall Road, Frank replayed the conversation he'd overheard behind the curtain. Dennis was obviously blaming Barry for making him 'blab to the cops' about some quarrel or other that involved a coloured person. But that didn't mean it had to be Nelson. The term 'wog' could apply to anyone who wasn't lily white. When he was working on the building site Frank had heard the word applied to all kinds of foreigners, from an olive-skinned Italian to a coal black Indian.

Frank hadn't noticed it was growing dark until street lamps flickered into life as he turned into the once-elegant enclave of Park Dale with its decaying square of Victorian mansions. Christine's place was a bedsitter on the first floor, above three second-year graphics students, who rented the ground floor flat. The heavy front door stood ajar, its varnish peeling, brass handle and knocker tarnished and dull. Frank stepped into a large, black-and-white-tiled hallway. He could smell damp foundations overlaid with the pungency of fried food, onions, bacon, or both. Male voices and laughter drifted from somewhere at the back of the house. Frank tiptoed up the wide staircase, using the dark stained bannister to balance himself. He wasn't sure why he was behaving like a burglar. Several doors led off the landing. Pasted to Christine's was an ad for Ajax All-Purpose Cleaner. It featured a smiling, neatly-coiffed woman standing in a sparkling bathroom holding the cleaner in both hands. The slogan 'Stronger than dirt!' was emblazoned across the top of the ad. Christine had drawn manacles in black magic marker, binding the housewife's wrists and ankles. Frank had been meaning to ask her if she was aware Ajax had sued the Doors for using the slogan and part of their jingle in one of their songs. He suspected her graffiti was more likely to be a comment on the slavery of housewives, but if it was also a nod to the Doors affair, how could he not worship Christine for the rest of his days?

"What the hell do *you* want?" said Christine when she answered Frank's knock. "You look like a drowned rat."

It took Frank a bit of pleading but eventually she let him

in on the condition they "just talk."

Once inside Frank felt safer, reassured by Christine's domestic clutter. Clothes were piled on the chair next to her bed. Art materials covered her table in a colourful muddle. A half-finished collage sat on a drawing board. Cuttings were pasted on top of others, but many were still unattached. Piles of old magazines sat on the floor nearby.

"You look like shit," said Christine. "You'd better sit down."

She lifted a pile of college library books from one of the armchairs that sat either side of a glowing electric fire and laid them on the floor. As Frank sank into soft cushions he noticed a Peter Blake portrait he admired, Babe Rainbow, on the cover of the top volume. It wasn't only the white bikini that appealed to him. Frank liked the laid-back tilt of the subject's shoulders and the fact that she was smiling, yet confrontational. The painting reminded him of Christine.

Frank conceded he probably did look like shit. He'd hardly slept the night before. He'd been woken in the early hours by a nightmare. He dreamt he was being threatened by shadowy figures in the Montego Club but was unable to find a way out. He eventually fell back to sleep but when he woke again he was keen to get to the police station. He'd rushed out of the house without shaving, eager to tell his story. He probably had grotesque bed head. Frank ran his fingers through his hair in an attempt to tame it. He wasn't surprised to find a soggy cobweb.

"Here," said Christine, thrusting a mug of steaming Nescafé into his hands. She sat in the chair opposite and observed him silently. Frank sipped his coffee, fingers of both hands wrapped around the mug.

"I went to the police," he said.

"Really?"

Frank was heartened by a faint tone of approval in Christine's voice.

"Told them everything," said Frank.

"So your Jamaican mate is off the hook?"

"For the moment."

"What do you mean?" asked Christine.

A surge of dismay swept over Frank. He stared at Christine, her enquiring blue eyes, honey hair swept behind her head in an unruly coil, barely kept in place by a crimson coloured pencil thrust into its centre.

"What the hell's wrong?" she asked.

Her question triggered a spate of verbal vomiting from Frank, he didn't – couldn't – hold back. He told her every detail of what had happened at the police station, dwelling on Nelson's hurt expression and how it made him feel even more of a bastard. He went through each stage of his frantic search for his working material, and described how it terrified him when he couldn't find it. He babbled on about Dennis Perkins, how they'd met at the building site, and how he'd seen the Brummie labourer at The Vine that evening. He described the conversation he'd overheard between Dennis and Barry, although he wasn't sure how it was relevant.

"I've made such a sodding mess of things."

He swiped a tear from his cheek with the flat of his hand.

"Nelson doesn't have a leg to stand on, and it's all my fucking fault."

He couldn't tell from Christine's expression whether she sympathized or was about to slap him.

"For Christ's sake, pull yourself together," she said.

She obviously wasn't too sympathetic, but then she continued.

"There must be something we can do."

The weight of the word 'we' hung in the air. Frank couldn't believe a two-letter word could be so reassuring.

"Don't look so bloody pleased with yourself. You're not out of the woods with me yet. I'm not one of those women who thrives on picking their menfolk off the floor every time they fuck up."

"I know, I know," said Frank, straining to look contrite.

They sat silently for several minutes, heat from glowing bars of the electric fire warming their legs. Frank's eye was caught by a folded copy of the *Express & Star*.

"This tonight's?" he asked, more as a diversionary tactic than out of any real interest.

"Not sure. It was delivered downstairs by mistake. I picked it up for possible collage material. I haven't looked at it."

Frank unfolded the paper to the front page. He hadn't reckoned on the headline causing cardiac arrest.

ASIAN VICTIM OF VIOLENCE DIES: JAMAICAN ARRESTED FOR MURDER

"Fuck me, look at this," he said, holding the paper up for Christine to see.

She snatched it out of his hand, examined it for a second, and then started reading aloud.

"Twenty-two-year-old Jamaican immigrant, Nelson Clarke, was arrested early this afternoon and charged with the murder of Mr Ramanjit Singh of Sandyfields Road, Sedgely, who died earlier today of injuries sustained by an assault on Sunday, April 14th, at his place of business, the Sunrise Boarding House, Wednesfield."

"Let me see," said Frank, tugging the newspaper away from Christine. There was only one further paragraph. They'd obviously just managed to shoehorn the police statement in as the paper went to press. Detective Inspector Gorman was quoted as saying, 'As well as other evidence,' – Frank's abdomen contracted with anguish – 'a witness has recently come forward with a first-hand account of an altercation between Nelson Clarke and Mr Singh in August of last year. The accused and the victim obviously had a history of conflict and disagreement. We have every reason to conclude it can only have been the accused who carried out this vicious attack.'

Frank leant back in his chair, closed his eyes, and moaned.

"Is it legal to spell out evidence before a trial? Somebody claiming they saw something?" asked Christine.

"They can do whatever they fucking want," said Frank. "I wouldn't trust the detective I saw as far as I could throw him."

Then, as if his brain had been kick-started, perhaps by the Nescafé, Frank remembered Dennis's words and put two and two together.

"It must have been that bastard Dennis. He told Barry 'It was your stupid idea for me to go and blab to the cops about the wogs' bloody quarrel.' And here's what the detective said in the paper." Frank read from the *Express & Star*. "'A first-hand account of an altercation.'"

"But why would this Dennis person be so upset if all he'd done was to give an account of a quarrel between Nelson and the Asian landlord?" asked Christine.

"Barry was holding the newspaper when he came into the bar after I overheard them. Dennis must have just read about Singh dying. I bet he didn't know about it until then. He blamed Barry for making him go to the police with his story of a quarrel. He said he'd been 'off the radar' before then. He was obviously unhappy about suddenly being mixed up in a murder case."

"But why would he be worried?" asked Christine.

"Nelson never told me about any quarrel. He's not the kind to get into a fight. Maybe Dennis was lying about it. And if he was found to have given false evidence during a murder investigation he'd be in deep trouble," said Frank.

"But why would he deliberately lie?"

They sat in silence for several minutes. Frank thought about his missing envelope and felt sick to think that without it Nelson might go to jail for a very long time.

"The one thing that mystifies me about this whole affair is how the police brought Nelson in mere hours after the photo was published" said Christine. "How did they manage to get hold of a copy of the student newspaper so fast? I mean, *VoxPop* isn't exactly the *News of the World*, is it?"

Frank felt irrationally defensive about the newspaper that had carried his first published photo.

"It gets around," he said.

They sat in silence for a while staring at the flame of the gas fire. Eventually Christine took a decisive intake of breath and sat up straight.

"We'll go to the local MP. His office is just around the corner, on Tettenhall Road," she said.

"What do you think he'll be able to do?"

"I'm not sure, but isn't that what MPs are there for? To help when all else fails? We can go first thing tomorrow."

"Does that mean I can stay over?" Frank asked.

Christine threw a towel at him. It hit him squarely on the head, swathing his face.

"As long as you have a bath," she said.

When Frank joined Christine in bed she smelt of Nivea cream. When he kissed her she tasted of Gibbs peppermint toothpaste.

"Remember to keep the orgasmic volume down," whispered Christine. "Those wankers downstairs tease me enough as it is."

Frank considered claiming it wasn't him she needed to worry about, but thought better of it.

DAY FIVE

Thursday, April 18, 1968

"Are you sure about this?" Frank asked. He and Christine were standing in front of a shop window almost completely covered by a poster of the Member of Parliament for Wolverhampton South West.

"Of course I'm sure. If you can't trust the police, this is your best bet."

"Why do they always photograph them looking like they've got a poker up their arse?" Frank asked, staring at the poster. "They should jolly them up a bit. Shoot them in their shirtsleeves. Make them smile at least."

"He does look a bit grim. Like Churchill all set to invade Germany," said Christine.

"More like Hitler about to invade Poland if you ask me."

Inside, the place resembled an office rather than a shop. Three desks were lined up one behind the other loaded with typewriters, blotters, staplers, and other detritus of office life. A Gestetner machine was the only other large accoutrement. A door stood open at the back to reveal what looked like a storeroom. Frank could see shelves piled with stationery and envelopes.

"May I be of service?" asked a woman sitting at the front desk. With her upper-class accent, tweed skirt and twin-set, she could have been a cartoon posho out of the pages of

Private Eye – Frank's preferred periodical of the moment. It occurred to him the singular word 'bust' perfectly described her formidable breasts, obviously contained by substantial undergarments and shrouded by a mauve sweater. A matching cardigan was draped over the back of her chair. Her steel-coloured hair was swept back in a stately wave. Her only make-up was a smear of crimson lipstick, which although precisely positioned didn't quite cover the extremities of her generous mouth. Frank would have expected a frosty reception from a woman of her ilk sitting in a Tory office, but there was something about her demeanour – she smiled with her eyes as well as her lips – that appeared genuinely welcoming.

"It's rather a long story, I'm afraid," said Christine.

"You'd better sit down then," said the woman. "Grab a couple of those chairs and bring them over here."

"First things first," said the woman. "My name is Mrs Verington-Delaunay."

Double-barrelled to boot, thought Frank. Even so, she seemed affable enough. Frank sensed something solid under her county clothes. Not only physically, although she must have been a stunner as a young woman. Frank liked the way she'd clearly made a decision about him and Christine that was obviously not negative. He could always tell when people over forty took one look and wrote him off as a deadbeat. Frank told his story almost from beginning to end. Mrs Verington-Delaunay nodded from time to time. She appeared genuinely interested. When he recounted the conversation he'd overheard in the Vine, Mrs Verington-Delaunay interrupted.

"This Barry you mentioned, is his name Dangerfield?"

"Yes. Do you know him?"

"He's been in here a few times to talk to Mr Powell. I believe he's concerned about illegal drinking clubs."

"He's got a bee in his bonnet about a West Indian club in Whitmore Reans he claims is taking his business."

"Yes, so I understand," said Mrs Verington-Delaunay.

She seemed genuinely shocked when Frank reached the end of the story and pulled out the previous day's *Express & Star* to show her the account of Nelson's arrest for murder. She read it carefully, put it aside and sat thinking for a minute or two.

"How did you come to fake the photo in the first place?" she asked.

Frank cursed himself. He'd been too embarrassed to tell about Barry suggesting the forgery, and his making the bet with his fellow students.

"So it was Barry Dangerfield's idea to fake the photograph?" asked Mrs Verington-Delaunay after he hesitantly explained.

"I can't believe I went along with it," said Frank. But then a thought hit him.

"You don't suppose the snake had some other reason to suggest it, do you? An ulterior motive of some kind."

"It wouldn't surprise me."

"Fucker!" said Frank, before he had time to consider.

"Sorry," he said.

"You shouldn't be," said Mrs Verington-Delaunay. "It's exactly what he is."

Frank was relieved – and amazed.

"As I see it we have two problems. The first is that since your friend lives and has been arrested in Birmingham, the affair really doesn't come under Mr Powell's auspices, not being in his constituency."

"But the original assault took place in Wolverhampton," said Christine.

"True and that may have some bearing. But the second problem is that Mr Powell is rather busy at present preparing for a speech he's to give on Saturday."

Frank was beginning to wonder if perhaps he'd misjudged Mrs Verington-Delaunay. Maybe she wasn't as amenable as he'd thought.

"But I'll be sure to tell him all about your friend's problem and ask him to at the very least make a phone call. Let the police know we know, so to speak."

Mrs Verington-Delaunay took down both Frank and Christine's phone number, promising to keep in touch.

"If only I could find that bloody envelope full of my working material," said Frank.

"There must be some other way we can prove Nelson wasn't at the demo," said Christine.

Mrs Verington-Delaunay picked up the copy of *VoxPop* they'd showed her and studied the photograph.

"Wouldn't the others substantiate your story?" she asked.

"Others?" asked Christine.

"What others?" asked Frank.

"These other people in the photograph. If they tell the police your pal Nelson wasn't in the march with them, it'll back up your claim that the photo's a fake."

"That's a bloody brilliant idea," said Frank. He was so grateful to Mrs Verington-Delaunay he didn't mind at all when she laughed and said, "I would have thought it was the obvious thing to do."

After Frank and Christine left the Tory office Christine suggested they walk through West Park on the way to college. Frank hesitated, he was eager to root out Steve MacDonald, who he prayed could identify the marchers in the photograph.

"Come on. It'll only take a few minutes more," said Christine, pulling him by the hand in the direction of the park.

When they walked through ornate iron gates Frank was glad she'd coaxed him. The clouds and rain had moved off to another part of England, leaving Wolverhampton rinsed of dust and gleaming in Spring sunshine. The air in the park smelt fragrant, hyacinths perhaps. Sunlight filtered through young leaves. An atmosphere of serenity enveloped Frank.

"How many shades of green do you think the human eye can see?" asked Christine.

"Must be hundreds, maybe thousands."

They rounded a bend, overtook a meandering procession of daffodils, and strolled along a lakeside path.

"I feel like we could be Adam and Eve," whispered Frank.

"Having not only tasted the apple, but eaten the pie and drunk the cider," said Christine, tugging playfully at the side seam of Frank's jeans. She kissed him, a loud smack on his cheek.

The water in West Park's lake was unruffled. A reflection of a glass-gabled conservatory shimmered on its surface.

Floating ducks seemed to glide in and out of white window frames. It struck Frank that everything in the park – elegant railings, crystal conservatory, ornate bandstand, cast-iron clock tower – were outstanding examples of the aesthetics and workmanship of 19th century Britain he'd learnt about in art history classes. In the pastoral atmosphere of the park it was impossible to believe that the filthy industrial hell where such handsome accoutrements were manufactured lay mere miles away.

"The Victorians knew a thing or two about designing a park, didn't they," said Frank.

"Can you imagine anything more English?" asked Christine.

As they rounded a bend they came within ten or fifteen yards of an arched iron bridge that separated the larger boating lake from a smaller expanse of water, home to flocks of wildfowl. On the bridge stood a group of Pakistani women enjoying the sunshine. They wore traditional pyjama-style pants with matching tunics. Each outfit was a brilliant colour: fuchsia, crimson, azure, emerald, and yellow. Every woman wore a scarf in the same hue as her outfit thrown loosely over glossy hair anchored by a thick plait. Two of the women leaned their elbows on the iron balustrade and murmured to each other. The other three stood gazing around them, obviously admiring the park's charms. One adjusted her headscarf. As she unwrapped it and tossed it back into place over her hair, gold threads glittered and dozens of slim bangles tinkled against each other on her arms.

"Wow," said Christine, stopping to stare at the women.

"Suddenly we're in the Punjab," whispered Frank, wishing to hell he had a camera.

"The Victorians were all over India like a rash, weren't they? It stands to reason they shipped over bandstands and conservatories and made parks identical to this. Is it any wonder these women look so at home? They've probably been in places just like this since they were born," said Christine.

Frank wasn't convinced the women looked as comfortable as Christine made out. They appeared relaxed enough, but Frank was sure they must be aware they were in a town in the middle of England, with all the attendant strangeness of climate, smell, and white-skinned observers – he and Christine, standing gawping, curious as zoo visitors. For his part he wasn't sure he could move halfway across the world to live permanently in a strange locale. Could he ever feel at home? How would he feel if he knew he was unlikely to ever see the country of his birth again? What was wrong with him that he'd started to ask himself all these questions? He laughed out loud.

"What?" asked Christine.

"You make me think about the weirdest things," said Frank.

"Isn't that a good thing?"

"It's not bad," said Frank. He kissed Christine lightly on the lips.

"Come on, I've got witnesses to find."

They strolled away. Frank felt slightly disoriented, as if he'd travelled thousands of miles in the space of a few seconds.

They emerged from the tranquillity of the park and onto New Hampton Road – a few streets away from the Montego Club. Rain-scrubbed air and sunshine did little to improve the prospect of dingy houses and broken pavements. They headed past the gates of Wolverhampton Wanderers football ground, climbed the steep incline to St. Peter's Church, stepped between tall pillars either side of heavy double doors, and into the dimly lit college hallway.

"See you later?" asked Frank.

"It wouldn't be a good idea to show your face in The Vine this evening. Why don't we go back to my place after classes? I make a pretty good spaghetti Bolognese," said Christine.

It wasn't until then that Frank realized he'd hardly drunk a drop the day before. Only a single Guinness. He was surprised to find the prospect of another dry spell didn't fill him with dread – an evening of domesticity with Christine was well worth the sacrifice.

"Sounds great. I should have names of the others in the photo by then. Maybe we can discuss who to approach first. If you want to, that is."

"Of course I do," said Christine.

* * *

Enoch felt some trepidation as he approached the office. Now that his speech was dispatched hither and yon he hoped not to hear any more resistance from Georgy. He'd always thought Pam was the only person whose approval he truly sought, but in the last couple of days he realized Georgy loomed large. Enoch once overheard someone say in relation to Pam that he'd married his mother, which was preposterous. His mother had been slight and rather pale despite her fierce determination. Pam was much rounder and, although stalwart in her support, was nowhere near as intense as his mother. Georgy, on the other hand, was a lot closer to the mark in terms of personality.

Enoch's mother was the more forceful parent throughout his childhood. Enoch's father was milder-mannered, less assertive. Both supplied an atmosphere of scholarship, but his mother galvanized his brain. Enoch's earliest memory as a toddler was of her putting letters of the alphabet around the kitchen for him to learn as she cooked. Despite her constant exhortations to excel, Enoch never thought there was anything oppressive about his childhood. If he could have remade it or reconstructed it, he wouldn't have known what to do to make it better. Anyway, he liked to believe the theory that the sort of person he was and the sorts of things he'd done – and would do in the future – were settled by the time he was born. However, as he approached the office, brain swirling with overlapping images of his mother, Pam, and Georgy, he began to doubt his belief in preordination and wonder exactly how much of his character was formed during his upbringing.

"Good morning, Enoch," said Georgy when he pushed open the glass door to the shop-front office. "Beautiful morning."

"Spectacular. Nothing quite like a sunny day in April," he said, relieved to see that Georgy seemed to bear him no ill will from their heated exchange the day before.

"Don't speak too soon. You've heard about April showers?" said Georgy.

"Yes, but they're purported to bring May flowers, are they not? So a blessing, perhaps."

Georgy smiled. Enoch was seized with a memory of the smell of baking. He always remembered the kitchen of his childhood at dusk during winter. A single light hung low from the ceiling, illuminating the kitchen table. Enoch remembers quite clearly the hissing of the gas mantle. His mother's boldly written alphabet stuck to the walls was barely legible in the dimness of the room's periphery. No toy or outing gave him as much pleasure as his mother's smile and her muttered "good" or "well done" as she sat at the table watching him copy letters onto a sheet of paper. Enoch was always struck by the sense that his mother was armouring him with education. He was left with the abiding impression that there was an unmentionable evil lurking outside the kitchen walls, the only antidote for which was irrefutable knowledge.

"Before you get stuck into anything, I want to tell you about a young couple who were in here this morning," said Georgy.

"But Georgy," Enoch interrupted her account. "If this young immigrant lives and was arrested in Birmingham there's nothing at all I can do. Nor, to be honest, do I see why I should intervene. It's a matter for the police and the judiciary."

"I know, but it seems your friend Barry Dangerfield may somehow be involved."

Georgy recounted a rather preposterous story about a

conversation supposedly overheard between Dangerfield and his nephew.

"And you did say, not that long ago, and I quote, that 'you'd set your face like flint against differentiation on the grounds of origin,'" concluded Georgy.

A great deal of water – and a spate of immigrants – had flowed under the bridge since he'd made that statement, but Enoch decided he'd appease Georgy. Better to humour her, given their altercation of the previous day. Not to mention getting her off the subject of Barry Dangerfield.

"I tell you what, you draft a letter to the Chief of Police in Birmingham saying that since the crime was committed in Wolverhampton the case has come to my attention, that I hope the fact that the accused is coloured and an immigrant will have no bearing on the investigation, etcetera, etcetera. You get the drift. Although I have to warn you, it's unlikely to make the slightest difference."

"At least my young friends will feel you've done something. And you never know, they may even vote for you after this."

There were no volunteers in the office. Georgy appeared to be busy stuffing newsletters into envelopes. Around eleven o'clock she stuck her head into the back room.

"Coffee, Enoch?"

After she'd put his cup on his desk, she lingered.

"I was thinking about your speech in bed last night," she said. "And how you've never really talked about your trip to America. So I was wondering, when you and Pam were there last year your must have been conscious of the race riots in Detroit. Do you think that influenced what you wrote?"

"As you know Pam was very much looking forward to revisiting New York, her old stomping ground when she worked at the United Nations, which as you may remember, was just before she came to work for me. I was less anticipatory about the trip. Admittedly New York is an exciting milieu, but I felt from the moment I stepped off the plane at a remove from everything that ultimately mattered, from all that gave one birth."

"You've never really explained what it is about America and Americans that you so dislike."

"It's like saying one doesn't like sugar in one's tea. *De gustibus non est disputandum.*"

"Sorry, Enoch, my Latin is a bit rusty."

"In matters of taste, there can be no particular rationale. No why or wherefore when it comes to things American."

"But what about that young American man who helped you with your history of the Lords? You liked him tremendously. Even gave him a glowing credit in the book. And he was a smoker, you usually detest smokers."

"Keith was the exception that proves the rule. And he was living in England at the time. He displayed good judgment in turning his back on America – if not on tobacco."

"Taste aside, doesn't travel, even to America, jolt one out of one's complacency about one's everyday life?"

"You use the word complacency as though it were a negative. You're implying one is ill informed and therefore ignorantly smug about one's quotidian life. But if one can see that the status quo is, on the whole, in excellent health and not to be meddled with for the sake of meddling, or not to be diluted – even polluted – by some misguided policy, then being complacent, in the sense of being satisfied with how things are, is exactly the correct way to behave."

"Are you saying the British can't learn anything from other nations?"

"Not at all. But we must be mindful that from this continuous life of a united people in its island home spring, as from the soil of England, all that is peculiar in the gifts and the achievements of the English nation, its laws, its literature, its freedom, its self-discipline. The unbroken life of the English nation over a thousand years and more is a phenomenon unique in history."

Enoch knew she'd heard it all before in one of his speeches or other, but he didn't see anything wrong in the eloquence of rhetoric, even in everyday conversation. Georgy rolled her eyes.

"China, for one, might dispute your claim of England's uniqueness," she said. "But to go back to my question, where you aware of racial tension in America?"

"Every single minute of every single day. You can't walk down a street in America without being aware of the difference between the Negro and the Caucasian."

"Even after all these years."

"The United States lost its only real opportunity for a solution to its racial problems after the Civil War, when it should have partitioned the old Confederacy."

"You mean make the old slave States for coloureds and the rest for whites?"

"Certainly. But now it's less a melting pot and more a

massive conglomeration of groups from diverse origins, all living alongside. I admit the country holds immense power by virtue of its size, but in terms of diplomacy and foreign policy Americans act like deluded bullies, who believe everybody lusts after becoming like them. So while they strive to shape the world in their likeness, yet they're also deeply suspicious of being overtaken."

"Why does the last bit sound familiar?" said Georgy. "But to go back to your idea of separating a country – or any other organization – by colour. It's unthinkable. "

"But not impossible. Take South Africa. Look at Liberia. It was ostensibly part of America when thousands of freed slaves were encouraged to move there in the nineteenth century. Repatriation wasn't the dirty word it seems to be now. The main rationale for American investment in Liberia was to avoid racial conflict within the United States by separating black from white. The plan was a stroke of genius. I said it while I was in New York and I'll say it to you now: integration of races of totally disparate origin and culture is one of the great myths of our time."

"One could argue that our immigrants do not come from such disparate origins and culture," said Georgy. "They're all from the former British Empire. And anyway, their children will be bona fide British citizens. Their version of English nationality may not include Houseman poems and fox hunting, but by virtue of being born and growing up here they'll have more in common with your daughters than you seem able to imagine."

"Your friend, Geoffrey Ayres, tried to claim the same

thing. I should have told him what I'll tell you now, which is that, while I grant that in law children of immigrants will become by birth United Kingdom citizens, they will be West Indians or Asians still. They will by the very nature of things have lost one country without gaining another, lost one nationality without acquiring a new one. I take you back to your question at the beginning of our conversation about my fears about us experiencing the kind of racial unrest we see in America – where, I hasten to point out, the negro is now a third or fourth generation American. I believe that within the lapse of a generation or so we shall at last have succeeded – to the benefit of nobody – in reproducing 'in England's green and pleasant land' the haunting tragedy of the United States."

Georgy sat down in a chair on the far side of Enoch's desk. She leant forward, her bosom almost resting on the polished wooden surface, and fixed Enoch with an earnest stare. It occurred to him she looked like somebody, a nurse or a social worker perhaps, about to impart a piece of particularly tragic news. She spoke in a low but emphatic tone.

"Let's cut to the chase, shall we Enoch? You and I are both perfectly aware that there's a world of difference between people whose forebears were wrenched from their homes, thrown into the hold of a ship in chains, and transported thousands of miles to work as slaves, as opposed to willing immigrants who come to a country with which they're more or less familiar to make a better life for them and their children. And I'm sure you remember as well as I that observers from America came to Birmingham a few years ago to see how successfully immigrants had been assimilated here."

Georgy sat back in her chair.

"So what's really going on, Enoch? Why didn't you voice more strident opposition to the Race Relations Bill to shadow cabinet? Why wasn't Central Tory Office sent a copy of your speech?"

Enoch employed his tactical silent stare. Georgy held her ground, eyes crackling with curiosity. Did he owe her an explanation? He thought back to his first year in Wolverhampton when he was living in his frigid bachelor flat in Chapel Ash. Despite the frugality, he relished the ascetic atmosphere – he had almost no furniture and slept on a camp bed. Georgy discovered he'd be on his own on Christmas Day and brought him a small Christmas tree, more of a sapling really. She dangled jelly babies from branches by way of decoration. He'd eaten all the black ones first. The liquorice ones proved to be his daughters' favourite too. Add Georgy's myriad acts of kindness to the invaluable work she'd done on his behalf, and the answer was yes – he owed her some kind of explanation.

"An element of surprise is never a bad thing," he said. "And the speech will go down well with hoi-polloi."

Georgy closed her eyes. Her head fell forward. Not unlike someone who'd just received tragic news. Enoch felt the smallest trickle of doubt – more a steady drip, but it threatened to become a torrent.

"You know I'd be the first in line to help you increase your popularity – especially if it meant you becoming leader – but I'm convinced this speech is completely the wrong way to go about it."

Enoch felt as though he'd been confronted with the unspeakable evil that lurked outside the walls of his childhood kitchen. Not that it was Georgy herself, but the sentiment she represented. The thing he most dreaded and that his mother had so vehemently opposed: any question or doubt in his mind whatsoever of the certainty that he was right.

* * *

Steve MacDonald was only able to identify one of the students marching alongside Nelson in the photo. He told Frank he recognized the demonstrator holding the placard as a first-year ceramics student named Denise James.

"She's only been here a term and a half, but she's already gained a reputation for being a bit of a shit disturber."

"How so?" Frank asked.

"She organized a sit-in to protest the probation of a couple of first-year students, even though their work was crap. And she was raked over the coals by the principal for 'aggressive confrontation' of a staff member. She threatened to cut the ceramic technician's balls off with a modelling tool after he addressed her as 'dear' or 'darling,' or some term of endearment she found demeaning."

"I had a run-in myself with that technician during my pre-diploma year. He's a condescending turd. Although threatening to castrate someone seems a bit extreme. But why was she so steamed about a couple of students being put on probation if their work wasn't up to snuff?" asked Frank.

"She doesn't believe in any system that 'imposes status,' as she puts it. She made a big to-do of pronouncing her end of term assessment irrelevant, even though it was excellent. She's a brilliant potter, fabulous glazes. She believes that as long as a student produces something – anything – they should be considered legitimate. She doesn't believe in quantifying quality of art with marks or grades. She doesn't seem to take into account that she got accepted to college ahead of hundreds of hopefuls who didn't make it. If that isn't imposing status I don't know what is. She's obviously cut from the same cloth as all those bloody vegetarians who sanctimoniously nibble dandelion leaves and nuts while swanning about in leather jackets."

Frank considered heading off to the ceramics department there and then, but decided it might be better to wait until he could take Christine along with him. He was spooked by strident women at the best of times. Denise James might wield her modelling tool over his groin once she learned his reasons for faking the photo. Better to have one of the sisterhood by his side.

Steve MacDonald had no idea who the other students were.

"I remember seeing this one at a few CND meetings," he said, pointing to a wild-eyed, bearded young man with shoulder-length hair and beads around his neck.

"He was so spaced out most of the time he could barely string two words together, and one of those words was always 'man.' As in 'Cool, man,' or 'Wow, man.' Maybe he's at the Tech, although I can't imagine what he'd be studying. I don't think Transcendental Meditation is on the curriculum."

"What about the other two?" asked Frank.

"She looks familiar. I have a feeling she's somebody's girlfriend."

"That gives me a lot to go on. And how would you like to be described as somebody's boyfriend?"

"I think the horsey one is in interior design, but I can't be sure," Steve continued, oblivious to Frank's dig and pointing to square-jawed girl in a duffel coat with a murderous expression.

"You're no bloody help at all," said Frank.

"This from the man who nearly got me killed," spluttered Steve, the veins on his forehead beginning to bulge.

Frank beat a hasty retreat to the college office to see if the secretaries could identify any of the students from the photo.

"Who do you think we are, dear, Interpol?" asked one of them.

"Why don't you put a notice in the common room?" another suggested.

Frank had no intention of broadcasting the story of his misdemeanour by appealing for assistance on the walls of the common room. At least he'd learnt a valuable lesson – from now on he'd make damn sure he knew the names of people in the shots he took.

His college work hovered in the back of his mind. At coffee break he came across the *Express & Star* from the day before that someone had left in the common room. Frank couldn't resist picking it up and rereading the brief but devastating couple of paragraphs about Nelson's arrest. Not wanting to be seen reading the article, he quickly turned over the page when someone sat down at his table. Inside the paper he read about a Sikh bus driver who'd been suspended from work for refusing to wear a regulation cap. A demonstration of Sikhs pushing for permission to wear turbans instead of regulation headgear on the job was planned for the following day in Wolverhampton. It sounded like an ideal opportunity for Frank to take some photos. Dave Bishop was only too pleased to lend him one of the Rolleiflexes and give him some film. Frank hoped to hell the weather cooperated. With a shoot lined up and equipment stowed in his RAF knapsack, Frank felt free to wander down to the interior design department to see if he could find the horsey girl in the duffel coat.

A couple of college departments, including interior design, were accommodated in a rambling succession of rooms on the upper floors of a nondescript annex building in a road off Darlington Street. A creaking staircase led up from the pavement. Frank was familiar with the art history lecture room on the first floor. Its low ceiling was supported by one or two columns, behind which Frank snoozed during talks by one or other of the art history tutors. But he'd never been inside the interior design department on the floor above. He was intrigued by the clutter of fabric samples, paint chips, and floor tiles surrounding three-dimensional models of rooms. He showed the photo to a couple of students, a heavy lad with frizzy black hair sporting a brown corduroy suit, and a slender fair-haired boy wearing a paisley shirt.

"That's Diana, Diana Throgmorton," said the heavy lad as soon as Frank showed them the photo.

"Is she here?" asked Frank.

"Canary Islands," said the fair-haired one.

"You what?"

When the bulky student explained that Diana Throgmorton had taken time off and gone on holiday to Tenerife, Frank asked what kind of an art student flies off to exotic locales in the middle of term – or any time, come to that.

"One whose Daddy's rich, and who's heartbroken after being chucked by her big bad sculptor boyfriend," said the paisley-clad lad.

Frank experienced a pang of sympathy for Diana at the mention of her being ditched by a sculpture student.

"When's she back?" he asked.

"Monday, if she comes back at all. She's susceptible to rough types. She's likely to marry a local goat farmer and live happily ever after – or for ten minutes anyway. Until she gets bored."

Frank asked if they knew where she lived.

"Out near Brewood somewhere," said the heavy lad.

"Just ask for Throgmorton Manor," said paisley boy.

"You're joking," said Frank.

"Not entirely," said the boy.

Frank had thought he'd be able to find all four students in the photo with no problem. He'd imagined triumphantly springing Nelson from police custody in no time at all. He'd even anticipated Auntie Irene's warm embrace of gratitude. The fact that it was clearly going to take more than a day or two took the wind out of his sails. He didn't have the heart to trek around the unfamiliar corridors of the Technical College asking questions about the two students he couldn't identify. He'd never been inside the place except to go to dances.

Frank thought about grabbing a pint instead, but the Vine was out of bounds for obvious reasons. The Giffard Arms didn't appeal, maybe a bad association from the night before last, when he'd spilt his guts to Steve and Christine. Another alternative was the Tiger, but Frank was put off by its flashy modern interior, more like a coffee bar than a pub. Nelson weighed heavily on his mind. Frank was gripped by the urge to find out exactly what was going on with his Jamaican friend. He didn't think Irene had a phone. He supposed he could try her at the hospital but he seemed to remember she usually worked nights. If he went to Handsworth by train Frank reckoned he had just enough time to see Irene and be back before he was due at Christine's that evening. Perhaps he could snap a few photos while he was there to justify the trip.

※ ※ ※

"They say they have a first-hand account of an argument you had with Mr Singh last summer. Do you want to tell me about it?" said Ruth Barton

Nelson stared at her. Touch of green eye shadow brought out the sea-water highlights in her eyes. He'd noticed as soon as he walked into the prison visiting room that her hair was clean and wavy. She had a jacket that fitted her better, didn't make her look so skinny. But he didn't like the hint of a frown furrowing her forehead – felt bad it was because of him. Nelson looked down and shifted in his chair.

"It wasn't no big fuss. Just a lickle disagreement."

Nelson described the incident with the bed sheets, his

phone call to Mr Singh, and Charlie's stunt of breaking into the linen cupboard at the Sunrise Boarding House.

"Trouble is, Nelson, you should have mentioned it before."

"Never took it for anything," said Nelson.

Ruth explained to him that now he'd been formally charged, he'd need the services of a barrister to defend him.

"Barrister? That cost?"

"That's the least of your worries. From now on you must tell me and the barrister everything, truthfully and in full, otherwise we can't help you."

"I tell you everything a'ready. Me no know wha' more fi say."

He smelt her perfume – flowery but spicy too – drifting across the narrow table separating them. The fragrance seeped into him and filled him with a longing so strong it threatened to overwhelm. How a smell make him sad so?

"Then why does it feel like you're holding back?" Ruth asked.

Nelson hurt even more to think Ruth suspected him of hiding something from her. She leaned forward, fixed Nelson with her aqua eyes and lowered her voice.

"You realize whatever you tell me, I don't have to tell anyone else unless you want me to? They can't make me talk about anything you might say to me."

"A true?"

"Yes, it's true. That's why they let me see you without a guard present, so nobody but us knows what's been said."

Nelson wanted to spill his guts to Ruth right then, what a relief to pour it all out, but he was confused. The flip-flop he'd felt in his chest, or was it his belly, when he saw her again – shiny hair the colour of Jamaica walnut – had confused him. Would he be right to 'fess up to Ruth, or were his feelings for her clouding his judgement?

"It can be anything Nelson. Even something you don't think is relevant to the situation."

Nelson leant forward, took a breath.

"I kill a man back home, but as there is a God, I no touch Mr Singh."

He didn't expect Ruth to just narrow her eyes and stare back at him. He thought she'd react, maybe reel back in shock and horror. On the contrary, she leant further in toward him.

"Were you charged?"

"No. That why me leave outa Jamaica and come here, stop them looking into it."

Then Ruth smiled. Nelson couldn't believe it.

"Me say me kill a man and you smilin'!"

"I'm sorry Nelson. It's just that I don't believe you're capable."

She eyed him for several seconds. Was Nelson dreaming, or did he recognize something he knew from the eyes of his mother and aunts? She jus' playin' or she like me so? he wondered.

"You're too good and gentle. Bit of a softie really, aren't you?"

Gratitude, relief ... indignation too. Ruth evoked them all in him, but mostly the warm honey in his veins sensation of being liked, maybe loved.

"Well, a true," he said, surprised to hear his voice hoarse. He coughed once to clear his throat.

Ruth looked at Nelson for a few seconds longer. Then she straightened up, sat back an inch or two. It seemed to him the colour of her eyes changed, from emerald shallows to deeper water.

"Tell me all about it, in detail. Don't leave anything out."

Nelson told Ruth everything. How, after one of the three toughies took hold of him while another cut his face, he was sure he'd be stabbed for real, maybe killed. Somehow or other – don't ask, is like a bad dream! – Nelson got free of the one holding him. But then, as he was tussling with the one with the knife, it ended up in the boy's chest. For a few seconds the world stopped. Nelson and the other two stared at the one stabbed, who held on with both hands to the knife still buried between his ribs. When the boy's knees buckled, Nelson took off faster than a dog pelted with stones.

"What makes you think you killed him?" asked Ruth.

"Next day in the *Gleaner* it write them find a dead body. Then we get fi realize them have mi wallet with name and address. Is the other two come kill me – that or the police come find me."

Ruth sat calm throughout Nelson's rendition of the story. But when he poured out the rigmarole about his cousin dying two days after the robbery and his mother saying it was Nelson that fell out of the tree so it would look like it was him that died so he could take his cousin's birth certificate and escape to the Mother Land, Ruth held up her hand.

"If asked, I'll deny you ever told me all that."

"You say them can't make you tell."

"I'd have to check, but if I know you're not who you say you are ... best we pretend you never said it. As for the rest, it sounds like an open and shut case of self-defence, so you'd only be charged with manslaughter at worst. And since the event has no bearing on Singh's murder we don't need to mention it again."

Is that simple? After he deal with fifteen month of sufferation? Nelson was in danger of watering up again. Ruth must have noticed. She put a warm, dry palm on top of his hand, which made him less able to hold things in.

"Try not to worry. We'll apply for bail later today."

She stood up and put papers in her case.

"Oh, and I never told you this, you understand? But if you or your aunt have any letters back and forth from Jamaica that mention anything about what you just told me, I suggest you burn them."

When Ruth reached the door she turned before opening it.

"I presume Nelson Clarke was your cousin. So what's your real name? Off the record."

Nelson considered for a second or two.

"If me tell you, me haf a run away with you and hide you and keep you close."

"Goodbye, Nelson," said Ruth.

* * *

Next up was Auntie Irene.

"Is a big mess fi see you held in prison for a murder you

don't commit, while your other t'ing back home ..."

"Tcha! Shush, Auntie!"

He glanced at the guard. Irene looked suitably shamefaced.

"Ruth ask for bail ... me soon come home," said Nelson.

"She tell you fi call her Ruth?"

Nelson rolled his eyes and shook his head.

"Me a her client. We close, you know."

"Mmm. Anyway, I never think I would see the day when I in here. I hate this place, is where they hang that bwoy, you know."

Nelson had heard the story of a Jamaican lad who killed a shopkeeper during a robbery a few years back, but he didn't know he was in the prison where the boy was executed.

"You lucky them ban hanging from when them kill him," said Auntie Irene.

"Them a go find me guilty?"

Irene had the good grace to appear apologetic.

"Is just me worrying how you acting so cool."

"Better me cry?"

Nelson felt his irritation prick. What she think, him turn into rude bwoy gangster overnight? Even before this latest trouble she was always warning him about law-abiding boys she'd known who – once the idea lodged in their head that they'd be picked up anyway – went right ahead and did things they wouldn't normally do. What it matter if a little stealing involved? They'd be accused, guilty or no. Why not hurt someone if it bring money in them pocket? They'd be pulled in by police whether they'd done it or not. Irene never claimed all the innocent boys who were picked on turned out that way, but she swore she'd seen it in young men as decent and good as Nelson.

Irene pulled a handkerchief from her pocket and dabbed her eyes. Her tears melted Nelson's irritation.

"Promise auntie, I never turn to crime. Me too 'fraid, you know."

Nelson could see why Irene worried about him acting cool. When Fowler had come out with the mumbo-jumbo about whatever you say will be used in evidence, he felt like part of his brain shut down and he forgot what fear of the future felt like. Nothing he could do about it so why be petrified? When prison doors slammed shut and were locked behind him, he didn't flinch. He wasn't nervous when a couple of Jamaican boys inspected him closely as he passed them on the iron stairs leading up to his cell. A white crocheted cap, like Pakistanis wore, was perched on each of their closely cropped heads. Nelson assumed the headgear was some kind of gang uniform.

"Wa'apen, star," they muttered as he passed them.

"Wa'apen," Nelson mumbled back.

He supposed there were some good things about his newfound fearlessness. He'd flirted with Ruth hadn't he? Teasing her about having to kidnap her if he told her his real name. Hard to believe he was so cheeky. But Nelson could see Irene's point. He'd have to watch himself.

"Anyway, listen. Frank waiting outside. But they say you have to agree fi see him," said Irene.

"You wait 'til now? Yes sa, me waan fi see 'im!"

* * *

Frank's rail journey took him over pea-green canals clogged with algae and filled with the accumulated detritus of neglect. The only leaf in sight was on an occasional spindly sapling struggling to survive in a crack of masonry. It was obvious how the area had acquired its name: the Black Country. It had to be the most concentrated stretch of soot-smeared 19th century industrial buildings in the world. As the train rattled past the back of one of the few remaining working foundries, Frank saw silhouettes of workers caught against the massive open door of a furnace with white-hot innards. He glimpsed a fountain of sparks from a welding torch illuminating a man wearing a gleaming space-aged face protector. He looked completely out of place in a filthy Victorian workshop, more like a character in Stanley Kubrick's latest film, set in outer space. Frank was relieved when the train reached Birmingham.

He wasn't able to remember the number of Irene's house on Newcombe Road, and all the houses in the terraced block looked the same. He hovered outside one he thought he recognized. The net curtains looked familiar, but almost all the houses had identical window covering. His indecision was made stronger by a thought that hadn't occurred to him until that moment – Irene might not exactly greet him with open arms. The front door of the house next door flew open. A man with an astonishingly large head of tight curls, extending from his scalp like a massive blackberry, stepped onto his front path.

"Wha' you need?" he asked.

When Frank explained he was looking for Irene, the man narrowed his eyes.

"I kinda 'member you."

"Yes, I'm a friend of Nelson, Irene's nephew," said Frank, relieved that the man recognized him from previous visits.

"A lotta sheggery happen. A lotta sheggery," said the young man. Then he puckered his lips, raised his eyebrows and made an astonishingly loud noise somewhere between a hiss and a kiss. He was obviously disgusted with events in relation to Nelson.

"Yes, terrible isn't it. But I'm trying to help get him off. That's why I wanted to see Irene," said Frank.

The man leaned over a low wall that separated the two front paths and pounded on next-door's knocker. As they waited the man examined Frank scrupulously, his eyes travelled slowly from the crown of Frank's head to the scuffed suede of his desert boots. Just as the man put his hand out to lift the knocker for a second time Irene's voice could be heard.

" Soon come," she called from inside.

When she opened the door dressed in a lime green velour dressing gown and matching bedroom slippers Frank launched into a profuse apology for disturbing her.

"Take time with me, Frank. I been awake fi a good half-hour. You want a cup o' tea?"

Satisfied that Frank posed no threat, the next-door neighbour turned to disappear into his house as abruptly as he'd appeared. As he stepped over his threshold the top of his hairdo brushed the lintel of his doorframe.

Over tea and the fiercest ginger cake Frank had ever eaten, he told Irene of his efforts to find the other people in the photo and persuade them to come forward to prove that Nelson wasn't at the march. Frank was relieved Irene didn't mention his working material. She probably didn't grasp how the material could prove the photo was a fake. Nevertheless, when a telephone rang out in the hall Frank was glad of the distraction.

"I didn't think you had a phone," he said.

"It Handsworth, Frank, not the bloody jungle."

While Irene answered the phone Frank washed the tea dishes and left them to dry on the kitchen draining board. After a few minutes Frank heard Irene thank the caller. She walked slowly into the kitchen.

"It was that solicitor woman. She tell me them never grant no bail. Nelson done for."

"But he's bound to get off eventually."

"It's the meantime I worry about. The longer they keep him in jail the deeper he'll sink."

She gazed at nothing for a few seconds. Frank didn't know what to say. He was relieved when she snapped out of her reverie, saying she should hurry and get ready so she could visit Nelson before she went to work, Frank jumped at the chance to go with her. Irene agreed to phone and see if she could arrange a visitor's pass for him.

"You have ID?" she asked.

Frank explained that he had a student card and a driving licence.

* * *

Winson Green prison was a short bus ride from Auntie Irene's terraced street. It more closely resembled a Victorian country house than a prison. The massive pile was constructed of stone, with carved decorations and embellishments that hid its utilitarian purpose. But once inside there was no doubt about its use. After they'd produced their identification, their bags were summarily searched. They held onto Frank's, saying cameras weren't allowed. It would be returned to him when he left. The echo of locks and metal doors followed Frank and Irene as they progressed toward the visiting area. Frank was struck by a constant cacophony. He could hear crockery or pans being roughly shifted around. The sound of voices, loud and whispered, seemed to be everywhere. Heavy footsteps came and went. The occasional distant shout or exclamation took on sinister meaning.

Frank had to wait outside double doors leading to the visiting room while Irene went in to check. Apparently Nelson had to agree to see Frank. Eventually Irene reappeared and beckoned him to go with her.

"Frank, me never think me woulda ever buck you up in a place like this," said Nelson.

Frank tried his best to smile.

"I could say the same about you."

He reached out to shake Nelson's hand the way they always did. He couldn't believe his ears when a guard shouted to him that he wasn't allowed to touch the prisoner. Nelson shrugged his shoulders and gave Frank one of his big-eyed expressions of disbelief.

"The newspaper said the reason the cops arrested you was because someone told them about some kind of quarrel you had with Mr Singh. Is that true? Did you fight with him?" asked Frank.

Nelson scowled and made the same tutting noise as Irene's neighbour had made with his teeth.

"Ruth Barton tell me say them find out 'bout that. It was nutten, just a little fuss."

Frank asked what it was about. Nelson explained about his bed not having been made up, his phone call to Mr Singh and the way Charlie had broken into the linen cupboard.

"A whole heap of 'em must 'ave 'eard me swear at Mr Singh. Me know me use bad language, but 'im mek me vex so, yuh know. In the end me pay 'im for a new lock and that the end of it."

Frank asked if Nelson remembered Dennis Perkins being there.

"Dennis would have been at the Sunrise when me phone Mr Singh. Him woulda bound fi hear what was going on. Me can't remember if him was there nex' mornin' when them say me broke the lock. Why you ask?"

Frank told Nelson about the conversation he'd overheard in the Vine. Nelson's eyes narrowed.

"That rass Dennis. Him always a-call me all kinda name. It make sense say is him that told the police."

Then Nelson's eyes fairly crackled.

"If you find Charlie, 'im can tell the police how the whole argument go … how is nothing. Not sure 'bout Charlie's phone, but Mr Murphy will know how fi reach 'im. Charlie can clear the whole matter up."

Patrick Murphy was the foreman of the crew, the same

man who'd hired Frank. Frank was doubtful if Charlie's word would hold much sway, but when Nelson recited Mr Murphy's number he jotted it down on a piece of paper Irene gave him from her handbag.

Once Irene and Frank were outside the prison they lingered on the damp pavement for a few seconds.

"I didn't have the heart to tell Nelson 'bout no bail," said Irene.

She didn't seem anxious to go off to work.

"I hate that place. I can't help but remember say is where they hung that Jamaican boy a few years back."

When Frank expressed shocked astonishment, Irene explained that the boy had been younger than Nelson and that he'd been hung in 1962, a year or more before capital punishment had been abolished.

Irene pulled her handbag tighter to her body. Frank felt the urge to hug her but he held back, uncertain that they'd recovered the amicable relationship of his summer visits to Handsworth.

"It seem like nothing compare to the rest, but I worry Nelson sweet on that solicitor woman."

"Wow! He's the dark horse, isn't he?"

No sooner were the words out his mouth than he realized what he'd said.

"I mean ..."

"No worry, Frank. I know what you mean."

"Would it be so bad? Him and her, I mean."

"It a hard road to travel. When them find that gyal Christine Keeler have a man from Antigua for a boyfriend, people slag her off more than for them white men she sleep with that cause all the ruckus."

Frank, who'd just reached puberty at the time, hormones raging, remembered the juicy scandal when it was revealed Keeler's lovers included, as well as the coloured boyfriend, both a Tory minister and a Russian spy. His father had cancelled delivery of the *Daily Express* because of their lurid coverage of the case, denouncing the newspaper 'full of smut.'

Just as Irene looked as if she was ready to leave, she turned to Frank.

"You find the stuff what prove Nelson not in the real picture?"

Frank had underestimated her – she'd understood perfectly about his working material. A couple more layers of guilt settled on his shoulders.

"Not yet," he muttered.

Waiting for the bus to take him back to New Street station, Frank remembered he was supposed to be working on his end of course project. He spent an hour taking shots of the surrounding shop fronts. He snapped a hairdresser's window – Sunset Snips – that featured photos of various styles, from a massive Afro similar to the one Irene's neighbour sported, to a short-cropped head with swirling designs made by shaving sections of hair down to the scalp. He adjusted the exposure so that through the window he captured the blurred figures of two men in white tunics bent over their clients' hair. He took several photos of a grocer's window piled with a display of cans and bottles. Their labels featured West Indian produce from canned ackees to mangoes to Pickapeppa sauce, all labelled in a riot of typographical styles. In his excitement over the photos Frank forgot about Nelson until he was on the train. Frank wouldn't have believed his return trip to Wolverhampton could be more depressing than his outward journey.

* * *

Frank remembered Patrick Murphy, the building site foreman, as an affable Irishman. One of his favourite lines, which he trotted out to announce the midday break, was, "Empty sacks won't stand up now lads, off and have some food." When Frank explained to Patrick Murphy from a phone box outside the station in Wolverhampton that he was trying to help clear Nelson's name, the Irish foreman said, 'Good man yourself' and coughed up Charlie's phone number.

Charlie picked up the phone on the first ring. He was reticent at first, but warmed up when he remembered Frank from the previous summer.

"I couldn't fuckin' credit it when I heard they'd done Nelson for murder. I don't know nobody less likely."

Frank asked him about the kerfuffle with Mr Singh. Charlie described Nelson's phone call to the landlord and the confrontation the following day in exactly the same detail as Nelson.

"Nelson was steamed, but he kept his cool and paid Singh for the price of the lock. I was pissed off about it, but Singh wouldn't believe anything I said."

"Yes, Nelson told me you tried to tell Mr Singh it was you that broke the lock."

"That's not strictly true. Nelson might have assumed it was me, but it wasn't. I just went along there to make sure Nelson hadn't made a mistake – that it really was locked tight. It was Dennis Perkins who jemmied the lock. But I didn't want to blow the whistle on him. You must remember what a vindictive bastard he is."

Frank's scalp tightened. He became aware of the stench of urine and stale cigarettes that pervaded the telephone box.

"Dennis Perkins?" said Frank.

"He'd obviously heard Nelson on the phone to Singh. He came along while I was examining the cupboard, broke the lock and handed me a set of sheets without saying a word. I must say I was a bit surprised. I wouldn't have thought Dennis Perkins would give a toss about Nelson having a comfortable bed to sleep in."

On the façade of the Grand Theatre across the road from the phone box where Frank stood, shoulders hunched, a man on a ladder was arranging oversized letters on the marquee to spell out the name of the next production.

"You know, I always thought it was odd that Nelson's was the only bed that hadn't been made up. I wouldn't put it past Dennis to have taken the sheets off in the first place," said Charlie.

"Why would he do that?"

"To stir up some shit. Dennis's idea of fun."

When Frank stepped out of the phone box he took a deep breath of relatively clean air. He looked across to the theatre. The man was packing his ladder away having finished arranging the letters. Frank glanced up to read the play's name above the theatre doors – Dial M for Murder. He couldn't bloody believe it.

* * *

Apart from Marjorie Jones, Georgy was the cleverest woman Enoch knew. And for political acumen she was streets ahead of the Tory men in his riding. Which explained why his trickle of doubt was proving difficult to dam. Georgy's unequivocal statement about the fecklessness of his speech had evoked for Enoch the fear that he was somehow missing a key piece of information or knowledge to combat a shapeless threat – the mysterious evil his mother hinted at, only to be held at bay by more knowledge, extra learning. Might the fact that he was reluctant to divulge to Georgy "what was really going on," as she had phrased it, point to a gap in his logic, a flaw in his thinking? Whatever the reasons, Enoch was in no mind to debate the matter further with her. He'd been mistaken – damn it – to think he owed her any explanation. He employed his icy stare and simply shut down any attempt to prolong the conversation. Enoch had noticed when Georgy became agitated her neck broke out in a mottled rash as though the heat of her ire was colouring her skin. In debate with her he looked for the tell tale marking as a sign that he was hitting a nerve. After several minutes of his cold shoulder, Georgy stormed off, neck blazing, bosom heaving. She sat bristling at her desk.

Enoch's thoughts kept returning to an outing he and Pam had made with Clem and Marjorie Jones a week or so before. They'd spent a few glorious hours wandering around Ludlow

Castle. Enoch had delighted in telling Clem and Marjorie all about the mix of Norman, Mediaeval, and Tudor architecture. As they strolled, Enoch heard a man tell his family in a stage whisper, "Look, that's Enoch Powell." The man's tone of awe triggered an early memory for Enoch of himself as a pre-schooler lecturing his parents' guests about his grandfather's stuffed birds. Enoch's recollection of the room where the birds were kept was hazy – wallpaper featuring trellises and trailing flowers was his only recollection. But he never forgot details of the habitat and breeding habits of the British birds immortalized in mid flight or arranged on a branch – barn owls, bearded tits, kingfishers. He was less sure of the foreign breeds. What was burned into his brain however, as vivid as a film playing, looping over and again on a screen in his head, were the expressions of admiring amazement on his parents' friends' faces, not unlike that of the man at Ludlow Castle.

After they left Ludlow, Enoch and his party had driven through the town of Telford to Ironbridge, home of the eponymous bridge, the first cast iron bridge to be built in England. Enoch, flush with the success of his talk about Ludlow Castle pointed to the bridge and pronounced, "... designed and built by Thomas Telford."

"No Enoch," Marjorie Jones piped up from the back of the car. "That bridge was built before Telford's time."

The second he heard the words Enoch realized he'd jumped to the conclusion that, because they'd just driven through the town of Telford, the man had engineered the bridge. The jolt of panicked doubt that struck him on that occasion had hit him again when Georgy had said so emphatically, "You know

I'd be the first in line to help you increase your popularity – especially if it meant you becoming leader – but I'm convinced this speech is completely the wrong way to go about it."

Despite the knowledge that he might possibly be wrong about the builder of the iron bridge, Enoch had insisted it was Telford.

"No Enoch, you're wrong," said Marjorie Jones. "I'm certain it was a man named Abraham Darby who built that bridge. I tell you what, there's a plaque. Let's stop and take a look."

Enoch immediately pressed his foot down on the accelerator.

"Steady on, Enoch" said Pam. Nobody spoke for several miles, but when Enoch glanced in the rear view mirror he could see Marjorie's expression of irritated astonishment.

Was he putting his foot down too hard on the accelerator now? It wasn't too late to moderate the speech. The version he delivered would be different to the transcript he'd sent out to the media, but did that matter? For the rest of the morning and most of the afternoon Enoch felt as if he were Jesus wandering in the wilderness. Was he being temped from the true path by the devil? Or was it the voice of reason?

* * *

"Goodbye, Georgy." Enoch tried to sound confident, unaffected.

"Goodbye," said Georgy without looking up. Her tone of voice was dismissive, as if she'd already written him off.

Enoch stepped through the door. A brisk walk was called

for to try and clear his head. He decided to take a long route home. As he approached Paget Road he saw a group of young people loitering outside the door of the pub on the corner. He glanced at his watch. Ten minutes to four o'clock. Perhaps they were waiting for the pub to open, Enoch would readily admit he was at sea about licensing hours. He was bemused by this group of rag tag students. The males' hair grew at least to their collars, one had tresses hanging down to his shoulders. They sported shaggy moustaches. As well as their top lips, the skin to either side of their mouths was unshaven so that whiskers extended as far as their chins. A couple of the females wore the shortest skirts Enoch had ever encountered. He resented the image of genitals and buttocks that their astonishingly naked legs brought to mind. Another young woman wore denim jeans fashioned like a sailor's bellbottom trousers. Up and down the legs she'd sewn patches of various colours and patterns. The effect was of a circus performer. As he walked past them he could see that most of them were smoking. He was almost compelled to snatch cigarettes from young mouths. Not so much from any indignation about the impropriety of smoking in the street, but more because the sight of them polluting their young bodies was too much for him to bear. This group of baby boomers seemed to Enoch as alien as a extra-terrestrials. He couldn't in his wildest dreams imagine what it must be like to be them – never to have experienced war, for instance. Can a person be patriotic when they've never had to fight for their country? Patriotism was to have a nation to die for, and to be glad to die for it – all the days of one's life. Enoch was truly regretful he hadn't been killed during World War II. He was abidingly envious of Tommy Thomas for his sacrifice. The recent anti-Vietnam war demonstrations appalled him. To Enoch they were an erosion of authority. What did these young people aspire to, if not the satisfaction of loyalty to one's country and the supremacy of a democratically elected government? Enoch had always thought that if one weren't to be powerful and glorious oneself it must be some compensation to at least belong to an entity that was. But now Britain's unique structure of power was falling victim to satire and scepticism and scorn. It seemed to Enoch that England was in danger of dying just as the Empire had died. He was frustrated by the lack of attention to the lessons that should have been learnt. To be one of the diminishing number of those who had actually witnessed the glorious phenomenon of British India and then to have watched its demise was like belonging to an extinct race which cannot pass its secrets on.

As Enoch strode away from the lolling gang of students he was hit by a sharp memory of one of his Indian servants who cried bitterly on the day Enoch left, like an abandoned child. The tears had trickled down his long henna-dyed beard. As naive as Enoch considered Indians to be, many of them were wise enough to realize the folly of British abandonment and the lunacy of partition of the subcontinent. They were aware only too keenly of the sleeping volcano of rampant communalism that would erupt with the violence of Krakatoa once the British left. Enoch looked straight ahead, but his vision was blurred. He saw two lampposts where there was only one. Fine details of facades were lost. Every single time

Enoch thought about Imperial India's demise he was moved to tears. The idea of England importing the red hot lava flow of sectarianism within its own borders was too much for him to bear. As he marched up Paget Road he repeated aloud one of the sections he was most pleased with from his speech, with its suggestion of Asia in the last few words. "Those whom the gods wish to destroy, they first make mad. We must be mad, literally mad, as a nation to be permitting the annual inflow of some 50,000 dependents, who are for the most part the material of the future growth of the immigrant-descended population. It is like watching a nation busily engaged in heaping up its own funeral pyre."

Yes, this was all good. He was working up a good head of righteous indignation. Just the ticket to combat Georgy's scepticism and the doubt she'd generated. He moved on to his next logical bugbear. The Commonwealth.

The idea that the Empire had metamorphosed into an equally magnificent Commonwealth was nothing more than self-deception. The Commonwealth was as insubstantial as a fragile, ornamental butterfly designed to dupe people into believing that the spirit of the Empire was not lost. Enoch wasn't above a bit of myth making, but his romanticism was at least grounded in practicality. The Commonwealth was an ethereal product of cowardice – let's all huddle in a corner and pretend Britannia still rules the waves. And the idea of the monarch as Head of the Commonwealth was a sham. Commonwealth countries would have their own governments and make their own laws. Their independence would leave no sense of self-sacrifice for the good of the whole that an Emperor demanded. Then, too timid to alienate citizens of the former Empire from Britain, a pretend citizenship was dreamed up. People who had no commonality with or allegiance to the United Kingdom were by law suddenly indistinguishable from a person born in the British Isles. It had been all very well to give freedom of movement, but what if the majority of migration was overwhelmingly in one direction?

As he walked up Compton Road Enoch's indignation energized him. There was a spring in his step. He admired large detached houses, each with the obligatory privet hedge surrounding a substantial front garden. The more distance he put between himself and Georgy, the easier it became to stem the drip of uncertainty she'd instigated.

* * *

When Enoch arrived home he found everyone sitting in the back garden. Pam, Clem and Marjorie Jones, their son Nicholas, together with his fiancée, Pat, who Enoch had never met before, were ranged around in deck chairs. The house's interior tended to be particularly gloomy in the late afternoon. Enoch's parents' furniture – installed along with his father when they first lived in the house – was dark and heavy. If the family spent more time in Wolverhampton they'd have replaced it after his father's death, but as it was it added to an atmosphere of impermanence. Whenever possible they escaped the shadowy rooms for the garden. Susan and Jennifer were kneeling on the grass, surrounded by three of their stuffed toy dogs. Topsy, the birthday girl, all white fur except for black ears and eyes, sat eyeing the proceedings like a watchful Lone Ranger. The sun still reached the lawn but was losing its heat. Enoch would be fine in his usual tweed three-piece suit, but the girls were dressed in T-shirts and shorts. He was concerned they might feel a chill.

"If you want another cup of tea I'm afraid you'll have to take lemon," said Pam Powell. "I forgot to pick up a bottle of milk."

"Don't you have milk delivered?" asked Marjorie Jones.

"The Co-op is the only company to deliver in this area," said Pam. "And we can hardly be seen to be patronizing the Co-op."

Enoch could tell the workings of Marjorie's brain by her facial expressions. First a creased brow of puzzlement, followed by the gradual raising of her eyebrows as the penny dropped. Then she burst into gales of laughter. Clem, however, was obviously stuck at the puzzled stage. He stared at Marjorie, clearly confused by her amusement.

"The Co-operative Society, Clem," she said. "Firmly in bed with Labour."

"Of course," said Clem. "How dense of me."

"I'm sure Socialist milk is as nourishing as any other, perhaps more so," said Enoch, desperate to be included. "But Pam is wise not to give the Opposition reason to ask questions in the House about our membership of an organization so closely allied to Labour as the Co-operative Society. On the other hand, a regular milk delivery might be good reason to change political allegiance."

"People have crossed the floor for less," said Clem. "It's worth considering."

Amid the ensuing laughter Enoch noticed Susan and Jennifer looking bemused. He briefly explained the history and principles of the Co-op.

"By 'share of profits' you mean people get money back?" asked Susan.

"Exactly," said Enoch.

"Let's join," said Jennifer. "We'd have milk *and* money."

Enoch was about to explain further but Pam second-guessed him.

"Let's leave the Party allegiance conversation for some other time shall we? Who'd like some of Marjorie's apple pie?"

It was a magnificent pie, boasting golden folds of pastry glazed with sugar. Each slice slid easily off the dish as Pam served it.

"I suppose you had to butter the plate a lot," said Pat, Nicholas's young fiancée.

"You mean 'butter the plate *profusely*,'" said Enoch, without a moment's thought.

Enoch wasn't unaware that the few seconds of silence that followed his remark were weighted. He glanced at the young woman. Her face was flushed, eyes downcast.

"I suppose you could have been politically pedantic and suggested the word 'liberally,'" said Marjorie. "But being an ordinary pedant was uncivil enough."

There was no mistaking the censure in her voice. It wasn't until then that Enoch was aware he'd been peremptory in so brusquely correcting Pat's choice of words. He was relieved when Susan and Jennifer decided it was the moment to sing

Happy Birthday to Topsy. Perhaps Pam was making too obvious an effort when she later questioned Nicholas and Pat in a friendly way about their activities. It would never have occurred to Enoch to ask, but he wasn't uninterested in what they had to say. He wondered if they were as different as they seemed to the youths outside the pub. Which led his thoughts back to the office and Georgy. Now that his customary confidence had returned, Enoch wondered if perhaps he should have told her his exact strategy from the outset. But there was a danger she wouldn't have gone along with his justification for what he considered to be exceptional means. He hadn't come to the conclusion easily, but now he was convinced it was the only way. How else was he going to be noticed by the media? And he wanted to make damn certain there'd be no repeat of the damp squib his Walsall speech had proved to be. Enoch remembered that after Jesus eventually managed to resist the temptations of the devil in the wilderness, he was attended by angels. At that moment he thought of Clem as his guardian angel. As well as his strategy of pulling out paragraphs for a cover sheet, Clem had come up with a timetable for his speech that would guarantee days of press coverage.

Clem's theory was that if Enoch gave a powerful speech during the day on a Saturday, it would be covered first on radio and TV that evening and then by the Sunday newspapers next morning. If Clem's theory proved correct, news of the speech would gather momentum. Radio and TV would cover the story yet again on their Sunday evening broadcasts. The Monday morning newspapers would pick up on the speech and include as much response as they'd been able to dig up. And later that day there would be in-depth reports in the evening editions. Editorials and op-eds were sure to follow on Tuesday, once editors and political mavens had time to gather their thoughts.

The story would have at least a forty-eight-hour life and be given massive exposure. Enoch was counting on the power of his rhetoric to guarantee a media feeding frenzy that would last for weeks. He looked fondly over at Clem. Enoch had some difficulty with the idea that Clem's philosophy of pacifism had made him a conscientious objector during the war, but he respected Clem's right to be one. And Enoch had to admit it was hard to imagine Clem in uniform. His round, often smiling, face was topped by an explosion of grey hair reminiscent of Albert Einstein. Owlish spectacles framed animated eyes. Enoch cast around for words to express his appreciation for the man who'd helped and advised him and whose company he relished.

"I'm going to make a speech on Saturday, Clem," said Enoch. "And you know how a rocket explodes into lots of stars and then falls down to the ground. Well this speech is going to go up like a rocket, and when it gets up to the top, the stars are going to stay up."

Enoch had the idea that boasting about the success of his speech would automatically imply his appreciation of Clem's part in the plan. He was surprised when Clem appeared not to grasp his meaning.

"I presume you sent a transcript to the newspaper. I'll have to root it out and take a gander," was all he said.

***

In the dining hall Nelson sat next to his cellmate, Brian, who was a soft-spoken marshmallow of a man. He looked like the picture of Jesus in Auntie Irene's prayer book – tangled yellow hair with blue eyes. Brian wasn't shy in revealing he'd been sent down for extortion and grievous bodily harm. Nelson knew about GBH, although he had trouble believing his mild-mannered cellmate was capable.

"Wha' extorshun?" Nelson asked.

"I used to look in on a couple of old ladies on pension day. If they made a fuss about openin' their 'andbags I threatened to give 'em one. They reckon that's extortion," explained Brian.

"I wasn't a total prat though. I always left 'em summat for food and that. Trouble was, one of 'em got a bit resentful. I 'ad to sort 'er out, didn't I?"

Nelson never saw a smile as pleasant as Brian's, eyes clear as a cloudless sky. His angelic cellmate downed the last forkful of dinner, and eyed the congealed stew Nelson had pushed to one side of his plate.

"You goin' to eat that?"

Nelson was happy to give up his greasy stew. All he'd managed were a couple of mouthfuls, the brown mess tasted bland and rancid at the same time. He'd managed to down most of his mashed potatoes and some of his cabbage.

After the meal Nelson didn't know what to do with himself. He'd been told by a guard he was free to either go back to his cell or sit in the recreation area, a large central space, containing half-a-dozen tables and accompanying chairs.

Iron stairs led to three tiers of balconies lined with cells. Massive skylights, forty or fifty feet above, illuminated the area. Because the day had been sunny the space had seemed relatively pleasant. Now that the light had faded, harsh overhead electric lights were switched on. Nelson noticed everything cast more than one distinct shadow. He sat at a table trying not to catch anyone's eye. He tried coming up with words for a new song, but when he couldn't even think of an opening line he sunk deeper into depression.

"Clarke!"

Because it was the name he'd taken from his dead cousin, not the name he'd been born with, Nelson sometimes took a moment to respond.

"Clarke!"

Nelson raised his hand, a habit from school.

"That me."

"Your counsel is here."

Nelson didn't understand. He hesitated.

"Look sharp lad, she won't wait all night."

When the guard showed him into the visiting room Nelson noticed Ruth Barton had taken off her jacket and hung it on the back of her chair. She was wearing a different blouse from the one she'd worn earlier in the day. Old-fashioned with a bit of lace on the front. When Nelson sat down opposite her, first thing he saw was the two top buttons were undone.

"How are you coping?" she asked.

"No bad. I make a friend with me cellmate."

"Watch out who you talk to Nelson, they're all criminals in here, you know."

She worse than Auntie Irene! Nelson was wondering if he should protest when he noticed Ruth's eyes shining. She smiled. He grinned.

"You look surprisingly well," said Ruth.

"You too, you lookin' good."

Nelson wished they were somewhere nice, like Auntie Irene's living room, instead of in a rass prison.

"It a lickle late for visiting men in prison, nuh?"

"As your solicitor I can have access to you any time I want."

She winked, which gave Nelson the warm honey in his veins feeling. But then her face changed.

"I'm here because I wanted to break the bad news to you in person. I'm afraid our application for bail was refused. It's insane but they think you might be a risk to Singh's family, or to the general public."

Him a public menace now! Nelson shrugged and tried to look like he couldn't care less. He didn't want Ruth to feel bad.

"Or maybe they're worried you'll jump on a slow boat to China. In which case I'd probably come with you."

Ruth smiled.

"You know ... like the song."

Nelson didn't understand. But he liked the idea of them being on a boat together.

"They've set your trial date. May 6th, so not far off. Puts me in the hot seat though. Even more reason to hope your pal comes up with his negatives and such."

Nelson grimaced. Being given a date made his trial

suddenly more real. And he remembered the look on Frank's face before he claimed it'd be easy enough to find whatever it was to prove the photo a fake.

"I wanted to ask you something, Nelson. I have a contact in Kingston, a Jamaican lawyer who went to law school with me. He went back home to practice."

Why she tell him this? Nelson wondered if this Kingston lawyer practiced on Ruth when they were at school together.

"I thought it might be a good idea to ask him to look into that thing you told me about. You know, when you were robbed?"

"You say we no need to talk about it."

"I know, but I can see it's bothering you. May as well see if I can shed some light on it, don't you think?"

Nelson was touched, but still wary.

"It cost?"

"No, no. My pal would be doing me a favour. And I wouldn't tell him about you. Just ask him to find out if there are any official records. If there was a body and a newspaper report the police must have been involved."

Nelson felt a glow. She want fi help and she go on so.

"Awright," he said.

She asked Nelson more details like exactly where the robbery had taken place, the date and time. He had no trouble remembering – he wished he could forget.

They sat silently for a few seconds. Nelson searched for more to say. He cursed himself for being so tongue-tied. Not so cheeky after all.

"If   Frank   comes   forward   soon   with   proof   the

Wolverhampton photo was fake they'll have to drop charges and release you," she said.

Was he imagining it or was she putting off having to leave.

"Make we hope," said Nelson.

Eventually Ruth stood and put on her jacket. The guard saw her through a glass panel in the door and came in to escort Nelson back to the recreation area.

"Goodnight, Nelson. Sleep tight. I'd tell you to watch the bugs don't bite, but in here it's too true to be funny."

Nelson managed a smile, but to see her leave made him feel as desolate as when his boat set sail from Kingston.

* * *

Nelson christened his prison bedding 'Brillo Pad blankets,' so scratchy any fibre involved was more likely to be steel than wool. They weren't at all warming, and Nelson was freezing his backside off. His feet felt like pure ice. He wrapped his arms around his knees, pulled them so close to his chest he could have kissed them. Combine the frigid temperature with Brian's snores roaring down from the bunk above and any hope of sleep seemed faint. There were other noises – muffled moans, metallic belches emanating from pipes above his head, heavy footsteps of a warden outside the cell door, the occasional grating of gears in the distance, followed by the revving of engines.

Frank's stricken expression of guilt floated in front of Nelson. He prayed his friend could find the things that would prove the photo a fake. He hoped he'd managed to reach Charlie. Then Fowler's pockmarked face pushed Frank's aside. It brought stirrings of anger in Nelson that threatened to turn into something more serious. Nelson didn't have to try too hard to find something pleasant to think about. He hugged his knees tighter and pictured Ruth Barton slumbering in sweet-smelling sheets, her hair draped on the pillow, like Sleeping Beauty in the fairytale. He sang to himself, softly so as not to disturb Brian.

You gotta love, no pick and choose
You gotta love, no pick and choose.
You gotta love, sisters, brothers too.

DAY SIX

Friday, April 19, 1968

Having reluctantly opened his eyes, Frank could see a suggestion of daylight seeping through gaps around Christine's curtains. A manic cacophony of birdsong confirmed that dawn was breaking. Frank rolled over onto his back. Christine murmured in her sleep and turned away from him. Frank stared at the shape of a plaster decoration on the ceiling, half-a-dozen concentric rings of various thicknesses that encircled the light fixture. Words to the Noel Harrison song, Windmills of Your Mind, floated into his brain. *'Round, like a circle in a spiral, like a wheel within a wheel, never ending or beginning on an ever spinning reel.'* Why was he thinking of that bloody awful song? He'd enjoyed the film, The Thomas Crowne Affair, but never latched on to the theme song. Maybe it was Harrison he didn't appreciate – too posh to be a pop star. But, now that he had first-hand experience, Frank had to admit the words of the song certainly evoked the frustration of an unsolved mystery.

How, if at all, did Barry and Dennis Perkins fit in to Nelson's situation? Frank pondered the revelation that Dennis turned out to be Barry's nephew. He wondered about Charlie's claim that Dennis might have instigated Nelson's dispute with Mr Singh over his bed sheets. But why? Just to be a bastard? Frank thought about Nelson in prison. What the hell must his West Indian pal be going through, locked up with a bunch of criminals and hard cases? He wriggled closer to Christine's warm back and, for the first time in his life, Frank thought what a jammy life he'd led.

Despite being such cold fishes, his parents had supplied him with life's necessities. They'd always thrown in an annual birthday and Christmas present. Even taken him on the occasional holiday. He hadn't been bullied at school. He'd never been beaten or physically abused in any way. He was a privileged post-war child who'd benefited from National Health, free milk, a good education, and a college grant. He'd dodged National Service by several years and never fought in a war. He'd never felt threatened – quite the reverse. The events of the last few days coupled with the feeling of menace he'd felt in the Vine the evening before last made him appreciate the security he hadn't realized he enjoyed. It wasn't as if Barry had held a knife to his throat, nevertheless the atmosphere had been heavy to say the least. Frank was deeply aware that a murder had been committed. The murder of someone only once removed from him. Despite the glow from a rising sun filtering through Christine's curtains, Frank felt chilled when he thought about the expression of malice he'd glimpsed on Dennis's face at the Vine, before the silver strips fell back into place. He turned towards Christine and buried his face in the nape of her warm neck. She smelt faintly of Nivea cream.

Christine climaxed first, arching above Frank's body and keeping her mouth wide open in an attempt not to moan. Then she leaned forward and held her hand over Frank's mouth. He breathed heavily through his nose as he struggled to be silent, eyes bulging.

"Praying Mantis has nothing on you, does it?" said Frank, after he'd caught his breath.

Christine collapsed on top of him and pulled the covers over their heads in the hope that their laughter would be muffled from the students downstairs. But their efforts appeared to have failed when there was a banging on Christine's door.

"Come on you two lovebirds. Rise and shine."

"Sod off, Donald," shouted Christine.

"Very ladylike. It sounds like your mother on the phone down here. You want me to tell her why you can't talk to her?"

"What a twat," said Christine. She pulled on a white cotton kaftan and padded to the door.

Frank must have dozed off. Next thing he knew Christine was back. She was struggling into a pair of jeans.

"It was that woman from the MP's office, Mrs Verington-Dee-something. Better jump to it, she's dropping in on her way to work. Turns out she just lives around the corner, on Clark Road."

* * *

"The house is a bit of a wreck, but this room suits me. And it's affordable," said Christine as she ushered Mrs Verington-Delaunay through the door.

"It's a beautiful room. In the old days, this is where the family would have entertained their guests."

The room ran the full width of the house and was illuminated by two deep sash windows with a view of dense foliage in the square beyond. Frank glanced around at elaborate moulding running around the perimeter of high ceiling. Christine had hung a pink paper Japanese globe over a dangling light bulb, and thrown a saffron paisley scarf over an ugly lampshade. A handsome iron fireplace with inset, glazed tiles was cluttered with Christine's bits and pieces – a Venetian mask, a Mexican doll, a glazed snow dome with the Eiffel Tower inside.

"A room of one's own," murmured Mrs Verington-Delaunay.

Frank had never thought about it before, but seeing the scene as if through her eyes and bathed in dappled sunlight he saw how much the room might have pleased one of the Impressionists. The shapes and colours, but also a sense of a personality – Christine's – pervading the room. Her books were piled on the floor next to the table, where her collage material, sketchbook, and pencils were laid out. Her caftan lay on the bedcover where she'd thrown it in favour of an Indian T-shirt decorated with embroidery flowers.

"I'd have given my right arm to be a student," said Mrs Verington-Delaunay. "Unfortunately, it wasn't enough. So I kept my arm and got married instead."

Christine made them all a cup of Nescafé.

"I hope you don't mind me barging in on you. I wanted to let you know what we've done for your friend. But to be absolutely truthful, when you mentioned on the phone this was where you lived, I was curious. I walk past Park Dale every day and often see students coming in and out. And since it's on my way to the office ..."

Her voice trailed away wistfully. Frank sensed her regret. He was about to downplay the joys of student life, say something about it not being all beer and skittles. But he thought back to his early morning revelation.

"Yes, we're pretty lucky to be handed four years of further education on a silver platter," he said.

Christine glanced at him. He supposed she was checking to see if he appeared at all sarcastic. Who could blame her?

"Yes, indeed," said Mrs Verington-Delaunay, in the same pensive tone. But then she seemed to pull her thoughts together. She sat forward in her chair. She told Frank and Christine about the letter Enoch had written to the Birmingham Chief of Police.

"But I'm afraid that's as much as we can do, for now. I'm afraid Mr Powell isn't in the most positive frame of mind at the moment when it comes to immigrants and immigration."

The frustration in her voice was palpable. Frank and Christine's silence begged an explanation.

"It's just that Enoch was in America recently, around the time of the race riots in Detroit. He seems to believe we're in for the same trouble here if we don't do something soon."

"Do you believe that?" asked Christine.

"It's not going to be easy, but I wouldn't go along with the dire scenario Enoch is predicting. He doesn't take into account that over time society in general is likely to bend to accommodate recent immigrants, just as it's accommodated other newcomers throughout history. The thing is we have absolutely no option but to accept them, so we may as well be doing all we can to help newcomers fit in, not trying to find ways to get rid of them."

Frank noticed a red-mottled flush appearing on her neck. He could almost feel the heat on her skin.

"Britain owes those people. We allowed thousands and thousands of their ancestors to be exported as slaves so we could benefit from cheap labour in the colonies. And in the case of Asia Africa, and the Caribbean, we overran their countries, plundered their resources, and tried our best to destroy their culture. You only have to look around almost any town or city in England to see evidence of the prosperity this country enjoyed – and still does to a certain extent – as a result of our occupations of other people's lands. Their presence here is a consequence we have a responsibility to accept. It's as simple as that."

Georgy sat back and sipped her coffee.

"Unfortunately Enoch is choosing not to agree," she said.

"I see," said Christine.

"So I'm afraid there's little point in approaching him further. If pushed, he's just as likely to suggest your friend be deported as help him."

They sat in silence for a few seconds. Frank watched dust motes float through sunlight slanting through the window.

"I don't know how I know this," he said. "But isn't your boss a bit of a poet?"

Mrs Verington-Delaunay smiled, clearly relieved by the change of subject.

"It's quite possible you read it somewhere, Enoch's poetry has been reviewed here and there."

"Bit of an odd pastime for a politician isn't it?" asked Christine.

"Enoch would say poetry and politics flow from the same source. In poetry the writer expresses something to the reader because he or she believes they'll feel the same sentiments if they're expressed effectively. He'd claim that the same is true of political speeches."

" Makes sense. Are his poems as expressive as you'd think?"

"Some of them are quite affecting. Highly influenced by Housman. Enoch knew him at Cambridge and was profoundly moved by his work. Enoch's poetry is a tad too romantic for my liking. His speeches are far more effective, mainly because he's such an impassioned speaker. His delivery would do credit to the best Shakespearean actor – he gives an amazing impression of strength in his beliefs. But, like Shakespeare, Enoch is sometimes difficult to understand. He uses poetic devices that sail over people's heads – metaphor, literary allusions, and the like. His speeches sometimes leave the audience a bit bemused. People are left feeling terribly impressed without knowing why."

"I can see how that would be a problem," said Frank.

"I tease him about a statement he made when he was Health Minister. It was just a dozen words, but I tell Enoch it was the most effective speech he's ever given. He was quoted as saying 'The hospital exists for the convenience of the patients and not the staff.' Those few simple words probably garnered him more support than any of the grandiose speeches he's made."

"I seem to remember my father talking about a speech Mr

Powell made about Kenya. It sticks in my mind because my dad couldn't believe he was praising a Tory."

"That would be his Hola speech."

"Funny name," said Frank.

"Yes, but actually the place was anything but fun. It was a detention centre for captured members of a rebel force in Kenya, which was still under British colonial rule at the time. But it was clear the Empire was in its death throes. Enoch was a staunch Imperialist – a firm believer that countries of the Empire would go to rack and ruin without white army officers to run them and a British monarch as Emperor. He was devastated when India was given independence ten years earlier."

"That was partition, right? I seem to remember my father saying there was horrible sectarian violence as a result," said Frank.

"That's true. And I'm sure it was something Enoch had foreseen. The way in which India was given independence may have been flawed, but the principle of independence for the colonies is a good one."

"But what about this speech about the place with the odd name?"

"The name came from the camp's location in Kenya. There was a big stink because eleven rebel prisoners were beaten to death by personnel, the deaths caught the headlines back in London and forced a political response. The Tory government tried to wriggle out of taking any responsibility. One MP even went so far as to excuse the deaths by calling the victims 'sub-human.' Enoch used ambiguous language to refute the term, but he did go on to describe them as 'fellow human beings' and he denounced the use of a double standard of justice for Africa as opposed to anywhere else. It was a remarkably impassioned speech. Enoch sat down and wept after it. Which is perhaps why your father remembers it positively. But Enoch made it clear from the outset that he was criticizing the Kenyan administration, which he believed was falling apart without firm British leadership. In his opening paragraphs he called the affair an 'administrative disaster." His Hola speech was as much a condemnation of the erosion of the authority of the Empire as it was an accusation of moral wrongdoing."

"You know, my father was in India during the war," said Frank. "He once described the locals he ran into as being 'like children.' I always used to wonder how the hell he knew when he couldn't understand a word they were saying."

"It's not unusual for colonialists to describe the people they're dominating as 'children,'" said Christine. "It legitimizes their assumption of superiority. As though they're omniscient and the poor bastards whose country they've appropriated are ignorant naïfs. I should make a print about it."

"Now you've done it, Mrs Verington-De..." Frank hesitated.

"Please, call me Georgy."

"Ah ... right," said Frank, slightly taken aback. He was pleased to be granted the honour, but couldn't help wondering why posh women came up with such masculine nicknames. "Once Christine gets an idea in her head for a print, there's no stopping her."

"Is this your work?" asked Georgy, pointing to the sketches and collage material on Christine's table.

Frank listened as Christine explained how she worked. God but she was beautiful when she expounded on her art. Her eyes sparkled and two pink circles appeared in her cheeks. Frank could swear her lips became tumescent as after a long snogging session. She pulled out some of her finished prints. Mrs Verington-Delaunay – Georgy – seemed intrigued with Christine and her work. She was an odd duck, obviously relishing time spent in a student dive. Actually, now that Frank thought about it, she seemed much less different than when he first met her. Not quite a fellow student obviously, but not far off.

"There is one other thing I wanted to ask," said Georgy before she left. "What can you tell me about Barry Dangerfield?"

"I think we told you pretty much everything. About the conversation I overheard, which the more I think about it, must mean he's somehow mixed up in my mate's, Nelson's, problem. And now we're almost certain his nephew, Dennis, was causing trouble for Nelson as long ago as last summer, at the boarding house where they all stayed. Why do you ask?"

"I'm fairly certain Dangerfield has given Enoch stories."

"Stories?"

"Anecdotes. Or in one case a letter with a story in it. The problem is I have no way of knowing if they're legitimate. But I'm fairly sure Barry Dangerfield gave Enoch a story a couple of months ago that he used in a speech. Then later it turned out it was completely untrue. Enoch looked a bit foolish."

"Sounds like something Barry would do," said Frank.

* * *

By mid-morning of his second full day in prison Nelson decided the worst part of jail was boredom. It seemed an eternity until the midday meal – if you could call a corned beef sandwich a meal. Afterwards Nelson was let out into a high-walled exercise yard for an hour. But the time outside seemed brief. Bracing while it lasted, but a distant memory after a few minutes back inside. He saw his cellmate, Brian, setting up a game of dominoes with a couple of other inmates. Nelson decided to go up to their cell. He'd have some time alone – or alone as it was possible to be in this rass claat place. Maybe he'd be able to come up with some words for a song. When he turned toward the stairs the two Jamaicans he'd seen when he first arrived blocked his way.

"Where you a-go?" asked the taller one.

"Me a-go a me cell."

"Satta," said the short skinny one.

He tipped his head toward some vacant chairs. Before he was arrested Nelson would have sat with the two men out of fear of what might happen if he didn't, but the lack of concern that set in the minute Fowler charged him with murder persevered. He sat with the Jamaicans for no other reason than it promised to be more interesting than staring at the walls of his cell.

"So is wha' make you kill the man?"

Brian had coaxed out of Nelson the reason he was there. He'd obviously blabbed.

"Me no kill nobody. Is pure fuckery, dat."

"Police samfie you?"

Nelson doubted they'd believe the story of Frank's fake photo even if he tried to explain it, so he simply confirmed the man's assumption that the police had framed him.

"Wha' you name, yuutman?"

"Nelson. Nelson Malcolm Clarke."

He wondered if he'd ever get used to saying his dead cousin's name. He always felt as though everybody must know it wasn't really his own.

"Better you call youself jus' Malcolm, yuh know."

Nelson frowned, puzzled. The two broke up laughing. Then one of them explained they'd been admirers of Malcolm X. Nelson seemed to remember the man had been an American hot steppa, as Auntie Irene called anyone she judged a troublemaker.

"Him did come to Smethwick, you know. A year from when the Tory them win election. Him say how him hear say coloured people over here live like Jews under Hitler. Malcolm X shake this hand here, you know."

The man held up his right hand and examined it, eyes shining.

"Not two week later them assassinate him."

"There was a time when him did say make justice and be free by any means possible," said the other Jamaican. "But him wander from the true path toward the end. Him get a lickle soft,"

As the two talked, it became obvious they admired Malcolm X for becoming a Muslim. Nelson was surprised with the extent of their knowledge. He assumed they were uneducated boys from Trenchtown, which they might have been, but they knew a lot more about Islam than Nelson knew about Christianity.

Churchgoing had never caught on with Nelson. The only pull had come from his mother when he was little. She held him tightly by the hand and hauled him into church, feet dragging. Whether he liked it or not he heard prayers and sermons about people burning up forever in a fiery furnace, or about love gushing from a mysterious source in the sky. Nelson couldn't understand if the Big Man loved all people how he could throw so many of them to hell's flames. He was alarmed by lurid depictions in prayer books of a white man nailed to two pieces of wood and bathed in blood. He wanted nothing to do with him. After Nelson grew too big for his mother to yank, she couldn't get him near a church. But it didn't stop her bothering him. And in England Auntie Irene took up the crusade. Time and again she tried to convince her nephew that church wasn't only about religion

"Is as much 'bout community as the good Lord. Congregation a safety net fi catch you any time you need it," she told him.

Nelson insisted church would still involve God, His Son, and the Holy Ghost – in which he could never believe any more than he could accept Obeah with all its witchcraft mumbo jumbo. But Irene never let up. Just like his mother. Was it any wonder Christianity for Nelson was like one of those devilish little fish bones, like brittle hairs, that caught in his throat? Not so sharp they choked him, but impossible to be rid of.

As the morning wore on, Nelson's two new friends spouted facts, figures, names, and dates. They told him about African Muslims, the Nation of Islam, and the Five Pillars of Faith. About not eating pork, or smoking, or drinking alcohol. It was only pork Nelson would miss – he loved a rasher of crispy bacon.

The two Jamaicans told Nelson about slave traders imposing Western names on captured Africans. How the boxer, Cassius Clay, became Muhammad Ali, and why he became a conscientious objector. Purposely or not they put things in simple terms that made clear the causes and effects. Nelson lapped it up. What had begun as a meaningless diversion from the boredom of a day in prison quickly developed into a genuine curiosity about everything the two were saying.

When one of the Jamaicans told Frank how Malcolm X had said that Islam was the true religion of black mankind and that Christianity was the white man's religion, Nelson realized he had a solution to fix the Christian irritation once and forever. Auntie Irene could hardly criticize him for embracing a religion, even if it wasn't Christianity. If he claimed to be a Muslim she might stop bothering him about churchgoing. And if she protested, he could point out that Islam was more suited to his skin colour. Hers too, come to that.

Eventually their conversation was halted by the appearance of a tea trolley. A huge urn was wheeled around and cups doled out by a mountain of a prisoner with flesh like lard. The tea dispenser was nicknamed Mother, for obvious reasons.

"So why you never serve coffee? You no know say is coffee gentlemen like we drink?" asked one of the Jamaicans.

"Isn't a good cup of English tea good enough for you bastards?" Mother asked.

"Cho! You think tea is English? The leaf come from India, mon. And the sugar from Jamaica. Mind sharp, the cow wha' the milk come from foreign too. Is only the water is English."

Nelson thought his two new friends were going to fall over laughing. He was so amused by their paroxysms of mirth that he laughed right along with them.

"Bunch of fucking niggers," muttered the tea dispenser.

The two Jamaican men sobered up in an instant. The tall one stuck his face an inch or two from Mother's nose and glared.

"All right, you two. You want to make love, do it somewhere private," shouted a warden.

The Jamaican backed away, but continued to give Mother the evil eye. Mother trundled away with his trolley. It thrilled Nelson to see a fellow Jamaican stand up to a white man. He always felt like he need lower his eyes around white people. It was only with Frank that Nelson felt like he was no different. No need to lower his eyes around Ruth Barton either, but that was something else.

"You know we have our own Malcolm X name Michael X?" the short Jamaican said. Nelson could see no sign he'd been affected or upset by the contretemps with Mother. They both acted like nothing had happened. Them cool so!

This Michael X character was news to Nelson.

"Him come in like a brother to John Lennon and a whole heap o' famous people."

"You know what is real fuckery?" asked the other.

"Wha'?"

"John Lennon and the Beatles singin' 'bout peace and love, and then them sing that song Penny Lane."

"Not catching you."

"Penny Lane name off o' James Penny, the biggest slave trader them ever have. Him fight hard fi keep the trade when them did want it abolish. And look 'pon John Lennon saying is peace him defend, and a sing 'bout Penny Lane. Is a fuckery."

Nelson' brain was buzzing with everything he'd been told. He was particularly taken with this Michael X character. Every West Indian in England knew about the Notting Hill Carnival, but Nelson hadn't known who organized it, or why.

Michael X have a bashment in the capital of England so large it make television news! Him big still!

* * *

Enoch spent most of the morning reading Party memos and circulars in the sanctuary of his living room in the house on Merridale Road. He sometimes found the subdued light, which lent a lugubrious atmosphere to the rooms, oddly soothing. Despite his insistence that he enjoyed his life since he'd married Pam and had a family – their obvious affection for him was undeniably comforting – Enoch found melancholia to be an occasional state of mind, not unwelcome for its familiarity from his early years. The smell of baking floated in from the kitchen, it transported Enoch back to his childhood home. The clatter of Pam working in the kitchen could easily have been the sound of his mother. He thought about the thousands of solitary hours he'd spent reading alone in front of the dining room fireplace as a teenager. With no siblings to divert him, was it any wonder he'd never acquired the knack of conviviality? But he'd learnt to be self-sufficient, so the scarcity of camaraderie in politics didn't bother him. Although he didn't enjoy the backbiting, acrimony, and name-calling that made Westminster unfavourable for enduring alliances. He himself became estranged from several people he'd once considered friends within the Party. He and Iain Macleod had been thick as thieves during the early years until Churchill appointed Macleod to the cabinet and Enoch was ignored. Although he professed to prefer the back benches, the green-eyed monster reared up in Enoch and he froze Macleod out of his life. Although not long after, when Mrs Macleod became seriously ill Enoch relented. He loaned Macleod a key to his London flat with instructions to stay whenever he needed. Afterwards Macleod had told a fellow Tory, "Enoch seems to take great pains, even delight, in hiding the fact that he is a kind and generous person." The backhanded compliment made its way by gossip mill to the Wolverhampton office, where it was a source of amusement to everyone except Georgy. Enoch was grateful when she pronounced Macleod "a mean-spirited ingrate."

Politics was certainly an unhealthy milieu for a depressive, although Enoch didn't think of himself as such. If he was stubbornly pessimistic, it was because he believed he saw clearly the ramifications of situations, which were, more often than not, negative. And he wasn't afraid to say so. When he was in the army, an exasperated fellow officer cursed him as "the most bloody-minded officer in the Middle East." Enoch considered it a compliment. Sometimes, when a downward spiral of gloom threatened his vitality, he liked to think of the more positive side of his political balance sheet. He gazed at a tree outside the living room where he was sitting, its recently unfurled leaves fluttering in a breeze. He would forever remember his achievements as Health Minister. Particularly the modernization of mental institutions, which had been horribly out of date. He'd commissioned new uniforms for staff to be designed by the Queen's dressmaker, Hardy Amies, who he'd met as an officer cadet and kept in touch with after the war. Less formal outfits for nurses might be considered lightweight by some, but it was all part of his effort to make the National Health Service a more humane place where patients had the right to be treated as intelligent persons, not cattle. He'd voted for the suspension of the death penalty, which he was glad to see, irritated his critics. It was difficult to pin the ultra right-wing label on him after that. He believed changes to the Rent Act he'd helped push through were excellent. He was at a loss to understand his Tory colleagues, who hadn't uttered a peep when Prime Minister Wilson's first act after being elected was to reinstate tenant's rights.

The one subject Enoch knew he must avoid when in a pensive mood was India, but he was immensely proud of the report he'd helped write for the Re-organization Committee following the end of the war. His projected figures revealed insignificant numbers of Indian officers in the army, which was criticized as untenable. Enoch had been at pains to explain the numbers were based on perfectly logical projections of suitably qualified men, but his approach was deemed too rigid. When the report was discounted it became obvious to him there were some who were rushing India's independence. He'd never forgotten Edmund Burke's words about finding the keys of India not in Calcutta or Delhi, but in the House of Commons in London. He realized if he were to prevent the erosion of British rule for the jewel in the crown of the Empire and eventually become Viceroy of India – as he believed he would – he'd have to inveigle his way into Westminster. It shouldn't have mattered which Party he joined to fulfill his ambition. It would have made more sense at the time to join Labour, who'd formed a majority government and looked likely to remain in power for some time. But a deep respect for the authority of institutions, such as the monarchy, was so ingrained in Enoch that his only honest choice was the Conservative Party. He had no inkling of where his unshakeable respect for everything in which authority was embodied had originated. Even physical locations, if they were the scene of some momentous event, gained his deep respect. He remembered his father's astonishment when he asked Enoch, who was only seven-years-old at the time, why he'd removed his school cap in a room in Caernarvon Castle. "Because this is where the first Prince of Wales was born," said Enoch, having read up on the castle before their trip. He'd once told Georgy he thought his deep regard for nationhood – meaning allegiance to a monarch and a democratically elected government – was "congenital." He remembered she laughed and said, "like idiots and liars."

Enoch glanced around the room at his parents' dark-stained furniture, the pieces he'd grown up with. Even had it been sunny, the room would have been dreary. He knew he oughtn't, but he couldn't help think about the sombre February day when he sat in the gallery at the House of Lords, where the Commons was meeting while their chamber was under reconstruction after wartime bomb damage. He listened, aghast, as Atlee told MPs that transfer of power would be handed to India no later then June 1948. Just ten days earlier Enoch had failed in his first attempt to become a member of parliament. Although his loss was expected in the staunch Labour riding he'd been given in West Yorkshire, it had been a blow to his pride. But the ignominy of defeat was like a gnat bite in comparison to the mortal blow that Atlee's words dealt him. The rug had been ripped from under his aspiration to be Viceroy. Enoch had been certain the position would someday be his. He was so keenly disappointed that even the sumptuous chamber of the House of Lords, with its lashings of gilt and rich red leather, failed to comfort him. And with India gone, the rest of the colonies were sure to follow. Enoch remembered staggering around London throughout the night in a daze of grief and disappointment, sometimes sinking onto doorsteps to sit, head in hands, and weep. It was a miracle he wasn't picked up by the police and placed in one of the mental hospitals he'd eventually modernized.

He resigned as secretary to the Tory India Committee. It was a mere gesture, but he hoped it was noted as an expression of his frustration that the Tories hadn't done a damn thing to try to save India from itself. He learnt a bitter but memorable lesson that his Party would not always agree with his ideas – nor him theirs. Pam had typed his letter of resignation. It had been one of her first chores when she came to work for him. Perhaps he'd realized even then on some unconscious level that she was his saviour. Certainly he surprised himself when, once he'd recovered from his disappointment, he discovered he'd become entranced by politics and the political process. Sufficiently enraptured by the working of the House of Commons to not want to run for the hills, even though his original motive had been snatched away. Three years later he won his Wolverhampton seat ... with Georgy's help.

But why was he dwelling on the past? It was all water under the bridge. And after his speech tomorrow all previous efforts would pale anyway. With that in mind, Enoch roused himself, shouted through to the kitchen to let Pam know he was leaving, and stepped out into the day.

* * *

Enoch was determined not to let Georgy threaten his resolve as she'd done the day before. He began as he meant to continue, with a curt nod as he stepped into the office accompanied by a brief "Morning." Rather than the morose mood he'd expected, Georgy appeared buoyant.

"I dropped in on those two art students I mentioned to you yesterday to tell them we'd written to the Chief Constable about their immigrant friend."

"And did you extract a promise from them to vote for me in the next election?"

"I'm not sure if they're old enough. But I'll be sure to tell them to register here the minute they turn twenty-one, so they vote in Wolverhampton rather than wherever their family homes are. Come to think of it, numbers of students are bound to increase when the Tech. and the Art College merge next year. The student population is something we'll need to work on."

Although Enoch had doubts about the numbers of young people they'd be able to rely on, Georgy's energy and enthusiasm never ceased to impress him. The least he could do was show willing.

"Good idea. Perhaps we could organize a debate at the Tech. with other candidates concerning issues of interest to students."

Georgy looked suitably impressed, if a little surprised.

"I'm sorry if I was a tad rabid yesterday," she said. "I know you always calculate the effects of whatever you say. It's just that I can't help wondering if you quite understand the trouble you're likely to cause – to yourself and others."

It was Enoch's turn to be surprised. It wasn't like Georgy to be so solicitous. He was about to reassure her he knew exactly the risk he was taking when she spoke, sheepishly at first.

"And I'm sorry to say what I'm about to, but it would be remiss of me not to point out the inaccuracy in the claim you make in this item in the newsletter – that you weren't aware of the birth rate among immigrants until recently. It might be as well not to repeat it in a more public forum."

Georgy picked up a copy of the newsletter and waved it, as if to emphasize her point. Enoch was wrong-footed, he was certain she was going to criticize his speech again. In order to buy some time to gather his thoughts he merely said, "But I wasn't aware."

"But you were Minster of Health back when maternity beds were in short supply. 1960 to 1962," said Georgy. "You visited the new maternity unit here at New Cross hospital. Who did you think needed the majority of those additional facilities if it wasn't immigrant mothers? I know for a fact that there were records as early as 1960 which showed the exact same proportion of births to immigrants – twenty-five percent – as the ones you're claiming not to be aware of until now. If I knew about them, so did you. Come on Enoch, admit it, you're using your claim of newfound knowledge of old figures to explain why you weren't riding on the immigration bandwagon during the last election campaign. Better be careful, Geoff Ayres won't be the only one who'll remember you hardly uttered a peep about immigration before this year, and absolutely nothing about restrictions. It's hard to believe that less than four years ago you were defending the right of dependents of immigrants to live here 'out of an inescapable obligation of humanity.'"

Rather than annoy him, Enoch – having recovered his equanimity – considered Georgy's reproach a test, not unlike a mock exam. If he could successfully manoeuvre his way through her trial-by-fire he'd be prepared for anything the Opposition could throw at him.

"Even had I known about the facts – which, despite your remarkable omniscience in the matter, I did not – the birth rate at that time was less alarming when compared to overall figures for the immigrant population. Now that those numbers have swollen, the proportion of immigrant births indicates an alarming trend, which, if allowed to continue, will result in a disproportionate number of children of immigrants."

Georgy looked down at her desk for a second or two. She glanced back to Enoch and held his gaze before speaking, as though calculating the wisdom of her next move.

"Disproportionate to whom?" she said. "And by 'children of immigrants' what you really mean are brown babies. Is it really so difficult to accept dark-skinned, native-born citizens walking around as British as everybody else? And if so why don't you say so? Why not be as overt as Peter Griffiths was when his Smethwick supporters came up the with the slogan, 'If you want a nigger neighbour, vote Labour?'"

Georgy certainly wasn't pulling any punches. Enoch felt as though he'd received a blow to the solar plexus. He struggled to remain cool and collected.

"As you clearly remember, it was not Peter Griffiths who originated such a contentious catchphrase but people outside his organization."

"Maybe, but he refused to condemn them for the slogan, let alone demand it not be used."

"Your remarkable recall must also enable you to remember that Griffiths won the seat by a comfortable margin. He ousted the Foreign Secretary in the process. He was the only Tory to buck the countrywide trend away from the Conservatives."

" I can't believe your modelling yourself on such a loathsome man. "

"If I'm emulating anything from the Smethwick experience it isn't the methods, nor the man, but the principle."

"Since you seem to be having memory lapses, you've probably forgotten that Griffiths was defeated the next time the country went to the polls."

She was right, of course. Enoch was well aware the immigrant population might have become more savvy about their right to vote, which could explain Griffiths' eventual downfall in Smethwick. But he still believed he had no option but to take the path he'd embarked on. He was convinced that, even in the unlikely event that his margin narrowed in his riding, it would be worth the attention and support he'd garner nationwide. He decided to dodge her argument by back pedalling.

"To go back to your unfortunate and unfair description of me not 'riding on the immigration bandwagon during the last election campaign.' I was adhering strictly to Party policy at the time, which dictated we mention more stringent immigration controls as only one of many issues. And to be at pains to point out that they would be beneficial to all, immigrants included. Whereas Peter Griffiths chose to break Party protocol and run with immigration control as his main platform. On reflection, I wonder if his hard-headed approach wasn't more honest."

"But surely Party policy was correct in showing consideration to immigrants as well as everybody else. Even you stressed the need for benevolence in assisting integration.

Nothing wrong with promoting compassion is there?"

"You cannot compel somebody to be compassionate; nor can you be vicariously compassionate by compelling somebody else. Compassion is something individual and voluntary. The Good Samaritan would have lost all merit if a Roman soldier were standing by the road with a drawn sword, telling him to get on with it and look after the injured stranger."

"I'm not sure you have to threaten anyone with violence. Wouldn't it be enough to just lead by example with kind and caring government."

"You can be certain that by being 'kind and caring' to a particular group one will be unkind to a different collection of people. Favouritism, which is what this misguided Race Relations Bill embodies, cannot be countenanced in government. Fairness is the only yardstick. Is it fair that somebody has no choice of whom they take as a tenant? Who they employ? Who they allow in their bar or restaurant?"

"But Enoch, can't you see that it's grossly *unfair* when the sole reason for refusing to rent, employ, or serve someone is because of skin colour, race, or national origins, when the person has been given the right to live here?"

"There you have it," said Enoch, delighted that he'd manoeuvred Georgy to say exactly what he wanted. "The main thrust of my argument is the number of people given the right to live here. What's wrong with talking about that?"

"Nothing. But you also stress the foolishness of the Race Relations Bill. 'Like throwing a match on to gunpowder' is how you describe it."

"I'm not professing to be against the Bill without qualification. I'm saying it's a disastrous move to make *at this time,* while feelings are running so high."

"I'm not about to flog a dead horse. I've already told you how off the mark I think you are about how high feelings are running, and I've made clear my opinion about how your speech will only serve to elevate any feelings that do exist. I'll just make one last point though, which is that even if I concede that, at the moment, race can be a uniform, indicating cultural difference, it's certain to change. You of all people know the myth about inflexibility of class distinction. You certainly bucked the assumptions your background suggested. The same will become true of race. Especially if we help the process along with legislation like the Race Relations Bill. Can you imagine how much faster society would have improved if there'd been a Bill against discrimination because of class distinction?"

Enoch was taken by surprise by a wave of emotion – unalloyed affection for this intelligent, insightful woman who seemed to understand him more than almost anybody. Perhaps more than Pam.

"Sometimes I wonder why you're a member of the Conservative Party," said Enoch, trying his best to adopt an affectionately teasing tone. "Have you ever considered a change of allegiance?"

"There are certainly some impressive additions to Labour's list of MPs, even if they don't have the pedigree I've always thought was paramount in a politician. I'm a big fan of actor Andrew Faulds. You remember him, he's the man who was very witty about you after the Walsall speech?"

Georgy was clearly trying to annoy him by mentioning Faulds. She knew how irritated Enoch had been when the ex-actor surmised out loud in the Commons that it must have been childhood trauma, perhaps overly strict toilet training that made Powell so "lacking in social generosity." But then Georgy appeared to relent.

"I wouldn't dream of switching parties at this point. Just as I would never exchange a thoroughbred for a workhorse simply because one's mount was suffering from lameness," said Georgy, speaking tartly, but smiling nevertheless.

"You think me lame?" asked Enoch.

"I believe you're more damaged than you realize."

"Are you suggesting I should be shot, as one would a worn out old nag?"

"I'm not sure you're that far gone. You could yet redeem yourself."

* * *

"I think it best if I root out Denise James on my own – we might need your testicles someday," Christine told Frank. How could he not love her? And with Christine on the case in the ceramics department, he was free to photograph the morning's Sikh demonstration.

Frank was as dumbfounded by the scale of the procession. An endless column of turbaned men wound its way from Cannock Road through the streets of Wolverhampton to the open area where the old market used to stand. A liberal sprinkling of young boys with topknots marched alongside fathers and uncles. Almost every man was bearded – from sparse pubescent tufts soft as silk, to mature inky bushes, to aged whiskers the colour of ivory. But what was most remarkable to Frank was that every single man and boy remained silent as the grave. They obviously believed that their banners would be enough to get their message across without any chants or shouted slogans.

Frank photographed a particularly expressive placard, held aloft by a tall man in an orange turban. It occurred to Frank that the succinct slogan would have gained top marks in a copy-writing project. The brief would have been to write a five-word response to accusations toward immigrants that they make no effort to integrate.

The sign read: MAKE YOURSELF AT HOME. HOW?

Frank fired off several frames. He'd come prepared and walked alongside the man long enough to write down his name. The man's accent was strong and Frank had to ask him to spell it out: G-u-r-i-n-d-e-r D-a-h-r-i-w-a-l.

Frank snapped an ancient man with a snowy beard brandishing a sign that simply said: WE'RE HERE BECAUSE YOU WERE THERE, signed by an A. Sivanandan. The man certainly looked old enough to have experienced decades of British rule. Frank soon realized some of the best photos would be of the reaction of passers-by, people who'd been going mindlessly about their daily business, when they were unexpectedly inundated by a deluge of dark-skinned men. He tried to include both sides of the equation – resolute Sikhs and stunned observers – in the same frame so the drama of the situation was evident. Each onlooker's response to the multitude of turbaned men told a different story.

One woman, hat clamped onto a recent perm and arm hooked through handbag handle, Queen Elizabeth style, slowly shook her head, eyes narrowed. Two male students, swathed in college scarves, smiled and nodded. A man in a cloth cap grimaced while dragging on a weedy hand-rolled cigarette. A teenager, no more than sixteen with closely-cropped hair, red braces, and Levis hiked up snug to his genitals, stared at the Sikh men, slack-jawed in obvious disbelief. Two young women standing arm-in-arm giggled nervously. It occurred to Frank that it had only been in the recent past that Wolverhampton's white inhabitants had clapped eyes on a solitary Sikh man – to be confronted by several thousand was obviously discomfiting.

Frank hoped the closed mouths of the marching men and the fixed expressions of the onlookers in his photographs would communicate the remarkable hushed silence of the event. He only heard a couple of comments. Somebody half-heartedly muttered, 'Fuckin' wogs,' and another nervously yelled, 'Pakis go home.' After the second remark an elderly woman in the crowd said loudly, 'They've as much right to be here as you.' 'Hear, hear,' said a man in a suit.

Having taken up half-a-dozen films with close-ups Frank decided he needed to take some long shots to capture the sheer volume of men. He ran along the pedestrian path leading past St. Peter's church and came out at the top of a flight of steps that led down to the large expanse of empty ground where the Sikh men were congregating, on the space in front of the Town Hall where the old market had been. Some of the top-knotted boys fidgeted and nudged each other, but the men stood impassive, silent as the grave. They remained until the last marchers arrived and the area was packed with turbans and banners.

Frank couldn't believe his luck with the weather. Spring sunshine persevered throughout, contributing sharpness and contrast to his shots. He took a series of photographs that took in the whole panorama. Wolverhampton Town Hall, built in French renaissance style with a sandstone façade and mansard roof, made a handsome backdrop. Frank wasn't good at estimating numbers but figured there must be upwards of four thousand men and boys wearing turbans of various colours and hues, from navy blue to saffron yellow. When Frank looked through the viewfinder he could almost believe the sun-drenched scene was in a colonial city on the Indian subcontinent instead of a dour industrial town in the British Midlands. Having made their point the men slowly filtered quietly away, down side streets leading to West Park, to the railway station, or to Cannock Road.

As Frank made his way back to college, traffic was resuming. Shoppers were disappearing into doors they'd been intending to enter before they were distracted by the march. Pedestrians had set out once again for temporarily forgotten destinations. Life appeared to be back to normal. But it seemed unlikely that anybody who'd witnessed the procession would forget the sight of four thousand brown-skinned men walking, unfaltering and wordless, through the streets of their town. Frank suspected the Sikhs' dispassionate demeanour had been more affecting than any noisy act of protest. You'd have to be a hard-hearted bastard not to feel some iota of sympathy.

Frank hurried back to college to develop his film, but when he reached his desk in the third-year graphics studio he found a note from Christine telling him to come and find her in the fine printing department.

* * *

"Brace yourself, she's a little scary," said Christine as she and Frank approached Denise James, who was waiting for them at the bus stop.

Christine told Frank she'd had no trouble persuading Denise to go with them to the police. In fact Denise had champed at the bit once she'd heard about Nelson's wrongful incarceration.

"So you're the stupid bugger who forged the photo."

Denise was a sturdy young woman, thick-waisted and broad shouldered with a mass of tight curly hair.

"Go easy on him, Denise, he's suffered enough."

Not only was Christine defending Frank, but she'd arranged everything. She'd even phoned to make sure Gorman would be available. They'd been fobbed off onto Fowler, but still. If it weren't for Denise, Frank would have given Christine the warmest hug he could possibly muster. As it was, with the ceramics student scowling at him suspiciously, Frank felt distinctly inhibited.

"Doesn't it strike you as funny that she's the spitting image of Pansy Potter, the Strong Man's Daughter," whispered Frank to Christine as they followed Denise onto the bus.

"Who the hell is Pansy Potter?"

"In the Beano. And Denise is a potter too ... get it?"

Christine frowned at him. She clearly had never read the Beano. Frank had gobbled it up every week when he was a kid. They followed Denise up the stairs of the bus where the two young women sat next to each other. Frank sat behind them. He could hear Denise bending Christine's ear all the way to the police station about the evils of the grading system for final diplomas at college.

"And there certainly shouldn't be any bourgeois honours shit, like seconds and firsts, for Christ's sake. It's art, not fucking algebra. The work should speak for itself."

Their visit with Fowler was less than successful. As soon as he ushered them into an interview room Denise accused him of blatant racism. He remained as impassive as ever. He interrupted her once to ask her name and home address. She ignored the question and continued her rant about 'racist pig policemen.' Christine told him her name, but Denise refused to give her address. Fowler wrote the name down on a piece of paper and left the room, which took the wind out of Denise's sails.

"For God's sake, cool it Denise. When he comes back just tell him about the demo," said Christine.

When Fowler returned, Denise managed to keep a lid on her obvious dislike of the police and explained that Nelson definitely wasn't at the march.

"I swear, not a West Indian face in sight."

At that moment a uniformed officer opened the door and handed Fowler a sheet of paper.

"You are Denise James of Upper Park Street, Toxteth, Liverpool?" he asked.

"Yes," said Denise, obviously miffed that he'd discovered her home address in Liverpool.

"You are at present on probation for public mischief and assaulting a police officer, I believe?"

"He attacked me first, the pig."

"Before that you were fined twice for causing a disturbance and using obscene language in public, am I right?"

"I refuse to be judged by such bourgeois standards," said Denise.

As far as Frank could tell, bourgeois seemed to be her favourite word.

"In every single one of those cases I was exerting my undeniable right to peaceably protest ... so screw you."

"Not exactly a reliable witness. I think we've finished here, don't you?" said Fowler, clearly relishing the situation.

"But she insists Nelson wasn't at the demo," said Frank.

"She can insist 'til the cows come home, but nobody will believe her."

At that point Denise completely lost control.

"You see they're all the same. Pigs. The law is an ass, my man. Have you even heard of Lady Chatterley's Lover?"

A uniformed cop led Denise out of the station with a firm grip on her upper arm. At least she had the good grace to appear slightly sheepish on the bus ride back to Wolverhampton. Frank and Christine sat together while Denise perched on the other side of the aisle.

"Just out of curiosity, what was all that about Lady Chatterley?" Frank asked.

"Nothing should be judged obscene, as the book wasn't. It's a question of standards."

"Shut-the-fuck-up. How about that for a non-obscenity?" said Christine.

Frank admired Christine's courage. She wouldn't have stood a chance if Denise, a.k.a. Pansy Potter, the Strongman's Daughter, had decided to get physical. But Denise kept quiet for the rest of the journey. She even murmured an apology as she turned away after they'd stepped off the bus.

"Wait. Do you know who the others are?" Frank asked.

He held up the front page of *VoxPop*.

"I know him. His name's Giles Shannon."

Denise explained that the bearded hippy lived with his girlfriend in a rented house in the countryside to the west of Wolverhampton.

"He's an electronics genius. An amazing guy, really brilliant. I was at his place once, it's cool. I can take you out there if you like?"

"Wouldn't it be easier to nose him out at the Tech?" asked Frank.

Denise explained that he was rarely at college.

"He's building a contraption out at his place using bits from transistor radios. His invention is going to change the world."

"For the better, I hope," muttered Frank.

"Giles says it'll empower the proletariat."

"I can't wait," said Frank.

The prospect of another outing with Denise was too much to contemplate. So Christine extracted directions to Giles Shannon's house after Denise warned them he had no phone.

"How about this one?" Frank asked, pointing at the young woman Steve had identified as somebody's girlfriend.

"I've seen her around. I think she hangs out with one of the third-year sculptors. Taffy Thomas."

"What is it with women and sculptors?"

"It's their rough hands," said Christine, and winked at Frank.

"I'm more turned on by an interesting glaze, myself," said Denise.

* * *

Once back at college they bumped into one of the Three Little Pigs, Jeremy Oakley. He was called Jerm by all and sundry. Frank found the nickname hilarious – if a virus was anthropomorphized it would look just like Jeremy Oakley.

"Ah've bin lookin' for yow. Eet's your lucky day," said Jerm, who was born and bred in nearby Dudley.

He handed Christine an opened envelope addressed to the chief Little Pig. The logo and London address of the Royal College of Art appeared in the top left corner.

"Seems that bloke from the Royal who came down to tek a shufty at your work got 'is feathers ruffled 'cos yow didn't apply. Well, goo on, read eet."

"May I?" asked Frank, as he peered over Christine's shoulder.

Christine moved aside slightly so he could see. The

letter was a short note from the tutor who'd been her outside assessor during the dispute with the Three Little Pigs. He expressed the hope that Christine hadn't been discouraged from applying to study printmaking at the Royal College. He went on to say that although it was late for an application for next academic year, Christine would be seriously considered were she to apply within seven days. The date on the letter was April 17. She had until the following Wednesday to submit.

"I don't know if I can get enough work together," she said.

"Sounds like a bloody shoe-in if yow ask me, just tek whatever yow've got," said Jerm.

"What do you mean?"

Jerm was uncharacteristically supportive when he urged Christine to make an appointment for early the following week, to buy a same-day return to London, and carry her prints down on the train. Then he spoilt it all by reverting to form.

"Sounds loike a leg-over job, if yow know what ah mean. Wink, wink, say no more."

Frank was about to come to the rescue of his damsel, but before he could act Christine saved herself in spectacular fashion.

"I doubt it. He's homosexual. Much more likely to want to get his leg over you than me."

Jerm made a noise like a startled piglet and scampered away.

"Well done!" said Frank.

Christine appeared puzzled. Frank realized she was

probably so accustomed to dealing with pricks like Jerm she didn't think twice.

"Is he queer, the Royal College man?" asked Frank.

"I'm pretty sure. Definitely no sexual vibes in my direction anyway. His letter makes you wonder about his motives though. It's a bit late in the day to be asking me to apply. Maybe they've had a batch of crappy applicants and are desperate for better. Or perhaps somebody was accepted and then dropped out."

"Or maybe, just maybe mind, it's because you're frigging brilliant."

Christine gave him a grateful kiss on the cheek.

"Whatever the reason, I'd better get to work. If I try, I could have that new print I was telling you about finished by Monday. Which means I won't have any time to help you find the other marchers from the photo. Sorry."

"But you could be testing Taffy out for rough hands."

"Good try, but I'll leave it to you to do the handholding. I'm off to the office to see if they'll let me phone the Royal College for an appointment. See you tomorrow."

"But aren't we …"

"I need a good night's sleep, Frank. And you need a change of clothes. A manly aroma is one thing, but days-old BO is another."

Frank took a sly sniff of his armpit and had to concede she was right.

"Sleep tight," Christine called.

* * *

When Frank eventually tracked down Taffy Thomas he was hacking away with a mallet and chisel at a massive hunk of wood in the yard of the sculpture department. Wood shavings clung to his black mat, more rook's nest than hair. Taffy's appearance was made swarthier by a tide of unshaven stubble. Bristling black caterpillars of eyebrows crawled across a prominent brow. Frank pigeonholed him as one of a breed of sturdy Welshmen well equipped for scaling mountains to retrieve lost sheep, or for hefting coal in a mineshaft.

"I remember that day. How could I forget? Bloody nightmare, it was," said Taffy when Frank showed him the photo in *VoxPop*.

Judging by the expression in Taffy's burnt-umber eyes the Welshman was deeply troubled. Frank was gratified to think his shot had had such a powerful effect, but he soon realized it was an unpleasant memory, not the photo, that was distressing. When Frank pointed out the woman reputed to be the sculptor's girlfriend, he thought Taffy might burst into tears.

"She was my girlfriend all right, but she dumped me, right after the demo. Worst weekend I ever 'ad, it was."

Taffy's voice was mellifluous despite his miserable demeanour. Frank had always had a penchant for the melodious rhythm of a Welsh accent. As a kid he'd been given a record of Richard Burton reading Under Milk Wood by a well-meaning literary aunt. He loved the sound of Burton's voice so much he played it over and again. Frank wondered if Dylan and Taffy Thomas were related, but didn't judge it a good time to ask.

"What do *you* want with her, anyway?" asked Taffy, his hang-dog expression suddenly transformed into that of a canine more likely to bite.

As a result of his fondness for the accent Frank had a tendency to unknowingly mimic the Welsh when talking to them. He'd come close to being punched by more than one Welshman for taking the piss. In his nervousness, Frank made a conscious effort not to slip into Taffy's vernacular – so much so that he inadvertently assumed the plummy voice of a public school boy.

"I just wanted to ask her for permission to use the photograph in my end of course exhibition, that's all," said Frank, his words dripping with posh vowels. He was determined not to admit to his counterfeiting, but he wished he'd come up with a more believable reason to talk to the object of the Welshman's affection. Taffy eyed him, mallet in one hand, chisel in the other. Frank assumed he was working out exactly where on Frank's anatomy to make the first cut.

"If you'd rather not give out personal information, I'd totally understand," said Frank.

At that, Taffy seemed to relent. He shrugged his shoulders, a stray wood chip fell from his oversize pullover.

"It's no skin off my nose, boyo. We haven't been together since that day."

Frank couldn't believe his ears. He thought only Welshmen in films or on TV used the term 'boyo.'

"Sorry to hear that. So ... you wouldn't know where I could find her would you?"

"Fashion department," said Taffy.

He enunciated the words fast and sibilant, bitter as bile.

"Oh, right. Great. Thanks," said Frank.

He proffered his hand for the Welshman to shake, thinking it'd be hilarious if he could report on the roughness of Taffy's palms to Christine. After glaring mournfully at Frank for a split second, Taffy shifted his mallet under his arm to free up a hand. The sculptor's palm and fingers felt disappointingly average – neither rough nor smooth. Another assumption shattered, thought Frank. Taffy returned to his block of timber and started to chip savagely away, shavings flying.

"What's her name?" asked Frank over the din of the mallet.

"Kathy. Kathy Stevenson," Taffy yelled.

Although sour, Taffy Thomas wasn't as irascible as Frank had assumed he would be. Where did the cliché of the short-fused Welshman come from anyway? Maybe it was Shakespeare's fault. The Bard of Avon always portrayed his Welsh characters with filthy tempers. Frank remembered from Henry V, the play he studied for his English GCE, that the Welsh officer, Llewellyn, was described as being 'touch'd with choler, hot as gunpowder' and 'quickly will return an injury.' He came across as a virtual psychopath. Maybe Frank should talk to Denise James about excising racial stereotypes from Shakespearean plays. It sounded like a crusade that Pansy Potter, champion of the proletariat, would throw herself into.

The fashion department was housed in the same building as interior design. Frank realized he'd better hoof it down there if he wanted to find Kathy Stevenson before classes ended. As he dodged pedestrians hurrying to their various Friday evening activities, Frank thought about Nelson mouldering away in prison. No payday pub night for him, poor bastard. The fiasco with Denise James and Fowler had been such a farce that Frank had almost lost sight of the seriousness of the situation. He was pessimistic about Giles the mad inventor being of much use, and Diana Throgmorton sounded downright undependable. He hoped to hell Taffy's ex was a normal, responsible human being.

When Kathy Stevenson was pointed out to him by a gaggle of fashion students in a massive top-floor studio littered with tailor's dummies and fabric samples, Frank's hopes soared. She was older than the average student, perhaps in her early thirties. She was slim, sported a stylish short-on-one-side-long-on-the-other hairstyle, and gave the impression she'd been round the block a few times. Frank came clean right away and told her every detail about the doctored photo.

After Frank had introduced himself, Kathy told him she didn't have much time – she had to pick up her young son from nursery school. Knowing she was a parent, it came as no surprise to Frank when she gave him what for.

"I can certainly understand your motives, Frank, but that was an extremely irresponsible act, I hope you realize that."

Frank couldn't understand why Taffy Thomas was so bereft at having been dumped by Kathy Stevenson, she seemed like a complete pain in the bum. But for his purposes she was perfect.

"I do. I do. But you will help, won't you?"

"I couldn't do anything else. You leave me no option," said Kathy.

Christ, but she was sanctimonious. How had Taffy put up

with her? When she put on her coat – mini length to match her skirt – to leave, Frank couldn't avoid walking out of the building and part way up Darlington Street with her. He racked his brains to make conversation, but all he could come up with were questions about her son.

Kathy explained young Eamon was four-years-old and that they lived with her mother in a council house near Fordhouses, a half-hour bus ride from the centre of Wolverhampton. She told Frank she'd left school at fifteen to work at the nearby Goodyear tyre factory, but she soon realized she wanted more out of life. She went to night classes and eventually passed enough GCEs to get into Art College.

"Once I pick Eamon up, we eat together and I put him to bed. Then I do an evening shift as a cleaner at a nearby school. I'm lucky to be living with my Mum, but it's still not easy having a kid and going to college full time."

Frank was beginning to think Kathy had every reason to be sanctimonious. He felt like a parasite compared to her. How could he object when she insisted the earliest she could go to see Fowler was Monday because she worked in the local Co-op grocery on Saturdays and was committed to spending Sundays with her son? When they reached her bus stop Kathy wrote down her phone number.

"Call me on Sunday evening and we'll plan where to meet."

Frank wandered up Darlington Street feeling at a loose end. He supposed he could drop in somewhere for a pint – he was missing his Guinness – but which pub? Then he remembered he hadn't developed his films from the Sikh march. He liked the idea of working in the college darkroom knowing that Christine was working downstairs in the printmaking department. Dave Bishop had left for the day, but Frank assumed it'd be more than permissible to use the equipment.

* * *

Developing film was Frank's least favourite activity. Each film had to be loaded into a developing canister in the dark. Once the canister cap had been secured, a light could be switched on. Then began the tedious work of pouring and emptying a succession of chemicals and washes into the canister – developer; stop bath; fixer; wash; and finally a product called Photo-Flo, which prevented spotting on the film. Frank had eight undeveloped films. Each canister held two films. To develop all eight would take him a good two or three hours.

As Frank went about his mindless task, he replayed the week's events in his head in the hope of making sense of it all. He went over every move from Monday morning, when Barry suggested inserting Nelson's image into the photo of the demonstration, to today's scathing dismissal by Fowler of Denise James as a credible witness. He reran the overheard conversation between Dennis and Barry several times. He was convinced their exchange must hold more of a clue to the reason for Nelson's troubles. He tried to recall every detail. To help fix things in his mind he pretended to be Dennis and spoke out loud.

"It's not going to blow over now, is it? I was well off the radar. I could have been kept out of it."

Frank racked his brain to remember what else had been said. Dennis had blamed Barry for making him go to the police.

"It was your idea for me to go and blab to the cops about the wogs' bloody quarrel."

The only reason Frank could see that Barry would want Dennis to tell the police about Nelson's quarrel was if the fat bastard wanted to put the young Jamaican in a bad light. Frank suddenly realized he'd lost track of how long the damn developer had been in the canister. He ought to be paying more attention to what he was doing, but he was distracted by a thin sliver of an idea that was beginning to dawn.

He emptied out the developer, poured in stop solution, agitated the canister to get an even distribution of chemical, and left it for sixty seconds or so. Then he emptied the canister and filled it with fixer. He glanced at his watch. Five minutes to allow the fixer to do its job would take him to a quarter to the hour.

Temporarily free to ruminate further on Barry's doings, the thin sliver of an idea suddenly became a glaring light bulb. Frank was staggered by an appalling thought. When Barry had tried to push Nelson into the mire with Fowler and D.I. Gorman by persuading Dennis to tell them about the quarrel, it had obviously been earlier in the day, before news of the arrest was reported in the *Express & Star*. In which case Barry must have known that Nelson was under suspicion for the assault on Mr Singh before it became public knowledge. Could Barry have been aware that Nelson was a person of interest as early as last Monday morning, when he suggested doctoring the photo? If so, Frank's suspicion that Barry had used him to incriminate Nelson might actually be true. Frank was sick at the thought.

"Shit."

Frank had left the fixer in the canister a few seconds too long. He quickly emptied it out. He filled the canister with Photo-Flo, agitated it for thirty seconds, and then poured out the solution. Now that the film was processed he could open the canister. As he hung up the film to dry, Frank struggled to come to terms with the idea that he may have been manipulated by Barry. After all, even if Barry had been cunning enough to suggest faking the photo, Frank may not have executed the switch. And even if he'd gone along with it and produced the photo, there was no guarantee *VoxPop* would publish it. And even if they did, it was unlikely a copy would get into the hands of Gorman and Fowler. Then Frank remembered Christine questioning how the student newspaper came to be in police hands so quickly – the same day as it appeared in print. If Barry was capable of persuading Dennis to tell the police about the quarrel, the slimy sod was perfectly capable of getting a copy of the student newspaper to Gorman and Fowler as soon as it was available. The more he thought about it the more possible it seemed. Frank was incensed by the idea that he'd been unwittingly manipulated by the greasy publican, especially since the plan had obviously been a stab in the dark. Barry could never have been certain his ruse would work.

Frank's first thought was to find Christine. Perhaps he was mistaken. Maybe the whole Nelson affair was just making him overly suspicious. He didn't want to risk spoiling the last couple of films by trying to develop them when his head was too screwed up to keep track of time. The first six films were quite safe hanging up to dry in the darkroom. He'd develop the other two later.

Christine wasn't in the printmaking studio when Frank went to look for her. He experienced a moment of resentment that she'd left, having told him she'd be working there all evening. The weedy Jerm, told Frank she'd gone home to find some material for her collage.

"I'd have thought her's a bit owt of your league, Frank."

"Sod off," said Frank.

He was in no mood for snide remarks from a little shit like Jerm Oakley. Frank considered jumping on a bus to Park Dale to find Christine, but she'd been adamant she wanted the night to herself. The more he thought about Barry's devious doings the angrier Frank became. He decided he was going to drop into the Vine in the hope that his presence would make the bastard feel uncomfortable. Frank couldn't care less about the menacing atmosphere that pervaded the place last time he was there. Barry couldn't do him any harm in a public bar, for fuck's sake.

* * *

Enoch made his way home through the gloomy late afternoon with a spring in his step, his mood considerably lighter. He thought he'd done well in countering Georgy's accusations, and in the process he'd wrung from her a hint of approval. He was confident she still thought well of him. Enoch believed he'd 'dodged the bullet' where Georgy was concerned, although he'd never uttered the expression in his life – being counter to his belief that one should always be ready and willing to die for one's country. It wasn't the first time he'd diverted disaster. Georgy seemed about to tip over from disgusted disapproval into outright mutiny some years ago during the Thalidomide affair. He was Health Minister at the time the news broke that more than four hundred infants had been born with physical deformities.

"I have to resist any sentimental treatment of the situation, which I see as only one type of maternal tragedy – others being mongol and abnormal babies," he insisted after Georgy remonstrated with him that the Government had to shoulder some of the blame. "Thalidomide was properly tested according to the knowledge of the time. No matter how rigorous the regulations, no drugs can ever be deemed absolutely secure. Even those prescribed by the medical profession should always be taken under advisement. Pregnant women need to be particularly watchful. Any prospective mother who takes medication during pregnancy is culpable for any adverse effects on her baby."

The angry rash that usually only appeared on Georgy's neck spread to her face. Enoch thought she was either going to strike him or suffer a stroke.

"For God's sake Enoch, it's not about being 'sentimental.' Can't you see there are occasions when empathy must trump ideology, even … *especially* … in a Minister of Health. You must drop this ridiculous obsession with Hayek and his misguided ideas about the perils of public regulation of private industry before it proves your undoing."

It was yet another occasion when Georgy appeared to know him almost as well as he knew himself, perhaps better. Then – adding to the misgivings caused by Georgy's insights into his inner thoughts and motivation – Enoch learned that supposed neutral information about the standard of testing for Thalidomide had come directly from the person advising the drug company who manufactured it. Not exactly an unbiased view of 'the knowledge of the time.' He decided it was in his interest to soften his hard line resistance to regulation of pharmaceutical companies. He took advice from his standing medical advisory committee and set up a safety committee to take an objective and unbiased examination of new drugs, which he maintained to Georgy would pave the way for future legislation.

"But," he told her, "I don't believe there will ever be absolute security. It is irresponsible to claim all danger is ruled out by controls or regulations, no matter how stringent. Each individual must take some responsibility for their own well-being."

It was several months until relations between them thawed, but at least she continued to work for him.

As Enoch crossed Compton Road – which he was beginning to think of as the River Styx, separating the Earth of white middle-class respectability from the dark immigrant Underworld – he wondered why he was lately dwelling on the past. It was almost as if he was watching his life pass before him, not in a flash, as it's supposed to do before an abrupt death, but unreeling in slow motion. He hoped it wasn't some kind of omen.

Georgy would settle down once the dust his speech was sure to cause had settled. Enoch was certain she'd be more loyal than she'd ever been after she realized the end had justified the means. Not that Enoch felt the means – his speech – was insincere in any way. He believed in its essential message. Maybe his language was a tad more extreme than his normal style, but it was necessary to be forceful. He knew he'd be vilified by those too blind to see or too cowardly to speak, but he was willing to take his knocks for the cause of those who were desperate for someone to speak for them. One only had to look at history to know that if there was something the majority of the population wanted to hear said, and if their representatives would not say it for them, they'd find a different and much less pleasant person to say it instead. Better it be him than an out and out racist – which in Enoch's book was somebody who believed one race to be superior to another. He was merely conscious of a difference between peoples, and could clearly foresee catastrophe for England and the English in the newcomers' incompatibility. If as a result of speaking out he gained approval from the population at large and therefore increased stature within the Party, so much the better.

When he pushed open the front door Enoch was met by the sound of his daughters' laughter coming from the sitting room. He could smell a robust aroma of meat cooking, a casserole perhaps, or maybe a roast. The hall lights were lit and it seemed to Enoch the house held an uncharacteristically festive air. He put his head round the front room door and said hello to Susan and Jennifer who were sitting on the sofa looking at a book. When he married, Enoch had fully expected to have a son. He was to be called David in a nod to his Welsh ancestry. Enoch had gone so far as to put his name down for Eton. But he'd been enchanted with Susan from the second he saw her. And he hadn't minded at all when his second child was also a girl.

"What are you reading?" he asked, sitting next to Susan and putting his arm around her shoulders.

"It's a lovely book about ruined castles," said Susan, thrusting the book in Enoch's direction so he could see some of the coloured photos adorning the page.

The girls listened in rapt silence as their father outlined the bloody history of Pontefract Castle, its ruined walls pictured on the pages Susan showed him. He told them all about its bloody history and its role in the bitter dispute between Royalists and Parliamentarians. He described how, once Cromwell gained the upper hand, he asked the townspeople of Pontefract to petition Parliament to have the castle destroyed. They were only too happy to comply, it having been a place of death and despair, with the deepest, darkest of dungeons.

"Why didn't he just tear it down himself?"

"First of all Cromwell wanted to make sure the job was done properly, but most importantly he believed in the democratic process. He would have been the first to proclaim that no government has the moral right to alter or permit to be altered the character and identity of a nation without the people's knowledge and their will. It is a moral issue, and it is a supreme issue today, perhaps more so than ever. Whatever our government is destined to achieve elsewhere with all its hopes, its determination, and its courage, if it fails in this, it fails in all, and its epitaph will be the verdict of children like you: 'They betrayed our inheritance while there was still time to save it.'"

"Oh," said Susan.

Satisfied his parenting was done, Enoch kissed his daughters on the tops of their heads and went to the kitchen to find Pam. She was standing at the stove, her back to the room. He found the fact that she was wearing oven gloves remarkably endearing. When Pam's mother heard of their engagement she muttered something about marriage to Enoch being the equivalent of taking a university degree. But she had to eat her words when she later learned that Enoch celebrated every wedding anniversary by presenting Pam with a poem, and a red rose for every year they'd been married. Enoch put his hands on each of Pam's shoulders. She murmured a hello and bent to open the door. Enoch felt heat from the oven and moved back to give her room. She hefted a cast iron casserole, placed it on the stovetop and lifted the lid. Steam rose from the surface of a stew studded with carrots and chunks of meat. Enoch smelt a delicious combination of beef fat and onions. Pam gently stabbed a piece of meat with the point of a knife. "Almost there," she murmured, replaced the lid and returned the casserole to the oven. She turned to look at Enoch.

"Everything all right?" she asked.

"Perfectly fine," said Enoch. "Georgy has voiced reservations about tomorrow's speech. I would be lying if I were to say her comments hadn't given me pause. But I've concluded her fears of dire detrimental effects are unfounded."

"It's a good forceful speech," said Pam. "I agree with every word. I heard what you told Clem about it going up like a rocket and staying there. But it's not likely to cause many more waves than any other of your speeches, is it?"

She looked questioningly at Enoch. He knew what was in her mind. She once commented – with only a hint of criticism – that he seemed to drop a bomb every few years that turned their lives upside down. The bomb before last was when he'd resigned from Macmillan's government, where he was Financial Secretary, over increased public spending, a tactic he believed would lead to inflation. If nothing else, Enoch's resignation meant he kept his promise to Pam of a life of poverty with a backbencher, made when he proposed marriage on bended knee. He scrabbled to supplement his modest Member of Parliament's income with fees from articles written, and from radio or television appearances. Then, in 1960, their life changed again when he was made Health Minister. The bomb that time, although not terribly wounding, was Enoch's bitter battle with fellow Tories over his intransigence about Thalidomide.

"If there are to be waves I'm sure we'll weather the storm as we've done in the past," said Enoch.

"Ted will be furious, of course," said Pam.

Enoch marvelled at the volumes of meaning she managed to insert into such a short statement. Mischievous delight. Toe-clenching alarm, but no more than at a good horror film. Slight anxiety nevertheless. A soupçon of reproach perhaps.

"That's not going to be a problem is it?" Pam asked.

"You know my rule about inserting at least one startling assertion into every speech as a precaution that our Leader will never be able fire me from shadow cabinet? Well, as you've seen, this one has a plethora of startling assertions."

Pam smiled, her qualms seemed to have been dispelled.

Enoch didn't blame her for considering Ted Heath's reaction. She'd have to be blind and deaf not to be aware that he and the Leader had been butting heads like testosterone-crazed Billy goats almost since the day Heath was elected as Tory head. During the short honeymoon period, immediately after Heath had appointed Enoch as Shadow Defence Minister, the Powells invited Heath to dinner. During the course of the evening Susan and Jennifer's pet hamster appeared to take a fancy to him – it sat on his lap and washed its face. Later, after Enoch realized he and Heath held divergent political beliefs, he'd told Georgy about it.

"We subsequently realized it was a momentary lapse of judgement by the hamster, but we didn't hold it against him."

"Better watch who you tell that story to," said Georgy. "You wouldn't want Ted to hear about it."

"Wouldn't I?" said Enoch.

Enoch was aware that things began to sour when it became obvious his and Heath's ideas of the role of a politician were poles apart. Enoch believed politics to be 'educational,' as he phrased it, whereas Heath thought it was all about coming up with concrete solutions for everyday problems and putting them into practice through the parliamentary process. Heath's habit of taking into account everybody else's view before he acted infuriated Enoch. He couldn't remember ever taking into account what anybody else thought before making a decision.

"One can't help but wonder how, living alone as he does, Ted decides what tie to wear in the morning, with no-one there to ask," Enoch said to Georgy.

He and Heath disagreed violently and publicly on an array of objectives and policies. Relations between them worsened by the day. The press had a field day when Enoch purposely distorted Heath's 'Action Not Words' slogan into 'Words Not Action.' Enoch was well aware his public demeaning of the slogan undermined the Party's manifesto as well as the Leader's authority, but his frustration with Heath's wishy-washy approach was mounting. Enoch had to admit Heath appeared anything but ineffectual when he raked him over the coals, or when he obviously leaked the fact that he'd done so to the press. The newspapers trumpeted that Heath had issued Enoch an ultimatum. One of them ran the headline: 'Toe The Line or Take Your Cards.' They also claimed, to Enoch's irritation, that 'Mr Powell shuffled meekly into line.' The Leader made it seem as if he was trying to mend fences a couple of days later when he put out a statement saying that there were few Tories who 'think so deeply and originally on politics as Mr Powell.' But Enoch thought it trite, hollow praise. More as if he were Ted's lap dog, and was being thrown a bone for obedience.

Soon afterwards, Enoch was infuriated all over again by a comment Heath made in the United States when the American press, who disliked Enoch for his suspicion of American foreign policy, asked Heath if he had 'Enoch Powell under wraps and would he stay there?' Heath was widely quoted in the British press as having replied, 'Yes to both questions. When I left he had talked about nothing but milk and the Co-ops.' Enoch still simmered at the memory.

He wasn't sure if it was then that his leadership aspiration bubbled to the surface. The desire was always in him to some degree. He remembered as a child standing on a kitchen chair practicing on his parents the speeches he planned to make when he became Prime Minister. He deeply regretted letting himself be persuaded to run for leader three years earlier, before he had his ducks in a row. It was painfully galling when he only accumulated fifteen votes to Heath's one hundred and fifty. He vowed never to let it happen again. Enoch would have to see exactly what effect tomorrow's speech would have, but he was counting on it to put him in a winning position during the next leadership race.

* * *

"Bloody 'ell, look what the cat brought in. Where 'ave you bin?"

"Around," said Frank.

He thought Barry might have appeared more worried. He must wonder if Frank had overheard his conversation with Dennis.

"The usual, my son?"

Frank nodded. The pub was only half full. Frank could remember Friday nights in the Vine when the place was so packed if you passed out there was no space to fall down.

Although reaching an unconscious state was virtually impossible because you had to fight your way to the bar for every single drink. Frank didn't recognize a soul except for three fine art students at a table, who were debating loudly the advantages of oil paints over acrylic. A typical painters' conversation – almost as boring as watching their bloody paint dry. Frank couldn't imagine graphic designers arguing as passionately about typefaces, or printing inks.

"There you go, my son."

Barry placed Frank's pint of Guinness on the bar. A seething frenzy of tiny bubbles swiftly settled to form the customary cap of creamy foam. Frank examined the publican's face as he handed over his change for any sign of awkwardness. Not a trace. Maybe Frank had added two and two to get five. Perhaps his brilliant deduction that Barry had actually manipulated him to fake the photo was mere paranoia. Frank nodded, turned his back, and carried his beer to a vacant seat in a corner opposite the bar. He gulped his Guinness and watched as Barry pulled a couple of pints. The more Frank drank and the longer he thought about it the more he convinced himself that he'd been right. The fact that Barry's ruse to have him doctor the photo had fucking well worked was even more annoying. Frank could think of nothing else. He barely noticed when the fine art students stumbled out of the pub. Barry watched them leave, his face stony, clearly irritated they were leaving well before closing time. By the time his glass was empty Frank was beside himself with anger and resentment. He was so enraged he was finding it difficult to think straight. It couldn't be the booze, he'd only had one pint. Although he realized he hadn't eaten much all day, some toast and marmite in the common room, but that was hours ago. He walked clumsily to the bar for another Guinness.

"You'm quiet tonight, cock," said Barry.

"You'd like that wouldn't you ... for me to keep quiet."

Barry frowned, feigning puzzlement.

And a double rum, too, demanded Frank when Barry handed over his Guinness.

You alroight? asked Barry, as he watched Frank throw back his rum.

"No thanks to you," said Frank, his voice husky from the harshness of alcohol on his throat.

"Look, my son ... "

Just at that moment Tina, the barmaid, called over that a barrel needed changing. Barry glanced at Frank before disappearing through the door that led down to the cellar. Frank walked, slightly unsteadily, back to his seat and started on his second pint. By the time Frank sunk his beer, Barry had reappeared and was chatting with a customer who was propping up the bar. Frank pushed his way past a couple of people sitting at a table. He stumbled slightly, and then bumped against the man Barry was talking to.

"Yow big lummock. Watch where yow'm gowin'"

"Gimme another," said Frank, banging his glass down on the bar. Fortunately he hit a towel emblazoned with a Banks Brewery logo, designed to sop up any slops. The fabric softened the blow otherwise Frank's glass may well have shattered on impact with the wooden counter. Barry began to pull Frank his third pint of Guinness. Frank glared at Barry, swaying slightly.

"A double rum and a bag of crisps too, you fat bastard," said Frank.

Barry reached for the crisps and put them down next to the pint of beer in front of Frank. He turned for the double measure of rum from a bottle hanging behind the bar.

"Yow'm never goin' to let him talk to yow like that?" said the customer.

"He don't mean it, do you Frank?"

Frank knocked back the rum and threw a bunch of change down onto the bar. He tottered back to his corner seat, slopping Guinness onto his hand and the floor in the process. Once seated, he ripped open the bag of crisps. He usually relished the ritual of searching for the plug of salt hidden in the bottom of every bag. There was something immensely satisfying about unwrapping the small blue square of greaseproof paper and dumping salt onto his crisps. A few sharp shakes of the bag to distribute the seasoning evenly and – voilà – the perfect snack. But on this occasion Frank ignored the salt completely, and unceremoniously wolfed all the crisps in a couple of handfuls. He washed them down with several large gulps of Guinness. Barry hadn't been evident for five minutes or so. Frank presumed he was down in the cellar attending to another empty barrel, but as he stumbled back to the bar for another pint, Barry appeared from behind the mirrored strips that led to his private quarters. He studied Frank as he approached.

"Ah think you've 'ad enough for tonight, cock."

Injury added to insult – Frank saw red.

"I know what you did ... you think I don't know but I do ... you, bastard ... pig. I'll swing for you ... I swear ..."

His words wouldn't put themselves in the right order. Barry lifted the flap that separated the public area from the space behind the bar. He put his arm around Frank's shoulders and propelled him toward the door. Anyone watching would have thought the landlord was gently easing Frank out of his pub, but Barry's fingers were curled around the back of Frank's neck in an iron grip.

"Fuck ... hurts," said Frank. He tried to turn away from Barry in an attempt to free himself. But Barry grasped Frank's upper arm to prevent him.

"Shit ... leggo ... bashtard."

Barry used Frank's body to open the door, banging his chest forcibly against it.

"Ow ... shit."

Once outside, Barry accompanied Frank a few yards down the street keeping a tight hold. Then he gave Frank an almighty push. Frank staggered for several steps, arms flailing to keep himself from falling.

"Bashtard."

"Go home, Frank."

Frank steadied himself. Fresh air came as a shock. It sobered him slightly. Which, ironically, made him realize how inebriated he was. He wasn't in the best condition to try and outwit Barry into confessing anything. Better wait until he was sober and with someone to witness whatever was said. Frank decided to throw in the towel and head for home. He turned and reeled away in the direction of his bedsit.

The house in which Frank had a room was a twenty-minute walk from the Vine. But in his uncoordinated condition it took Frank a full twenty minutes just to reach the halfway mark, the point where a railway bridge arched above the road. As Frank stumbled into the murky shadow of the bridge – most of the lights had been vandalized, bulbs smashed – he heard heavy footsteps behind him. Frank turned to see a burly figure walking quickly towards him on the same side of the road. Frank wasn't so drunk that he didn't realize he was staggering. He decided to lean against the bridge wall while the man passed. It wouldn't be a good idea to bump into anyone, the last thing he needed was to get into a scrap. Frank was no Henry Cooper. On the few occasions in his life when he'd been physically threatened he'd managed to talk his way out of any rough stuff.

In his alcohol-induced fatigue Frank was having trouble holding his head up. His chin rested on his chest. He could tell from the sound of footsteps the man was almost level. A heavy-booted foot came into Frank's field of vision. In the dim light Frank could see it was black leather. The boot had an unusually high top, it was tightly laced. A blue jean leg was rolled up above the ankle. Another boot came to rest beside the first.

"Alroight?"

"Yeah, fine, thanks. Just having a bit of a breather."

When the man didn't budge, Frank made an effort to lift his head. In the split second before an explosion of excruciating pain, Frank saw a foreshortened freckled face

– it was Dennis Perkins. Dennis's chin was lowered slightly in order to deliver a head butt that hit Frank square in the nose. Frank reeled back against the bridge wall, one hand covering his face, fingers growing sticky with blood. He tried to steady himself, scrabbling at the wet wall with his other hand, but his fingers slid on the slime of its sopping mossy surface. Dennis saved Frank from falling by grasping him by the shoulders, but then he kneed him in the groin. Frank's breath was yanked out of his lungs. He doubled up in pain. With the aid of a booted foot and a hefty shove Dennis tripped Frank, sending him sprawling. Somehow, from some primeval corner of his being, Frank knew to curl up, one arm protecting his head, the other his abdomen. Nevertheless, Dennis got several vicious kicks to the unprotected side of Frank's head and a few more to his chest. Frank tasted snot, or was it blood, trickling into his mouth. Dennis yanked Frank to his feet. He pulled him to within inches of his face. Frank could smell Dennis's breath – pickled onions and cigarettes.

"Keep fookin' quiet about that bloody snapshot of yours, you 'ear?"

Frank tried to tell Dennis to fuck off. All he was capable of was an indistinct splutter. Dennis relaxed his hold. Frank's knees buckled. He fell to the ground.

"Fookin' nancy boy."

Frank was barely aware of Dennis's footsteps receding, back toward town, from where he'd come. A World War II air raid siren was screaming in the ear Dennis had kicked. Frank's testicles were throbbing like jungle drums. He knew now that his mouth was filled with blood. It tasted too metallic to be snot. Frank wasn't sure how long he lay on the ground. He was vaguely aware of the lights of several cars driving past. A train clickety-clacked across the bridge above him. The first time Frank tried to stand, the pain in his ribs was so sharp he collapsed. The second attempt was marginally better. He used the wall to ease himself upright. Frank had no idea how long it took him to reach home. He stopped every dozen or so steps to stand immobile. After the relative lack of pain when he was motionless, it took Frank superhuman effort to continue.

Frank's room was on the ground floor. The bathroom he shared with two other tenants lay at the back of the house, where the kitchen had been before the house was made into bed-sitting rooms. Undressing was a nightmare. The pain was so intense Frank thought he might throw up. He managed to reach the bath taps and plug by bending at the knees rather than the waist. He stepped into the tub, leaning both hands on the edge and slowly lifting each leg over the rim. Once both feet were in, he twisted slowly around so he could slide into the bath to a sitting position. After the initial shock of hot water on cuts and bruises Frank was able to relax a little, anaesthetized by delicious heat that permeated his body.

Frank woke up God-knows-how-long later in a bath full of lukewarm water. Putting on clothes was unthinkable. Frank didn't give a damn if anybody saw him limp, naked as a new born but tentative as an octogenarian, to his room. He cried out in pain as he manoeuvred himself into bed. Astonishingly,

he found a position where nothing hurt and fell soundly to
sleep.

DAY SEVEN

Saturday, April 20, 1968

Frank was woken by the relentless ringing of the coin phone in the hallway outside his room. He was buggered if he was going to answer it. Just the thought of climbing out of bed was enough to make him cringe. Eventually he heard someone, probably one of the gang of Technical College students who lived in the rooms above him, run lightly down the stairs.

"Hello," a voice said, followed by a long pause.

"Just minute."

The sound of footsteps from phone to Frank's door. A knock.

"Frank? You there?"

Frank tried to call out, but his lips were too sore. He made a whining sound deep in his throat.

"Frank?"

Just open the sodding door, thought Frank. Miraculously, as if he'd voiced his thoughts, the doorknob turned and Chan, an engineering student from Hong Kong, poked his head around the door.

"You a'right, Frank?"

"Do ah lick ahrite?"

His mouth hurt like hell.

The Chinese student moved toward the bed and eyed Frank from under a furrowed brow.

"Wha' happen to you?"

"Fell off fickin' barshtool," said Frank.

Chan shook his head and returned to the phone.

"He look like train run over him. Blood all over pillow."

Frank tried to inspect his pillowcase, but yelped in pain after no more than a ten-degree turn of his head. From the hall Frank heard Chan giving more lurid details of his injuries, followed by the metallic chattering of somebody on the other end of the phone.

"Okay," said Chan and put down the phone. Seconds later his head appeared round the door.

"Friend coming soon."

The door closed and footsteps made their way across the hall and up the stairs. Thanks for nothing, thought Frank before he drifted back to sleep.

"Jesus, your Chinese friend wasn't exaggerating. What the hell happened?"

Christine's face, mere inches from his.

"Bashtard got me under a bwidge."

"Which bastard? What bridge?"

"Dennish bashtard. Bwidge on the way home."

"Barry's nephew bastard? Home from where?"

"Mmmm," said Frank.

"Home from where?"

Frank described his confrontation at the Vine and explained as briefly as he could his theory that Barry had persuaded him to fake the photo to incriminate Nelson.

"That's why the bashtard had his nephew beat me up ... to stop me trying to prove it's a fake," Frank said.

Christine had some Disprin in her handbag. On a quick trawl through the rest of the students in the house she managed to turn up Dettol disinfectant and cotton wool. By the time she returned to Frank's room he'd managed to sit up and had swung his legs over the side of the bed. His head was pounding. He was having trouble distinguishing between hangover pain and injury soreness. Christine gave him two Disprin in a cup of water. After he gulped down the dissolved aspirin she swabbed the cuts on his face, ear, and lips with Dettol and water.

"Do you want me to do down there too?" asked Christine, indicating his groin.

"Very funny," said Frank, the pain in his mouth easing with the effects of the aspirin.

"Your testicles are very swollen."

"You think I don't know that?"

"And the most amazing colour. A beautiful pale indigo."

"Just drop the artistic appreciation and pass me my sodding Y-fronts."

He pulled on his underwear, flinching when fabric hit the bruised skin of his scrotum, but once in place the support eased his discomfort slightly. Nevertheless, the prospect of snug-fitting jeans filled him with dread. Christine fished out an old pair of baggy corduroys from the bottom of his wardrobe. With her help Frank managed to pull them on. Now that he was up and moving, the pain wasn't quite so debilitating. But as the soreness eased, the enormity of what had happened threatened to send him staggering back onto his bed.

"Can you fucking believe this?" asked Frank.

"Believe what?"

"This," said Frank.

He gestured, hands slightly outstretched palms upturned, indicating the extent of his injuries, eyes wide in an expression of disbelief.

"I'm not in the least surprised. We're dealing with a couple of psychopaths, Frank. Not some rowdy art students on a Rag Day prank."

Frank groaned and sank down onto his bed. His sheltered life thus far hadn't prepared him for violence. He'd seen television footage and heard reports, but he'd never been confronted by the real deal. But it wasn't as if Christine had grown up in Belfast or Cyprus. How come she was so worldly? So pragmatic?

"Have to pee," Frank muttered.

"Do you want any help?"

Frank was too daunted by the prospect of a long walk to the bathroom to come up with a witty retort. It took him a good ten minutes to get there, do his business, and limp back.

"As long as I walk like Wyatt Earp, it doesn't hurt as much as you'd think," said Frank, hobbling bow-legged over to a chair. He sat down gingerly and closed his eyes.

"Look, Frank. This is serious. I think we should go to the police," said Christine.

"There's no way I'm going to the fucking police."

Christine recoiled. Her head jerked back, almost as if he'd slapped her.

"I'm sorry. It's just that whatever I tell the police about

why Dennis beat the shit out of me will sound half-baked. I've no proof Barry and Dennis are in cahoots, or that they're trying to shut me up about faking the photo. Which the police don't believe I did in the first place."

"But it'll be in police records that it was Dennis who reported the argument between Nelson and the Sikh landlord. If you tell a policeman – anyone other than Fowler – that you believe he and Barry are trying to make it look like Nelson beat up Singh they might look into it."

"But they'll ask why Dennis and Barry would be trying to screw Nelson and I've no fucking idea."

Frank felt somewhat bereft when Christine appeared perplexed. He realized he'd been counting on her to come up with a solution to his problem.

"At least you should phone Nelson's solicitor. Ask her advice and, if you haven't already, let her know you're trying to rally the students in the photo."

Christ, but she was good. He knew she'd come up with something constructive.

"I'd better go and rescue Don. He's waiting outside," she said.

"Don who lives underneath you?"

Christine explained that, when Chan had answered the phone, she'd been calling to tell Frank she needed to work on her print and couldn't accompany him to see Giles Shannon as they'd planned.

"After I put the phone down from your Chinese friend, I ran into Don in the hall. He saw I was worried and after I explained, he offered to run me over here in his car."

"He's got wheels?" asked Frank. There were few students at college who owned a car.

"Yeah, on old Austin A40."

While Christine went out to find Don, Frank grabbed some coins to call Auntie Irene to ask her for Ruth Barton's number. The aspirin had done its job. It wasn't until Frank put the receiver up to his injured ear that he received a painful reminder of the damage Dennis had wrought.

"Fowler's behind this, you can count on it," said Irene.

Despite his misgivings about Fowler, Frank found it hard to believe Irene was right. The white Jamaican was a policeman, surely he'd have nothing to do with GBH attacks by a thug like Dennis.

"Why do you think Fowler's got anything to do with it?" asked Frank.

"It no easy to explain, you know. All I can tell you is when Jamaica got independence the cry went up, 'Out of Many, One People.' We have a sweet in Jamaica made from sugar and coconut. It hard like glass and dark like rum. We call it Bustamante Backbone – named after the first prime minister. He was hard as them sweets, and he was for the people, without question. Him never take orders from nobody, least of all the whites who lord it over everyone for centuries. Fowler's family had their fingers in lots of pies – bauxite, sugar, whole heap o' stuff. Well, their finger soon got pull out after Bustamente was put in power. Whites like Fowler get vex. So Fowler is a bitter man who hates everyone – he blames coloureds for takin' his birthright and the British for givin' it to them."

"But that must have been a long time ago," said Frank

"Where you been, Frank? Is only six year since Jamaica independent."

"But why would the police here employ such a man?"

"'Cos they don't know nothin' 'bout him. They see him as a Godsend, a white man who understand what it is Jamaican people say. They no realize the harm him can do. Or maybe they know damn well, but don't care. All I know is he's like a shark, once he get his teeth in something he never let go."

Frank assured Irene he'd be careful, asked her to give his best to Nelson, and then phoned Ruth Barton. Her opinion was that going to the police about Dennis's attack would achieve little. It might even screw things up if Irene was right about Fowler.

"I've been doing a bit of digging into Fowler. He's a nasty bastard. Best steer clear of him and hope he puts a foot wrong. It'd be better for now to get those students in the photo to come forward. But Frank, write down an account of the assault while it's still fresh, exactly where it took place, and so forth. And take photos of your injuries if you can."

Christine's downstairs neighbour, Don, grimaced when he saw Frank's face.

"Bloody hell, you really got the stuffing knocked out of you didn't you."

"You should see my balls," said Frank.

"No thanks," said Don. "But I know what it's like to be thumped in the manhood. It happened to me a few times playing rugby. A week's rest and a few hot baths and I was right as rain. Time's a great healer in that department."

When Frank told Christine what Ruth Barton had said she suggested it might be easier if Frank recounted to her exactly what happened and she would write it down for him. Frank gave her an account of Dennis's attack from the opening head butt to the concluding kick. Christine became concerned all over again.

"Does it hurt when you breathe?" she asked.

"Not really."

"Your ribs are probably not broken then."

Frank owned an Instamatic camera he'd had since he was a teenager. There were a few unexposed frames left on its film. He stood in the light from his bedsitter window while Christine photographed the cuts and bruises on his ear, cheek, and mouth.

"Your lips look like Mick Jagger's, but bigger."

"You're enjoying this far too much," said Frank.

"One frame left. Drop your pants."

"I'll meet you outside," said Don, making for the door.

"No need to leave. There's no way I'm letting Lady Snowdon here take a shot of my privates," said Frank.

He grabbed the camera from Christine.

"My mangled face is evidence enough."

"You'd better put your feet up for the rest of the day. I'm sorry but I can't hang around to play Florence Nightingale. I'll never get my print finished if I don't get to college," said Christine.

"I can't sit around here waiting for my … you-know-whats to recover. I've got to find Giles Shannon."

"You can't go all the way out there on a bus, not in your condition," said Christine.

Denise James, the mad potter, had told them that the place where Giles lived was a half-hour walk from a bus stop in the middle of nowhere – just over the Shropshire border, seven or eight miles to the west of Wolverhampton.

" How the hell else can I get there?"

"If you must go, I'll run you out," offered Don.

* * *

On their way through town, Frank and Don dropped Christine off at college. They continued westward on the quest for the elusive hippy electrical genius, Giles Shannon.

"One thing about Wolverhampton, it doesn't take long to get out of it," said Frank.

They'd been driving for only half-an-hour and already they'd left Wolverhampton's meagre suburbs behind. Gently rolling hills clad in a patchwork of fields stitched together by fat hedges lay on each side of the road. Frank was struck by the marked contrast to his recent trip in the opposite direction, when he travelled from Wolverhampton to Birmingham through an unrelenting landscape of factories and warehouses.

"There are worse places than Wolverhampton, you know," said Don somewhat defensively. Frank remembered Don was born and brought up in the town.

"Like Dudley, you mean?"

"You're joking, but you're right too. Dudley assumed the grubby mantle of industry early on, mining coal and making iron. But Wolverhampton's roots have always been in agriculture."

Don waved a hand at the surrounding fields.

"Its proximity to all this saved it from being as soot-stained as the rest of the Black Country. Wool was its making. The fleeces from millions of sheep that thronged the border country were brought to Wolverhampton. Hence all those street names that end in 'fold.' And Woolpack Street itself, of course."

They were silent for the next half dozen miles. Frank thought how little he knew about the history of the town where he'd been a student for almost four years. Or anywhere else come to that – he hadn't exactly been attentive at school. But he realized he was probably aware of Britain's heritage whether he was conscious of it or not. It was impossible to move without running across some vestige of the past, recent or distant. A name, like the street names Don had mentioned, a building, or a statue were daily reminders of the weight of English tradition.

There was surprisingly little traffic on the road, given it was a sunny Saturday and warm for the time of year. Here and there bursts of snowy blossom sprang from branches. A green haze of feathery corn shoots swathed neatly furrowed fields. Sunlight penetrated the flimsy tissue of immature leaves. Trees and bushes glowed as if lit from within.

"Quintessentially English, isn't it?" said Don.

Frank had to admit the scene was identical to ones he'd seen rendered by Eric Ravilious, the British illustrator he admired, for posters advertising the joys of the countryside.

Even though the surrounding landscape was no artist's device, it seemed irrelevant.

"Acres of suburban mock-Tudor semis would be more representative of England today, don't you think? The idea of blacksmiths pounding contentedly away at horseshoes and pink-cheeked locals picking apples is a fairy tale. And even if anybody ever did live like that, life was probably bloody hard."

"You're just a crazy romantic at heart, aren't you?" said Don.

"Sod off," said Frank.

Don had a heavy foot. Frank knew the signs with a white circle dissected by a diagonal black line meant no speed limit, but they were taking the bends more or less on two wheels.

"Steady on. I think the road we want is just up ahead."

A couple of hundred yards further on they reached the side road Denise had mentioned. The first building should be the gatehouse where Giles Shannon was living. It was built on the perimeter of a local estate, the wall of which ran along the side of the road. They followed the wall for a good two miles before rounding a curve to find two massive stone gateposts about fifty yards ahead. Carved into the stone of both posts were initials in a flowery script, presumably belonging to the family who owned the land. The letters were so ornate and weatherworn they were illegible. Just inside one of the posts sat a single-storey building. A line of faded and tattered Tibetan prayer flags had been pinned above the front door.

"You wouldn't think his lordship would look kindly on

heathen artifacts draped over his property," said Frank as they turned into the driveway.

"He probably never sees them. This is obviously the back entrance to the estate."

"How can you tell?" asked Frank.

"Country houses usually have an avenue of trees at their front entrance, there's none here. There are no gates either. They were probably never replaced after they were carted off during the war for metal to build tanks or aeroplanes. But you can bet the front gates, where the family go in and out, were reinstated PDQ after the war was over."

" PDQ?"

" Pretty Damn Quick," said Don, in the tone of voice people use when they can't believe they haven't been understood.

When they stepped out of the car they could see a large kitchen garden to the side of the lodge. The skeletal stems of Brussels sprout plants, now stripped of their bounty, stuck up here and there. Potato plants had been plundered, their leaves and stems tossed to one side to rot. On an expanse of bedraggled grass a line of limp laundry flapped languorously in the breeze. A young woman with astonishingly long but greasy hair emerged from between two bed sheets. She was barefoot, dressed in a floor-length Indian print skirt and a purple kaftan. Frank noticed she wore a ring on one of her toes. Her feet were ingrained with dirt.

"Welcome to Nirvana Lodge," she said, smiling with such intensity one might have thought Frank and Georgy were long-anticipated family members.

"My name's Moonglow."

"Frank," said Frank. "Is Giles around?"

"He split a couple of days ago."

"Split?" asked Frank.

"Yeah, split," repeated Moonglow, still smiling, although less warmly now that she'd picked up on the ridicule in Frank's voice.

"Where did he go? For how long?"

"California. For good. Happily ever after."

"California! What is it with all these bloody students flying round the world?"

Moonglow couldn't maintain her smile, forced or otherwise, in the face of Frank's exasperation.

"It's a free world, isn't it?"

"We'd like to think so," said Don.

"I thought he was working on an extraordinary Earth-shattering invention?" said Frank.

"He was … he is. That's why he went to America. Giles wrote an article for a trade magazine about the computing device he was working on. A fellow in California read about it and offered a lot of bread for Giles to go and develop it there, so he went."

"Computing device? Bread?" asked Frank.

Moonglow's brow furrowed, as though she were wondering from what planet Frank originated.

"I'm following him out there," she said. "We're going to live near San Francisco. Flowers in our hair and all that."

Moonglow reverted to the blissful expression with which she'd greeted them as skilfully as an accomplished actress slipping into character.

"Come inside, take tea," she said.

"Love to," said Frank.

The Disprins Christine had given him were wearing off. He'd brought more with him and needed to dissolve them. As well as sore, he felt incredibly weary. He was dispirited at having come to another dead end. He hoped to hell the self-righteous single parent, Kathy Stevenson, didn't let him down.

Apart from the string of tatty prayer flags, the exterior of the lodge couldn't have appeared more traditional whereas the interior couldn't have been less so. Jimmy Hendrix was wailing 'Are You Experienced?' on the record player. The living room walls were lined with psychedelic posters. A huge reproduction of singer/musician Marc Bolan's head was stuck with yellowing fragments of Sellotape on the wall above the fireplace. The musician's mass of curls were depicted in rainbow colours and writhed like a nest of vipers around his head. A stylized sun rose behind him, its rays radiating to the poster's edges in hot pink and bright yellow. Under his chin lime green letters, hand drawn and barely legible, picked out the name of his band – TYRANNOSAURUS REX. There was no furniture in the room to speak of. A few mattresses were bent into L-shapes and propped against walls for seating. Indian rugs of various sizes covered the floor in front of them. Compared to the bracing air outside, the room was heavy with the scents of musk oil, stale tobacco, and marijuana. Old coffee mugs sat about, rimed with rancid milk. A half-eaten plate of congealed brown rice had tipped over onto one of the mattresses. Jimmy Hendrix crashed to a conclusion. Frank remembered that Are You Experienced? was the last track on the album. He hoped Moonglow would give the record player a rest. His head was pounding.

"Mint, evening primrose, or camomile?" she asked.

"Haven't you got any ordinary?" Frank asked.

"I think there's a packet of Typhoo."

"Lovely. Milk and one sugar, please," said Don, who was staring distastefully at the grubby mattress where Frank was sprawled. He hesitantly lowered himself and perched, legs awkwardly outstretched, on the cleanest of the other mattresses.

"You really should have taken the evening primrose, it has amazing analgesic powers," said Moonglow when Frank plopped two Disprins into his cup. In a ridiculous attempt to make light of his cuts and bruises Frank claimed he'd fought off a gang of Hell's Angels intent on raping his girlfriend. He hadn't the energy or the inclination to tell the real story. needn't have bothered – Moonglow couldn't have been less interested. She chattered about her new home in California as though it were the Promised Land, eyes wide, pupils huge but glazed blackly.

"It's actually a place called Menlo Park where Giles is doing his thing. Doesn't it sound amazing?"

"Fantastic," said Frank. He would have said or done anything for some peace and quiet. He longed to stretch out and sleep for a week or two.

"We should be off," said Don, clearly longing for fresh air.

"It'd be cool if you wanted to take any posters you like. I may take the one of Frank Zappa on the toilet. It's my favourite. But you can have the rest," said Moonglow.

She managed to hold on to her blissful smile in the light of Frank and Don's refusal of her offer. She was still grinning dementedly as she waved them goodbye, prayer flags fluttering around her flowing hair and skirt billowing in the breeze.

"That'll end in tears," said Don as they drove away.

Before they left, Moonglow had written down Giles's address in California on the back of an old envelope. Frank didn't think it could hurt to write to Giles with a clip of the photo and ask if he remembered the demonstration and Nelson not being there. He turned the envelope over and glanced at the name on the front.

"You'll never guess what Moonglow's real name is," said Frank.

"What?"

"Rita Higginbottom."

* * *

After the hilarity of discovering Moonglow's real name, Frank and Don relaxed into amiable silence during the rest of the drive back to Wolverhampton. But as countryside gave way to houses Frank became more and more concerned that he was losing witnesses from the faked photo – two out of four – faster than water through a sieve. They rounded a bend in the road and were confronted by a wisteria-draped pub. The facade of the ancient building dripped with swollen clusters of mauve flowers. A biscuit tin lid scene of Ye Olde England.

"Let's stop," said Frank, more a command than a suggestion. Don deftly pulled the car in front of the pub. The brakes squealed slightly on the cobblestoned forecourt.

"You feeling ill?"

"No, I need a drink" said Frank.

Don looked slightly dubious. Frank guessed he was wondering if Disprin and alcohol might not be an ideal combination. It had occurred to him he probably shouldn't mix, but sod it. How bad could it be?

"I used to come to this place quite a bit when I was in the sixth form," said Don, once they'd settled into the pub's comfortable lounge, Frank with his habitual Guinness, Don with a gin and tonic. They sat admiring hundreds-year-old beams that supported low ceilings of the pub's tasteful but cosy room. Despite being in a convivial public lounge, Frank was despondent about the day's lack of results.

"If only I hadn't listened to Barry," he said.

When Don asked what he meant, Frank realized he'd only heard the details of his beating. He hadn't been told about the reason for his drunken antics in the Vine nor been given a full explanation for exactly why Dennis had beaten the living daylights out of him. Frank filled Don in on the whole sad story, ending with his suspicion that Barry had set him up by suggesting he insert Nelson into the demo photo.

"It seems like such a long shot on Barry's part. He couldn't have been certain you'd do the switch," said Don.

"He had nothing to lose, so why not lob the idea out. And as it happens it found the sodding mark, didn't it?"

Frank stared into his Guinness. Perhaps it was the addition of alcohol, but the Disprin didn't seem as effective as the first he'd taken. His face ached and his groin was starting to throb, lightly but insistently. Maybe one's body become resistant to medication, but surely not that quickly. And then, with the increasing pain, came a disturbing thought. Now he knew Dennis was more than capable of beating the shit out of someone, Frank wondered if he might have been the one who'd attacked Singh. If Barry knew about it, he might have suggested the switch in the photo to incriminate Nelson and take the focus away from Dennis.

"While I don't doubt that this Dennis character is capable, why would he beat the poor bastard half to death?" asked Don, after Frank shared his theory.

"I don't know ... but remember the confab I told you I overheard behind the curtain at The Vine? Barry said something about it being Dennis's fault in the first place, that he'd got 'carried away with the bloody Paki.' Then Dennis said he was out of his mind with worry that he was 'on the cop's radar,' as he put it."

"But hadn't your pal Nelson been charged with the murder by then? Why would this Dennis maniac be worried?"

"If you found out you'd murdered someone rather than just roughed them up, wouldn't you be worried, even if somebody else was charged for it? Especially if you knew how flimsy the evidence was. I'll bet any money Dennis did it and that Barry knew all about it. He grabbed the chance to help his nephew when he saw my shots from the demo."

Frank became incensed all over again for falling for Barry's lame ruse. He bristled with anger, which didn't help his aches and pains.

"But Barry would have to be aware that Nelson was under

suspicion. How would he have known?" asked Don.

Frank mused about this as he drank his Guinness. He remembered Auntie Irene's warning about Fowler being behind the beating he'd had from Dennis. Although he'd been sceptical, he supposed there were stranger threesomes than the creepy detective, Dennis, and Barry. Then Frank remembered, when Fowler was throwing cold water on his story about faking the photo, that the detective used the expression "bosom pals" to describe Frank and Nelson. Frank didn't remember saying anything to Fowler about them being friends. All he'd said was that he'd taken photos of Nelson at the building site. Fowler must have heard from somebody that he and Nelson were more than just workmates. Frank also recalled Fowler describing the two of them as being "close as twins." It was an odd expression to use about the two of them, one coloured and one white. If the dodgy detective had been talking to Barry he may well have told Fowler that Nelson and Frank joked about being twins, in the pub the summer before. The more he thought about the Jamaican detective's 'close as twins' comment the more he was convinced Fowler and Barry must be connected.

"It wouldn't surprise me if it was Barry who put the rotten Jamaican cop on to Nelson in the first place."

"But if Barry had been the one to first finger your pal why would he need to have you insert him into the demo photo?"

"If he and Fowler were in cahoots, Barry probably knew that Nelson was claiming he was at home in Handsworth on the day Singh was assaulted. And that Auntie Irene was backing his story. A photo showing Nelson in Wolverhampton would suggest they were lying. Come to think of it, Barry was on the phone while I was looking at the photos in The Vine. I remember he hung up pretty fast once he saw them laid out on the bar. I bet he was talking to Fowler."

"I can understand why the cop might go along with a tip-off from Barry and pull Nelson in for questioning, but why would he bother to phone Barry and tell him about Nelson's alibi?" Don asked.

"Maybe they're all in this together. Perhaps Fowler knew it was Dennis who assaulted Singh but wanted Nelson to get done for it. If so, I imagine he would want to keep in touch to make sure Barry kept Dennis under control and out of the limelight so the trumped-up case against Nelson would stick."

"Even if your version of events didn't sound like a paranoid conspiracy theory – which it does – it brings us back to the question of why Barry's nephew would assault Singh in the first place. And why would the cop protect him?"

"God only knows," said Frank. He emitted a loud sigh of exasperation. His brain hurt.

Don insisted on dropping Frank back at his bedsit.

"You look bloody awful. You need to lie down."

Frank didn't argue. As he pushed open his front door he could hear Sergeant Pepper's Lonely Hearts Club Band blasting from one of the rooms upstairs. Nevertheless, Frank tumbled into a dreamless slumber on top of his tousled bedcovers the moment his body discovered a position that didn't hurt.

* * *

"For Heaven's sake, Enoch, stop making such a fuss."

Enoch barely registered the words. His eyes were screwed shut to avoid suds seeping into them, and his ears were blocked with water he would have described as scalding. He hated having his hair washed, but Pam insisted he have clean hair on this of all days. He was inundated by another jug load of hot water.

"Surely it's thoroughly rinsed by now," he said, but the taste of Silvikrin shampoo told him otherwise. He would have thought it might have had a more pleasant flavour, given its Lemon and Lime label, touted in magazine ads to 'super clean greasy hair.' He supposed the fact that Pam bought the shampoo for him meant she considered his hair oily, what little there was beyond his receding hairline. When his ears eventually cleared he could hear Jennifer and Susan giggling outside the bathroom door. They found his protestations hilarious. He had to admit to exaggerating his wails of complaint for their benefit. Once the washing process was finished, Pam left him to towel himself dry.

"Come along girls, the show's over. Downstairs with you," Enoch heard her say.

Pam had laid out his charcoal wool suit and a white shirt in their bedroom. Enoch switched the tie she'd chosen for his Old Edwardian's tie. It seemed only fitting since the Midland Hotel, where he was to give the speech, was a mere stone's throw from the school where he'd excelled. King Edward's had moved in the 1940s to a new building in Edgbaston, but Enoch remembered with pride walking into the original Gothic Revival building in New Street on a sunny September day in 1925 as a thirteen-year-old scholarship boy. The building was designed by the same architect who built the Palace of Westminster, another institution that embodied the sense of tradition Enoch so revered – and where he believed he'd shone and would continue to triumph. As he fitted his old boy's tie around his shirt collar he experienced the powerful sensation that he was completing some kind of mystic circle by returning to New Street to give a speech that might well propel him to the leadership – even to Number 10 Downing Street. It certainly seemed auspicious that the speech was to be made within such a short distance of where he'd won the accolades that so pleased his mother. Her expression of approval hovered in his mind. He was blindsided by a wave of grief to think she wouldn't be there to witness his performance that afternoon, or be around to relish its effects in the days to come. His image in the mirror grew blurred. Enoch swiped his eyes, then refolded his handkerchief and placed it carefully in the top pocket of his jacket, leaving only the neat V-shape of its corners showing.

* * *

Pam and Enoch dropped the girls off at the Jones' house on their way out of town. Clem and Marjorie had offered to look after Susan and Jennifer for the afternoon,

"With the embargo on your transcript, I'm afraid I haven't had a chance to take a gander. Other priorities you know," said Clem. "But I brought it home to read later."

Enoch was happy to hear people abided by the embargo. It was usual for press releases to be given to the media on the condition they weren't published before a particular date and time. In this case Enoch knew Georgy had made certain the cover sheet to his speech had specified it not be made public until after he'd delivered it in Birmingham that afternoon.

"Be good you two," called Pam as the girls trooped behind Clem into the house.

As they made their way to Birmingham, Enoch, sitting in the passenger seat, gazed out of the car window. It was true the urban landscape wasn't pretty, but he always thought of it with affection. He'd grown up in the shadow of dark satanic mills of the industrial revolution and was accustomed to their forbidding appearance. In late morning sunlight even the most depressing factory and foundry seemed to Enoch to have a majestic quality to it. The buildings reminded him of the might and power of English manufacturing and of all the products made in the Midlands – trains, cranes, machinery – that were shipped worldwide to help speed the progress of the Empire. Enoch was proud to think Britain could never have been so mighty without the smelters and kilns of his Black Country birthplace.

Inspired by the sunny landscape Enoch recited aloud his favourite verse from James Thomson's poem, Rule Britannia.

To thee belongs the rural reign;
Thy cities shall with commerce shine:
All thine shall be the subject main,
And every shore it circles thine.
Rule, Britannia! rule the waves:
Britons never will be slaves.

The words never failed to trigger a surge of emotion. Enoch was grateful to Pam when she took up the refrain. Eyes fixed on the road ahead, she belted out the song version at the top of her voice.

When Britain fi-i-irst, at heaven's command,
Aro-o-o-o-ose from out the a-a-a-zure main,
Arose, arose from out the azure main,
This was the charter, the charter of the land,
And guardian a-a-angels sang this strain

At which point Enoch jumped in and sang along with her.

Rule Britannia!
Britannia rule the waves
Britons never, never, never shall be slaves.

They parked the car near the new Bullring Centre. Enoch had heard the much trumpeted shopping centre, the first in Britain, was experiencing problems. Retailers shunned it because rents were high, and people were reluctant to walk through subways under ring roads circling the mammoth building like mediaeval moats. The shopping centre sat like a modern-day concrete castle isolated from the rest of town. Enoch remembered Georgy's criticism of Wolverhampton's new market and thought how right she'd been to wonder why modern buildings need appear so austere. He was relieved when they turned into Stephenson Street and saw the back entrance of the Midland Hotel, with its reassuring traditional style, letters of its name hewn from stone above leaded windows. In between each letter the mason had carved ornate foliage, which was echoed in the arched tympanum above two of the second-floor windows. Two stone figures stood solemnly supporting one of the arches.

The receptionist directed them to an upstairs dining room where Reginald Eyre, MP for Hall Green was waiting, together with a hundred or so members of the Conservative Political Centre. Eyre was the man Enoch had thought was Geoffrey Ayres, Georgy's friend who worked for the Commonwealth Welfare Council, but the two men were like chalk and cheese. No matter Enoch's opinion of Geoffrey Ayres, he had to admit he was a good-looking man, and charismatic to boot. Reginald Eyre was pudgy with a bland face only relieved by dark-rimmed spectacles. His mouse brown hair was swept back and plastered to his head, slick and shiny as a photo from a Brylcreem ad. He spoke softly, and only looked Enoch in the eye as he finished what he was saying, as though checking to see if his words were well received.

Large mirrors lined the walls of the room where lunch was to be served, which gave an impression of airiness. Once Enoch and Pam were seated at the head table Enoch felt the frisson he always felt before giving a speech. A tightening of his abdomen. A heightened sensitivity to his skin, which imparted a vague tingling sensation to his hands, feet, and lips. It was not unlike the anticipation of imminent sexual activity. He ate sparely, not wanting to fill his stomach before he spoke. He barely registered any conversation. He made only monosyllabic replies to his neighbours. As coffee was served Enoch was delighted to see an ATV camera crew was allowed entry and was setting up a camera and microphone to record the proceedings. A BBC radio man was also admitted with his sound recorder. Anybody else might have have taken the opportunity to excuse themselves to slip to the toilet before giving a speech, but Enoch believed the slight tension of a full bladder added a dimension – urgency perhaps – to his public speaking. Finally, with TV camera rolling, Reginald Eyre rose to announce their speaker. He kept his introduction mercifully short.

When Enoch stood he felt as if the room entered into slow motion. He glanced around him. Most people sat immobile, but some lifted coffee cups to lips or inhaled on a cigarette. The smoke they exhaled hung in the air in front of them, imperceptibly drifting. Enoch took a breath. He used to have to tell himself to slow down at this point. The biggest error in public speaking was to rush one's words. But he'd learnt early on to speak unhurriedly, making each word drop separately from the next, a steady drip rather than an uninterrupted trickle. Ever since he'd given his first speeches about his grandfather's stuffed birds as a preschool child, standing on a dining chair to make himself seen, he'd know the exhilaration of holding an audience's attention. One of the wonders of being a member of the House of Commons was when he actually had his fellow parliamentarians in his hand. The moments in which he played upon the members as on an instrument were like no other Enoch had experienced. His Hola speech had been the watershed. He'd been so affected by the power of his own eloquence, the authority of his articulation, that he broke down and wept after his concluding sentence. His reputation as a cold fish was temporarily forgotten. He was stunned by the revelation that his oratory could be so affecting. Ever since that moment he'd worked to hone his craft, as he thought of it.

Enoch began speaking in a fairly low key, employing the tone of a lecturing professor. He laid out the function of statesmanship and the duty of politicians to draw attention to potential "evils," even if to do so made for unpleasant and undesirable listening. It had been a stroke of genius to define himself as a Martin Luther type, the principled man of conscience, who had no moral option but to deliver an inconvenient truth.

"Here I stand, God help me, I can do no other."

Enoch could see himself in one of the mirrors that lined the far wall. His reflection was partly obscured by the television camera. Although tempting, he decided it would be a mistake to keep observing himself. Nor did Enoch allow his eyes to linger on the lens of the television camera. If he were to give a truly credible performance, it was vital he engage with his live audience. He made sure his eyes rested on a different individual when he made each point, or for the duration of each complete sentence. In that way a majority of people would have the impression he was speaking directly to them. He dropped the first of his 'startling assertions' in the form of a quote from a constituent.

"In this country in 15 or 20 years' time the black man will have the whip hand over the white man."

He was slightly disappointed there wasn't more of a

reaction. No shocked intake of breath. No 'hear hears.' He continued with a prediction, in the belief that, by describing the effect his words would have, he'd take the wind out of the sails of his detractors.

"I can already hear the chorus of execration. How dare I say such a horrible thing? How dare I stir up trouble and inflame feelings by repeating such a conversation?"

Then again the Martin Luther device.

"I do not have the right not to do so."

The line received a chorus of 'hear hears.' Enoch seized the opportunity and looked expectantly out across the diners. He was rewarded with mild but obviously heartfelt applause. He felt the excitement of an angler who feels his line tighten when a fish takes the bait.

"I simply do not have the right to shrug my shoulders and think about something else."

Secure in the knowledge he had the entire room's attention, he began to ratchet up the drama in the next few paragraphs to offset the rather dry presentation of facts and figures. He sprinkled statistics about the extent of immigration to Britain with poetic allusion in order to magnify their scale and significance. He lengthened the spaces between words and added more tonal range to his voice, rising higher on some words, then lowering to almost a rumble on others.

"Those whom the gods wish to destroy, they first make mad. We must be mad, literally mad, as a nation

to be permitting the annual inflow of some 50,000 dependents, who are for the most part the material of the future growth of the immigrant-descended population."

Enoch paused, scowling around the room as though actually confronted by the insanity he described.

"It is like washing ... watching ... a nation busily engaged in heaping up its own funeral pyre."

He cursed himself for his slight stumble, but nobody seemed to notice. Every face in the room stared in his direction. Activity around the television camera distracted him slightly. He could see the cameraman changing a reel. Just as well perhaps – the next section was somewhat dry, it wouldn't matter if it wasn't recorded. He evoked "Conservative Party policy" three times in the next nine paragraphs of description of possible "solutions" to the question of how the dimensions of immigration could be reduced. He was truthful about the basic three points of Party policy strategy, but he inserted emotional expressions of alarm and dismay at the consequences should they not be implemented. Enoch relished the thought of Ted Heath's reaction as he implied that all he was doing was repeating "Conservative Party official policy," intoning the words like a mantra, when in fact he was doing precisely what Ted had demanded he *not* do by fleshing out the bare bones of the policy with extreme and provocative language.

Despite knowing he probably wasn't being recorded, Enoch didn't let up on his oratory talents. He put all his effort into making the paragraphs of figures as dramatic as possible. He tempered his voice, employing emphasis at key phrases and glaring around the room, almost as though challenging the "evil" he repeatedly mentioned to show itself from where it might be hiding behind chairs or under tables. People seemed untroubled by any lack of justification for the use of the word "evil," with which he peppered his speech. Enoch knew that to dissect the nature of the evil would dilute the power of the word. He'd learnt as a child that it was most feared when it was amorphous –like the evil his mother hinted at, prowling outside their kitchen window, only to be kept at bay with the weapons of learning and academic knowledge. It was much more effective to prompt people into imagining their own worst nightmare of what immigration might bring.

This was precisely why he'd avoided sending a copy of the speech to Tory HQ, he knew Heath would never agree to such tactics. That, and the other of his 'startling assertions,' such as the rabble rousing nature of his *coup de grace* – the letter from the old lady. But before he delivered the concluding blow he must first introduce the subject of anti-discrimination legislation, by throwing in the implication that the liberal press were no better than Nazi naysayers from before the war.

"There could be no grosser misconception of the realities than is entertained by those who vociferously demand legislation as they call it 'against discrimination,' whether they be leader-writers of the same kidney and sometimes on the same newspapers which year after year in the 1930s tried to blind this country to the rising peril which confronted it."

Enoch purposely fixed his stare on a middle-aged man, perhaps in his mid-fifties, who in all likelihood fought during the Second World War. Enoch could almost see the man's synapses paving the way for the logic Enoch was relying on. In equating the "rising peril" of naziism with anti-discrimination legislation, the entire issue of immigration became as much a monstrous bugbear as anything Hitler could have dreamt up. The man's eyes widened, then he nodded vigorously. It was extraordinary how an iota of skewed logic could evoke the degree of alarmed indignation the man was clearly feeling. Enoch would claim he was only enabling expression to what the man already felt, but he knew he'd have difficulty persuading Georgy – for one – of that.

After pausing for several heartbeats, Enoch moved on to a paragraph he'd inserted with his debate with Georgy in mind about comparisons between British immigrants and American slave descendants. In all the letters he received after his Walsall speech by far the most common bone of contention was that immigrants who were accepted into Britain were instantly given rights and privileges of "full citizens" – the ability to vote, free treatment under the National Health, and others. Enoch realized it was this that set the British immigrant apart from American slaves, who'd only been awarded franchise and other rights slowly and in recompense for past misdeeds against them. He deduced that if resentment at the automatic entitlement of immigrants in Britain was rife in the people who'd bothered to write to him, so must it be in others. By making the comparison between 'deserving' American negroes and the instantly privileged immigrant to Britain, he hoped to imply that the latter were unworthy. He was careful not to mention Georgy's point that the granting of rights to Commonwealth immigrants could be justified as payment for the exploitation of their country by a British colonial power. Instead Enoch threw in a paragraph to make clear that if, having been granted such privileges, immigrants experienced "drawbacks" it was their own fault. He tempered his accusation by claiming that their problems would be no different than "those personal circumstances and accidents which cause, and always will cause, the fortunes and experience of one man to be different from another's." But that wasn't his main rationale for making the point. He moved on to the effects on the "native population" of the granting of rights to so many immigrants – people were confronted by crowded maternity wards and their children forced to study in overflowing classrooms. Their neighbourhoods were being transformed against their will. He applied words to the British public such as "defeated" and attributed to them the feeling that they were "unwanted." Powerful words to use so soon after World War II. Having painted a scene of utter degradation of ordinary native citizens as a result of immigration, Enoch touched again on the proposed Race Relations Bill, the legislation that had given him a golden opportunity to speak. He described to his audience an Act of Parliament that would "give the stranger, the disgruntled and the agent-provocateur the power to pillory ordinary Britons for their private actions." He didn't doubt half the room had no inkling of the exact meaning of an agent-provocateur, but it was another of those words that he was sure would instil fear precisely for its enigmatic menace.

Then Enoch stood poised to deliver the climax to his speech, the crescendo that he believed would lend humanity and empathy to all his rhetoric. He had the impression that this twenty minutes in a Birmingham hotel dining room was the culmination of his total experience thus far. His life seemed to have been lived for those moments. He gazed at faces, holding his audience's stare for several minutes, as though breathing expectancy into their very lungs.

Enoch began by describing the hundreds of letters of validation he received after his Walsall speech from "ordinary, decent, sensible people" too afraid to sign their name for fear of "penalties or reprisals." He didn't elaborate what form the supposed punishments might take – like "evils," they were more potent left unspecified. But he did state that being part of this "persecuted minority" was something that those "without direct experience can hardly imagine," knowing full well his saying so would actually encourage his audience to conjure up their own heart-stopping versions.

Enoch told the room he was going to let one of these unfortunate people speak for him, and began to quote his version of the letter Barry Dangerfield had supplied.

"Eight years ago in a respectable street in Wolverhampton a house was sold to a Negro. Now only one white (a woman old-age pensioner) lives there. This is her story. She lost her husband and both her sons in the war. So she turned her seven-roomed house, her only asset, into a boarding house. She worked hard and did well, paid off her mortgage and

began to put something by for her old age. Then the immigrants moved in. With growing fear, she saw one house after another taken over. The quiet street became a place of noise and confusion. Regretfully, her white tenants moved out."

There was tutting from the Birmingham audience and one cry of "shame."

"Her little store of money went," continued Enoch. "And after paying rates, she has less than £2 per week. She went to apply for a rate reduction and was seen by a young girl, who on hearing she had a seven-roomed house, suggested she should let part of it. When she said the only people she could get were Negroes, the girl said, 'Racial prejudice won't get you anywhere in this country.'"

Somebody in the audience hissed, obviously a condemnation of the girl, not Enoch. He surged ahead

"She is becoming afraid to go out. Windows are broken. She finds excreta pushed through her letter box. When she goes to the shops, she is followed by children, charming, wide-grinning piccaninnies. They cannot speak English, but one word they know. 'Racialist,' they chant."

This led Enoch to the last, but he considered it the most persuasive, arrow in his anti-immigration quiver – the lack of integration. He conceded that integration was difficult "where there are marked physical differences, especially of colour," but not impossible. Enoch relished the fact that he could use the words of a Labour MP, John Stonehouse, to highlight the fact that there were factions in the community, Sikhs in this case, who not only made no effort to integrate, but went so far as to display blatant communalism. Remembering Georgy's insistence of the harmlessness of the Sikh's so-called 'communalism,' Enoch failed to mention it was the turban issue amongst bus drivers to which Stonehouse was referring. In his final slam to the Race Relations Bill he described the dispute in 'us' and 'them' terms so beloved by the people he was appealing to.

> *"It is the very pabulum they need to flourish. Here is the means of showing that the immigrant communities can organize to consolidate their members, to agitate and campaign against their fellow citizens, and to overawe and dominate the rest with the legal weapons which the ignorant and the ill-informed have provided."*

Enoch paused, gazed into the distance – actually at his own image in the mirror on the far wall – and summoned as much drama as he could to pronounce the words he'd debated about saying in English or in the original Latin.

> *"As I look ahead, I am filled with foreboding; like the Roman, I seem to see the River Tiber foaming with much blood."*

He didn't think Laurence Olivier could have done better. Then, just in case his poetic allusion had missed anyone in the audience, he spelt out in plain terms his prediction that there would be race riots in Britain that would be easily as violent as those in the United States.

As his voice tailed off to a sanctimonious hush, he repeated the self-sacrificial words of Martin Luther.

"All I know is that to see, and not to speak, would be the great betrayal."

Considerate applause ensued, together with a couple of "hear hears," but certainly not the standing ovation Enoch would have preferred. He glanced at Pam for reassurance. She was the picture of solidity, appearing calm and dressed in a pale suit with a collar of darker fabric. She smiled and nodded once, as if to say, "Good job. Well done." Despite her obvious approval, Enoch was overwhelmed by a sense of anti-climax. He knew better than to expect instant gratification. Hadn't he engineered the whole event – the timing, the venue, the speech itself – for long-term gain? Nevertheless, a bit more spontaneous praise wouldn't have gone amiss. Reginald Ayres didn't refer to the speech at all. He merely thanked Enoch for coming, more like a relative going through the motions of gratitude to a family member who'd dropped in for a cup of tea on the way to somewhere more important. So when the BBC sound-recording technician muttered "devilishly clever speech" to Enoch as he and Pam were walking past on their way out, Enoch stopped to thank him.

"It wasn't a compliment," said the man, turning from packing the recording equipment into a black suitcase with silver latches. The man had silver hair with bristling black eyebrows and a lined face.

"What I meant was that it was very clever in the Machiavellian sense."

Before Enoch could make a comment, the man continued.

"I've been doing this job for almost forty years now. I was in Munich before the war and recorded Hitler. I taped Franco on more than one occasion. At one point today when I was paying more attention to the sound levels than to what you were actually saying, it struck me you had cadences of both. The manic urgency of Hitler together with the strained indignant tone of Franco. Some of the self-righteousness of Churchill too, if I were honest. But then, when I began to take in what you were actually saying, I realized I'd never heard such a manipulative load of ..."

"Enoch we really should be going," interrupted Pam. "Clem and Marjorie will begin to think we're never coming for the girls."

Undeterred the man continued.

"You used the word evil over and again. Let me tell you, yours was the most evil performance I've ever witnessed."

As he spoke the man continued packing away his equipment. He slammed the lid of the case shut. Enoch noticed his hands were shaking.

"I only pray you're pilloried from pillar to post for what you've done today," he said.

"I believe the pillory was abandoned as a form of punishment in the nineteenth century," said Enoch.

"More's the pity." said the man. He grasped his case by its

handle, hefted it off the table where it had been sitting, and strode away. Even his gait was irate.

"At least I seem to have elicited a definite reaction," said Enoch.

Pam frowned slightly.

"You're aware you used the expression yourself?" she said. "In the speech."

"What expression?"

"Pillory."

"So I did," said Enoch. "So I did."

* * *

"You on uppers?" asked Irene.

"Wha'?" said Nelson.

"I hear you find more drugs in prison than hospital. If you a dog your tail be wagging. You on Benzedrine ... Preludin, maybe?"

Nelson supposed he might look like he was happy. Prison didn't seem as bad since the two Jamaican boys befriended him. He liked them telling him about Islam. Mostly because it was something to fill prison time, but he still had hopes it would keep Irene quiet about going to church. But he wasn't ready to call himself a Muslim just yet.

"Tcha! Jus' make couple friend. Some other Jamaican."

"Hope is not no rasta. Them is rasta?" asked Irene.

"Not rasta. Muslim."

"Indian?"

Nelson knew why she asked. Back home, if you're not Christian or Rasta, you must be Indian. There was a family of Indian children in Nelson's school, sister and two brothers. Their grandparents were shipped over years ago along with a whole heap of others to work in the plantations. Everyone called them 'coolie.'

"Them don't come from India. No."

"So what them name?"

Nelson hesitated. Then pushed his shoulders back and jutted his chin out.

"One name Abdul-Hakim Haddad, the other Jamaal Al-Asmari."

The day before Nelson had made the two men write their Muslim names down. Afterwards he lay on his bunk repeating them over and over.

Each word sound good, but look 'pon them together and the two Jamaican bwoys large so! Abdul-Hakim Haddad, Jamaal Al-Asmari.

Nelson drifted off to sleep imagining himself on trial, called to the dock by his new name – even in a dream he didn't know enough about Muslim names to come up with one for himself. Nevertheless he stood, wrongly accused, as the whole world knew, wearing headgear like the ones his two new friends wore. In his dreams Auntie Irene had crocheted the hat and placed it, like a crown, on his head. In court, as the judge pronounced 'Not Guilty,' flames licked at Nelson's feet. But the fire didn't burn him. A bank of TV cameras whirred and press bulbs flashed.

Irene asked Nelson for the boys real names. Nelson wouldn't have told her even if he'd known. He just repeated word for word what the two had said about rejecting their names because they'd been given them when their great great grandparents were brought to Jamaica.

"So these are names their African family had?" Irene asked.

Nelson knew she was testing him. He explained all over again, but slowly, as if she was six-years-old, how African names were lost when traders and owners gave slaves British surnames.

"Where these two hot steppas find this Islam? Lyin' in the cash register they stole from? Maybe it in the pocket of the man them beat up when them thief his billfold?"

"You believe I murder me landlord just because policeman say so? Make sure you know people before you judge."

Irene pursed her lips.

"Well, I'm glad they make you feel so upful, she said."

* * *

The latest face-off between Mother and Abdul-Hakim was thrilling, but Nelson had to admit to growing tired of the back and forth of insult and threat every time the tea trolley appeared.

"Why don't you go back where you came from, bleedin' jungle bunnies?" said Mother.

"Don't romp with you bloodclaat life, me friend. Don't romp with you life," said Abdul-Hakim.

"You realize say him no understan' when you talk patois, right?" said Nelson.

"Your mate's spot on there, Sambo. No nignog spoken here, you know," said Mother.

He mimicked Abdul-Hakim, making incomprehensible blubbery noises interspersed with the odd 'rass' and 'bloodclaat.' A couple of his pals smirked. Mother moved on with his trolley.

"Just through you face look like rudie no mean say you can talk to me any way you want," said Abdul-Hakim.

Nelson hadn't thought about his scar since he was first pulled in. It was funny the Jamaican boys had taken it as a sign of a thug – exactly what he'd been afraid of with the police. He thought these two would have known better.

"No bother skin up you teeth with we," said Jamaal.

Nelson hadn't realized he was smiling. Jamaal spoke stern enough, but his eyes were fearful. His body tense, head down, shoulders hunched. He reminded Nelson of a cat confronting a dog, ready to flee if necessary. Nelson saw an opportunity.

A niggling worry of Nelson's had always been that he was lacking in masculinity. Maybe because he was raised by a bunch of women. Nelson was no batty bwoy – girls were the object of his masturbatory fantasies – but the little house he'd grown up in was awash with female hormones, the place always cluttered with women's undergarments and beauty products. They make him less like a man? As an adolescent he tried hard to appear masculine, sometimes scowling, and talking in a gruff, abbreviated tone. Now was his chance to prove his manhood once and for all. If he matched Jamaal and Abdul-Hakim's tone but came on even stronger, the two would back off for sure. But once won, could he sustain the macho-male Don Gorgon position as head bad bwoy?

Nelson eyed Jamaal, then glanced at Abdul-Hakim. What if he succeeded, which seemed likely? Nelson pictured a spiral, like a picture he'd seen at school of one of those tropical storms that hit Jamaica now and again. It could carry him far above everything, but he had no control of how high the spiral reached or where it went. He could hear Auntie Irene: I tell you wha' happen when you mix up with them kind! Nelson decided to rest on solid ground.

"Me never mean nothing by it, star."

Jamaal relaxed.

"You lucky," muttered Abdul-Hakim.

The moment passed. The three fell into an uneasy silence.

At supper they sat together as usual. Jamaal announced he'd volunteered them for clean-up duty.

"Is good fi serve the whole community. Not jus' we Moslem."

Jamaal shot a look at Nelson, clearly challenging him to deny his inclusion in their group. Nelson didn't think this was the moment to say that he was still on the fence when it came to Islam. He liked the idea of a Muslim name – he'd changed his name once, why not again? Abdul-Hakim had suggested Omar, but Nelson worried it sounded like some place in America. The sacrificing of booze didn't horrify him, and if pushed he was even prepared to forego bacon sandwiches. But he began to suspect Jamaal and Abdul-Hakim didn't know what the hell they were talking about when it came to some aspects of Islam. Nelson supposed he'd been too dazzled by their crocheted hats and solemn air of authority to notice that their Muslim practices included smatterings of Rastafarianism. Nelson thought he remembered that the greeting they used – reespeck – was a Rasta salutation. And Abdul-Hakim had mentioned he wanted to take the Haj pilgrimage by saying, 'mi waan fi go a Zion.'

"Is not Zion," said Nelson.

"Wha?"

"Is Mecca where Muslim pilgrim wan' go."

But then Nelson felt guilty. So what if Abdul-Hakim got a little mixed up in his geography? Who was he to judge these Trench Town boys. He'd had the benefit of regular teaching until he was fifteen. Who knew if these two ever went to school? It was their enthusiasm that counted. But they were sometimes a bit too mean-spirited for Nelson's liking. Their cuss-cuss fights with Mother were too intense. Brian told Nelson that Jamal and Abdul-Hakim had been jailed for inciting murder – the killing of white men who touch coloured women. He described how Michael X had been convicted for the same thing.

"Silly barstard made a big performance of sayin' it in a public meetin' in Reading. You wouldn't fink any bugger in Reading would give a toss, but the press was there and since Michael X had called all reporters white monkeys they made sure the police heard about it."

Abdul-Hakim and Jamaal had been vague about their convictions, but insisted they'd done nothing wrong.

"Jus' like you," they told Nelson.

As soon as they finished supper Jamaal jumped up and started piling dirty dishes and cutlery onto a trolley. Abdul-Hakim and Nelson helped him. Once the trolley was loaded

Nelson didn't see any point in three of them taking the trolley to the kitchens so he started to walk away.

"You is part-time or what?" asked Jamaal.

"You need me fi push a trolley?"

"We need all hands on deck fi unload it. So stop you coming and come."

Nelson followed as the two Jamaicans trundled the loaded trolley into the kitchens. He'd never been in this part of the prison before. Mammoth stainless steel ovens like furnaces lined one wall and black iron ranges ran down another. Beyond was a pantry area in a short corridor where tall cupboards sat above wooden counters. A large boiler sat on one side with a tea urn positioned under its tap. Having passed through the pantry, Jamaal and Abdul-Hakim trundled their trolley into a room with bathtub-sized sinks and draining boards the area of single beds. They all three started to unload food-encrusted plates and cutlery from the trolley onto one of the draining boards. Two prisoners with rubber aprons, more suitable for an abattoir than a kitchen, plunged the dirty dishes into frothy water, white with suds.

"Come on you lot get a move on," said one of the washers-up.

Abdul-Hakim and Jamaal were taking their time. They kept glancing towards the pantry area between the two kitchens. Suddenly they speeded up. Plates were in danger of being shattered as they almost threw them onto the draining board. Cutlery clattered on stainless steel. The trolley was emptied in double-quick fashion.

"Take it easy," said Jamaal to the two washers who were

now fully occupied trying to cope with a mountain of dirty dishes, knives, and forks.

He and Abdul-Hakim strode toward the pantry. Nelson followed. Abdul-Hakim stood at the doorway for Nelson to enter the pantry area while Jamaal walked quickly ahead. As soon as Nelson stepped inside, Abdul-Hakim closed the door to the washing-up area. Nelson could see a figure in prison clothes stooped over the hot water boiler. Jamaal was already at the other end of the short corridor and was closing the door to the kitchen.

At the sound of both doors shutting, the figure at the tea urn straightened. It was Mother. Presumably he was preparing for the last of the endless rounds of tea he trundled out during the long hours of the day. The after-supper cuppa was the last.

"What the 'ell do you fuckin' monkeys want?"

As Jamaal approached Mother he pulled a knife from his pocket. Nelson recognized it as one of the dull-bladed table knives they were given to eat with. They were so blunt the prisoners were lucky if they could saw into soggy Spam or cut sopping vegetables in two. But Nelson could see Jamaal's blade had been sharpened to a vicious point.

"Hold this," demanded Abdul-Hakim and thrust a similarly honed knife toward Nelson's hand.

Thank God he hadn't pretended to be a tough gang leader earlier because he'd have been exposed within the hour. It was little more than sixty minutes since Nelson had debated acting the 'bad bwoy wid cutti-cutti face' that his two compatriots had taken him for. Now Nelson looked with horror at the weapon being forced on him. Abdul-Hakim nudged Nelson's closed fist with the handle.

"Hold him rassclaat and stab him. Jook out him bloodclaat!"

Nelson had a flashback of a knife sticking out of the chest of the toughie who'd robbed him, back home. He was so nauseous he thought he'd lose his dinner. Jamaal was closing in on Mother, who, his back against the counter, resembled a cornered pig, wild eyed and breathing heavy. Nelson couldn't get out of the pantry fast enough. He yanked the door into the kitchen and burst into an empty room. Not a soul in sight. He hurried back to the empty dining hall and on into the recreation area.

Mus' calm meself! Rest man, rest!

He walked in measured steps to the iron staircase where a warden was standing.

"Me no feel so good. The food ..."

He held his guts and tried to appear sick.

"My heart pumps piss for you, Clarke. What do you want me to do about it?"

"I going lie down in me cell. Maybe that will make me feel better."

Nelson, having had the wit to conduct a conversation with a warden, who, God willing, would remember it and the time the exchange took place, climbed the stairs, one hand still holding his belly. It wasn't difficult to put on an Academy Award winning performance. Nelson felt as sick as a three-day drunk at the thought of what might be happening around the tea urn. He prayed to God to please, please, not let him be named in what was going on in the pantry. He prayed to Auntie Irene's God, a Christian God, because, when push come to shove, he realized it was the only God he could trust.

* * *

When the Powells emerged from the Midland Hotel Enoch could see the sunny morning sky had given way to leaden clouds, their charcoal underbellies seemed almost within reach. After giving a speech Enoch usually felt lighter, as though relieved of the burden of meaning his words had held. A problem shared is a problem halved. Wasn't that the expression? But if anything, he felt more encumbered after this afternoon's performance. He'd known the speech would elicit extreme reactions. He'd acknowledged – actively sought – tumultuous consequences of his speech, but being confronted by the unexpected rage of the BBC sound technician had given Enoch pause.

When he and Pam drove into Wolverhampton, it started to rain. The illuminated shop windows on Darlington Street were reflected in wet pavements thronged with Saturday shoppers, most brandishing umbrellas. When they arrived outside the Jones house Pam dispatched Enoch to pick up the girls. The front door opened as he walked up the wet path. He could tell by Marjorie's expression all was not well. However the girls seemed perky enough. They were pulling on their raincoats, all ready for the off.

"You girls go ahead," said Marjorie. "I want a word with your father."

Jennifer immediately skipped down the path to the car.

Susan was a little slower off the mark. Before walking away, she glanced at the two adults, obviously aware of the serious tenor of Marjorie's voice.

"Clem read the transcript of your speech. He was appalled by it, and asked me to read it too. I'm sorry, Enoch, but we can no longer see you."

Enoch held Marjorie's gaze. She in turn didn't flinch. He'd known that people he liked and admired would disagree with his speech. He'd taken into account that some might find it unacceptable to the point where they'd want to disassociate themselves from him. But he certainly never dreamt the first to go would be Clem and Marjorie Jones. They and Enoch had maintained a respectful constraint around political debate in the past, hardly mentioning issues they were unlikely to agree on. Enoch had expected the same in relation to his speech. He imagined Marjorie in particular might react negatively, but the worst he anticipated was a reproachful comment or two.

They stood eye-to-eye at the doorway. Marjorie was resolute, with one hand holding the edge of the door as if ready to slam it. Enoch hovered on the doormat, feeling like a troublesome salesman. He felt a rivulet of rain find its way down his scalp toward the back of his neck. He managed to summon up enough righteous antagonism to disguise his true feelings. He repeated in his head the Martin Luther quote he'd used in his speech, 'Here I stand, God help me, I can do no other.' But he couldn't conceal the sharp intake of breath he needed before he was able to speak.

"Well, I suppose that's the end of a wonderful friendship."

"Goodbye, Enoch," said Marjorie, and closed the door.

As he walked down the garden path to the car, Enoch was struck by the identical nausea he felt when his mother became exasperated with him as a child. Pam looked at him quizzically when he climbed into the car, as if to ask 'what was that all about?' Enoch shook his head slightly, indicating it might be best not to discuss it in front of the girls. An expression of comprehension passed over Pam's face. She wiped condensation from the windscreen with a gloved hand, turned the ignition, glanced over her shoulder to check nothing was coming, and eased the car away from the kerb. Did Enoch imagine it or had her actions been more deliberate than usual? Was there an air of resignation to them? He guessed she'd come to the conclusion that one of Enoch's 'bombs' had indeed dropped, as she thought it might. Enoch had never considered how reaction to his speech might affect Pam and the girls. He knew Pam would remain loyal, she knew enough of politics to know it was best to ride out any storms before abandoning ship. But the girls had lost their canine friend, Topsy. How much more might they be forced to endure until they began to blame their father?

When they reached home the house felt cold, damp, and dark. Enoch had always viewed it as a utilitarian house. He supposed he'd always thought of Wolverhampton as a means to an end, Westminster being the end in question. Was it any wonder the semi-detached at 79 Merridale Road never seemed as homely as their Georgian terraced house on South Eaton Place. Like many Londoners, the Powells had bought only the leasehold on their London house. The freehold was held by the Grosvenor Estate. Enoch liked the idea that the rights to his property were held by the Duke of Westminster.

"Are the Italians feeding you, or shall I heat up the left-over casserole?" asked Pam.

Enoch cursed under his breath. He'd forgotten all about the Italians.

"It's hard to believe, but there's to be no food at the Italian event. I've just been asked to address their members after their monthly meeting."

"Casserole it is then," said Pam.

"I might just catch the six o'clock news on the television," said Enoch.

Pam looked meaningfully at Enoch before addressing the girls who were hanging their macs on the coat stand in the hall.

"You girls go to your room and read until teatime. I'll yell when it's ready."

Enoch realized she was preventing – protecting? – them from seeing the news which would almost certainly cover the speech.

The newscaster simply reported without any fanfare or editorial comment that Enoch had made a "controversial" speech in Birmingham that afternoon. The television people obviously couldn't broadcast the complete speech, it was too long. Instead they included a series of extracts, mainly from the first half. Enoch was glad to see they'd quoted one of the literary allusions he'd isolated on the cover sheet that was sent out. There had clearly been no time for ATV to elicit any opinion or editorial view about his performance. As a result the item was fairly short. By the time the newscaster moved on to the next item – about a local lad who went missing in a sleepwalking episode – the Powells' recently installed telephone was ringing. Enoch had seen little point in having a phone. Anybody wanting to reach him in Wolverhampton could do so at the office during the day. But Pam had thought it a good idea so that arrangements for the girls' riding lessons and other activities could be more easily made.

"I just wanted to congratulate you on a job bloody well done," said a Wolverhampton accent when Enoch confirmed it was him the caller had reached. "It needed saying and it's just as well is was you. It'll put Wolver'ampton on the map, that will," said the voice.

As soon as Enoch returned the phone to its cradle the phone rang again with a similar caller expounding the excellence of Enoch's speech. After the sixth call Enoch left the phone off the hook. He could have stood and taken congratulatory calls all evening, but Pam was calling the girls to wash their hands and then come down for tea.

* * *

"What the hell's going on there?" asked Christine when someone eventually fetched Frank to the phone. She could barely hear him for the sound of hammering and agitated voices.

"The Bolshie bastards upstairs are planning some kind of protest. They're using the hallway to make placards. There's bloody paint everywhere. It seems Georgy's man in Westminster made a speech today that this lot think is downright fascist. They're up in arms about it. I can't think why they get so upset about things. Where are you?"

"Still at college. But I've finished a run of the print I was telling you about. You'll never believe this, but Jerm came in to help me out."

"What's that weasel doing sniffing around?"

"Claims he came in to clean up, but all he did all day was help me, spreading photo emulsion onto screens, making positive films, preparing paper, and generally making himself useful. When I couldn't achieve the transparency I wanted on the final layer of ink I almost wept. Jerm took over and mixed pigment and transparent base to give exactly the strength I needed for other colours to show through. I almost feel guilty now for bunching him in with the other Little Pigs."

"He probably fancies you," said Frank.

"I doubt it. I was so grateful I gave him a kiss on the cheek when he left. When I told him he'd gone a nice shade of scarlet he turned tail and fled."

"Just as well."

"You're not jealous of Jerm Oakley for God's sake?"

"Take it as a compliment to the power of your charms."

"You smoothie. Listen, I thought I'd come over there. I hope you can manage a cup of chicken noodle and some soggy bread."

"You're going to have to kiss me better first."

"Oh, all right then, if I must. See you soon," said Christine.

Frank was sitting on the stairs watching a young woman mop red paint off the black-and-white-tiled floor in the hallway when Christine arrived. A dozen placards were stacked up against one wall. A large black and white photo of Enoch Powell, obviously ripped from an old campaign poster, had been mounted onto one of the placards. Earlier Frank had watched as the girl with the mop had daubed a toothbrush moustache and fringe in black paint onto the photo. Then she'd drawn an armband featuring a bright red swastika. The likeness to Hitler was startling and the armband stood out like a beacon.

"Did you do this?"

The girl nodded, obviously thrown off guard by the abruptness of Christine's question.

"It's brilliant. I mean the idea. The message itself is worthwhile too, of course. But the concept and implementation are mind-blowing."

"Huh?" the girl said.

"You're not an art student, are you? You must be at the Tech.?"

"Yeah, I'm in Catering and Hospitality."

"I bet your cake decorations are amazing," said Christine.

"You know sarcasm is no form of support," said Frank once he and Christine were in his room with the door closed behind them.

"I don't mean to be bitchy, but whenever I see people frittering away their talent I just see red. Catering, for Christ's sake. With the flair it took to create that sign the girl could be making amazing art."

"We can't all be Marcel Duchamp, you know."

"I know, I know," said Christine.

After she'd heated soup on Frank's hotplate they drank

it out of mugs, dunking bread between mouthfuls. Frank winced occasionally as steaming noodles hit his swollen mouth. Afterwards they retreated to the coverlet on top of Frank's single bed. Frank lay on his back, leaving enough room for Christine to lie on her side next to him.

"Don't get any ideas. You might regret it in your condition," said Christine.

Frank laughed, mirthlessly.

"How are things down there, anyway?"

"Shrinking ... I think."

"Oh dear."

"To their normal size, is what I meant."

"That's all right then," said Christine.

Frank told Christine the theory he'd come up with in the pub that afternoon.

"I'm convinced it was Dennis who beat up the Asian landlord. And I'm willing to bet it's why Barry suggested I put Nelson in the photo – to take the heat off his nephew. And it looks like that creepy cop is somehow involved too."

"It's all a bit of a stretch though, isn't it? You've absolutely no evidence."

"Auntie Irene is convinced Fowler's a bad apple."

"How would she know?" said Christine.

Frank told Christine the things Irene had said about Fowler – him being from a white Jamaican family with no reason to rejoice when the country gained its independence.

"Wow, that's wild," said Christine.

They lay listening to the kerfuffle upstairs. A female

voice dominated the unintelligible but obviously heated conversation.

"I hope to hell that's the catering student," said Christine.

A Cream album began playing loudly in another part of the house. Frank was relieved when it drowned out the anguished voices from upstairs – their aggressive tone had prompted a replay in his mind of Dennis's attack. By the time Sunshine of Your Love went into the second verse for the first time, Frank was so relaxed he began to doze off. His chest rose and fell in time to the muffled surge and retreat of Clapton's guitar. Christine nuzzled closer, gingerly laid an arm across his chest. She quietly sang the chorus: 'I've been waiting so long, To be where I'm going, In the sunshine of your love.' Then she wriggled to a more comfortable position. Frank fell asleep.

It seemed like only a few minutes later he was woken abruptly by a man's voice thundering from the room above.

"Those whom the gods wish to destroy, they first make mad. We must be mad, literally mad, as a nation to be permitting the annual inflow of some 50,000 dependants, who are for the most part the material of the future growth of the immigrant-descended population. It is like washing ... watching a nation busily engaged in heaping up its own funeral pyre. So insane are we ..."

Bellows of abuse and noisy curses from the room upstairs drowned out the rest of the man's words. The row was so loud Frank's neighbours and their radio may as well have been right there in the room.

"What the fuck?" said Frank.

He never enjoyed having his sleep disturbed at the best

of times. The bloody Tech students were always making a commotion about something. He swung his legs over the side of his mattress and reached for a broom he kept by the side of his bed. He stood and hammered on the ceiling with the end of the broom handle. The uproar diminished slightly, the man's oratory shrunk to an inaudible rumble. It was obvious they'd turned the radio down.

"Quick, turn on the wireless," said Christine.

When Frank just stood and blinked, half-awake and irritable, she cursed and hurried across the room. The clipped enunciation of Enoch Powell's delivery reverberated around the room in otherworldly stereo sound, a version streaming from Frank's transistor side by side with the low growl from the radio upstairs.

"... discrimination and the deprivation, the sense of alarm and of resentment, lies not with the immigrant population but with those among whom they have come and are still coming. This is why to enact legislation of the kind before parliament at this moment is to risk throwing a match on to gunpowder. The kindest thing that can be said about those who propose and support it is that they know not what they do."

The announcer's voice followed. He described the reaction after Powell's speech from those who attended the Tory meeting at the Midland Hotel in Birmingham. Everybody was said to be full of praise for the Honourable Member's bravery in speaking out.

"Turn if off, it's sickening," said Christine.

She was obviously grumpy too. Frank realized it had been a hard day in the printmaking studio for her and, while she was obviously happy with the results, she was probably dog-tired.

"First turn it on. Now turn it off," said Frank, jokingly.

He hobbled across the room and flicked off the radio. In the ensuing quiet anguished mutterings could be heard from upstairs.

"I had no idea Powell had a Birmingham accent. At least he's not one of those posh public-schoolboys like all the other Tory wankers," said Frank.

"Is that all you can say? Can't you see beyond the sound of his fucking voice?"

"I don't know why everybody's getting their knickers in such a knot. It sounds to me like he's just voicing his opinion."

"Have you heard his opinion? The man's a Nazi."

"Chri-st-ine," said Frank, as one might to an unreasonable child.

Christine started gathering her things together. She tugged a sleeve of her jacket over one arm.

"Do you have any idea what you sound like?" she said.

"Steady on. I'm just saying ... where are you going?"

"Home. I'm not sleeping in that bed, it's too narrow ... just like your mind."

Christine stomped out of Frank's room leaving the door wide open. The voices upstairs grew louder again. People shouted over other people. Frank grabbed the broom and hammered violently on the ceiling. A few pieces of plaster chipped away and fell on his pillow. It made little difference. The students upstairs were intent on competing with each other to see who could sound the most outraged.

Frank had no idea what the hell he'd said that was so offensive. He strode over to the door, wincing as he went, and slammed it shut.

* * *

Enoch had been so preoccupied with his afternoon's performance he hadn't decided exactly what to talk to the Italians about. But he wasn't concerned. He had a couple of hours to come up with something. He preferred original thought whenever possible, but Signora Macchia's friends and acquaintances formed only a small local group. Neither they nor anyone else would know if he revived a past speech. And if he spoke in Italian he was confident he could inject enough life into his delivery, even though he'd said it all before in English. He sorted through a stack of his most recent speeches for one he could revive.

He'd given a particularly jocular account a day or two before of the dangers of government interference to a group of Wolverhampton businessmen at the Molineux Hotel. It was short too, so translating it wouldn't be time consuming. In the speech he'd described a survey, which typified the ludicrous lust for facts and figures on which the government relied to base future policies and regulations, which Enoch believed were meddlesome and did more harm than good. He fished the speech out from the pile and scanned a paragraph to judge if it might work.

*The candidate of the survey is now in a position
to approach the more advanced parts of the
questionnaire. For instance: how many fizzy drinks,*

non-alcoholic by the glass do you drink per week, or, if you take sugar on your breakfast cereals, are the spoons you use tea spoons or dessert spoons, and are the spoonfuls level or heaped?

Enoch chuckled at the next line he'd written:

Don't fill that in if you are like me, and prefer porridge, for there is a separate entry on its own for those who take porridge.

Why in God's name did people claim he didn't have a sense of humour? The sting of seriousness only appeared in his concluding words.

… these government minions are all from branches, some tiny, some large, of this same pervasive, poisonous upas tree of contempt for the independence, dignity and competence of the individual.

He must remember to take out the 'upas tree' reference. It became evident, when he likened the branches of an interfering government to the upas tree, that Wolverhampton's businessmen had never heard of the tree. So they obviously hadn't known that every part of it was highly toxic. His audience looked bemused by Enoch's conclusion rather than incensed with indignation, as he'd hoped. Sometimes he despaired at people's ignorance.

Then Enoch remembered a speech he was to give in May, for which he'd already written a good draft. It was about the machinations of government – much more appropriate for the Italians. He pulled out his transcript and started scribbling an

Italian translation, editing it down in the process to keep it short.

* * *

It always struck Enoch as wrong to be sipping strong Italian coffee and being offered *vin santo* in a draughty Victorian house in the middle of Wolverhampton. Signora Macchia passed around plates of *biscotti*. He'd never understood the allure of the semi-sweet biscuits, rocklike enough to break a tooth, but he took one to be polite. He was aware one was supposed to dip them into one's coffee or sweet wine to soften them, but that would be dunking, which, as his mother had drummed into him, was impolite. Whenever he attended one of the Italian gatherings he thought about his old friend Andrew Freeth, who he met in Rome before the war. Freeth, an aspiring artist, was studying engraving, while Enoch was poring over Thucydides manuscripts in the Vatican library. One of the first things Enoch told Freeth when they met was that he was praying the Pope, who was ill, wouldn't die. Freeth thought it hilarious when Enoch explained, poker-faced, that his fear was not for *il Papa's* demise, but concern for his studies if the Vatican library was forced to close while a new Pope was appointed.

Enoch had once heard that one could only count one's true friends on the fingers of one hand – he found the thought comforting, although he wasn't sure he could fill up a whole hand. But one finger he knew would always be occupied by Andrew Freeth, to whom Enoch felt unusually close. Freeth had made quite a few likenesses in various media of Enoch over the years – the most recent was a painting. If it'd been any other artist Enoch would have had no bones about complaining that the rendition wasn't quite right. He looked like a constipated owl. But since it was Andrew Freeth, he kept mum. Wasn't that what friendship was all about?

"Allora, Signor Powell. Siamo pronti."

Enoch was pulled away from fond memories of Rome and Andrew Freeth. He stood in front of Signora Macchia's ornate iron fireplace, adorned with gold encrusted rococo vases, and stared at the forty or so people ranged around. No need to stand on a chair to be seen as he'd done as a child. Most of the Italians were seated, and anyway, they tended to be short. Enoch was the tallest in the room. They were all, except for a couple of bottle blonde women, dark-haired. Many were dark-skinned, probably from the south, Calabria or Sicily.

Enoch apologized for having to consult his notes, by which he meant his translation. He was aware of speaking more profusely than if he were speaking English. Language imposed certain characteristics – Enoch assumed slightly different personalities depending which language he was speaking. He was quite effusive in Italian. In French he expressed more scepticism, in Urdu he was extremely polite. He wasn't sure what he was when speaking mediaeval Welsh. More romantic, perhaps. He launched into his talk describing the government's prices and incomes policy as a "sustained and successful conspiracy against the common sense of the public." His audience perked up visibly. Aha! He knew the phrase 'conspiracy against common sense' would do the trick with an Italian audience. He continued confidently, savouring the pronunciation of each sentence.

"Unfortunately it is not without precedent for a small group of interested people to succeed in hoodwinking the vast majority of their fellow citizens and thus bringing them under their own control."

There were murmurings of *"certo"* and *"si, si"* among the Italians.

"One of the devices employed is the principle of 'divide and rule.' Look at Labour's recent policy to control inflation. Like all artful dodges, it is basically simple. They tell the consumer the real object is to reduce 'price inflation,' as they call it, by keeping prices down, which they say the wicked producers are trying to raise. They then turn around and tell the producers the intention is to keep 'wage inflation' down, which manufacturers approve of because it'll increase their profits. So employers balk at pay increases, while the workers demand lower prices, each feeling righteous in blaming the other for rising inflation. While the true culprit, government and its profligate spending, appear to be doing their best to moderate the situation."

Enoch paused and glared around the room. People nodded and someone called out *"cattivi."* Enoch prided himself on thinking on his feet during public speaking. "Villains indeed," he said. Then consulted his transcript before continuing.

"This is the method by which tyrants have often risen

in the past – they make each class in the community
unpopular with the rest, so that they can always
command a majority of support for each step in the
usurpation of power."

There were more cries of *"cattivi"* and a few other epithets
thrown out throughout Enoch's condemnation of the
underhand behaviour of the Government. At the end of
his talk he received a round of applause and a shower of
gratifying '*bravos*' that wouldn't have been out of place in La
Scala. Then Enoch was besieged by people wanting to tell him
their own stories of the evils of government. After the hubbub
died down, a married couple came up to talk to him. Enoch
guessed the man was in his forties, but his wife appeared
much younger. He was slight, and handsome in a swarthy
fashion. Had he been Spanish, Enoch might have pegged him
as a bullfighter. She was short, but full figured, with a tight
skirt, waist cinched by a wide black patent leather belt.

"That was quite a speech you gave in Birmingham this
afternoon, by the sound of it," said the man in English with
no trace of an accent.

Enoch thanked him, despite being aware of the lack of any
compliment.

"Forgive me," said the man. "Forgetting my manners. I'm
Enrico Belli and this is my wife Daniella."

"*Felice,*" said the young woman and extended a hand
bedecked by several rings. The display of gleaming gold and
sparkling gemstones seemed excessive to Enoch. Pam and
Georgy only wore slim wedding bands and single diamond
engagement rings. Enrico Belli explained he'd been born

in Wolverhampton after his parents moved there following World War I.

"My Dad made a good friend of one of the British soldiers who fought alongside him in the Alps. After the war there was little or no work in Italy for my father. His English friend suggested he and my Mum and my two sisters move here. It worked out well. My Dad went to work at Goodyear, and my sisters ended up working at the Courtauld factory. Until they married anyway. In those days they only hired single girls. If you got married you were out."

Daniella explained, in Italian, that this was no longer the case. She got a job processing rayon yarn at Courtauld's when she moved to England after marrying Enrico. They'd met in Italy when Enrico went there to visit family.

"You must feel terrible pangs of homesickness," said Enoch.

"*Niente affato,*" said Daniella. "I come from a small town. It's very poor. There is nothing for me there now my parents are dead. I have two brothers in America, but no other close family."

Enoch looked at her with suspicion. He was struck by a brainwave. This was the perfect opportunity to conduct a small experiment.

"If I were to offer you … say two hundred pounds each, to return to Italy to live. Are you sure you wouldn't grab the opportunity to reunite with your homeland?"

Daniella looked at Enrico, who stared at Enoch for several seconds.

"I only speak a few words of Italian, and only dialect at

that. Why would I want to move somewhere where I couldn't understand a word people said?"

"So you didn't understand my little talk?"

Enrico looked down.

"Hardly a word, I'm sorry. I only come to these evenings for Daniella. Although I like meeting all the people. And Signora Macchia's *biscotti* are better than my mother's, but don't tell her I said so."

He laughed.

At that moment Signora Macchia intervened and swept Enoch away to meet somebody else in the group. Enoch wasn't quite out of earshot when he heard Daniella say, *"Quell'uomo e pazzo."* That man is crazy. He hoped, somewhat pessimistically, that Enrico couldn't understand her.

DAY EIGHT

Sunday, April 21, 1968

Not even seven o'clock. But with the warden shouting less than two feet from Nelson's bunk he'd better move his backside.

"Rise and shine, Clarke. Grab your stuff. You're going on a little 'oliday."

"No need fi loud me up, you know," said Nelson, emerging from under a coarse prison blanket.

The warden watched, arms crossed, as Nelson pulled on his jail clothes over his underwear, navy blue trousers and light blue shirt.

"Is where you take me?"

"Not to Butlins 'oliday camp, I'll tell you that much," said the warden.

All Nelson could think was that Abdul-Hakim and Jamal must have made out he was part of Mother's stabbing. His mind in a jumble, Nelson picked up the Koran that Abdul-Hakim loaned him. It was a handy place to stash the few sheets of paper where he'd written his songs. Last thing he'd do is ask the warden to return the bulky book – the less he was roped in with them two villains the better. He wrapped the Koran in his spare shirt and trousers and took his toothbrush from his side of the sink. Since he'd been in prison Nelson had the feeling he was disappearing into thin air. Who was he, with so little stuff? People fleeing from war had more. He patted his shirt pocket to make sure his only Biro was safe.

"Send us a postcard, there's a pal," said Brian from the top bunk.

Through thin fabric Nelson felt the warmth of the warden's hand on his back as he was gently eased out of his cell. Nelson thought he could hear angry shouts coming from other cells, as yet unlocked, but it wasn't until he stepped onto the concrete landing that he made out what the prisoners were yelling through the bars in their doors.

"You're a dead man, you black bastard!"

"We'll do for you, you coloured cunt!"

By the time the warden steered Nelson along the landing and down the first flight of metal stairs, a hundred or more men had joined in. As Nelson descended from one landing of cells to the next, a barrage of vitriolic bellows echoed around the prison walls. He clutched his few belongings tighter to his chest. When Nelson and the warden reached the ground floor the hubbub above them sounded like an almighty roar. It felt to Nelson like he was caught under a towering wave that pounded him into hard sand, his heart hammering, vision blurred, breathing hellacious. Muscles melted, his feet didn't land where they were supposed to. He faltered and glanced over his shoulder.

"Just keep walking," said the warden, not unkindly.

Nelson took meagre comfort from the man's warm hand glued to his shoulder blade.

Slowly, with interminable pauses while a succession of doors were unlocked and locked again, the din receded.

Finally Nelson was escorted to an outside exit and out of the building. He thought he may have staggered down the doorstep, 'cos the warden moved his hand from Nelson's back to support him with a tight grip on his upper arm. When confronted with open doors of an armoured van in the prison yard, Nelson balked. Where was Ruth Barton to come save him?

"Me solicitor need telling, you know," he said.

"Don't worry, son, he'll be informed," said the warden.

"It a she."

"Whichever."

The warden steered him toward the van.

"Is where we going?" Nelson asked a uniformed man he assumed was the driver.

"We're off to sunny Stafford. Your two Jamaican mates stabbed another prisoner last night. Unfortunately his friends don't see too well, they can't tell you lot apart. So you're being moved for your own good."

Nelson thought he might faint with relief – if Jamal and Abdul-Hakim had tried to finger him, they obviously hadn't been believed.

"Is who them stab? Mother? The big one who serve tea?"

"How d'you know it was him?" asked the warden.

"I mean ... them always quarrellin' ... so him dead? Him no dead, right?"

"Lost a kidney. He'll have to piss with just the one now, won't he? The bugger went down fighting though – managed to drown your chums in scalding hot water."

"Them no chums o' mine. I don't really know them you

know. I don't really know them at all," said Nelson.

The sturdy sardine can of a transport van was divided into four cubicles, each no bigger than a water closet. Nelson was locked into a compartment with a single seat and a sliding frosted glass window, a foot or so square, up near the roof. The window was partly open. Through a six-inch gap Nelson glimpsed blue sky, a fluffy cloud, and telephone wires. It wasn't until he sat down that he relaxed his iron grip on his belongings. As the van gained speed, cool air blew against Nelson's face from the open window. It felt better than the freshest island breeze back home. He took one deep gulp after the next. Rhaatid! Nelson thought he'd never breathe again when he heard them prisoners scream for his blood. He supposed he should be thanking Auntie Irene's God for answering his prayers and delivering him from evil.

* * *

"Jesum piece! Look 'pon this place," said Nelson when they pulled him from the van at Stafford prison.

High brick walls surrounded a four-storey building with postage-stamp windows. Deep-set panes were almost obscured by rows of thick metal bars. Every inch of the place screamed penal retribution. Once inside, Nelson was thoroughly searched. Although what they thought he could have picked up between Winson Green and there was beyond him.

"Now son, you're going in the hole for your own protection until your trial," a warden told him.

Nelson discovered the hole was a row of one-man chambers

on ground level, tucked away under three landings of ordinary cells. When the warden swung open a three-inch thick metal door Nelson could see his new home was no bigger than the coal cellar in Auntie Irene's terraced house in Handsworth, and not much lighter. A single barred window, no bigger than a record album, sat too high up to look through. An acrid smell of damp bricks and mortar stung Nelson's nostrils when he walked inside. A'least is me alone, thought Nelson. No more Brian staggering out of his bunk in the middle of the night to piss louder than Dunn's River Falls a foot or two from Nelson's head.

"You'll be let out twice a day. Early morning for solitary exercise, and once after evening lock-up to empty your slops. You'll be given meals in 'ere ... just like being at a five star 'otel."

"Thank you, mister," said Nelson, before the door slammed and the lock was turned.

Nelson hadn't known how to address the wardens. He was damned if he was going to call them sir. Yet them deserve a lickle respect too, nuh? Mister sounded like it'd keep everyone happy.

On a shallow porcelain sink a fresh bar of prison-issue carbolic sat beside a single tap. He ought to complain – what five star hotel have only cold water? Nelson liked the smell of the antiseptic soap but was beginning to suspect it was the cause of his scratchy skin. He placed his toothbrush on the vacant space on the other side of the tap. There was no place to hang clothes. No pegs on prison cell walls – too much of an invitation to hang yourself, according to Brian. Nelson put his spare trousers and shirt on the only chair, an upright wooden one. He placed the Koran on a narrow shelf above his mattress, lay down, put his hands behind his head, and crossed his feet.

Nelson couldn't shake those curses from the prisoners in Winson Green. He had no doubt the men would have gladly ripped him limb from limb if they could get their hands on him. And not necessarily because he'd attacked their countryman – most of them had to have known he never laid a hand on Mother. The fuckery of it was Nelson knew for a fact that some of the prisoners who'd been yelling hadn't even liked the man – they couldn't care less if Mother was stabbed. Nelson could let the anger and resentment simmering gently in a corner of his mind boil over. But he'd lost control before, with those gangsters in Jamaica. An' look what happen then! Better to turn down the heat, maybe wrestle with why the men in Winson Green went on so. If he could understand that, then maybe he'd settle.

Looking at his skin, Nelson knew nobody would guess he had a white-skinned forebear. He'd been told his mother's grandmother was the daughter of a Scotsman who'd come to oversee a plantation for an absentee owner. But Nelson's skin was so dark it sometimes appeared deep purple. Especially in England, where he was cold more often than he was warm. Nelson remembered men in Jamaica boastfully concluding the list of their most recent girlfriend's charms with the words, 'an' she fair skin too.' Everybody knew lighter was better. So why his dark colour so much threat to them men – all white so?

"We is all the same under the skin," his mother used to tell him.

It might seem like something people say to make them feel better, but Nelson knew it to be true. Not far from the house where he'd grown up was a goat farm, which supplied meat to butchers and restaurants in nearby Port Antonio. Their coats ranged from all white to all black, some with patches of both colours. Nelson and the other pickney dared each other to sneak into the farmyard to watch from their hiding places, behind a tractor or around the corner of a shed, when goats were slaughtered. Little Nelson looked on, sickened but fascinated, as an animal was strung up by its back feet, its throat slashed, and its bulging stomach cut open. Blood spurted, steaming heaps of innards ranging from lurid pink to livid maroon slithered out of the goat's abdomen. Then the job of skinning began. Nelson saw muscles, tendons, fat, and connective tissue slowly revealed as the goat was laboriously flayed. It didn't matter what colour the goat had been before it was skinned – black, white or patchy – every goat was identical once its coat was pulled away.

Nelson held an arm out in front of him. He imagined if his skin were peeled away his arm would look similar to a flayed goat. Nelson was about the same size and bulk as Frank. If both their arms were skinned, nobody could tell them apart.

"So is just the skin them hate," said Nelson.

He thought about it for several seconds and concluded it obviously wasn't so simple. What it was then? He stared at the ceiling. A tattered cobweb hung from a metal cage surrounding a bare light bulb. It drifted gracefully in a draught. Nelson stared, brow furrowed, 'til his face was in danger of freezing. He gave up, turned on his side.

"Fuckery that," he muttered.

* * *

Despite deep curiosity about how the press may have handled his speech, Enoch adhered to his self-imposed rule never to look at the Sunday newspapers. But when Pam sent him to the corner shop to buy sugar for a pie she was making, the man behind the counter waved a copy of the *The Sunday Times* in the air and pointed to Enoch's photo on the front page. Enoch was pleased to see a particularly expressive archival photo of him in full oratorial flight, eyes blazing.

"Well done, Sir," said the man. "It needed to be said."

As well as the thrill of achievement, Enoch experienced an element of surprise that the 'rocket,' as he'd described the speech to Clem Jones, had performed even better than he'd expected. Every single newspaper on the newsagent's counter covered his previous day's performance, with or without a photo. *The Sunday Times* article only took up a couple of short columns, but Enoch wasn't disappointed. A quick scan told him the editors had fallen for Clem Jones' ploy and copied verbatim the extracts from the cover sheet sent out with the transcript. Enoch noticed Susan, who'd accompanied him to the shop, appeared bemused by the shopkeeper's behaviour. She examined the newspapers with wrinkled brow. When they left the shop he decided she deserved an explanation.

"It would seem the speech I delivered yesterday in

Birmingham is the subject of some interest. It's likely to cause a bit of a fuss."

Susan nodded her head slightly in acknowledgement. Enoch was often amazed by the depth of intelligence in his daughters' eyes. Today was no exception. He didn't see any reason to expand on what he said, but he was touched again by concern for the possible effect of the speech on his family. He doubted if Clem and Marjorie would have been so unthoughtful as to discuss it in front of the girls before he collected them, but he wondered if perhaps Susan had overheard Clem and Marjorie's comments – which would have been far from complimentary.

At the thought of Clem and Marjorie Jones, Enoch was overcome with sadness. They'd been good company, he would miss them. He hoped Clem didn't regret all the advice he'd given, *gratis,* as one friend to another. Apart from the cover sheet, there'd been Clem's tip about the timing of the speech, which seemed to be unfolding exactly as he'd predicted. The brevity of the articles Enoch had glimpsed meant the Sunday papers hadn't been able to reach anybody for comment before they went to press. The paucity of rebuttals was sure to give Enoch's words an air of indisputable authority. Enoch thought with glee about the next few days of media coverage – TV and radio news tonight, more newspaper articles the next morning, followed by reaction and in-depth reporting on the following days. With a bit of luck the story would run for a week. Enoch grinned at the thought of the media frenzy he was virtually guaranteed, as long as some unforeseen news item didn't bounce him off the front pages.

"You look pleased with yourself," said Pam, when Enoch handed over the bag of sugar.

"I have no reason not to be," said Enoch

"Hmm," she said, and smiled. Then she called to the girls. "Better start getting ready for church, you two."

* * *

The interior of St. Peter's never disappointed Enoch. The previous evening's clouds had dispersed and sunlight streamed down from a row of windows high above sandstone arches on the south side of the nave, which was divided into three, lengthways, by a series of graceful columns. Straight ahead, behind the altar, a single pointed arch directed Enoch's eye, not only to Heaven, as designers of the Perpendicular style had intended, but also, closer to earth, to an impressive array of organ pipes. They ranged, in three gleaming sets, above the full width of the altar. Some reed thin, others the thickness of a young tree trunk. The wooden ceiling was studded with gold bosses and supported by a series of gilded beams. St Peter's was rife with the attributes of religious authority that Enoch revered. The organ played softly as people filed in. Enoch was aware of a few heads turning as he, Pam, and the girls took their places in a pew near the front. Enoch sat on the aisle, attempting to keep his back ramrod straight.

The organ moved into a higher gear, morphing smoothly from a plodding dirge to a lively processional. Clergy and choir trooped down the aisle. Proceedings began. Enoch spoke assertively during the general confession, hardly glancing at his prayer book. He intoned, along with everybody else,

"Almighty and most merciful Father we have erred and strayed from thy word like lost sheep. We have followed too much the devices and desires of our own hearts."

A hymn was announced. Pam had, of course, seen the list of hymns posted and already found the appropriate page in both their hymnals. She handed Enoch his, and held hers in such a way that Susan and Jennifer could read the words. The organ played the introductory chords. Enoch opened his mouth to sing, but was struck dumb when Georgy appeared, wraith-like, at his side. She stood in the aisle holding out a white envelope and waggling it gently in front of him. Her face was clearly illuminated from the row of windows above. Enoch could see lines and wrinkles he'd never noticed before on her forehead and around her eyes. Her eyes themselves revealed stony resolve, but also deep regret. Or was he imposing these emotions on her, having realized from the second he saw the envelope that it held her resignation? There was certainly no doubt in his mind of the turmoil she must have gone through – and then to summon up the lack of inhibition her extraordinary act required. She'd have known he'd be at church. Did she think the symbolism of confronting him there might affect him more than anywhere else? In the office, for instance? The voices of the choir and most of the congregation filled the church, "All people who on Earth do Dwell," but Enoch and people around him weren't singing. Pam stopped after the first line, once she realized what was happening. Everybody within sight stared as Georgy pushed the envelope into Enoch's chest. He took the envelope, but immediately dropped it on the pew next to him. He certainly wasn't going to give Georgy the satisfaction of seeing that she'd rattled him. He studied his hymnal and sung the second line, "Sing to the Lord with cheerful voice." Georgy stood motionless, examining his face. Was she hoping for some kind of acknowledgment? A sign that she'd finally, by this dramatic act, persuaded him of the lunacy of his speech? Enoch scanned the third line, lifted his hymnbook higher, and began to sing, eyes to the front. Georgy turned, and disappeared. Drama concluded, people picked up the lines of the hymn. Enoch sang louder, "Come ye before Him, and rejoice." He stared at a massive metal cross standing in the centre of the altar. Perhaps his vision wasn't what it used to be, the lines of the metal edges were distorted. Enoch was glad there were four more verses during which he could compose himself.

***

Like the rest of the congregation exiting the church, Enoch shook hands with the rector at the door. The Right Reverend Francis Cocks had been a chaplain in the Royal Air Force, and was a Cambridge man. He and Enoch had compared notes on university and their war experience on several occasions. He was normally quite affable toward Enoch, but when they shook hands the clergyman failed to make eye contact, and was quick to move on to the next parishioner in line. Enoch's mental list of those from whose favour he'd fallen was growing quickly. When the Powells emerged from the church porch they were besieged by a gaggle of reporters. A shrew-faced man thrust a fleece-covered phallus of a microphone in Enoch's face. A cameraman hung over the man's left shoulder like an appendage. Two or three other reporters duelled with microphones in an alarming competition for proximity to Enoch's mouth.

"Mr Powell, Mr Powell, would you care to comment on your speech in Birmingham yesterday?"

Enoch would have thought the shrewish man might have come up with a better line of inquiry. He was clearly not in the upper echelon of television personnel. Enoch refused to grace the question with a pertinent answer. Instead he smiled at the camera, but with his brow slightly creased as if in befuddled bemusement.

"Have I really caused such a furore?" he asked.

At that moment he caught Susan's eye. His elder daughter regarded him through narrowed eyes. It suddenly occurred to Enoch that she may well have heard him telling Clem the speech was "going to go up like a rocket, and when it gets up to the top, the stars are going to stay up." Even if she hadn't, he himself had told her earlier that morning that it might cause a fuss. Did she consider him disingenuous by asking members of the press if he'd "caused such a furore"when she knew damn well he'd anticipated that very thing? Enoch told Pam it might be just as well they all wait for him in the car while he dealt with the reporters. She ushered the girls away. Then Enoch agreed to do a short interview with the ITN news crew. The others packed up and sloped off, sullen as children overlooked for a part in a school play. After the questions he'd anticipated and to which he gave pat answers about his duty to speak, and that he was just reflecting the views of his constituents, etc., etc., the interviewer asked a final question, which took Enoch by surprise.

"Mr Powell, I'm curious to know if the speech was cleared beforehand by Mr Heath."

"No ... one doesn't. It was a speech entirely on the lines that he had set out ... I was speaking the official line."

"When you say 'one doesn't' what exactly do you mean?"

"It's normal practice to put the speech out through the West Midlands Area CPC rather than through Tory Central Office. This is my normal practice when addressing such a group and when I am its chairman."

At that point Enoch called a halt to the interview, insisting they had more than enough for a news item, and claiming he couldn't keep Pam and the girls waiting any longer.

"How did it go?" asked Pam, when Enoch slid into the passenger seat.

"Fine," he said.

As Pam turned the key in the ignition Enoch turned to look at his daughters.

"Are you two all right back there?" he asked.

"Fine," said Susan.

***

Frank spied Georgy, slumped on a low wall at the bottom of a grassy slope leading down from St Peter's. She was staring disconsolately at a ring of stone dolphins noisily spewing water into a fountain.

"Are you okay? You look like a lost orphan ... if you don't mind me saying," said Frank.

She looked up as Frank lowered his RAF knapsack from

his shoulder and sat gingerly down next to her.

"And you look like an orphan who's been badly abused. What on earth happened to your face?"

Frank recounted as briefly as he could the story of his beating at the hands of Barry's nephew, and his suspicions about the publican's part in Nelson's troubles.

"The man's a complete bloody menace," said Georgy, frustration and pain obvious in her tone of voice.

"But you haven't explained why you're sitting here looking so rattled. Is there anything I can do?" asked Frank.

"I'm beyond help, I'm afraid. I just made a complete fool of myself by handing Enoch a letter of resignation in the middle of a church service."

"Is this about yesterday's speech?"

"Things have been building, but the speech was the straw that broke this Tory's heart, so to speak. Did you read any of the extracts?"

Frank explained how he and Christine had heard the odd sentence on the radio. He told Georgy they'd fallen out over it.

"Or rather, Christine fell out ... apparently I'm narrow-minded."

Georgy seemed not to hear.

"I'd expected to feel relieved about resigning, but I don't," she said. "Unspeakably sad and angry, yes – but not a jot of liberation."

"Maybe it'll take time," said Frank. He was chuffed at being Georgy's confidante, but doubted he was qualified to offer much help.

"I've worked for that man for nearly twenty years. Since 1949 when he first came to Wolverhampton. God, but he worked hard."

"Really?" said Frank.

"That first Christmas, when I found out Enoch would be spending Christmas Day alone in his bachelor flat. More like a Buddhist cell than a flat, just a camp bed and a folding chair. When I found out he'd be on his own I bought him a small Christmas tree, just a sapling really. I decorated it with jelly babies by way of decoration. Enoch grew all misty eyed when he saw it. He can get quite emotional, you know."

"Really?" said Frank, then immediately cursed himself for sounding like a broken record.

"I remember him telling me his favourite where the black ones. Funny that, isn't it?"

Frank wasn't sure how to answer. But Georgy didn't seem to mind. After a second or two she pulled her shoulders back and sat up straight.

"What are you doing here anyway?" she asked.

"I'm going to ask permission to take photos in the church this afternoon. They're holding a memorial service for Martin Luther King. It'll be wild because the congregation from Waterloo Road Baptist Church will be there too. Can you imagine all those uptight white chaps mucking in with a bunch of coloured gospel-singers? After the service here they're all walking down to the Baptist Church, so even if they won't let me shoot inside I'll get some good stuff of them on the move."

Georgy examined Frank's face. He could imagine what

she might be thinking. When he looked in the mirror that morning he saw that the skin around his bloodshot eye had turned an alarming shade of purple. He had a cut on his forehead and black-scabbed abrasions on his cheek and chin. One side of his mouth was swollen, giving him a lob-sided appearance. He couldn't face the thought of shaving, and his hair probably needed a wash. He hadn't changed his clothes from the day before – a wrinkled collarless shirt and a pair of baggy threadbare corduroys. He hadn't thought much about it, but now he realized how he must appear. More like a dosser after a three-day binge than a serious student of photography. It was unlikely any self-respecting vicar would let him anywhere near their church.

"Tell you what," said Georgy, "let's wander over to Lyons and see if it's open. I'll treat you to a coffee. Once the morning service is over and everybody's cleared out, I'll go with you to ask permission. The rector knows me slightly, it might carry a bit more weight if I'm there."

She stood up tentatively as though testing her legs.

"Right you are," said Frank, trying to sound nonchalant despite being delighted to be taken in hand by Georgy.

* * *

After a bit of persuading from Georgy the rector had given Frank permission to take photos at the memorial service. Worried he may not have enough film, he'd rushed back to college and cajoled the caretaker on duty to let him in to pick up a couple more rolls from the photo department. When he approached the church doors he was amazed to see Nelson's

Auntie Irene talking to a group of people.

"What are you doing here?" he asked.

"What it look like I doing here, Frank? Olive invite me."

Frank recognized the woman standing next to Irene. She'd been at Irene's house on one of his visits there. She'd told him how she and Irene had met in nurse's residence the day they both arrived in England. Irene from Jamaica, Olive from Trinidad. They'd shared a room for a couple of years. Olive told Frank how she'd grown frustrated with always being given menial jobs – emptying bedpans and cleaning up the incontinent. One day a geriatric patient shouted at her to keep her filthy black hands off him and screamed blue murder for a white nurse.

"You should ha' just washed the ol' fool's backside anyway," Irene said.

But Olive had had enough. She applied to a scheme for Commonwealth immigrants to receive teacher training. After she qualified, she was offered a job in a junior school in Wolverhampton. She'd stayed there ever since. Irene had hung on as a nurse. She took courses in her spare time to improve her skills – and so that nobody could refuse her requests to be given more responsibility. She told Frank how she graduated from bedpans to bandages, and was eventually promoted to the casualty department.

"Lord Frank, you look like hell. You no 'ave ointment for your face?" asked Irene.

Frank sheepishly explained that Christine had washed his wounds with Dettol. Irene wasn't impressed.

"You mek sure to buy some antiseptic cream."

The rector of St. Peter's had extracted a promise from Frank not to use any flash lighting during the service. Fortunately, the sunny weather persisted. The interior was well lit by natural as well as artificial light. But to be safe Frank had brought along a lens with a wide aperture and was planning to use fast film. He'd also brought a tripod. As long as people didn't jiggle about too much, he should be okay with relatively slow shutter speeds. Even if they did move around, Frank thought the resulting blurred effect on a photo taken at a slow speed might be interesting. All a bit of a gamble, but he was pumped and ready.

The crowd couldn't have been a better balance. As well as Irene and Olive, there must have been two or three hundred coloured people, mostly West Indians by the look of them. There seemed to be roughly the same amount of whites mixed in. Frank almost shouted in delight when he set up his first shot, looking along a pew. The faces in his viewfinder were as sequential as keys on a piano – three black, a couple of white, two black, a cluster of white, some more black, and so on until the end of the row. Apart from the corny captions that popped into his head – 'playing beautiful music together' and 'a harmonious gathering' – Frank couldn't have been happier. He adjusted the depth of field until the closest faces were pin sharp and the furthest were slightly blurred. It was almost pathetic how something as simple as a variation of focus in a single shot got him fired up.

The rector had also told him to keep out the way. Which was fair enough, but Frank was willing to bet having a photographer there added to the sense of occasion. At one point he noticed Denise James in the congregation sitting with a couple of other students. Denise wore a short skirt and a sleeveless blouse that showed off her sturdy limbs. Tight curls sprang away from her head in thick clumps. She looked more like Pansy Potter, the Strongman's Daughter, than ever. But then it dawned on Frank – a thunderbolt – that Denise may be part coloured. Could it be? It would never have occurred to him were it not for the occasion.

Once proceedings began, Frank got some dramatic shots looking straight down the aisle at a skinny young white man with a guitar slung over his shoulder as he gave a heartfelt speech about the apathy shown by most Britons to the "colour problem." He looked as if he was about to burst into tears. The rector frowned at Frank when he inserted himself between the congregation and a Methodist chaplain to snap a close-up. The Methodist was a giant of a man with horn-rimmed glasses. White robes contrasted with burnished-mahogany skin. His voice was as impressive as his appearance, his delivery almost as dramatic as Martin Luther King's.

"The genius of Dr King was that he aroused a sense of dignity in the negro," the chaplain boomed.

His speech elicited loud and frequent amens. The baptist choir in purple robes and white hats belted out Mine Eyes Have Seen The Glory Of The Coming Of The Lord. Frank purposely took some longer exposures in the hope that he'd capture a sense of animation among choir members, being slightly out of focus as they swayed in unison, sometimes thrusting their arms in the air to clap their hands. When everyone sang We Shall Overcome Frank took a series of close-ups of a little girl standing in the front row with white bows in her braided hair. No hymn sheet for her, she clearly knew the words by heart.

At the conclusion of the service Frank positioned himself near a memorial book to take photos of people signing as they left the church. Next to the book was a placard with a photo of Dr King and a caption that read in large letters, 'A soldier of peace. January 15, 1929 to April 4, 1968.' It would make a dynamite shot as an introduction to the rest of Frank's photos. He was so psyched throughout the service he hadn't noticed the lingering soreness in his scrotum until that moment.

**

When Frank emerged from St Peter's he was impressed yet irked to find a television crew with camera and sound recorders set up outside. What the hell were they doing there? On one hand he was thrilled to think he'd been shooting an event considered important enough for television, but he also felt oddly hostile toward the crew. He supposed he'd never cared enough about his work in the past to feel particularly possessive about it. The cameraman and two others craned their necks to examine the last dribs and drabs of people as they filed out of the church. Then one of the two others, who held a microphone limply in one hand, turned to his colleague.

"Waste of bloody time. I knew Powell wouldn't show up at a circus like this."

Aha! So their interest in the memorial service was quite

different to his. But then Frank had a flash of self-doubt. Why wasn't he pursuing Powell? The man was the biggest news item since God-knows-what. And the Honourable Member was right on Frank's doorstep. Georgy might even help him gain access. But common sense prevailed – all Frank could hope for were a few candid snaps of Powell. They would add nothing at all to his year-end work. Better he keep on the course he was following.

The television crew was packing equipment into a nearby van when Frank followed the congregation as it wound its way along cracked pavements in the direction of the Baptist church. He hovered on the fringes, RAF rucksack slung on his back, gingerly holding a camera up to his face every now and again.

"Hello, Frank. How are the family jewels doing today?"

He lowered his camera. Christine must have joined Denise James when he wasn't looking. She'd obviously been watching him for some time. Her remark coupled with a hint of sympathy in her expression made him think she'd opened the door, by a chink at least, to reconciliation. He thought about how he must appear to her – scabby faced, black eyed, tousle haired, but totally immersed in his photography despite his injuries. An image Christine would doubtless appreciate.

"I notice you're still in love with me enough to ask."

"There's a huge assumption in that statement," said Christine.

Frank rolled his eyes. Trouble was, Christine was technically correct. The L-word had never actually crossed either of their lips. But Frank was so high from the success of his morning of photography nothing Christine could say could bring him down. In fact, in the spirit of the occasion, he felt buoyant enough to spill his guts. What the hell, he had nothing to lose.

"Well, I love you. Probably always will," he said.

Christine's eyebrows shot up.

"Ooh-ooh-oooh!" said Denise.

Mission accomplished, Frank moved off.

"Gonna grab some more shots. See you at the Baptist Church. They're putting on a bang-up tea later"

"He's obviously been drinking," Frank heard Christine say, an obvious fluster in her voice, as he moved toward the front of the line, where the choir was in full voice.

As the procession came in sight of the junction with New Hampton Road, a hundred yards or so up ahead, a crowd emerged from the adjoining street. They were a boisterous group, mostly men, vigorously waving red and white flags. Even from a distance the sound of drums and shrill flutes could be heard. Had the Baptist Church group been on the other side of Waterloo Road their procession would have been on collision course with the other parade, which was heading towards them, into town. But, since each faction kept to the pavement on opposite sides of the street, they were separated by an intermittent stream of cars.

As the two columns grew level Frank realized the flag-bearers were part of a Saint George's Day parade. A bit premature, there were a couple of days to go. But Frank guessed they'd taken the Sunday as an opportunity to amass a good crowd. He could see from across the street that almost the entire Saint George's mob was dressed in costume. A couple of blokes were dressed as Crusaders in metal helmets, their shoulders draped in chain mail. They each carried a sword and a shield emblazoned with a red cross. Others were dressed in costumes that appeared to Frank, despite his hazy knowledge of history, to be from a later period. Drummers sported flat floppy hats and shirts with wide lace collars under serge tunics. Others were dressed in similar styles but instead of drums they carried long poles. The few women in the crowd wore white bonnets and shawls with aprons over long skirts. Even a couple of kids were got up in appropriate attire. Frank debated dodging a couple of cars to cross the road and fire off some shots.

Not everybody was in costume. A group of six or seven lads who brought up the rear were in everyday clothes, although they sported a uniform of sorts. They all wore Levi jeans with bright red braces. A couple sported white T-shirts, the others wore polo shirts. Just as he'd decided the Saint George's Day mob was off topic and a waste of film, one of the lads in the rear bellowed across the road at the memorial procession.

"Bloody wogs. Why don't you go back where you came from?"

Frank had sensed nervousness among the West Indians in the Baptist Church group when the Saint George's Day people first hove into view. Now their pace quickened, heads held high, eyes fixed straight ahead. After slightly faltering, the choir sang more lustily.

A taboo of sorts having been broken by the racial slur, the

yobs at the back of the Saint George's group obviously felt at liberty to let loose with violent abandon. They bayed like a pack of hyenas. The Baptist Church members were pelted with a hail of abuse. They marched resolutely ahead, ignoring the invective hurled at them from the other side of the road.

Frank was quick to realize the potential of the situation. He scurried across the road so he was in a position to photograph the lads hurling insults. They made astonishing shots. Saliva spumed from their mouths as they bellowed expletives. Tumescent veins snaked across necks and foreheads. Their faces were so purpled with hate they looked as if the skin might split, like overripe plums. Frank wished to hell he was using colour film.

Beyond the howling hooligans the faces of the Baptist Church crowd were clearly visible in his viewfinder. Frank had seen expressions like theirs before, in photographs from World War II – tight mouths, jaws clenched, eyes fixed on a point ahead as though searching desperately for refuge. Traumatized people trudging through shattered glass and smashed furniture past gun-toting men who didn't need to scream or gesticulate – the swastikas on their uniforms spoke loudly enough.

After he'd shot half-a-dozen frames he noticed a figure in the crowd on the far side of the street who appeared anything but terrified. He looked up from his camera. Denise James was waving her fists and screaming at the top of her voice. Christine was trying to reason with her, obviously urging her to ignore the Saint George's Day mob and keep walking.

In the other camp the two Crusaders began remonstrating with the troublemakers, telling them to cool it or leave the parade. But by then the opportunity for confrontation had diminished as the Baptist Church group receded down Waterloo Road. Frank had been so involved with shooting he hadn't noticed the television crew set up a few yards away. The cameraman was intent on checking his camera, having obviously shot some footage. The other two were wreathed in smiles, clearly as pleased as Frank about having recorded the confrontation.

"Fuck!" Frank said out loud.

He was beginning to appreciate the full weight of meaning in the word 'scoop.' Frank scowled at the crew as they packed up. He was preparing to cross the street and follow the Baptist group when he glimpsed a figure among the retreating costumed crowd turn to look back directly at him.

Jock McAffrey, Frank's fellow graphic design student, was wearing a large broad-brimmed hat and a sleeveless brown-leather tunic over a white shirt with billowing sleeves and a floppy lace collar. A broad red sash completed the picture. Jock, at five foot five inches tall, looked like a hobbit from the Tolkien books everybody, Frank included, had been reading the year before. He was worth a photo, if only as a joke. Frank ran back toward the retreating soldier.

"Hey Jock. Smile for the birdy."

Rather than smile, Jock's expression was one of obvious shock.

"My God, look at your fucking face," he gasped.

Something about Jock's tone – clearly aghast at the

seriousness of Frank's injuries, but not surprised by them – set off a series of revelations for Frank.

As he'd been shooting the screaming hooligans he'd thought they looked vaguely familiar. They were all dressed the same. Like mods, but their hair was cropped shorter. Their jeans were rolled up higher, way above the tops of their boots. And their braces, as well as being red, were wider … much wider than the narrow ones sported by mods. He realized it was the exact look Dennis Perkins affected.

Then, like walking through a series of doors into a succession of rooms, Frank revisited a number of scenes: the back of Dennis's closely-cropped head disappearing out of the door of the Vine on Jock's heels; Jock being alone in the third-year studio when Frank had returned from the common room with a copy of *VoxPop*; the way that Jock had barely glanced at the demo photo but praised it nonetheless.

"You're a pal of Dennis Perkins, aren't you? He got you to nick my negatives and stuff didn't he, you little fucker? And you know it was Dennis who beat me up."

He grabbed Jock's arm and yanked him to one side of the parade.

"Everything all right, Jock?" called one of the Crusaders.

"Yeah, fine. I'll catch up."

Jock stumbled through his explanation. He'd met Dennis at a Sealed Knot battle re-enactment. He and the other yobs were in the audience.

"I think it was Nantwich. That was a corker of a battle. We managed to whip up a couple of hundred soldiers on each side."

"I'll bloody well whip you up in a minute. What the hell was Dennis doing there? My guess is he wasn't posing as a roundhead."

"He believes in the upkeep of English heritage, doesn't he?"

"Watching a bunch of wankers playing soldiers to some tosser of a King, who, by the way, was Scottish."

"Yeah, but he was the King of England too."

"Do you have any idea how pathetic you sound?"

Jock had the good grace to look sheepish. He took off his broad-brimmed hat, as though in capitulation.

"You must have realized Dennis was a psycho. Why the hell did you get mixed up with him?"

Jock stammered a limp excuse about sympathizing with what Dennis espoused.

"England for the English and all that."

There was a halting, indignant tone to his voice, as though desperate to justify his actions. But Frank had only to shoot Jock a threatening look for the pint-sized Cavalier to break down and confess that Dennis had persuaded him to steal Frank's material.

"I banged into him a couple of days ago right outside college. He claimed it was a coincidence, that he'd just been passing, but now I wonder," said Jock.

Jock claimed he'd refused to cooperate when Dennis first asked him to filch Frank's stuff, but that Dennis had threatened him. Jock thought once he'd delivered the material, that would be the end of it. But Dennis kept turning up, telling Jock they needed insurance. Next thing Jock knew, Dennis was boasting about having "seen to" Frank.

"I never dreamt he was capable of this though," Jock gestured weakly at Frank's face.

Jock McAffrey stood, eyes downcast.

"What did you do with my negs and stuff?" asked Frank.

"Gave it all to Dennis. I'm really sorry, Frank, honest."

Frank couldn't summon up any anger. All he could manage was disgust.

"You're a complete wanker, you know that? And I'd keep away from Dennis and his cronies in future if I were you."

Jock assured Frank he was having no more to do with them.

"Actually, Dennis told me to come to a meeting with him and some others upstairs at the Vine tomorrow night. But it's the last place I'll be."

"You mean in Barry's flat, above the pub."

"Yes. Something to do with his obsession about keeping England English, but if that means more of the carry-on we saw just now I'm having no part of it."

"Why wasn't the bastard here today with the rest of his maniac mates?"

"I dunno. He said he had some business to see to."

Frank watched as Jock scurried away. He looked like a frightened kid beating a hasty retreat after realizing the play battle was no pretence and the fake blood was for real. Frank turned to catch up with Christine and the others.

* * *

When Nelson woke from a long nap, he decided being in

solitary was no bad thing. In Winson Green he'd barely been able to sleep at night, let alone during the day. But at Stafford the upstairs clamour of slamming cell doors, heavy footfalls, and raucous voices was muffled. The hole might not seem so agreeable if he knew he'd be there indefinitely. But, even if Frank didn't get him out sooner, his trial date was only two weeks away. It soon come! Nelson picked up the Koran that Abdul-Hakim loaned him.

"The least dat rass bwoy do is gi' me this book," he said.

Nelson was always trying to get his hands on something to read. At school he learnt whole sections of David Copperfield by heart from a tattered copy he shared with his classmates. At the time, whenever Nelson was asked to do anything around the house, he sang out 'Barkis is willing' in his imagined version of an English bumpkin.

"Him have too much sun?" his puzzled mother asked, laughing all the same.

Nelson decided to give Abdul-Hakim's English translation a try, even though the Koran was an inch or so thicker than David Copperfield, the longest book he'd ever read. He immediately came across a lot of stuff that didn't seem any different from the Bible, about following the true path and being punished if you didn't. Nelson was surprised to run into characters he already knew – Adam, Moses, even Jesus. But whoever wrote the Koran didn't have the entertainment angle down as skilfully as the authors of the Bible, whoever they were. The tale of David and Goliath was one of the few stories Nelson enjoyed. But in the Koran the whole thing was summed up in one sentence: By Allah's will they routed them and David slew Goliath. That no kind of story! And he had difficulty wading through all those instructions about who you could marry and divorce, and exactly when and how many times. It had taken Nelson all day to slog his way through the first two chapters – only one hundred and twelve to go. But by the end of it he was beginning to think Allah was pretty cool. If you didn't have anything to eat but pig and were likely to starve, no worry, go right ahead and tuck into a bit of pork. Or if you couldn't make a pilgrimage 'cos you were ill, just sacrifice a goat instead. Compared to Father, Son and Holy Ghost floating around in heaven, it felt as if the Muslim Jah was right next to him – a real bashy fadda – looking out for him like a father should. Lurking at the edge of Nelson's mind was the man Jamal told him about, the American who said that Christianity was the white man's religion and that Islam was the true religion of black mankind. If it make Cassius Clay fi change his name, it must be so, thought Nelson.

But the one thing both the Bible and the Koran seemed to have in common was the concept of an afterlife. Nelson could never swallow the idea.

"When you finish, you finish," he said.

The thought of death took Nelson into dark territory. He dropped the Koran to his lap and started to think what would happen if he was found guilty and convicted of murder. He'd rot in solitary confinement for the rest of his days. Which wouldn't be many because, even if he was kept in the hole, he'd be killed. Cut down in his prime by a worthless bait like Mother, who'd find a way to get to him when he was emptying his slop bucket in the latrines. He'd bleed to death on a frigid cement floor, lying in a pool of shit and urine.

He shrugged off this version of events and tried to imagine life after Frank proved the photo was a fake and secured his release. After being set free Nelson would lead the life he'd hoped for in the Mother Country. He'd own a house with a three-piece suite, a stereo, and a television. He'd marry – Ruth Barton hovered in his imagination, but he didn't dare stand her next to him, not yet. He'd go back to Jamaica with his family every year with gifts for his mother and his aunts. He dreamed of doing something that didn't involve lugging metal rods up and down ladders all day long. He itched to get a group together to play some of his songs. He was sure Wesley could cajole some of the boys that haunted his music shop to give it a try. Why not? All them famous Jamaican musicians – Jackie Mittoo, Clancy Eccles – just ordinary youths once, must have started somewhere.

When he was older he – and maybe, Ruth – would move to Jamaica full time. He'd buy a house on the hill overlooking Port Antonio. But not like the shack where he grew up. His retirement place would have a proper bathroom, nice furniture, a wide veranda, and a hi-fi. Nelson squirmed slightly, found a less lumpy part of his prison mattress, and let his imagination run free. He pictured him and Ruth in their golden years, sitting together on a shady veranda listening to records of his biggest hits, of which there would be many. Below them a tangle of lush greenery tumbled down the hillside to pastel-coloured buildings and a turquoise bay that mirrored a cloudless sky.

But he could only maintain that fantasy for so long before

the alternative script about his conviction and early death kicked in. Nelson sat up and reached for the sheets where he'd written down the lyrics he wrote after Fowler, the white nyega policeman, brought him in for the second time. Now he had the melody formed in his head he wanted to try singing it full force, heartfelt as any singer back home. What it matter if the wardens and them other prisoner hear?

You gotta love all, no pick and choose
You gotta love all, no pick and choose.
You gotta love all, sisters, brothers too.
The path not always smooth,
And you not always in the groove,
So don't go accusing others,
Gotta make them all your lovers.

Nelson stopped for a second or two, he took a few deep breaths.

Some do their best to change you,
Try to rearrange you,
But it all up to you,
You gotta stay true.
You gotta stay true.

"Raasclaat, it good so!" Nelson said out loud, partly to justify his face wet from crying. Even with nobody there to see him, he still worried he looked like a sissy.

* * *

The Waterloo Road Baptist Church was a severe red brick

building devoid of frivolous decoration. Three arched and leaded windows gave only a vague hint of religious affiliation. A squat tower with a pointed top sat uncomfortably on one side of the roof like an afterthought, as though someone had added it hastily once it became obvious the brick facade lacked presence. The interior of the building was as unassuming as the exterior. Bare white walls met an unpolished wooden floor. A dozen bell-shaped glass shades with plain electric bulbs hung by metal rods from a high ceiling. They cast an even light over a few dozen rows of simple chairs. Were it not for a table at the front bearing a large brass cross, Frank would scarcely have known he was in a church.

Several rows of chairs at the back had been shunted to one side. Two long tables were set up just inside the front door, laden with tea urns, cups and saucers, and platters piled with sandwiches and assorted cakes. Frank detected an atmosphere of cautious relief in the hubbub that surrounded the tables, as though people were well aware they'd made it unscathed through the shadow of the valley of threats – for now at least. People chattered, smiling and laughing as they sipped their tea or scoffed baked goods. Frank spied Auntie Irene, Olive, and Christine. They were standing, seemingly transfixed by Denise James, who was holding forth.

"… grew up in Liverpool. My Granddad was a sailor."

"But where was he born?" asked Olive.

"I think it was Grenada. My Gran told me that's where he was raised. I can hardly remember him. I was only ten when he died. He was quite a bit older than her."

"And your Gran was British?" asked Olive.

"Scottish. She was born in Glasgow. She had lovely skin, like marble. And I've got her blue eyes."

"It can't have been easy in those days, being married to a coloured man in Liverpool," said Christine.

"It wasn't as bad as you'd think. My Gran used to say that negroes, as she called them, were considered quite the catch. They weren't as wild as white sailors. More into family, and all that. And don't forget, all the posh bits around Liverpool, those Georgian terraces? All down to the slave trade. Scousers were used to seeing black faces around the place, descendants of the odd African who'd been marooned in Liverpool."

Denise had her audience spellbound.

"My Granddad saved up and bought a house next door to a Chinese family. We moved in there with Gran after he died. Kids in our neighbourhood were all colours, like Liquorice Allsorts."

"But you don't have the blue ones, surely?" asked Irene.

Everyone laughed, slightly too heartily. Although Denise spoke emphatically – Frank supposed it was a Liverpool characteristic – she seemed less edgy than the last time he'd seen her. There was none of the reckless bravado she'd shown on the day they'd gone to the police station to see Fowler. He decided Denise was actually quite attractive, more like a young Cleo Laine than Pansy Potter.

When Christine noticed Frank watching she came over to him.

"When are you going to see Kathy Stevenson?"

"Christ, thanks for reminding me. I'm supposed to phone her this afternoon. I should get going."

"I'll walk with you," said Christine.

Frank tried to appear cool, but was sure his elation must have been obvious. As they said their goodbyes Frank made a point of telling Irene to reassure Nelson there'd be good news soon, that Frank was sure he'd sort things out with Gorman and Fowler in the next couple of days. Frank was betting everything on Kathy Stevenson, the self-righteous fashion student. She obviously had the conscience of a saint – there was no chance she wouldn't come through.

"You doin' everything you can do, Frank. Nelson appreciate it, you know," said Irene.

Frank was relieved she seemed to have relented as far as he was concerned.

* * *

"Did you realize Denise James was part coloured? asked Frank once he and Christine were outside the Baptist Church.

"You mean you didn't? Jesus, Frank, you're thick sometimes."

"If you're referring to my naïve nature, all I can say is that it puts me at a distinct advantage to other, more jaded, people."

"How's that possible?"

"No preconceived biases."

"This from the man who, at first sight, without knowing the slightest thing about a person, names her after an unflattering comic character."

The thought struck Frank that he probably wouldn't have come up with the Pansy Potter comparison if he'd realized from the get-go that Denise was coloured. Once he was aware of her background, he was quick to compare her with a more favourable image – Cleo Laine, the accomplished singer. Had he fallen over himself to find a more positive image for Denise only after the penny dropped about her background? And if so, was it true that prejudice, in whatever form, was absent when one was colour blind about race? There he went again, thinking about things. It was all Christine's fault. He'd realized early on she wasn't going to agree with everything he said, but he hadn't expected she'd trigger so much reflection. She certainly made the world more interesting, if a bit bewildering. Not that he savoured Christine's fiery spirit when she bollocked him as much as she'd done lately. Where was the positive stuff? Love and consideration?

"You must be knackered. You've been shooting non-stop all day. I bet you've got some great stuff though," said Christine.

It was as if she'd been reading his mind.

She thrust her arm through his and pulled it tight to her body. His elbow ached where Dennis had kicked it, but Frank didn't care. His bicep was pressed against Christine's breast. He could feel its heft through his jacket sleeve.

"Fanfuckingtastic photos. If I wasn't so shattered I'd go and develop the film right now. I can't wait to show you the shots of those sub humans at the back of the Get Knotted parade."

"Of the what?"

"All those idiots dressed like bad extras in a cheap film are members of something called the Sealed Knot. They re-enact Civil War battles."

"How weird. I assumed they were just a one-off, in aid of Saint George's Day."

Frank filled Christine in about running into Jock McAffrey. He told her about his epiphany about Jock's involvement with Dennis and his theft of the negs and working prints.

"The little weasel. If Dennis has his hands on your working material, you can kiss it goodbye," said Christine.

"It won't matter too much as long as Kathy Stevenson spills the beans. There's a phone box on the corner of Darlington Street, just up from the Milano. Have you got any pennies you can lend me?"

Christine crowded into the phone box with Frank. 'Kilroy Was Here' was scrawled in black magic marker over the list of emergency numbers above the phone. Damp fag ends littered the floor, but the reek of stale tobacco was soon overwhelmed by the smell of Christine's perfume, Eau Savage – designed for men, but, as she always said, "who gives a fuck?" It was comforting to have Christine pressed up against him, which was just as well, given Kathy's bombshell.

"What do you mean you can't help? What happened to you not being able to do anything else?" Frank shouted down the phone.

He rolled his eyes at Christine who frowned and gestured for him to put her on the line. But Frank could tell Kathy was in no state of mind to tolerate the kind of guilt trip Christine would lay on her. The fashion student was clearly completely freaked, her voice quavered on the other end of the line.

"There was a man here. Great brute of a thing. I looked out the front window and he was kneeling on the grass talking to Eamon. I didn't recognize him. He's not from our estate. I went out and asked him what the hell he was playing at. He dragged me into the alley at the side of the house and told me if I wanted to keep my son safe I'd best keep my mouth shut about the demonstration and the photograph. He scared Eamon to death. I'm sorry, Frank, but I'm terrified he'll hurt my little boy."

"Did this wanker have really short hair?"

"I've got to go now Frank."

"Wait. Just tell me what he looked like."

"What little hair he had was ginger. Blue jeans rolled up to the calf. Thick-soled black-leather boots, high-cut above the ankle, with leather laces," said Kathy, ever the fashion student.

She couldn't have done a better job of describing Dennis Perkins. So this was the business that had kept him away from the Saint George's Day parade.

"Frank, please don't phone me again. I'm begging you."

Frank cursed under his breath.

"Okay, okay. But you should really go to the police about this."

The line went dead. The dial tone clicked in.

"Fuck. Fuck, fuck."

Frank burst out of the telephone box as if it was filling up with mustard gas.

Two women walking by glanced nervously at him. They shook their heads at Christine, her Art College scarf draped around her neck.

"Bloody students," one woman said to the other.

"How the hell did Dennis know I was going after the people in the photo?" asked Frank.

"He must be sharper than we've given him credit for. Or Barry guessed you'd be on to them. I hate to say this, because we didn't think of it, but it doesn't take Einstein to work out they'd be the ones to back you up about the photo being fake. Dennis or Barry probably guessed you'd try to persuade them to come forward once you realized your working material had disappeared. Barry probably asked around in the pub and found out who they were."

Frank was suddenly aware of the throbbing of his wounds.

"Let's go to the Milano for a coffee," said Christine.

"I need a proper drink. The Giffard will be open by now. I think I can stagger that far."

The bar in the Giffard was almost empty. A couple of older men in flat hats sat stolidly smoking in a corner. Half-a-dozen students Frank didn't recognize were playing billiards. Frank knocked back the rum chaser he'd ordered with his pint of Guinness as soon as he and Christine sat down.

"Don't give up hope. You've still got the interior design student, maybe she'll come through," said Christine.

Frank grunted, obviously unconvinced.

"If only that little bleeder, Jock McAffrey, hadn't snaffled my negs and stuff, poor old Nelson would have been sprung days ago. In fact, he'd never have been locked up in the first place."

Frank had hardly eaten all day. A couple of dainty sandwiches and an Eccles cake from the Baptist Church bunfight weren't enough to sop up a pint of Guinness and a shot of rum. The booze hit him hard, but not pleasantly. His head ached.

"I've a good mind to crash that meeting at the Vine tomorrow night."

"What meeting?"

"Jock told me Dennis was holding some sort of gathering upstairs at Barry's. Some rubbish about England for the English. That mob who were screaming their heads off today will probably be there."

"So you're going to walk in there and do what exactly?"

Frank narrowed his eyes. His head sagged. When his chin hit his chest, he jerked his head up, battling the overwhelming compulsion to fall asleep in his chair. Christine reached over and put her hand on top of Frank's.

"They'll crucify you, Frank," she said. The warmth of her palm almost brought Frank to tears. Christ, but he was knackered. He'd never felt so defeated.

"The windows to Barry's flat must be on the Broad Street side of the Vine, right? There are no upstairs windows on Stafford Street," said Christine, sipping her half of cider.

"I suppose so. What's your point?"

"My friend, Jackie, rents a place on Broad Street, right opposite the Vine. Upstairs in a building on the other side of the street. It's just one big room with a sink and a hotplate. The bathroom's down the hall. Her windows must look right into Barry's place. What time's this meeting?"

"I dunno, Jock didn't say. He just said tomorrow night."

"It'll be dark by about eight. Barry doesn't look like the

type to have curtains. With a bit of luck they'll have the lights on. Does the photo department have one of those long lenses?"

"A telephoto? Yes. But what would a few grainy shots of a bunch of yobs in the upstairs room of a pub prove?"

"You never know, and you've got nothing to lose."

"Thanks for reminding me. Want another?" asked Frank, draining his glass.

"No, and neither do you. You can barely stay upright as it is. We'll go to my place. I've got a Vesta curry in the cupboard, it won't take long to whip that up. And then we can have an early night. I have to be up at the crack of dawn – my train to London is at some ungodly hour in the morning."

"Are you sure you want me molesting you all night? Don't you need to be bright-eyed and bushy-tailed for your interview?"

"The state you're in I doubt you could molest Julie Christie, let alone me."

Frank closed his eyes and nodded in weary acknowledgement that Christine was probably right.

"It's just, it'd be reassuring … you know … to have you there … that's all," she said.

Frank was astonished. Was Christine showing signs of nervousness about her Royal College interview?

"Vesta curry and an early night it is then," he said.

Frank congratulated himself for not having teased Christine. He took her hand, pulled her to her feet, and kissed her – long and hard on the mouth. Christine reciprocated enthusiastically. Frank's bruised lip hurt, but he didn't mind.

The gaggle of billiards-playing students whistled and jeered. Frank and Christine pretended not to notice.

* * *

The telephone in the hallway was ringing when the Powells arrived home from church. The minute he put the phone down, it rang again. Enoch was regretting the decision to have the damn thing installed at all. The only consolation was the overwhelming majority of calls by people congratulating him for "having had the courage to speak out," or similar expressions of approval. The loud tone the receiver made if he left it off its cradle proved almost as annoying as the phone's constant ringing.

"For Heavens sake, Enoch, we'll all go insane if this continues," said Pam. "Can't you phone the Post Office?"

"Certainly Mr Powell, sir," said the operator, when Enoch asked if it was possible to have the line cut. He was vaguely disappointed she didn't voice any opinion of his speech. "We can arrange for just incoming calls to be held, if your prefer. That way you'll still be able to dial out."

Serenity restored, Pam served a hearty Sunday lunch of roast beef with Yorkshire pudding, followed by an apple pie, made with British Bramleys, and custard. Enoch and the girls helped clear the table. It occurred to Enoch there was no day as pleasant as a Sunday – church, followed by a family lunch, and a quiet afternoon of reading. What could be more quintessentially English?

* * *

A little before six Enoch decided to watch the ITN news to see how much of his interview they ran. He was gratified to see his segment was first, with an explanation and excerpts from his speech for the benefit of anyone who hadn't heard about it. Can't be many of those by now, thought Enoch. He was pleased with his performance outside St Peter's, but annoyed when they cut him off before his last statement explaining policy surrounding distribution of the speech. The last sentence they aired, his imprecise line stating "one doesn't" when asked if Heath had been sent the speech, made him appear defensive. He was about to turn the TV off when the commentator made it clear they were staying in Wolverhampton for the next item. The first shots were of people emerging from St Peter's – whites and coloureds in apparent accord, smiling and shaking hands. Enoch was puzzled, there were no coloureds in the regular congregation. But then the commentary explained the footage was from the afternoon's Martin Luther King memorial service. Some wily producer must have deduced it was a perfect companion piece and rushed the footage through. The scene switched to Waterloo Road and shots of a procession as participants proceeded towards the Baptist Church. The newsreel showed another group approaching on the other side of the street. The commentary described it as a Saint George's Day parade. The characteristic Saint George Cross flags were being waved enthusiastically by people in traditional costume, children smiled for the camera. All seemed harmless, until the camera zoomed in on a group of young men dressed in modern-day clothes, jeans with braces and T-shirts. They were shouting angrily and gesticulating with clenched fists. The camera panned to show the object of their rage to be the procession of coloureds and whites on the other side of the street. The commentary stopped long enough so that the racial slurs and insults could be clearly heard. The camera played on the young men's faces, horribly distorted with hate.

Enoch had known their type would be emboldened to crawl out from whatever stones they'd been hiding under, but he hadn't anticipated the rawness of their emotion, the animal intensity of their aggression. Among the curses and vituperation he heard a lone voice begin to shout, 'Enoch is right. Enoch is right.' As soon as the words were audible, the mob of young men in the Saint George's Day parade roared in unison, 'E-NOCH. E-NOCH. E-NOCH.' Enoch's first reaction was to glance around to make sure his daughters weren't in the room. They'd been ensconced upstairs all afternoon doing something or other with Pam, but what if they'd come down without him noticing? When Enoch looked back at the television, contorted faces filled the screen shouting, 'E-NOCH. E-NOCH. E-NOCH.' He sprang up to turn off the TV. Then he backed slowly away, watching the white dot in the middle of the screen fade and disappear. He was slightly surprised when his legs hit the sofa's edge. He offered no resistance, but sank down onto it.

* * *

"Enoch, there's someone at the door."

Pam's shout coincided with a sharp rapping. Enoch looked up to see a face at the window.

"Are you alright Mr Powell? I was knocking for ages, and then when I saw you sitting, eyes staring and looking like death, I began to wonder ..."

"Still alive and kicking. Just in a bit of a reverie. Sometimes the intensity of one's thoughts leaves no room for anything else."

Enoch ushered Jim Brown, the Tory constituency agent, inside.

"I'll come straight to the point," said Brown. Why did people always say that when the point was invariably unpleasant? "Mr Heath phoned and asked me to come round and request you phone him immediately. Apparently he's been trying to reach you."

Enoch explained about the phone and thanked him for his trouble. Just as he was about to close the door on him, Brown turned.

"I just wanted to say, sir, that in my opinion and in that of many of us here in Wolverhampton, it would be entirely wrong that a man who is seeking to represent the views of his constituents, not only now but in the future should, because of a speech made by him, lose his position in the shadow cabinet."

"I doubt it'll come to that," said Enoch. But he couldn't help but wonder.

"I suppose you'd better phone him," said Pam, when Enoch explained.

"I'll wait 'til nine o'clock. Then, if whatever he has to say is newsworthy, it's unlikely he'll have time to leak it to the television chaps."

"Do you think it will be ... newsworthy?" she asked.

"Only time will tell," said Enoch, purposely eyeing his wife. If he avoided her gaze she'd know the answer was yes.

Enoch went up to tuck Jennifer in and to tell Susan not to stay up much longer. The next couple of hours were the longest Enoch experienced since the war, when he'd occasionally waited for an inevitable enemy offensive to begin.

"I'm sure you've guessed the reason I wanted to talk to you so urgently," said Heath. "I'm deeply upset ... saddened, and offended as well as angered that you should deliver a speech which is racialist in tone and liable to exacerbate racial tensions, particularly as I have asked you specifically on more than one occasion not to do so. Also, you've behaved shabbily toward your colleagues by purposely failing to mention your concerns with them at the last meeting of the shadow cabinet. This calls into grave doubt your loyalty to the Party, not to mention your belief in any democratic process."

"But Ted, I was merely expounding Party policy."

"Come off it Enoch. Any claim that you're only echoing party policy is disingenuous ... downright mendacious in fact. You know as well as I that the language and tone of your speech can in no way whatsoever be considered consistent with the party line. Not only this, but it's perfectly obvious that the timing is deliberate, and a strike directly at my authority."

Enoch decided to remain silent. An apology wasn't on the cards and any other comment would have sounded brazen. He stared at a picture hanging on the wall above the telephone. It had belonged to his mother. It was a hand-coloured engraving of the buildings of her school, Merevale Ladies' College in Shropshire. She went there to live with her grandparents after her father became a hopeless alcoholic.

"I have no option but to remove you from shadow cabinet," said Heath.

Enoch understood the words well enough – although Edward Heath was a grammar school boy he'd acquired a well-articulated upper-class accent at Oxford. But for a second Enoch's only thought was how disappointing it must have been for his mother to have a drunkard for a father. He turned his back on his mother's engraving.

"You must do what you think is right," he told Heath, but he was damned if he was going to lie down and roll over, legs in the air, like a subservient dog. This was likely to be the last occasion on which they talked – backbenchers had little access to the Leader, even if he was amenable. Enoch was determined to say his piece.

"I believe you will be Prime Minister of this country, and that you will be an outstandingly able Prime Minister, perhaps even a great one. There is one cause of anxiety which I hope that time will dispel. It is the impression you often give of playing down and even unsaying policies and views which you hold and believe to be right, for fear of clamour from some section of the press or public. I cannot help seeing in this light the fact that you stigmatize my speech at Birmingham as racialist when you must surely realize that it was nothing of the kind."

Heath didn't hesitate for a split second.

"Ever the wily fox, eh Enoch? Play the wrongly accused

racialist and everybody will overlook what you're really up to. Next time – although it's highly unlikely there'll be a next time – I suggest, before you make a play for power, you make sure you're not alienating the very people whose support you seek. How do you think we, who have to put the Party's policy to the Commons next week in the form of an amendment, were going to appear in the light of your extremist ravings? Did you think we'd all throw up our hands and downright oppose the Bill after our measured and well-considered debate at the shadow cabinet meeting? No Enoch, I'm afraid you've badly misplayed your cards. You may have the public's support for a few days, weeks even. But the people who matter will never forget."

The line went dead for a few seconds, and then the dial tone buzzed in Enoch's ear. He put the phone down and looked up to see Pam standing at he end of the hall, silhouetted by the light from the kitchen. Her face was indistinct, but he knew from the tension in her figure she'd guessed the outcome.

"He's frightened out of his wits, and, scenting danger, he's running for cover," said Enoch.

"Danger?' said Pam.

"The threat of my popularity."

"Yes, of course. Stupid of me."

They stood silently, unmoving, for a second or two.

"I'll make a cup of tea," said Pam.

Enoch was overcome by the uncharacteristic desire to talk to someone. He decided to phone Jim Brown.

"I knew what was afoot, but obviously I couldn't tell you directly," said Brown. "I talked to a pal in the press office this afternoon. Apparently Heath had them calling all the biggies all day to find out who they're supporting. The ones that matter are going with Ted. It's really only the yellow press that are supporting you – *News of the World,* the *Mirror,* and the rest. Apparently *The Times* is going to attack you with the headline 'An Evil Speech.' They're claiming this is the first time in our postwar history that a serious British politician has appealed to racial hatred in such a direct way. Ted told them he intended to fire you today and they're congratulating him for having the nerve. Apparently they're going to say it's better for Ted to have you as an enemy than a friend."

Enoch was shaken. He'd underestimated Heath. Never dreaming he'd be so canny to check on the tenor of the press before delivering his *coup de grâce* – on a Sunday of all days.

"There's something else," said Brown. "Heath put out a statement, but with an embargo. He'll have had it lifted as soon as he finished talking to you. Your firing will almost certainly be on the ten o'clock news."

Enoch was dreading watching the television. Sure enough, the segment ran with clips from his speech, and yet again they ran footage of the youths in the St George's Day parade. He studied Pam to gauge her reaction. Would the disgust any decent person would experience attach itself to him after the hooligans chanted his name in amongst their vitriol? If she was shocked she didn't show it, her face devoid of expression. Then the newsreader recited a brief statement from Heath saying that he'd "sacked Mr Powell from shadow cabinet with the greatest regret for delivering a speech that was racialist in tone, inflammatory, and liable to damage race relations in this country. I am determined to do everything I can to prevent racial problems developing into civil strife. This means that these questions must be treated with moderation and with toleration."

Before either of them had a chance to turn off the television there was a loud knock at the door.

"That can only be the police, or a journalist," said Pam. "And it's probably the latter. Just as well I drew the curtains."

Judging by the pandemonium when Pam opened the front door – voices shouting disparate questions – several reporters were at the door.

"My husband has gone to bed. He will write to Mr Heath tomorrow and has no further comment to make tonight."

With that Pam firmly closed the door and shot the bolt into place, making it perfectly clear she meant what she said.

"They'll be back in the morning," said Pam. "Once we're sure they've left, I suggest we bundle the girls up and drive to London."

"Doesn't that have echoes of the flight into Egypt?" said Enoch.

"Quite the reverse. If we go to London it will appear you're addressing the issue head on from the capital, not cowering in your constituency."

Pam was the voice of reason, as usual. She cleared out the kitchen, packing up whatever food they had, while Enoch roused Susan and Jennifer. Susan stood looking on with bleary-eyes as he explained to Jennifer. "I made a speech that all the newspapers and television are interested in, so we must go to London right away so I can talk to them about it bright and early tomorrow."

Enoch was aware of Susan looking on, bleary-eyed but attentive. As he led the way downstairs carrying suitcases, he heard Jennifer say something to Susan about a classmate.

"I bet Helen Lloyd's daddy never has to rush to London in the middle of the night."

"Helen Lloyd's daddy doesn't make speeches," replied Susan.

DAY NINE

Monday, April 22, 1968

"I thought Winson Green was bad. Wha' make them bring you here?" asked Irene.

"Them say is for me own protection," said Nelson.

"Is wha' kinda trouble you go get youself into?"

"The two Jamaican fellows I was talking 'bout attack another guy, a white guy and … tcha … anyway, them say is better for me here … revenge and so forth."

Irene frowned, but said nothing. Nelson knew there were probably a hundred thoughts Auntie had about them hot steppa Muslims now. He knew full well she bit her tongue for his sake. He wished he could jump the table and squeeze the daylights out of her.

"At least you not going on like you high," said Irene.

He couldn't hug her, but at least Auntie Irene had one less thing to worry about because of him. She told Nelson she'd seen Frank at the Martin Luther King memorial service – that he'd run into a bit of trouble.

"Wha' trouble?"

"That bwoy you work with beat him up."

"That rass Dennis?"

"Watch your mouth! Yes, Dennis, but Frank no hurt so bad. Superficial cuts and bruises is all. He jump around with that camera lively enough. He say to tell you everything will be all right soon."

"That funny Frank say that, you know. I have a dream where him set me free. I finish back home, but in a real bashy house on a hill by Port Antonio."

"Pray God it come true."

"You going back to Jamaica when you done work?"

"Maybe a holiday, but here is my home now."

"You no miss things?"

"No a lot to miss after twenty year. I forget more 'bout Jamaica than I remember. Grey day 'pon grey day in England I sometimes think 'bout the way sunlight bounce off water back home. When I a gyal I lie on me back and look 'pon them banana palm. Leaves big so, like elephant ears. With sun behind, them glow like a church window. Whole heap of different colour of green, dark then bright depending the breeze. From when I first come to England I try everything – paraffin lamp, hot water bottle – but nothing warm me like the Caribbean sun. My new electric blanket come close. I slide between them hot sheets, close my eyes, and pretend I look 'pon banana palm leaves. It work for five minutes 'fore I worry fi fall asleep and the thing electrify me to death."

"Them make you retire some day, nuh?"

"And if I go back what I going do there?"

"Wha' you a go do here if you no work?"

"Whole heap of stuff to do here after nursing finish. Old people need looking after. No shortage of hair to straighten."

"Gyal want coolie hair in Jamaica too, you know."

"I tell you Nelson, I will miss things here if I live back there."

"What things?"

"Christmas. Christmas Day feel wrong to me now if it hot so, like in Jamaica. And what about Coronation Street? I wonder what happen to Ken Barlow, or who Elsie Tanner shack up with next. And you caan beat a British strawberry with double cream ... or a pork pie from the butcher in Bull Ring market."

"Plenty good food back home too."

"Look Nelson, it take me long enough to get accustom to this damn country for me to leave it when I old."

Auntie Irene's laughter set her rolls of fat jiggling. A warden, who'd been standing behind her, expressionless as a rock, smirked. Nelson laughed despite himself. For a few minutes he forgot about where he was or why he was there – he could almost have been home joking with his mother or one of his other aunts.

"Anyway, it may be that none of us stay. Enoch Powell have his way we all going back on the next boat."

Nelson crashed back to earth – and to the prison visiting room.

"Who? Wha' you a say, Auntie?"

Irene told him about how the government man was stirring up trouble for immigrants.

"After I come to England he was Minister of Health. Him greet nurses and doctors from back home with open arm. Now his arms not so open. Is like him invite us to a party, but just when we having a good time we have to leave."

Nelson was surprised how troubled he was at the thought of being forced back to Jamaica. And it wasn't only being found by the two gangsters who saw him knife their friend, or by the local police that disturbed him. His dream of a three-piece suite and a stereo would never come true if he left England. And more times than not lately Ruth Barton was sitting on the settee next to him as they listened to the Pioneers on the record player.

* * *

On the way to see Diana Throgmorton Frank idly thought about the shapely female figure that the name Diana never failed to conjure up. The actress Diana Dors was probably to blame. She'd once described herself as, 'the only sex symbol Britain has produced since Lady Godiva.' Frank was always childishly amused by her real name, Diana Fluck.

Then there was Diana of the song that rocketed Canadian crooner, Paul Anka, to fame. Frank had heard Anka's Diana was a member of his church. Whoever she was, she must have had impressive charms, as Anka alluded to them, to inspire such a heartfelt – if soppy – song. Frank wondered if her charms matched those of Diana Dors, which were legendary.

And finally there was Diana, Roman Goddess of the hunt. The depictions Frank had seen of her in Art History classes portrayed her as rather mannish, more god than goddess.

If Diana Throgmorton resembled any of the three, it was the latter. Although Frank had to hand it to her, she obviously tried. The interior design student looked like Princess Anne after a makeover by Honey magazine (tagline: 'Young, Gay, and Get-Ahead'). But no amount of blonde hair dye, mascara, or eye shadow could soften Diana's horsey visage. She had a nose that never seemed to end, and a mouth full of more and bigger teeth than any one human would ever need. Diana's attempts at being 'young, gay and get-ahead' had obviously not extended to her wardrobe. She was as county as a fox hunt meet. She wore tan brogues, a below-the-knee tweed skirt, and a lamb's wool twinset the Queen Mother would have been proud of.

"Hell-owe," she boomed, her hand outthrust. Her handshake was as bone crushing as Christine's fiddle-playing folkie friend, Big Al.

"These chaps were telling me you were trying to get in touch."

She held on to Frank's hand for a couple of seconds too long. Out of the corner of Frank's eye he could see the 'chaps,' the heavy student with frizzy black hair and the slender, fair-haired boy, hands clamped to mouths, barely able to contain themselves.

"So sorry I've been so dreadfully elusive," said Diana. Her dramatic delivery, plummy vowels, and clipped consonants reminded Frank of actress Celia Johnson in one of the last scenes of Brief Encounter: *'I felt the touch of his hand on my shoulder for a moment. And then he walked away … out of my life forever.'*

Frank launched into his confession about faking the demo photo and the serious implications for his friend, Nelson. He hadn't even shown Diana the photo before she interrupted him.

"Tell you what, let's trot over to the Giffard. You can buy me a barley wine and tell me *awll* about it."

If it hadn't been for the context Frank wouldn't have known it was the word 'all' he'd heard. Diana was a woman after his own heart – to suggest a drink barely five minutes after opening time. Nevertheless, he felt like a working stiff being humoured by an aristocratic charity do-gooder. And a flirtatious one at that. Diana leaned in a little too closely when she talked. Frank could smell Nescafé on her breath. And she frequently dampened her lower lip with a plump tongue. She practiced a bit of quasi-demure lowering of eyelids followed by quick glances. She obviously fancied him. Frank remembered one of her fellow students saying she liked rough types. Perhaps she found his injuries appealing, now that they weren't quite so horrific. The swelling around his eye had diminished, a careful but thorough face washing had helped reduce some of the scabs, and the other bumps and bruises were on the mend. Perhaps he could finagle Diana's obvious attraction to him into persuading her to go to the police. Frank wasn't above using a bit of masculine allure if it would get Diana to cooperate.

Fortunately they were the Giffard's first customers of the day. Frank was relieved he could play the part without anybody seeing him. The barmaid was too intent on stocking the bar with bottled beer to take any notice. He made a point of taking a seat next to the coquettish interior design student on one of the leather benches that lined the walls so that he could occasionally let his arm or thigh brush up against hers.

"You must surely remember, Diana," said Frank.

He'd read somewhere that using a first name in a sentence

was a turn-on for women. He flashed her a smile and tapped the copy of *VoxPop* he'd placed on the table in front of her in the hope she'd actually look at the photograph instead of gaze at his mouth like a ravenous predator.

"It would be very helpful if you could just tell the police that my friend Nelson here was definitely not at the demonstration."

Frank tapped the photo again, but to no effect.

"That day was such a blur, Frank."

Was she employing the same first-name flirting tactic?

"I was a dreadful mess. Taffy had been such a brute."

"Taffy Thomas, the sculptor?"

"Yes, do you know him?"

"Er, yes. Everybody knows Taffy, don't they?"

"A damn sight too many people are intimate with Taffy, if you ask me. I only agreed to attend that ridiculous demonstration – against my better judgement I might add – because Taffy would be there."

"Let me get this straight. You and he were ..."

"Together? I believed so. I let him into my bed, for Heavens sake."

Frank almost winced at the image that popped into his head, but managed to hold what he hoped was an expression of sympathy.

"But then – it must have been mere minutes before you snapped the photograph – he had the nerve to tell me he was seeing another student. And to add insult to injury he told me he'd brought her along to the bloody march."

"Kathy Stevenson."

"Good God. Does everyone in the whole art college know her but me?"

"That's her there," said Frank, pointing to the photograph. Diana snatched the newspaper from the table and stared at the photo.

Finally!

"The unspeakable sod," said Diana.

"I don't remember seeing Taffy when I took the photo."

"The little *bahstard* took off just after he broke the news to me. But I had no idea the other woman was standing mere feet away."

Diana was laying it on thick – a foul-mouthed RADA-trained actress going for an Oscar. She rifled in her handbag and unearthed a wrinkled handkerchief. She dabbed her dry eyes.

"Really, Frank, the man's a monster."

"You're definitely better off without him, Diana. Now about my pal Nelson …"

"You're remarkably empathetic, Frank."

Diana pressed her thigh against his.

"Perhaps you'd like to come out to the house this afternoon. I have my own flat, quite separate from my parents' quarters."

Frank wasn't prepared to go as far as a private tryst. He put on the brakes.

"I think my girlfriend might have something to say about that."

It was immediately obvious he'd put his foot down too hard. The atmosphere turned as frigid as Aberdeen in December. Diana dropped any pretence at tears. She put her handkerchief back in her handbag. She sat back, pulling her thigh well away from Frank's, took a sip of her drink, and glanced around the pub.

"So, do you think we could fix on a time when you can come with me to talk to the police?"

She examined Frank as if she'd barely been aware of his existence, an inconsequential minion suddenly attracting notice.

"Are you completely insane? Daddy would have a complete meltdown if he found out I'd been marching in a student demonstration. I had to beg him to let me go to art school in the first place."

"So you were marching in an anti-racist march, but you won't lift a finger to help my wrongly accused Jamaican friend?" said Frank.

"I couldn't have cared tuppence what the stupid march was for. I was only there because of Taffy. As far as I'm concerned, they can send every single one of those people back where they came from."

She put her glass down, crossed her arms and glared at Frank, a show-horse filly refusing to jump.

"You know I always considered Enoch Powell to be a bit of a pill. We knew him from the Albrighton Hunt. He left after he made a complete idiot of himself over a perfectly lovely woman member."

Frank considered pointing out that Diana didn't appear exactly rational when it came to her own romantic involvements, but a rebuffed posh person isn't easy to interrupt. And if he were honest, he'd have to admit he was slightly scared of her. The intimidation of the privileged classes was hard to withstand, even for Frank.

"But Enoch proved his mettle in Birmingham on Saturday.

He delivered a corker of a speech. Daddy says he may not have gone to the right schools but his policies are top notch. If the rest of our men in Whitehall had half of Enoch's backbone the party would be in much better shape."

Frank wouldn't have believed it, but Diana's eyes actually flashed. He had to hand it to her she was passionate. He could see why Taffy might have been drawn to her.

"Ted Heath's a socialist ninny compared to Powell," Diana concluded.

She glared at Frank.

"So there's no chance you'll help then?" he asked.

Diana's loud exclamation of frustrated disdain reverberated through her upper class adenoids. She grabbed her bag and stalked out of the pub. The barmaid, who'd moved on from stacking bottles to polishing glasses, looked at Frank, eyebrows raised in puzzled sympathy.

The encounter had been completely absurd – like a twisted TV comedy sketch from That Was The Week That Was. Frank might have been inclined to laugh, but when he thought of the sinister overtones of Diana's remarks, not to mention the ramifications for Nelson, he put his head face down on the table and groaned.

* * *

Enoch was relieved to be back in his house on South Eaton Place. Bellowing Black Country youths seemed as remote as a tribe of Amazonian Indians from the respectable stucco facades and graceful wrought iron railings of Belgravia. Enoch had been on the telephone more or less all morning, fielding calls. Since his London number was unlisted he was fairly certain if he picked up the phone he wouldn't hear some frenzied fanatic, bellowing about it being "about bloody time somebody said something," or a so-called liberal calling him every obscene name known to man. He'd arranged various interviews with the press, which stopped them from pestering him, although a couple of reporters skulked on the pavement outside the house. Without exception, calls from colleagues were positive. Fellow MPs Duncan Sandys, Gerald Nabarro, and Teddy Taylor all voiced their unqualified support. But Enoch was more interested in who *hadn't* called. Not a single member of the shadow cabinet, but Heath would have seen to that. Nevertheless, Enoch thought he might have had a discreet communication from Margaret Thatcher. She'd often voiced her admiration. And Enoch heard she'd told Heath she was convinced Enoch was no racist, however selective quotations from his speech may have sounded. But Thatcher was obviously playing it safe, steering well clear of someone the Leader denounced as a pariah. Not a peep either from his old friend and sometime nemesis, Iain Macleod. They'd had their ups and downs but Enoch still held a glimmer of a hope Macleod would come through.

When the phone rang again it was Jim Brown, the constituency agent, calling from Wolverhampton.

"I just wanted you to know, Mr Powell, we're about to put out a statement deploring your unjustified dismissal from the shadow cabinet."

"Thank you for telling me," said Enoch. "Local support will help those too blind to see that I was entirely correct in my assessment of the situation in Wolverhampton."

"We've touched on that too, pointing out that you've had the courage to expose the true facts about the constituency. And we've expressed our appreciation of your eighteen years of energetic assistance and dedicated service to all your constituents, regardless of race or colour."

Despite Brown's stuffed-shirt tone, Enoch had to swallow to find his voice.

"Thank you, the support of everyone in the constituency organization is very important to me, as always."

Just as he was about to ring off he had a thought.

"Are you in the office at the moment?"

"Why, yes," said Brown. "We've been using the Gestetner to make copies of our statement."

"I wonder if you'd mind looking up Mrs Verington-Delaunay's home phone number in the staff directory?"

"Five Four Two Nine," said Georgy when she picked up the phone. Enoch found it endearing that she hadn't lost the habit of reciting her phone number when answering.

"I hope I'm not disturbing you."

There was a slight pause.

"No more than usual," Georgy said. He didn't know why the sound of her contralto voice took his breath away. He'd heard it a thousand times.

"You'll have heard the news," he said.

"Did you phone to give me the satisfaction of saying I told you so?"

"A battle may be lost, but I could yet win the war."

"Delusional as ever," said Georgy.

"The rest of your colleagues in the constituency seem to be throwing their support behind me."

"Ex-colleagues. And, as you well know, I have little regard for their political acuity."

Georgy had always known exactly where to thrust the dagger.

"I see the liberals of the world are queuing up to denounce you," she said. "Didn't I read something about Jeremy Thorpe believing there might be a *prima facie* case against you for incitement?"

"It's incumbent on him to say something dramatic, he's the leader of the Liberal party. As underdogs they always have to do everything possible to draw attention to themselves."

"True, but isn't Ted Leadbitter, a lowly Labour MP, making noises about referring you to the Director of Public Prosecutions?"

"Even were I to grant that there was a case against me under the law – which is preposterous – I don't think anybody would dare charge me. The provinces would be up in arms."

"It'd be a travesty if that was all it came down to, wouldn't it?"

"To what exactly?"

"Your perceived provincialism pitted against the political pooh-bahs in Westminster. I'll say one thing about that speech, Enoch, it's exposed the massive divide between the country and the Establishment. Which is good fodder for the press but let's face it, the Establishment – Heath or Wilson, it hardly matters which – will persevere. They always do. And where will that leave you?"

"The tide of public opinion against Heath – against all the old political leaders of every stripe – is beginning to turn. As you've implied it's becoming obvious I spoke for the majority of the country."

"We could debate that, but without empirical evidence – actual numbers – there's little point. One thing is certain, Enoch, the manner in which you spoke meant you weren't speaking for the Conservative Party – or any other existing party. And without an alliance you have no power. What are you going to do, form your own political party? Someone less in thrall to tradition may one day be able to, but not you. You're too committed to the old order, the monarchy, and all the other archaic institutions you revere."

Enoch stood at the floor to ceiling window gazing at the porticoes of the houses opposite, supported by pristine cream-coloured pillars. He hadn't realized until that moment precisely why he'd phoned Georgy. He became acutely aware of a longing he'd rarely felt since he was a child. Pam was marvellous, stood by him no matter what. But he craved the on-going support and motivation Georgy had supplied in the past – the same hard-bitten succour he'd received from his mother.

"It's true 'the manner in which I spoke,' as you put it, might not reflect the Conservative Party as it exists at present, but has it not occurred to you that the Party could change?" said Enoch. "It can't simply ignore somebody within their ranks who has successfully articulated what a huge segment of the population have been thinking, but were unable to express. Doesn't the idea of working for such a person excite you?"

"You're half right, in that the Party won't ignore the phenomena you've created. You of all people should know Conservatives believe in the value of the lessons of experience, and that past events should shape policy as much if not more than hypotheses. They'll sort through your ideas and your statements like buyers at a jumble sale, and grab the ones that have struck a chord or proved effective. But they will ignore *you*, Enoch. They'll marginalize you into complete and impotent oblivion. So in answer to your question I ask you – why would I work for a man who's condemned his career to the wilderness, and in the process wounded, perhaps mortally, the country he loves?"

Enoch turned away from the pillared portico of the house opposite and stood with his back to the window. He floundered, searching for something, anything, to say that might persuade Georgy she was wrong. But he couldn't think of a single solitary word or phrase.

"How, in God's name, have I wounded the country?" he eventually asked.

"I don't suppose you've heard about the attack on the Crooks family?" Georgy asked.

The name rang a bell but Enoch drew a blank.

"You remember Wade Crooks. The affable window cleaner who used to wash our windows at the office?" she said.

"I think I remember," said Enoch. "A Jamaican, wasn't he?"

"That's the man. Wade was hosting a christening party for his grandson yesterday when fourteen white youths burst in. They asked Wade why he didn't go back to his own country and when he didn't reply one of them slashed his face. Wade needed eight stiches above his left eye."

"This is exactly the type of violence I've been warning about," said Enoch.

"No Enoch, this is exactly the type of violence you have fomented. As they slashed his face the youths chanted 'Powell, Powell.' When I saw Wade this morning he told me nothing like this had ever happened since he arrived in Wolverhampton in 1955. But today incidents like it are taking place in cities and towns the length and breadth of Britain, where they've never happened before. And the perpetrators are chanting, 'Powell, Powell.'"

Enoch closed his eyes.

"Congratulations, Mr Powell," said Georgy.

The line went dead.

* * *

"Enoch, why are you standing staring into space? I've been calling you. We're on our way now."

Pam held a newspaper in one hand and what appeared to be a letter in the other.

"It's just as well Jeffa is going to stay in Buckinghamshire for a few days. She's admitted to feeling a bit peaky. Complains about her stomach churning."

"Shouldn't she see a doctor, in the eventuality of it being something we should be concerned about?" asked Enoch.

"No need, she's just upset because she's heard people saying horrible things about her precious father. You know how she adores you. Best to get her out of London for a while."

Enoch wondered if being out of London might be any better. But his younger daughter would be with friends of Pam, which assured some insulation from his critics and naysayers.

"It was a miracle I spied this letter from Diana in the mountain of letters the Royal Mail just delivered," said Pam. "It's rather sweet. I thought you might like to read it."

She handed Enoch a couple of pale blue sheets of Basildon Bond covered with the exuberant handwriting of Pam's friend with whom Jennifer would be staying. The address was typeset at the top of the first sheet.

The Manor
East Witticombe
Knotty Green
Beaconsfield
Buckinghamshire

Dear Pam,

Splendid speech, splendid Times *front page today after yesterday's debacle. In their present frame of mind they must have given themselves schizophrenia printing that headline. One would really think that the editor was Malcolm X.*

Thank goodness for Enoch – all the others pussyfoot round in terror of saying anything that means anything, & too blind to see half a generation in front of their own noses. I reckon Ted the Teeth is about to lose his queen in two moves (one could be funny about this retrospectively, but I resist because it would be actionable).

I hope you've got a vast bevy of extra secretarial assistance prudently laid on. This is fan mail that needs no answer – looking forward to seeing you when you drop Jennifer off and hearing it all from the horse's mouth. That sounds dreadfully insulting, but you know what I mean,
Much love, Diana

"What does she mean by the 'splendid *Times* front page?'" Pam held up the newspaper she was holding. It featured a large photo of her and Enoch as they emerged from St Peter's. Enoch was struck by how untroubled they appeared.

He looked particularly affable, smiling broadly. The headline screamed 'Powell out of Shadow Cabinet,' but there was a smaller headline to the left, the one Diana must have been referring to. It read 'Tory MP speaks of tragedy.' Enoch took the newspaper from Pam. It quoted a Tory MP, John Jennings of Burton, who described Enoch's dismissal as a 'tragedy that one of the few men who really abide by fundamental Tory principles should be sacked from the Shadow Cabinet, when so-called progressives, who have laid the Tory party open to the charge that there is no difference between it and socialists, are still allowed full rein.' No wonder Diana wondered about the newspaper's 'schizophrenia.' They were obviously flailing around to find someone who'd balance the condemnations they'd printed the day before. Enoch wasn't sure he'd ever met John Jennings. But whoever he was, Mr Jennings must be delighted to have made the front page of the *Times*.

"I must get off, Enoch. Jeffa is waiting," said Pam.

"Do you believe Susan to also be upset in any way over this affair?" asked Enoch.

"Well, I'm sure she's not happy about it, for the same reasons Jennifer isn't. But she's resilient. And I suspect a father's career is fairly low down on a teenager's list of things to worry about."

* * *

Christine had been spot-on about the location of her friend's room. Three large windows looked directly across the street at the upper floor windows of the Vine. Thirty feet at most separated Frank from the upstairs rooms of the pub. He could see a few desultory pigeons lurking on the Vine's windowsills. Jackie, Christine's pal, was a freckled redhead from Yorkshire with a blazing mane of copper-coloured waves.

"Fantastic hair," said Frank.

"My great-great-great-great grandmother was raped by a Viking," said Jackie.

"I'm sorry to hear that," said Frank.

"She wasn't the only one to mother Nordic offspring. ScandiYorkies like me are ten a penny around the Dales."

Jackie went off to an evening class, telling him to make sure he closed the door when he left. Just as well she didn't hang around. Frank would need to keep the lights off so he wouldn't be spotted if anybody happened to look across from the pub. To be doubly sure he set up his tripod and camera in the shadows a couple of feet back from the window.

Earlier that day, after Diana Throgmorton stalked out of the Giffard, Frank had used the coin phone in the pub to phone Ruth Barton. He knew it would be one of the most difficult calls he'd ever make. Frank was forced to admit to Ruth that he'd totally failed in persuading anybody to attest to the fact that Nelson wasn't in the group he'd photographed. And he had to tell Ruth that he was unable to produce his working material to prove his photo was a fake. In his nervousness he banged on to Ruth about his travails with the four students in the photo.

" Can't you force them to be witnesses?" he asked.

"There'd be no point in trying to subpoena the one in America. And I wouldn't trust the young Tory. From your description it sounds like she might claim she actually saw Nelson at the demo. And the prosecution would discredit the cop-hating Denise James in a nanosecond. I suppose we could lean on the mother of the little boy to come forward, but given the threats she probably couldn't be relied on to say categorically that Nelson wasn't there. But supposing she kept her oath and told the truth. I don't know about you, but I couldn't sleep at night if something happened to her son after we forced her to testify."

"Are you sure a jury are going to believe Nelson was in Wolverhampton just because of the bloody photo? Especially after I explain how I faked it. And what about Auntie Irene's evidence? She'll swear black and blue Nelson was home with her."

"Clutching at straws, Frank. Think about it. A young, rootless, Jamaican labourer with previous history of quarrelling with the deceased. One family member provides his only alibi. A drinking mate – an art student – recounts an unlikely and unsubstantiated story about faking a photo that places the accused near the crime scene at the time of the assault. As it stands Nelson doesn't have a snowball's chance."

"Rootless? You make him sound like a complete dosser."

"You and I both know he's an honest, intelligent, handsome bloke who deserves every break he can get ..."

Bit much, thought Frank, even if she was his solicitor. Was it possible she fancied Nelson? Frank hoped so for Nelson's sake.

"... but as things stand, Nelson's a lost cause. Counsel aren't supposed to cherry pick defence cases, but it's been like pulling teeth to find a barrister to take him on."

In desperation Frank had told Ruth about the yobs at the march and the evening meeting at the Vine. He filled her in on his intention to try and grab some photos.

"That's good. Tell me again how this meeting was described? And where exactly is this pub?"

She sounded surprisingly upbeat when Frank rang off. He, on the other hand, felt like a complete shit. It had been all he could do to resist staying at the Giffard and drowning his sorrows. But he had to keep it together. Maybe tonight's photo shoot would turn up something.

Frank was nodding off when the lights in the upstairs room opposite flicked on. Without looking through the telephoto Frank could see Barry and Dennis. Barry was taking beer bottles from a crate and ranging them on a table. He pulled several bags of crisps from a cardboard box. Dennis arranged a few chairs in a loose semi-circle. Frank couldn't believe his luck when he saw that the chairs faced him, with the open end of the semi-circle near the window. Whoever sat in them would be clearly visible, faces and all.

Almost immediately the lads who were at the Saint George's Day parade arrived, but there appeared to be more of them. Frank counted ten people, including Barry and Dennis. So a couple more had been added to the half-dozen who'd been on Waterloo Road the day before. This club, or group, or whatever the hell they were, seemed to be growing. The yobs milled around for a good fifteen minutes while Barry opened beer bottles and handed out packets of crisps. There was a lot of horsing around and laughing between Dennis and the others. They were on their second or third beer when another figure hove into view. He wasn't dressed in the Levi's, braces, and boots that the others, except Barry, were wearing. He looked completely out of place in a suit, white shirt, and tie. When he appeared the others quieted down. The newcomer and Barry greeted each other warmly. Barry put his arm around the man's shoulders as they chatted. Frank put his eye to the viewfinder and adjusted the lens to get a clearer look.

"Fuck me sideways," said Frank out loud as the focus sharpened and the man's face became clear. It was Fowler, the ghoulish cop, pockmarked cheeks and all. No doubt about it.

Frank immediately fired off a few shots. They'd be grainy photos, and the window frames sometimes encroached, but he was sure faces would be recognizable. He was so excited by Fowler's presence his fingers trembled. His suspicions were confirmed. Fowler and Barry were definitely intimate, as it were. Frank suddenly felt the need to pee. Why did it always happen at the most inconvenient times? Barry disappeared from the upstairs room and the rest of them sat down. Fowler settled himself slap bang in the middle of the semi-circle of chairs, facing the window. He seemed to be doing all the talking. He pulled out what appeared to be a map and held it up, pointing at various locations. He wrote things down in a notebook he kept on his lap. The others nodded a lot. Sometimes they became animated at something Fowler or Dennis said – they slapped each other or raised fists in the air. Frank shot almost two rolls of film. But as the meeting progressed, his attention wandered. He took a pee in Jackie's sink and ran the tap for several minutes to flush the drain. Three quarters of an hour passed. Just as Frank was beginning to think he'd had enough, Fowler and the rest stood up. They stretched out their arms in front of them, slightly higher than shoulder height, with fists clenched. They all held the pose long enough for Frank to snap the rest of the frames left on his second film. The room slowly emptied except for Dennis who stayed behind to crate the empties and gather up empty crisp packets. He disappeared, and the lights snapped off.

Frank waited in the dark for half-an-hour hoping they'd

all be long gone by the time he hit the street. He kept his head down as he walked quickly the couple of hundred yards to the Art College.

· ✱ ✱ ✱

"There was a time when you hardly darkened the door and now we can't keep you away," said Dave Bishop when Frank ran across him turning out lights in the photography department. He smiled his usual magnanimous smile, but Frank was wary. He was suspicious of the enigmatic photography teacher ever since he'd been manhandled by him. Maybe that had been Dave Bishop's intention, to keep Frank on his toes.

"All right if I develop a couple of rolls of film tonight?" asked Frank.

"As long as you're out before they lock the front doors at eleven. Otherwise you'll be in for the night. Listen Frank, I came across some of your old contact sheets and proofing prints this afternoon in the rubbish bin. Hope you don't mind but I want to show them to a friend of mine who may be interested."

After he'd torn himself away from the Giffard that morning and having phoned Ruth Barton, Frank had spent all afternoon making prints and rejecting them until he had the quality he wanted. He made prints of the Sikh men on the march, and of the Martin Luther King memorial. But his pride and joy were the ones he'd made of Dennis's mob going bananas on Waterloo Road with the Baptist congregation looking rattled in the background. His shots were spectacular. But he should have been more careful about discarding his rejected prints. He ought to have torn them up instead of throwing them in the bin whole – especially after the fiasco with his material from the *VoxPop* print. Frank thought about telling the photography tutor he didn't want some Tom, Dick or Harry seeing substandard work, but he couldn't help feeling slightly chuffed.

"They weren't exposed right, or framed properly, you know. That's why I ditched them," said Frank.

"Not to worry. My friend won't show them to anyone else. If he likes them it could go well for you."

Frank's ambivalent thoughts concerning Dave Bishop intensified. He wondered what the hell the photography tutor was up to.

By the time Frank had developed and dried the two films he'd shot through the windows of Barry's flat he only had time to print off a couple of frames: one of Fowler holding up the map, and one from the end of the meeting when Dennis and all the yobs appeared to be saluting, fists raised. Something about the grainy quality of the print, reminiscent of an earlier era, made them look even more like a bunch of fascists than they'd appeared in the flesh. He hadn't tried to disguise the fact that it was a covert photo, shot with a telephoto lens and taken though a window – the circumstances added to its malevolent atmosphere. Frank was beginning to realize how much the style of his shooting and printing could affect what the shot said almost as much as the subject matter itself. Frank placed the two damp prints carefully between blotting paper and put film and prints in an envelope. He wasn't going to risk leaving them in the dark room. He made a point of tearing the one working print he'd made into shreds so Dave Bishop couldn't get his hands on it.

Before he left the darkroom he put on the bright overhead

light to make sure he'd put everything away and cleaned up properly. When he'd thrown the torn print in the rubbish bin he mistakenly dropped a few pieces of ripped paper on the floor. They were lying at the base of one of the units that lined the room. The built-in cupboards were similar to those found in a kitchen. Counters above, and shelves below, with doors to protect their contents. Most kitchen counters had kick boards attached, for appearances and so that dropped food wouldn't find its way under the cupboards. Frank supposed it was to save money that the units in the college darkroom had been built without kick boards.

When he bent down to pick up the pieces of shredded print, he noticed something in the shallow space under a nearby cupboard. There were a couple of old prints, edges curled, lying barely within reach. He knew he'd destroyed the only working print he'd made that night, but being extra-careful, Frank nevertheless kneeled down and stretched his arm into the space to retrieve the prints. When he pulled them out into the light he could tell immediately they belonged to somebody else. They were studio portraits of a first-year student. The prints were obviously from a project that involved taking photos of classmates. The exercise was a lesson in how to use modelling lights. Frank threw the prints into the rubbish bin from his kneeling position. He was about to stand up when he noticed a strip of two-and-a-quarter-inch negative film lying in front of him where the prints had been. When Frank pulled the prints from under the counter he'd obviously dragged the film with them. He picked up the strip of negatives and held it up to the light.

When he saw what was on it he almost swallowed his tonsils. The strip of four frames was part of the original film that he'd taken at the demonstration. It must have dropped on the floor when he was stuffing all the material into the envelope that Jock McAffrey eventually stole. Frank struggled to catch his breath. Still kneeling, he held the negative film up to the light. It was scratched a little. He must have inadvertently kicked it under the cupboard after he'd dropped it, which would explain why he couldn't find it when he'd scoured the darkroom later. Each frame captured five figures. Giles Shannon, Kathy Stevenson, Denise James brandishing the placard, Diana Throgmorton, and ...

Frank felt like banging his skull on the floor. The fifth figure for fuck's sake! The person he'd obliterated when he pasted Nelson on top of the original print. Why hadn't he thought of it before? Frank felt like he'd won the Football Pools. Surely to God Gorman (Frank wouldn't touch Fowler with a barge pole after the evening's goings-on) would have to believe he'd faked the photo when he produced his piece of original film. But if Frank did need back up, the chances were good – one in five wasn't bad – that the fifth student would cooperate. Plus the evening's photos of Fowler at the Vine with the yobs would prove there was something shady going on between him, Barry, and Dennis. Frank carefully placed the strip of original film in his envelope with the negs and prints from the evening's shoot.

"Anybody there," a voice shouted from the corridor outside.

After his good fortune Frank was so full of bonhomie toward the world he could have kissed the caretaker as he held the front door open for him to leave. As it was, Frank grabbed the man's hand to shake, holding on to it for several seconds of vigorous pumping.

"A very goodnight to you. All the best. Thanks a lot."
Frank bounded away, clutching his envelope.

"Bloody students," he heard the caretaker mutter.

DAY TEN

Tuesday, April 23, 1968

"How was London?" Frank asked.

"Big."

Christine's frown was ominous.

"You all right?"

"Fine."

"What's the idea of the one-word answers?"

Christine's serious expression dissolved into laughter. She hugged Frank so hard his ribs ached. And he'd thought they were on the mend.

"They offered me a place. Can you believe it? I'm going to the Royal College of Art."

Several students turned to look. Normally it wasn't done to take notice of extroverted behaviour in the common room. The last time Frank could recall a similar reaction was when one of the painting students who was pissed out of his head at the end of term had climbed on a table and performed a striptease. Even then, those who considered themselves ultra-cool barely glanced as he shed his clothes. Maybe because, as one of the female students had said witheringly, 'there wasn't much to see.' Student stripteases weren't exactly rare, whereas Frank couldn't remember a fellow student being accepted at the Royal College of Art. Some people tried to appear unaffected by Christine's success, but quite a few looked on as she spun Frank around and planted loud kisses on whichever part of him she could reach. Some smiled, some frowned. Christine was regarded with esteem and/or a good deal of envy.

Frank was so pleased for Christine and chuffed about her obvious show of affection toward him, he grew tearful. He swiped his eyes, hoping nobody would notice.

"You'll have more letters after your name than in it – Dip.A.D., F.R.C.A., S.E.X.Y."

It took Christine a second or two.

"How do I qualify for the last degree?"

"Well, there's a rigorous oral test."

She slapped him on the arm.

"You pig."

They sat so that Christine could fill him in about her interview.

"Before I left they showed me the printmaking studios. They're absolutely amazing."

Her excitement threatened to overwhelm Frank. He was in danger of becoming tearful all over again. The only unpleasant dimension to his pleasure at Christine's success was the nagging worry about what would happen when term ended. She'd go off to London, but could he? His normal cockiness escaped him. He may have a portfolio of amazing photographs but would it be enough to secure his fortune in the Big Smoke?

"And how did you get on with Jackie last night? Not too terribly well, I hope," asked Christine.

"She played at being a Viking marauder. I had to pretend to be a compliant Anglo-Saxon farmer while she had her way with me."

"So she told you the story about her ancestor being diddled by a Viking. And you imagined the rest."

"You'll never guess who turned up at the meeting in the Vine? And you'll never guess what I found under a cupboard in the darkroom."

After a slight hesitation Christine agreed that finding the negatives was great news. Frank was relieved. If she'd given him shit for accidentally dropping his film, inadvertently kicking it, and then not seeing it in virtual darkness three feet under a cupboard, he'd have been annoyed to say the least.

"You have to tell Ruth Barton. About the negatives … and about Fowler. There must be something to be gained from telling everyone the creepy bastard associates with racist scumbags."

At that moment Steve MacDonald ambled into the common room. He beamed at Christine.

"Beautiful, and talented too. Congratulations."

"How did you know?" asked Christine.

"As editor of the student newspaper I have my ear constantly to the pulse of this institution."

"Your metaphors are mixed. But since you're so plugged in, have a look at this neg. and see if you recognize the chap next to Denise James. You remember her, she's the bird holding the placard," said Frank.

"It's a fucking negative. How am I supposed to recognize anybody? Everybody's in blackface."

"Exactly. All white-skinned faces. No coloured people."

Steve gave a low whistle, eyebrows raised.

"So this is the Holy Grail, an original negative from the demo?"

When Frank described the serendipity of his stumbling across the strip of negs in the darkroom Steve grew particularly venomous.

"I'm glad for your Jamaican pal that you found them. But as for you, Frank McCann, you are such a jammy bastard. You don't fucking deserve any one of the good things that seem to just fall into your sodding lap."

He glanced at Christine.

"Thanks for the support. Now ... if you really can't tell who it is from the negative I'll make a print, but on the off chance, take a closer look," said Frank.

Steve held the film up to one of the overhead fluorescent lights. He removed his tortoiseshell-framed specs and peered.

"I'm pretty sure it's Victor Manning."

"What department is he in?"

"He isn't."

"Please don't tell me he's dead, or moved to the Outer Hebrides."

"Alive and kicking, and living here. But he's not a student. He's a part-time instructor at the Tech'."

"How do you know him?"

"He helps typeset and print *VoxPop*. And I know him from Meeting House too."

"He's a Quaker?"

"Yes."

"A man with a conscience, thank God. Where can I find him?" asked Frank.

"He only teaches in the evening. During the day he's a copy editor at the *Express & Star*."

"He'll be there now?"

"Should be. They'll be putting the paper together to go to press this afternoon."

"You're sure it's him?"

"Ninety-nine per cent. Slight, mop of hair like an old

Beatles' cut. And I think I recall him saying he'd been at the demo. He complained about the cold, said it was brass-monkey weather."

Frank cajoled Christine into going with him to find Victor Manning.

You can use your womanly charms on him," said Frank.

"Okay. I'd like to rub the Royal College thing in the Little Pigs' faces, but I have an idea for a print I want to think more about before I see them. Hanging around with you will give it time to percolate."

On their way to the *Express & Star* she told Frank about her idea. On her train journey back from London she'd celebrated her Royal College triumph by treating herself to a three-course meal. She'd noticed all the waiters in the dining car were male.

"It got me thinking about the hierarchy of gender in restaurants. How come women are always relegated to work in more modest establishments, like cafés, tearooms, and pubs? The posh places never have female waiters. Trouble is I can't imagine how the hell I'd portray the idea in a print. Any ideas?"

Frank was at a loss. And rather than make a joke he wisely decided to just shake his head.

It was astonishingly easy for them to find Victor Manning. It was a cool day so they walked quickly to the building on Queen Street where the newspaper offices were housed. When they asked for Manning at the front desk, they were directed to the composing room, along a corridor that led to the back of the building. When Frank pulled open one of the double doors he couldn't believe the din. Several rows of ten-feet-high machines filled a space the size of a couple of tennis courts. A man sat at each machine banging away on a huge keyboard. There were at least a couple more rows of keys than on a normal typewriter. Nevertheless, it was obvious they were incredibly adept at transcribing from sheets of typewritten text held by clipboards mounted on the machines in front of them. At the side of each machine a long cylindrical bar of metal dangled from a chain. The end of each cylindrical bar sat in a small bowl of molten metal. As the metal reached the crucible it was obviously heated to a high temperature. No wonder it was so bloody hot in there. The machines used the molten metal to fabricate type, which Frank assumed was used for printing the newspaper.

The whole scene – ranks of men typing furiously, the smell of molten ore, unaccustomed heat, the hubbub of keyboards, and the constant chink of metal – thrilled Frank to his core. He felt as if he was inside a massive organism, whose power was irresistibly intoxicating.

Christine got the attention of the nearest machine operator and shouted Victor's name. He pointed to a small office to one side of the composing room with large windows looking out over the machines. Christine knocked at the door and peered through the adjoining window. Over her shoulder Frank could see a small man in his thirties, who looked up from a thick pile of paper and beckoned for them to come in. Once Frank closed the door it seemed blissfully quiet in the fishbowl of a room.

"Hello. You're a sight for sore eyes."

It was only after Victor Manning had spoken that he seemed to notice Frank – until then he'd been staring at Christine.

"Literally, I mean. After six hours of proofreading my eyes feel like they're on fire."

Frank had to admit Victor Manning was handsome, in an elfin way. He had bright, slightly slanted eyes, sharp cheekbones, and full lips.

"What can I do you for?" he asked.

Frank went through the whole rigmarole about his photo and Nelson's imprisonment. Christine told Victor it had been Steve MacDonald who'd identified him. Then she showed Victor the issue of *VoxPop*.

"I didn't see this issue. I was away last week, when it went to press. Otherwise I'd have bollocked you, Frank. You completely eliminated me. It's very well done, though. With those talents there's a bright future for you in journalism."

Frank warmed to the pixie of an editor.

"The *VoxPop* photo was just a misguided moment. He's a bloody good photographer actually," said Christine.

"Why can't I find a girlfriend like you?" asked Victor Manning.

Christine coloured slightly. It occurred to Frank that it was only fair to tell Victor about Dennis.

"Physical intimidation doesn't scare me. I may look like a nine-stone weakling, but I'm a black belt in judo."

"But aren't you a Quaker?"

"You obviously know sweet F-all about Quakers, or judo."

Frank forgave Victor his bluntness when he went on to say he'd be delighted talk to the police.

"I finish here at noon. I'll grab a quick bite and meet you two at High Level station at one o'clock."

* * *

Ruth Barton was disappointingly enigmatic when Frank phoned her to tell her his good news, and to ask her to meet them at the police station.

"I suppose I should stop looking for a barrister then."

She definitely sounded unsurprised. Frank presumed it was all in a day's work for Ruth. Or perhaps she was thinking about lost income if Nelson's case was dropped.

Frank and Christine walked to the railway station from the Art College. As they crossed Princess Street they could hear chanting. A column of a several hundred men, some swathed in scarves, many wearing flat caps, was heading toward them. A few men brandished crudely made signs with daubed capital letters:

BACK HIM NOT SACK HIM

SUPPORT ENOCH THE MAN WHO SPEAKS THE TRUTH

An onlooker told Frank the men were workers from the local brewery.

"Who the hell's making the beer? That's what I want to know," said Frank.

During the journey to Birmingham, Victor told Frank and Christine his life story, starting with his grandparents who were Russian, from Leningrad.

"It was called Petrograd when they lived there. My grandfather was a worker in a machine plant. He liked to boast that he and his friends began the Russian Revolution when they went on strike in the spring of 1917. He was a committed socialist and staunch anti-Imperialist, but he couldn't condone murder. When the Bolsheviks massacred the Tsar and his family, my grandfather saw the writing on the wall. He and my grandmother left Russia and found their way to Birmingham, where he got work in a foundry. His last name was Manin, Sergei Manin. It was changed to Manning when they came to England."

" Funny how many English names seem tailor-made for foreigners to assume. Our family name was Becker, but it became Baker when my father's forebears arrived here from Germany," said Christine.

"Christ Almighty, is nobody English any more?" Frank asked.

"I always thought you must be part Irish," said Christine.

"Me! I'm more English than sodding Stonehenge."

"All right, calm down. You'll be marching alongside Dennis and his gang next."

When they reached the police station Ruth Barton was waiting for them outside, smoking.

"I've told Gorman you want to talk to him," she said.

"But we don't want that bastard Fowler in on the conversation," Frank interrupted.

"No worries there," said Ruth, grinning. She ground the nub of her cigarette into the pavement with a heavy heel leaving a narrow smear of mangled tobacco, ash, and paper.

"Thanks to you I managed to pass word along to a police pal about last night's meeting at the Vine. He sent a couple of undercover blokes. Fowler's been charged with inciting racial violence. They're pulling in Dennis Perkins and tracking down the others as we speak."

For the second time that day Frank was in danger of losing his composure. He looked away down the street, his vision misted. The sun was trying its best to cut through a thin layer of cloud. It shone a bright but even light on the landscape.

Drab houses and cracked pavements appeared dreamlike, almost lyrical. Frank squeezed his eyes shut.

"That's ... that's ..."

A pregnant pause. He worried about what Ruth Barton might think of him but he couldn't utter a word.

"Wonderful. That's wonderful," said Christine.

She wrapped an arm around Frank's shoulders, more a motherly gesture than anything else. Ruth diplomatically averted her eyes for a second or two. Then she explained that her friend in the force worked in a special unit set up to nail the likes of Dennis and his pals. She'd called him as soon as she heard from Frank. He sent two of his appropriately dressed colleagues who'd conned their way into Dennis's group.

"They've had their suspicions about Fowler for a while so they thought they'd died and gone to heaven when he showed up. The two of them can corroborate that Fowler and Dennis were organizing the others to carry out attacks on coloured patrons at clubs and pubs catering to immigrants."

"That would be Barry's doing," said Frank, wiping an eye with the heel of his hand.

"The landlord? He insists he had no knowledge of what was going on. And since he wasn't in the room during the meeting, Gorman doesn't think they can touch him."

"The cunning bastard," said Frank.

"But they were able to nip this group in the bud. Which is just as well. This lot are so far out they've even been banned from the National Front," said Ruth.

"The National what?" asked Christine.

"It's an agglomeration of ultra right-wing groups who got together after the election. They're hardcore white supremacists. They claim thousands think the same way, but are afraid to speak out," said Victor.

"After seeing the size of that crowd in Wolverhampton today you can't help but wonder if they might be right," said Christine.

"With the undercover officers' testimony, and Frank's photos of the meeting, Fowler is screwed. He may be deported back to Jamaica – I'm not sure about the legalities of that. But he'll never work for the police again."

Across the road the same net curtain was twitching as the last time Frank had stood outside the police station. Let them go ahead and have a good gander – he couldn't care less.

"Unfortunately Gorman will have his work cut out to build a murder case against Dennis Perkins. There are no witnesses, no real motive."

"Hate isn't a motive?" asked Christine.

Nobody replied. Frank noticed that they avoided each other's eyes. Except Christine, of course. When he glanced her way she was eyeing Ruth as though willing an answer from her.

"What about him beating the shit out of me?" Frank asked.

"Again a tough one. No witnesses, but I'd be willing to give it a try, if you're game."

Frank shrugged. Despite his earlier euphoria, he felt as if something had been snatched away.

"You can take come comfort from the thought that at least Fowler and Dennis will be languishing in jail for a while," Ruth said eventually.

"Will they really go to jail?" asked Christine.

"There've been precedents of a prison sentence for

convictions of inciting racial violence. Michael X, for one. Although he was playing for the opposite team, obviously."

The meeting with Gorman was short and sweet. Frank handed over a print he'd made from the original negative together with a cutting of the *VoxPop* photo. He told the story of his deception one more time – the last, he fervently hoped. Victor gave a statement swearing that it was him in the original photo, that he'd attended the march, and that he'd seen neither hide nor hair of Nelson in Wolverhampton on that day.

Gorman was his usual inscrutable self. He grunted a few times. He asked if he could keep the two photo prints Frank had made of Fowler at the meeting in the Vine. Finally he thanked them all briefly and left.

"Bit of an anti-climax really," said Frank.

"I doubt Nelson will see it that way," said Ruth.

* * *

"It's your lucky day, Clarke," said the warden.

"Wha' lucky 'bout it?"

The warden threw some clothes at Nelson. Trousers, a startlingly white shirt – starched and ironed – and a jacket.

"Put those on. Can't release you in your prison overalls, can we now?"

The man was one of the friendlier officers. But still, Nelson stared at him, eyes narrowed.

"Come on lad, shake a leg. People might think you don't want to leave us."

Nelson allowed himself a glimmer of hope.

"Them give me bail after all?"

He didn't consider the alternative.

"All charges dropped. End of story."

"Wha' ... wha' happen?"

The warden claimed not to have any idea. But he grinned, clearly pleased to be the bearer of good news. It came as a surprise to Nelson that the man might like him.

The shirt fit okay, but the jacket and trousers were too big. Nelson considered asking what happened to his own clothes, but decided not to rock the boat. At least his billfold came back to him. Amazingly it still contained the few pound notes that he'd had when it was taken from him after he was arrested.

* * *

"Winson Green, and now Stafford. You've certainly got me running all over hell's half acre," said Ruth Barton.

The Head Warden sat behind a desk. Nelson and Ruth sat on the other side facing each other. She was smiling, but she looked tired. Her hair was droopy, like when he first saw her. Still, Nelson had a momentary fantasy of them lying somewhere – in a bed – him holding her 'til she fell asleep.

"Sorry," he said.

"Don't be sorry, it's all part of the service. Government's paying for my time."

A fragment of hope broke away from Nelson and floated away. Was she official so because them in the Head Warden's office, or she mean to be cool?

"Is just your job fi come get people out of jail? That all?"

"Mostly."

"Today?"

"What's your game, Clarke? Let your solicitor do her work or we'll have you back inside," said the Head Warden.

There were papers to sign. Then the Head Warden told Nelson he never wanted to see him in prison again.

But is them a fuckery! They should be saying sorry, not talking down to him, like he was a delinquent.

"Keep in mind, Warden, my client was wrongfully charged. He's committed no crime. Nor is he likely to."

Ruth Barton good so! Nelson radiated rays of love so strong he was sure they could be seen. He hoped so.

The Head Warden coughed and avoided his and Ruth's eyes. Ruth and Nelson left the prison together.

"My car's just around the corner," said Ruth and took a few paces up the street.

Nelson hesitated.

"Come on then," called Ruth.

Nelson almost ran to her side.

"Frank find the photo stuff? Is so me get free?"

Ruth told Nelson everything. About Frank finding his negs and about Victor Manning's statement saying Nelson wasn't at the demonstration. She told him about the meeting with Fowler, Dennis, and the other shaved-headed hooligans above the pub, and how they were all charged with planning violence against coloureds.

"Them like ska, you know."

"You defending a bunch of racists on account of their taste in music?"

Nelson looked over at Ruth. She glanced at him. They both laughed.

Ruth's car grew stuffy but Nelson was glad of the warmth. With just an ill-fitting jacket and open-necked shirt, Nelson had been cold on the short walk from prison to the car. It was nearing the end of a chilly afternoon and he'd been able to see his breath – something that had amazed him the first time he'd experienced it, on the deck of the boat coming over. At least it was bright. The setting sun was only half-hidden by a thin veil of pearly cloud cover suffused with a rosy glow.

"You know how I lucky so? I got the best solicitor in England."

Ruth's face turned that delicious pink. Nelson's fragment of hope floated back to him, double the size it was before.

"At the risk of more flattery I've got another piece of good news. I heard back from my lawyer pal in Jamaica. The official word on your so-called murder is that it was a fight between Kingston gang members. Apparently gangsters all inscribe the gang insignia on the blade of their knives. Because the body had a gang knife in it when it was found, the police assumed he'd been stabbed by a fellow member. They didn't look into it, never thinking they'd be able to pin it on any particular individual. Probably just happy to have them killing each other off."

"That good. But what about them other two bwoys? Them know me from my billfold stuff."

"A few days later an informant told the police which two gang members were with the dead man the day he died. They'd all three gone to Port Antonio – was it? – together. Of the other two, one was shot dead before the police could pick him up. The other disappeared with no trace. Probably dead too by now."

All that stuff people talk about when a problem solved – weights lifting and such – Nelson never knew what they meant. Until then.

"Wha' 'bout my billfold?"

"No record of any wallet. They probably took the cash

and threw it away. It's what robbers usually do."

Nelson watered up so much he couldn't hide it. Ruth leaned over and flicked open the glove compartment in front of him.

"Kleenex," she said.

"Sorry."

"Don't be. It's attractive in a man."

For a split second Nelson thought she was teasing him. Ruth know his worry 'bout him no manly? But when he looked over at her, Ruth's expression was serious, staring at the road ahead.

As Nelson swatted moisture off his face he thought about his mother. He shouldn't write to her about what Ruth just told him – best play it safe still – but he'd find a way to let her know. She'd be relieved, but she'd wish he hadn't run off to the Mother Land when there was no need. He glanced at Ruth who threw him a quick smile. At least he could tell his mother coming to England was the best thing ever happened and not be lying.

One of his mother's sayings was 'what don't break you, make you strong.' Nelson thought the expression stupid. He could see how unhappy she was when there wasn't enough food on the table, or when the school uniform his brothers wore before him was altered and re-stitched because she couldn't afford a new one. But now he wondered if perhaps there was something to what his mother said. He felt more tenacious than ever. And he supposed that, in the end, justice had prevailed. Nelson felt an undercurrent of anger about the indignities he'd suffered. He knew the future might not be easy, but he resolved as the car sped toward Birmingham not to let his vexation surface. If he let it out and something bad happen, people like that rass Head Warden smile like they win a million pound. A couple of lines of his song floated through his head. Maybe this was his chance to impress Ruth, show her something more than the put-upon bwoy she'd seen so far.

"Gotta make them all your lovers.
Some do their best to change you,
Even rearrange you,
But it all up to you,
You gotta stay true.
You gotta stay true."

"What a great song," said Ruth. "Who sings it? It's really catchy."

"It mine. One day I surprise you with the recordin'," said Nelson.

Ruth said it wouldn't be much of a surprise, now that he'd told her.

"Not that I'd be surprised anyway, having noticed your other attributes."

He didn't dare ask what she meant in case she was just teasing him.

Ruth looked in the rear-view mirror and tugged at her hair.

"I must look a wreck. Rough morning in court, two clients sent down and one given probation."

"Good thing me no reach court ... wi' your record."

Ruth punched him lightly on the arm.

"That no way fi treat a client, you know."

"You aren't my client any more, Nelson. Case closed."

Nelson put on a sad little boy act. He stuck out his lower lip and frowned.

"It's okay, there are advantages to not being my client."

"Wha' advantages?"

"If you were still my client I couldn't tell you how handsome you look in that white shirt. It wouldn't be very professional to tell you how much I like you. Or to say how nice and clean you smell."

Ruth leaned towards him, eyes still fixed on the road. She sniffed the air a few inches from his face.

"That carbolic? Lifebuoy's a turn-on, but carbolic works too," she whispered.

Nelson felt her breath warm on his cheek.

"You don't need to look so scared, Nelson. I promise not to crash the car."

"Is just me never dream ... that a pure lie ... me dream, but ..."

* * *

"Tell you what, let's go to the Vine to celebrate. We can rub Barry's nose in it," said Frank when he, Christine, and Victor arrived back in Wolverhampton.

"I'm not sure that's such a good idea," said Christine.

"Come on. Just a swift pint. Are you with us Victor? It's on me."

Victor agreed, so Christine went along with the idea.

For a few seconds after he pushed open the door Frank revelled in the familiar smell of beer and cigarette smoke. Half-a-dozen students were huddled at one table, heads together, talking in low voices. An older man sat on one of the leather-clad window benches scanning the pages of *Sporting Life*. He leant forward to circle something with a nub of pencil on a page of the newspaper, a cigarette clamped between his lips. Garlands of blue-grey smoke hovered above his head. But the idyllic scene was soured by the sight of Barry Dangerfield grinning at Frank from behind the bar. The landlord seemed completely unfazed by their appearance in his pub.

"'ello stranger. The usual? And what about your beautiful girlfriend? And you, sir?"

Once drinks were dispensed Frank tried to pay, but Barry was having none of it. He waved Frank's money away with a magnanimous wag of his meaty paw.

"On the 'ouse, Frank. You can 'elp me celebrate."

Frank was floored by Barry's behaviour. He'd expected to be refused a drink, not greeted like a prodigal son.

"What have you got to celebrate? You realize Dennis will be put away? Maybe even charged with murder."

"It's a shame abowt Dennis. He's forever getting himself in trouble ... ever since he was a nipper. But I can't help that. I'm just happy that bloody jungle-bunny club's been shut."

"You racist bigot," said Christine.

"It's got nothing to do with colour, duck. They could have been sky blue for all I care. Unfair competition, that's what it was. I'd have got 'em shut down, no matter who they was."

"How could a useless tosser like you get anything closed?"

"You'd be surprised, cock. Let's just say I've a friend in high places who gave me some insider information. Turns out the club owner was a town councillor."

Barry was virtually crowing. He named a Tory representative on Wolverhampton Town Council. A white man, of course.

"I don't believe you," said Christine.

"I don't give a toss if you believe it or not. All I know is the bugger closed the place down bloody quick when I threatened to go to the press and tell them how a town councillor was reaping the profits from a dodgy club for wogs. Bastard near shit his pants."

Frank looked at Barry with narrowed eyes. Something Georgy said the day she visited Christine's flat came back to him.

"And why would this 'friend in high places' of yours obtain such information for you? Unless, of course you'd done him a favour. Maybe he owed you one?"

"I'm saying nothing," said Barry.

Frank turned to Christine.

"Remember the morning Georgy – Mrs Verington-Delaunay to you, Barry – dropped by your flat? Do you recall her telling us about a letter our landlord here gave to Enoch Powell?"

Frank glanced at Barry. He'd stopped smiling. His teeth were bared, but any hint of amusement was extinguished from his eyes.

Christine thought for a second. God but she looked beautiful to Frank when she was concentrating, forehead furrowed and her eyes endlessly deep.

"Bloody hell," she said. She stared at Barry.

A bead of perspiration trickled from the publican's hairline and down his left temple.

"You must know about the 'piccaninnies' your mate, Enoch, mentioned in the speech he gave on Saturday," said Christine. "The ones who he claimed only knew one English word – 'racialist.' What language did they speak if not English? You must know. It wouldn't be Indian, would it? Not if they were 'piccaninnies.'"

Christine emphasized the word, laced it with the disgust it warranted.

"They'd be negro children. Almost certainly West Indian.

Odd that they didn't speak English then, isn't it?"

Barry said nothing, merely pursed his lips.

"You realize somebody, sometime, will discover the whole story is a set up?" said Frank.

"But Enoch wouldn't put it in a speech if it wasn't true, would he?" said Barry.

"You tricky bastard," said Christine.

"Listen, duck, it taykes two to bloody tango" he said.

At that, Frank looked down at his Guinness. Barry was right, of course. Powell must have gone along with it. A surge of anger welled up in him at how totally fucked up the world was. Nelson's freedom seemed like a hollow victory. The thought of what had happened to his Jamaican friend enraged him all the more.

"You suggested I put Nelson into that photo to take the attention off your fucking nephew, didn't you?" he said. "That's why you got Dennis to beat the shit out of me. When I threatened to stir things up."

"Look cock, I don't know what you'm on abowt."

"You fat bastard."

"Frank, mate, I thought we was friends."

Barry leered, jowls glistening with perspiration.

"Leave it, Frank," said Christine.

"You're never going to win, Frank. May as well just sit down and enjoy your Guinness," said Victor.

Frank trailed behind Christine and Victor to a table as far from the bar as possible. Whatever victory Frank thought he was going to wave in Barry's face seemed ineffectual to say the least.

"Some celebration this turned out to be. More like a wake," said Victor.

"I wonder if we'll ever know exactly why Dennis beat the shit out of the Sikh landlord in the first place," said Christine.

"I shudder to think," said Victor. "I'm willing to bet he doesn't know himself. His type may think they know – some rubbish about foreigners taking jobs or not speaking English – but actually they have no logical reason whatsoever for hating immigrants."

"Maybe it was all part of an elaborate, if creaky, plan to screw Nelson," said Christine.

"Barry doesn't seem to give a shit about his nephew. So why was he so keen to incriminate Nelson?" asked Victor.

"Perhaps giving West Indians a bad reputation was part of Barry's twisted strategy to get the Montego Club closed and make sure it stayed closed," said Frank.

He looked over at Barry, who was leaning against the bar talking to a customer, chatting and smiling.

"I never thought I'd say this, but I can't finish this fucking Guinness."

Christine took a last gulp of her cider.

"Come on then, let's go to the Giffard."

"Couldn't we just go home?" asked Frank.

"Who are you, and what have you done with the real Frank McCann?"

Victor, taken by surprise by Christine's quip, choked on his beer.

On the way out Frank realized Pete Scallion and Mick Collins were among the students sitting at the table of students. They'd obviously been keeping their heads down during the contretemps with Barry.

"You bastards owe me a fiver each for that bet we had about the demo photo," said Frank.

"You'll have to wait 'til next term, mate," said Pete.

"Yeah, we just spent the last of our grant money," said Mick.

"You know bloody well I won't be here next term."

"Oh dear. I completely forgot. You're going out into the big bad world, aren't you Frank?"

"You'll be earning so much you won't need our measly fivers."

The two second-year students collapsed in giggles.

"Wankers," said Frank.

When he stepped out of the pub door Frank gazed miserably at the dirty facades of buildings. The only light spots were walls beneath window ledges, where bricks were caked with cascades of chalky pigeon shit. He was smarting from the sarcastic dig Mick and Pete had made about him earning loads of dosh. What the hell *was* he going to do at the end of the college year? He thought again of Christine disappearing to London.

"You know Powell is partly responsible for grant money," said Victor.

"How's that?" said Christine.

"He supported nationalization of the universities. Making all post-secondary education to be overseen by government."

"He's a bloody weird Tory, isn't he?"

"He's a renegade, that's for sure," said Victor. "I suppose I should use the past tense. He won't be doing much of anything now."

After they said goodbye, Frank and Christine headed for Park Dale and Christine's flat.

"The sooner we're all coffee-coloured the better," Christine suddenly said.

"Where the hell did that come from?"

"I was just thinking that that's what we'll all be. Well, not us, but our great-great-great-grandchildren. Once everybody gets mixed up, the dominant genes will be the ones for darker skin, won't they? Everybody will be brown."

'I suppose so," said Frank.

"I think I'll do a print showing the Royal Family as brown-skinned people. Liz, Philip and the kids waving from the balcony of Buckingham Palace, but all with dark skin. It'll be fucking brilliant."

Frank wrapped his arm around her and pulled him to her. His pleasure at being with such an amazing person was only overshadowed by the thought of losing her at term's end.

As they passed the back entrance to the art college they ran into one of Frank's classmates, Gwyneth Williams, a compatriot of Taffy Thomas.

"Dave Bishop's looking for you. Frantic he is," said the student.

When Frank wondered aloud why the photography tutor was so desperate to find him, the Welsh girl claimed not to know.

"He's still in there, mooning around like a spurned lover or summat," she said.

"I'd better go and see what he wants," said Frank.

Christine opted to wait for him outside.

"Where the hell have you been?" demanded Dave Bishop.

Frank started in on an explanation, but the photography tutor was clearly not interested.

"Remember me telling you I was going to show some of your test prints to a friend of mine?"

"Yes, about that ..."

Frank was intending to protest Dave Bishop's cheek, showing his working shots to God-knows-who.

"He's offered you a job," said Dave Bishop. His eyes were shining. He looked maniacal.

"Doing what? Where?"

" Cleaning shithouses in Timbuktu. What do you think? At the *News of the World* of course. My mate's the photo editor, we were at college together. When I saw your shots I thought he might be interested. I had him up here for the day today to talk to the second year students about the real world. He was super-impressed with your photos of the Sikh march. And he wants you to send him some good prints of the ones of those maniacs screaming at the West Indians. They want to run them to go with an article on Enoch Powell. He wanted to meet you, but he had to go back to London. Here's his business card. Just make sure you phone him first thing tomorrow."

Frank stared at the card. It featured the newspaper's logo and an address in Fleet Street. The paper's motto, 'All human life is there,' was emblazoned under the logo.

"The *News of the World* newspaper? In London?"

"It's the biggest in the world, Frank. Nearly nine million circulation. You'll probably just be looking after the dark room at first, but it's a bloody good foot in the door."

Frank continued to gaze at the card.

"This doesn't mean you can wriggle out of your year-end exhibition, Frank. Don't forget, I made you, and I can break you."

Dave Bishop slapped Frank on the shoulder and strode off down the corridor. Frank wandered out into the street. The sun was winning its battle with cloud cover as it sank toward the horizon. A pink light suffused the sky, as delicate as a water colour wash.

"You'll never guess what's happened," Frank said to Christine.

* * *

Enoch could tell from the cacophony of voices that The Members' Lobby was crowded even before he stepped through the doors. The House promised to be packed – nobody wanted to miss the vote on the amendment to the Race Relations Bill. There was also little doubt in Enoch's mind that his presence at Westminster was contributing to an atmosphere of anticipation. People must be wondering if he'd dare speak as he'd spoken in Birmingham, and were probably speculating how his colleagues in the Shadow Cabinet might react. Was there a slight diminishment in the clamour when he stepped through the Lobby doors? Did he imagine heads that swivelled in his direction were immediately turned away? He couldn't be certain because he purposely avoided looking at his fellow MPs. He averted his eyes to the soaring Gothic arches of the Lobby walls. Enoch's pulse quickened at the sight of intricately carved stonework and distinctive ornamentation of elongated lanterns. Even the shame of being reduced to a backbencher couldn't diminish the thrill of again being in this historic building. He studied the nine massive ceiling panels fashioned from solid English oak. The frisson he felt wasn't for the craftsmanship necessarily, but for the weight of history and the sheer authority that the building represented.

"Afternoon, Enoch."

He looked down to see Iain Macleod standing with a

Labour member, Anthony Wedgwood Benn. Enoch took Macleod's greeting to mean that relations were cordial. He was relieved. Despite not having always seen eye to eye, Enoch regarded Macleod as a friend. It was obvious, however, that Macleod's companion was feeling anything but cordial. Tony Benn glowered at Enoch, his face flushed. He was ten years younger, but had been elected at the same time as Enoch, and was for a time the youngest MP in the house. Enoch regarded him as a bit of a softie. He much preferred Labour politicians who were more hard-line, like Aneurin Bevan – one knew where one stood with them. However there was clearly nothing wishy-washy in Benn's opinion of Powell.

"The flag of racialism that you have raised over Wolverhampton looks like the one that fluttered twenty-five years ago over Dachau and Belsen," said Benn, his face flush with emotion. He glared at Enoch for a second, turned on his heel, and marched away. Several MPs standing nearby smirked. Macleod shook his head.

"I'm not sure I'd have put it quite like that, but you should know I'm in agreement with the sentiment."

"You, of all people, must know perfectly well that what I said was not motivated by what is crudely called racialism," said Enoch.

"One can't help but wonder exactly what it was motivated by, Enoch," said Macleod, raising his eyebrows.

"The real and present danger of racial strife as a result of the threat to Britons and their way of life by the immigrant population. If those thousands of people protesting my dismissal seem to be able to understand why I've spoken, why can't you?"

"When situations are difficult and people struggle in life,

reactionary ideas like yours seem an easy fix,"said Macleod. "People latch onto them. You have portrayed Britain today as a tradition under siege, which you may well believe. But having exaggerated the situation, you then validate blatant prejudice by citing it as the only viable solution. Who can blame those poor stiffs, who you've whipped into a frenzy of resentment, for marching and demonstrating. Some will even commit acts of violence, God help them and their victims. But in the end human empathy and common sense *will* prevail."

Enoch fixed Macleod with his trademark stare. Enoch never knew quite how to react when confronted by his old acquaintance's idealism.

"I remember you once gave a speech at a St George's Day event we attended," continued Macleod. "Exactly seven years ago today. You talked with great affection and respect about the various regional differences among Britons, but also expressed wonder and awe at 'the homogeneity of England being brought about by the slow alchemy of centuries.'"

Macleod fixed Enoch with watery eyes. His shining pate made him seem to Enoch guileless, almost as though the lack of hair exposed his inner thoughts. Or maybe it was just that Enoch had always known him to be scrupulously sincere.

"The alchemy will continue, Enoch. And make no mistake – I'm unspeakably sad that neither you nor your poor brilliant brain will play a part in it. Please give my best to Pam. You and I will probably never speak again."

Macleod walked away, toward the door to the chamber, following other members who were trooping into the House. Enoch knew if he wanted a seat he'd better hurry – there wasn't enough space for all members – but it felt as though Macleod's words had robbed him of the use of his legs. It would be ignominious enough sitting on the back benches, but being forced to stand at the door and listen with other latecomers was unthinkable. It took him some physical effort to put one foot in front of the other but eventually Enoch regained his equilibrium. He was relieved when he was able to squeeze himself in at the end of the uppermost bench. He'd been dreading having to sit in the middle of a row, where, given the crowding, he'd be forced into physical contact with fellow Tories. Arms, hips, thighs would be squeezed together in the crush, too intimate a situation for Enoch at the best of times. Although he agreed with Churchill's urging, when the chamber was reconstructed after bomb damage during the war, to maintain its rectangular shape. Enoch conceded that a circular room would have accommodated more people. Churchill argued the square shape of the chamber, with two distinct sides, was responsible for the two-party system and should be kept. And at that point whatever Churchill said, went. Enoch was also convinced that the daunting prospect of 'crossing the floor' of the rectangular configuration, to abandon one's party for the other, was responsible for fewer defections.

Jim Callaghan led off for the government with a forty-five minute speech putting the case for accepting the Bill as it stood, without any amendment. Enoch was comfortable, even relaxed, throughout. He was particularly pleased when Callaghan insisted the opposition say in plain terms whether they opposed the Bill or not. Callaghan was obviously well aware the whole House would know he had Enoch's speech in mind. He even glanced in Enoch's direction as if to make it clear. Enoch smiled to himself. It would be difficult for his former colleagues to wriggle out of Callaghan's veiled accusation of ambiguity. But then Quentin Hogg rose to speak. Enoch sensed danger when Hogg immediately alluded to the Birmingham speech in an obvious effort to distance himself and the Opposition in general.

"I said that I would have to speak about my Right Honourable Friend the Member for Wolverhampton, South-West's speech over the weekend. This is where I fall foul of my Right Honourable Friend. I am bound to say so, for this reason. There is nobody that I admire more in this House than I do Mr Powell. We have so much in common. We have the same love of Greek literature. We have the same devotion to the same political party. We have the same religion, the same religious beliefs. But if one is going to say – and this was my Right Honourable Friend's analogy, not mine – that the streets of our country might one day run with blood – and make no mistake, it is usually the innocent, usually the defenceless, and sometimes just the ordinarily good, who are the victims of that kind of violence – then surely one ought to consider whether, in the more immediate future, one's words are more likely to make that happen, or less likely to make that happen."

Enoch's perch at the end of the topmost bench was becoming increasingly less comfortable. He fidgeted, unusual for him. He crossed, then uncrossed, his arms.

"It was not as if my Right Honourable Friend did not know what the effect of his remarks would be. He did, because he said in terms that he could imagine the

outcry he would cause. He did not come to me. He did not give me a sight of what he was going to say. He did not ask my advice, though, goodness knows, that advice is fallible enough. He summoned two television networks so that I could see him saying it. He sent a hand-out to the Press, by-passing the Conservative Office. He said what he said without a word to any of his colleagues that he was going to say it..."

One or two people on both sides of the House cried "shame." Enoch's extremities felt cold. He grasped one hand with the other in his lap in an attempt to warm them. The lifeblood couldn't have leaked out of him faster if Hogg's assault had involved knives and daggers, rather than a mere character assassination. He looked down, beyond the ranks of nodding Tories, to the front bench and stared at the back of Hogg's head. The realization that Hogg had delivered the deathblow to any hope of him ever regaining any position of power or influence hit Enoch like a lumbering tank. He barely registered what else Hogg was saying. All he could think of were Georgy's words. They repeated over and again, like a song he couldn't get out of his head – "they'll marginalize you into complete and impotent oblivion."

The debate droned on. Several MPs mentioned Enoch specifically in negative terms. One or two expressed sympathy with the thrust of his speech. But Enoch remained silent, in a kind of vegetative state, almost comatose, hardly shifting in his seat. The vote seemed to him to come surprisingly quickly, although the debate lasted almost five hours. Enoch towed the Party line and voted for the amendment. But the Government persevered – the noes won, the amendment was thrown out, and the Bill went forward to a second reading.

As soon as the vote was announced, Enoch fled.

As he left Westminster he was confronted by a ravening gang of reporters, microphones bristling and flash cameras popping. Enoch stood facing them for several seconds until the hubbub died down. One or two reporters glanced at each other, puzzled by Enoch's silence. He stood, his face more a death mask than a living countenance, the only movement was in the glittering of his icy blue eyes. Then he spoke, a brief statement before pushing his way through the melee.

"I have no regrets, all political careers end in failure. No office, and no apparent achievement, but I see myself being proved right. What I said will be repeated."

A MAIDEN SPEECH

Tuesday, June 29, 2010

Paul Uppal's amber eyes stared back at him from the mirror. His broad forehead, usually seamless, was slightly creased as he concentrated on knotting his blue silk tie. Kashmir, his wife, had pointed out, with her lawyer's acumen, that it didn't matter if the tie wasn't a Tory blue. She argued that the paler shade of sky blue was a better choice, given the celebratory nature of the occasion. As Paul worked on his tie he was aware of the kara that encircled his right wrist. The steel bracelet rested against the crisp cuff of his white shirt – a reminder of its wearer's commitment to lead a life of righteousness, and to make every deed and action true and honourable. While the occasion of Paul Uppal's maiden speech could be said to be about his achievements – considerable for someone born in working class Smethwick of East African Sikh immigrants – his kara reminded him that the day was actually more about his future and what was expected of him as the newly elected Member of Parliament for Wolverhampton South West. Satisfied his tie was neatly knotted, he slipped into the jacket of his pale grey suit. Warmer than average temperatures swathed Britain. London had hit thirty degrees at the end of May. No need to endure the discomfort of a dark wool suit for the sake of outmoded propriety.

Another, less simple, debate than Paul's choice of tie had been whether or not he would evoke the name of Enoch Powell in his maiden speech. He was aware it was customary to acknowledge previous incumbents, and of all the politicians who'd represented the riding, Enoch Powell was probably the most well-known. Not only to parliamentarians, but to ordinary Britons. The irony of his situation – not only the first Sikh MP, but in Enoch Powell's old riding to boot – was such that Paul knew in his heart of hearts he couldn't *not* mention the man who delivered the infamous 'Rivers of Blood' speech. Paul's father, Surjit Singh, confirmed the inclination that he had no option. In their discussions Paul was reminded of his father's stories about the palpable atmosphere of danger in the weeks following Enoch's speech. Having left East Africa for England, would Surjit and his young family now be forced to migrate somewhere else? And if so, where? They couldn't return to Kenya, to the thriving electrical business they'd been forced to sacrifice in the move to England. India seemed out of the question, Paul's father hadn't lived there since he was eight-years-old. The country would be almost as strange to him as to any white-skinned native-born Briton. But eventually, when Powell was relegated, powerless, to the back benches and the policy of 'repatriation' was mentioned less and less, Surjit Singh Uppal and his family breathed easier.

A seed of an idea for his maiden speech began to form in Paul's mind concerning an eerie similarity of his electoral victory to that of Powell's. He delayed the speech until the seed had grown into a few well chosen sentences, leaving him free to work on the more salient points he wanted to make. By the time a draft was completed, the Enoch reference was a small part, and had receded in importance in Paul's mind.

The new Member for Wolverhampton South West walked from Waterloo station along the south bank of the Thames to Westminster Bridge. At the far shore a Thames Clipper glided gracefully away from Westminster Pier and drifted eastward, following the river's current as it flowed inexorably toward the City. Paul strode up the steps to Westminster Bridge and rounded the corner in front of an imposing stone lion which, although a powerful guardian-like presence, seemed to be smiling benevolently down at him as he passed. The Palace of Westminster sparkled in brilliant sunlight. Every detail of the seat of British Government stood out in sharp relief, from the Victoria Tower at the south-west corner to the tower at the eastern extremity that housed Big Ben. As he crossed the bridge Paul was suddenly and unexpectedly hit by an image of Enoch Powell addressing parliament, his trademark eyes glittering. He'd seen numerous photos of Powell and watched footage of the Rivers of Blood speech, but Paul hadn't realized the man's features were so clearly etched into his brain. So vivid was the image that he could almost believe Powell was addressing the House of Commons at that moment, not two hundred yards away. Then, more than ever, Paul Uppal was aware of the full weight of history resting on his shoulders.

When the Deputy Speaker introduced him, Paul was conscious of the fact that he was by no means the first to experience the sensation that everything in his life thus far had led him to that moment. But he doubted there were many whose background was as unlikely to have carried them there. John Major, perhaps. Seeing the working-class boy from Brixton elected as Conservative Prime Minister in 1992 had sealed the deal for Paul in his decision to join the Party. He was aware that anybody who'd known him as a shy brown boy from Birmingham would have scoffed at the idea that the lad who'd been placed in a remedial class at junior school because it was assumed he couldn't speak English – in fact more English was spoken in the Uppal household than Punjabi – would ever rise to address the House of Commons as a Member of the British Parliament.

After the etiquette of a thankful introduction, Paul launched straight into the few succinct sentences which formed his nod to Enoch Powell.

"I have not traditionally been an individual who has subscribed to a fatalistic view of life, but I have found my skepticism tested by the fact that my majority of 691 that has bought me to this great House is exactly the same as that of another young Conservative Member of Parliament who won the seat of Wolverhampton South West for the first time in 1950 – one Enoch Powell."

Then the touch of humour designed to lighten the mood, and disallow the message that the Powell name was still capable of delivering.

"I make that statement with my tongue firmly pressed against the inside of my cheek and an ironic smile on my face."

Paul was rewarded by a ripple of laughter spreading throughout the House.

"I also appeal to all Members of the House to take me to one side and proofread any of my speeches should I feel compelled in 18 years' time to make a controversial speech at the Midland Hotel. That is unlikely to happen, primarily because the hotel is no longer there, but I have lived enough of a life to know that one should never say never – I ask the Hansard reporters to note

that my tongue is now firmly affixed to the other side of my cheek."

More appreciative laughter. That was it. Two short paragraphs. Job done as far as Powell was concerned. Paul continued with a playful statement surrounding his position as the first Sikh MP in the House of Commons before moving on to the main task at hand, to laud the town of Wolverhampton and its citizens. His closing statement elicited enthusiastic applause and a round of 'yeas' from Members on both sides of the House.

"This great House is nothing if not a reflection of the individual stories of its Members, and I hope that by adding my perspective I have added to the strength of its foundations and the breadth of debate."

Paul Uppal sat down on the green leather members' bench, his head a swirl of thoughts and memories. He thought about his family grouped around television at home watching his performance on the Parliament Channel. He thought about his uncle who, at thirteen, in Kenya, went to work so that his young brother, Paul's father, could attend school. He thought about the difficulty of the brothers' early days in England, with both families crammed together in a single terraced house in Smethwick. He thought about his family's move to overwhelmingly white working-class Northfield. And, almost unwillingly, he thought about a Friday in the late 1970s, when he was the only dark-skinned student in his technical drawing class. The deputy head, who was teaching the class, asked the boys what they were planning on doing that weekend. "Is anybody going out Paki bashing?" he asked. Whenever the memory invaded Paul's thoughts, he again experienced the spine-tingling horror he'd felt at the time. But then, perhaps coincidentally or maybe purposely to dispel the memory, Paul Uppal thought about his children. He thought about how their white-skinned friends didn't bat an eyelid at his father's turban, and how they were totally at home sitting at his and Kashmir's table eating Punjabi food – samosas, roti, or shabji.

At that moment the Deputy Speaker's voice impinged as he gave the floor to the next speaker. The business of the House of Commons continued. Paul Uppal could finally start work as nothing more or less extraordinary than the latest Member of the British Parliament.

Andrew Smith's first novel, *Edith's War*, won a gold medal at the Independent Publishers' Book Awards, U.S.A. His short fiction has been included in the Journey Prize Anthology and shortlisted for the CBC Literary Awards. His travel writing has garnered a Western Magazine Award. He has published two non-fiction books: *Strangers in the Garden*, the secret lives of our favorite flowers, and *Highlights*, an illustrated history of cannabis (co-author).

"The competent way Smith handles structure, moving between time periods and places, is really impressive ... a terrific accomplishment." Jack Batten, literary critic.

"*Edith's War* is an intricate study of war, love, and survival. A must read." Zoomer Magazine.

ACKNOWLEDGEMENTS

I owe a huge debt of gratitude to Nicholas and Pat Jones for sharing their personal recollections of Enoch Powell and his family, and for their ongoing support. Thanks to Velma Pollard, Jamaican poet and fiction writer, for imparting her expert knowledge of Jamaican patois. Thanks to author Colin Channer for his wise advice on early drafts of the manuscript. Thanks to Anna Davis at Curtis Brown Creative for her firm and insightful guidance. Thanks to the Churchill Archives Centre, Churchill College, Cambridge for access to Enoch Powell's political and personal papers. Thanks to Robert Shepherd and Simon Heffer, whose biographies (*'Enoch Powell: A Biography'* and *'Like The Roman: The Life of Enoch Powell'* respectively) were invaluable. And thanks to all the other writers, too numerous to mention, whose books, papers, and articles about Powell were so helpful in completing the man in my mind. Thanks to Paul Uppal for so generously recounting to me his experience of becoming Member of Parliament in Enoch Powell's former constituency of Wolverhampton South West. Thanks to author Brian Masters for assiduously reading my final manuscript and commenting on it so succinctly and articulately. Thanks to Matthew Smith of Urbane Publications for his enthusiastic encouragement and faith in my work. Last, but by no means least, thanks to my fellow writers at Curtis Brown Creative workshops for their invaluable input and constant support.

Urbane Publications is dedicated to
developing new author voices, and publishing
fiction and non-fiction that challenges, thrills and
fascinates.

From page-turning novels to innovative
reference books, our goal is to publish what
YOU want to read.

Find out more at
urbanepublications.com